CORK CITY LIBRARY

Tel: (021) **4277110**
Hollyhill Library: 4392998

This book is due for return on the last date stamped below.
Overdue fines: 10c per week plus postage.

Class no. _SAR_   Accn no. _4579271_

Despite the
Falling Snow

Also by Shamim Sarif

The World Unseen

Despite the Falling Snow

SHAMIM SARIF

'She Tells Her Love While Half Asleep' by Robert Graves,
published in *Complete Poems in One Volume*
by Carcanet Press Limited, 2001,
edited by Beryl Graves and Dunstan Ward
and reproduced by permission of Carcanet Press Limited

Extract from the closing sequence of *The Dead*, DUBLINERS
reproduced by permission of the Estate of James Joyce

First published in Great Britain in 2004 by REVIEW

An imprint of Headline Book Publishing

10 9 8 7 6 5 4 3 2 1

Cataloguing in Publication Data is available from the British Library

ISBN 0 7553 08670 (hardback)
ISBN 0 7553 2015 8 (trade paperback)

Typeset in Garamond by Avon DataSet Ltd, Bidford-on-Avon, Warwickshire

Printed and bound in Great Britain by Clays Ltd, St Ives plc

Papers and cover board used by Headline are natural, recyclable products
made from wood grown in sustainable forests. The manufacturing processes
conform to the environmental regulations of the country of origin.

HEADLINE BOOK PUBLISHING
A division of Hodder Headline Limited
338 Euston Road, London NW1 3BH

www.reviewbooks.co.uk
www.hodderheadline.com

For Hanan, Ethan & Luca
For the revelation you have bestowed –
that every moment of life can be wondrous and beautiful

Acknowledgements

T HE FOLLOWING PEOPLE were invaluable during the process of researching this book:

My sister Anouchka who accompanied me to Moscow, and who introduced me to Nazim Walimohamed, who was so generous with his time and contacts. Marina Rabinskaya took on the role of guide and proved to be a superb interpreter. She also helped me to find people who remembered Khrushchev's leadership. Galina Dronova, Yuri Bychkov and Zinaida Gurevitch provided an overall sense of the late 1950's as well as much important nuance and detail in their recollections of the period. Michael Weinstein helped to consider the most probable plotlines over (not too much) vodka in Moscow. Thanks also to Yasmine Naber who introduced me to Varvara Underwood here in London, and to Zinaida Chnitko, who took the time to answer the questions that arose later in the writing process.

Thanks to my agent Euan Thorneycroft for his excellent guiding comments and to Rosie de Courcy, for her delicate editing. Thanks also to David Pitblado and Katharine Priestley for an excellent final reading. Thanks to Karl Ghattas, for providing unfailing support and constant illumination. And immense gratitude to my partner, Hanan Kattan, for everything, not least her brilliant, thorough and incisive close reading. It is a rare dream for a writer to have an involved, sensitive reader who knows what you wish to convey, and is unafraid to tell you if you have not quite managed it. It is a thankless task, but I thank her for it.

She tells her love while half asleep,
In the dark hours,
With half-words whispered low:
As Earth stirs in her winter sleep
And puts out grass and flowers
Despite the snow,
Despite the falling snow.

— Robert Graves

Chapter One

Boston, November 2000

SHE HAS BEEN sitting on a wooden bench in the courtyard of this office building for some time – about twenty minutes, she guesses – and she is briefly grateful that the large quadrant is enclosed from the ice-hard blasts of wind that seemed to burn through her as she walked here; only the soft purity of the blue sky above is caught between the tops of buildings. The space is explicitly welcoming, yet she cannot help but feel oppressed by the ungainly height of the structures around it. The shiny, varnished seating, the eerily immaculate late-autumn flower-beds, the studied restfulness of the trickling fountain – all these lead her to regard this corporate resting place with subdued contempt. She resolves that she will not check her watch – not just yet – and turns her attention back to the novel. She is on page five (of seven hundred and forty-three) and decides to begin the page again, since she has read it without absorbing a single word.

It is hardly more gripping the second time round, and she wonders whether, at the age of sixty-one, she might not be excused from reading things that don't grab her at once, taking into account that even in the best of circumstances she can't have *that* much time left

1

in this world. Her husband has advised her gruffly to read Proust, to revel in his refinement of thought, to admire his delicacy of phrase. She is intelligent enough and perceptive enough to recognise both of those things, even within the small portion she has read, but something is lacking *here*. Unconsciously, she touches her heart. Perhaps it will come later, if she will but give the novel a chance. She eyes her handbag with a sidelong, slightly guilty gaze, like a child trying not to stare at a forbidden toy. It contains two slim volumes: one, a Hemingway novel, the other a book of stories by Salinger. Her husband is unimpressed by both, but holds a particularly sarcastic contempt for the Salinger. Nevertheless, she likes it, admires the direct simplicity of the sentences. She had been hesitant to read the stories again after Professor Johnson's vehement assertion that they possessed no real merit, but she found to her pleasure that they had come through unscathed, and were as poignant and relaxed and cleanly written as she had first thought them.

Her eyes are drawn back to the looming building before her. The endless squares of darkened glass and polished steel are uninviting, inscrutable, protective of the activity going on behind them. She is rarely in the business district. It is a section of the city that is unfamiliar to her, that has no relation to the Boston she loves. Hers, rather, is a world of red-brick houses and streets lined with trees that are coolly shady in summer and starkly proud in winter. The calm, broad sparkle of the Charles river, and the sweeping energy of the Back Bay. The small specialist shops of Newbury Street, the cobbled streets of old Beacon Hill, and the faint rumble of traffic that counterpoints the delicate quiet of the public gardens. The coffee-houses around the many university campuses where you might stumble on a reading or some music. Still self-consciously avoiding the book in her hands, she glances away from the structure before her, and looks for comfort to the solitary tree that soars up from the concrete. It is half stripped of leaves, but those that remain still show deep, burnished reds and darkening browns: the fading colours of a New England autumn that has come late this year, and is now almost at its end.

She becomes aware that something is buzzing. She glances round, seeking the source of the noise, but there is no one else in the courtyard. Then she feels a vibration against her feet. Inside her handbag. She reaches in, pulls out her mobile phone and slams shut the Proust. The handset shudders in her hand like a thing in pain. She focuses on it – none of the buttons appear clearly marked. She pushes a black one, then a green one, then holds it to her ear. Nothing.

'You're not used to it, are you?' says a voice.

She turns her head. Beside her, watching her, stands Alexander Ivanov. He is neatly wrapped in an understated but expensive navy cashmere coat and a russet scarf, which emphasises his silver hair. He removes his hat when she turns but she is too surprised even to notice the polite gesture.

'All the buttons look the same,' she says. She drops the handset back into her bag.

'You should get your daughter to teach you, Estelle,' he suggests.

'Maybe over lunch today,' she tells him. He says nothing to this, and she wonders if his silence is meaningful, coupled as it is with the fact that Melissa is nowhere to be seen. She shifts over on the bench, conscious that she is taking up the only available seat, and he sits down, keeping a correct distance, and smiles at her. His eyes are large and dark brown and softened with age – the warm pools of colour look textured, like worn velvet, she thinks.

'It's good to see you again,' he tells her. 'We didn't really get a chance to talk much the first time.' He has an accent when he speaks, a precision of utterance that is well defined but also musical.

There is a heaviness on the letter L that she is most aware of when he says her name.

'It was kind of you to let me wait in your office that day,' she says.

'Why didn't you come up today? It's cold out here.'

'I like the fresh air,' she says simply. She does not attempt to explain her ill-defined antipathy to the building – she has only met him once, and he is unlikely to understand her irrational whims, particularly since he owns the building in question. 'Anyway, if the meeting's done . . .' she says.

'Actually, it's still going on. I played truant, that's all.'

She is still wondering how someone can play truant from the sale of his own multi-million-dollar company when his telephone rings.

'Perhaps that's them,' Alexander says, reassuringly. She looks back up at the tree for something to do while she tries not to listen to the clear voice at the other end. Something about some final queries and wouldn't he like to come back to the meeting. 'Not especially,' he says. 'Why doesn't everyone break for lunch? I believe Melissa has another appointment . . .'

There is quiet at the other end, some conferring, perhaps, before the metallic voice comes back on the line. 'She says it's nothing important. She'd rather get this thing hammered out and finished.'

She can see him press the phone more closely to his ear, trying to block the words from floating out to her across the crisp air.

'Very well, I'll be back in a couple of hours,' he says, his tone terse. 'Try and have it done by then, will you?' He snaps the phone shut, then switches it off. He looks at Estelle, and there is a moment of quiet communication between them. She knows what has happened, and wants to save him the trouble of finding a tactful way to tell her that her daughter will not bother to come.

'I saw the article in *Business World* the other week,' she says. ' "The King of Catering".'

'Those headlines . . .' He gives a shake of his head.

'I thought it was interesting,' she replies. 'Especially about your background. Your life in Russia.'

He nods briefly, enough to acknowledge the comment politely, but says nothing. Estelle considers asking again, for the few lines about Alexander's early life gleaned from the article suggested a story worth hearing. She decides against probing too much – after all, she knows him only slightly. She pulls a hat from her bag, a preliminary to leaving.

'I'm sorry about lunch with Melissa,' he says. He hesitates, and a quick smile moves across his face, which otherwise looks concerned, even nervous. 'Would you care to join me instead?'

Estelle pauses, and while she is considering, decides against trying to put her hat on while he is watching. Instead she uses it to keep her hands warm. 'Shouldn't you be going back in?' she asks.

'What for? They all know what to do.'

She raises an eyebrow. 'I hope so. She may be my daughter, but I don't mind telling you that Melissa has the manners of a piranha when it comes to closing a deal.'

He laughs, surprised at her tight appraisal of her own child, and tells her that he doesn't mind, that tough negotiations are a part of most business transactions.

There is a short pause between them, a moment when he seems to be debating whether to reveal or explain something. He looks up at the glass building. 'That's where they are. Twenty-sixth floor.'

Once again she looks up. It is the type of inaccessible building that she usually associates with her daughter, clean and lean and functional.

'I was sitting there, fifteen minutes ago, sealed inside, look-ing out of the window like a restless schoolboy who can't concentrate on his math lesson. All I could see was the sky, and beyond that the city and Back Bay. When I finally came to, someone was asking me something, and I had no idea what it was. Nor did I much care what it was. So I excused myself and came down here.'

'It can't be easy, watching someone else take charge of your business.'

'I suppose that must have something to do with it. But I'm not sorry to let it go. It's time.' He rubs his hands together to keep them warm and fixes her with a mischievous look. 'So, will you come for lunch? Melissa did promise we'd get together the last time. You can help me play truant.'

'It's kind of you, but not at all necessary . . .'

'Martha, my housekeeper, is at home if you feel happier with a chaperone,' he says.

'Trust me, it's been decades since I worried about men being gripped by uncontrollable bouts of passion at the mere sight of me,' she tells him. 'Don't worry, I'm not scared of you.'

'Good. It's settled, then?' He stands up, as though it is.

She feels a prickle at this hint of presumption, but her curiosity about this man has been building. There is nothing she likes more than a good story. And she is cold and hungry, and does not feel like returning to the desolate rooms of her apartment or sitting in a restaurant alone.

He takes out his phone again. 'Why don't I call Melissa and have her meet us when they're done?'

She is grateful for his consideration – that her daughter knows where she is and will join them gives her a measure of security, a final encouragement. They walk out together, across the squares of sunlight that cover the courtyard. A scatter of auburn leaves floats to the ground before them, and there is something touching to her in the way that Alexander reaches out to feel one as it drops. In the sight of his hand, a little curved and battered from old age and Boston winters, probably from Russian winters too, extending involuntarily to greet a stray leaf that falls right before his eyes. He watches it settle, feather-like, upon the ground. Then he guides her out to the main entrance of the building, where the doorman tips his hat and whistles down a cab.

She slides into the red vinyl seats, and Alexander is half inside too, but stops to hand the doorman a tip. His wallet is flipped open – a rich, brown leather casing, which is beginning to show the grainy softness of age. He pulls out a bill and hands it to the man, but Estelle's attention is on a photograph that is exposed inside the open wallet. She sees it for only a second, perhaps two, and it is old and black-and-white, perhaps even very slightly out of focus. But the woman in the picture is arresting – she is also young and quite beautiful. Estelle can tell that much despite the fact that the woman is squinting into the camera because the sun is in her eyes. There is something about the photograph, something seductive, something she has no time to think about or define – but it strikes her as one of those images that contain a whole attitude and atmosphere and that would make anyone stop to take a second look if they could. As Alexander enters the cab, his thumb brushes lightly and quickly over the picture, and his glance falls on Estelle; then the wallet is closed, and the woman is gone.

He gives the driver his address, and Estelle clears her throat, but hesitates to ask the question on her lips. He looks at her, expectant, an open gaze with those polite brown eyes, and she can tell nothing at all from them. She sits back in her seat and looks ahead as the cab moves off.

*

7

His house is an old red-brick building dating from the days when high ceilings and grand rooms were common. From the days when a growing city could afford to be expansive.

'It's nice to see a place like this that's unconverted.'

'Lots of stairs,' he replied. 'Keeps my old bones moving.'

'We don't live all that far from each other. We're in a brownstone – it's a lovely building but we have an apartment. Small, but worth it to be in the centre of town.'

He understands this – he has always lived right in the middle of cities; even in Moscow he had that privilege. Most people who wanted larger apartments – or any apartment of their own – were forced to move to Khrushchev's new buildings, hastily thrown-up, thin-walled and grey, on the outskirts of the city. And many people were happy with that: those blocks gave them space they had never had before. Unless you did well for the Party, or worked in the government, rooms at the hub of Moscow were tiny and overfilled.

He holds open his front door for Estelle and she steps into a wood-panelled hallway that instantly brings to her mind an English country house. Instead of portraits of ancestors on the walls, there is a selection of art, some abstract, some figurative, all relatively modern. She half expects a butler to appear, but the only other sign of life is the understated hum of a vacuum-cleaner upstairs. While Alexander hangs their coats and scarves, she looks at the artwork. There are a couple of paintings that she feels immediately pulled into. Strangely, they are abstracts, the kind of non-representative pieces that usually she cannot find any empathy with. But these evoke a certain emotion within her, a feeling of lost love or deep sorrow, which unsettles her. She examines the paintings well, trying to ascertain how the patches of textured colours could create such a sensation. She is about to say something to Alexander when he

8

returns, but cannot find the words to articulate what she is thinking without sounding pretentious or confused.

'Are you sure about this? I hate to trouble you,' she says. 'We could just go get a sandwich somewhere.'

'Absolutely sure. Cooking is a kind of therapy for me. It will be a simple meal.'

Estelle follows him into the living room, a large, light space, with leather armchairs and sofas and a wall full of books and a grand piano. A drawing room from a novel, she thinks. Windows stretch from the ceiling to the floor, showing a small garden beyond. She looks out at it while he fetches a bottle of wine from the kitchen next door. The plants and trees have a feeling of fullness even now, in the late autumn, and she can tell that the slightly overgrown, lush, romantic quality of the garden is carefully nurtured. He returns with the bottle, and opens it smoothly, with close attention. Estelle gives him a glance of query, then goes over to the piano. She studies the photographs ranged over it, and picks up one. 'She's very attractive.'

'Lauren, my niece,' he says. 'She's an artist. Those are some of her pieces in the hall.'

Estelle turns, her interest caught. 'Really? I thought they were amazing. But I don't know why. I'm so ignorant about great art, and how it's made and yet . . .'

'Yes?'

'And yet if there's anything I would have liked to be it's a writer.'

And there it is, she has said it out loud, the thing that she keeps so quietly within herself.

He takes a sniff of the wine and concentrates. When he offers Estelle a glass, she takes it, swirls the liquid around as he has done, and inhales deeply. The scent is soft and smoky, a deeply comforting smell, of dried fruit and spice and warm tobacco, and it is a world away from the everyday wine she is used to.

'Why didn't you?' he asks. 'Become a writer.'

She winces, then takes a quick sip. 'Don't make it sound so simple.'

'Why not?'

She makes no immediate answer. When she does speak, quietly, she feels him leaning in to catch her words. 'Because if it is that simple, I've wasted too much time.'

It is a clear, open statement and she is almost embarrassed by it.

'Do you write now?' he asks.

She is dismissive, back in control. 'A little. Here and there. Not enough, I guess.' Her eyes escape back to the piano, and it is then that she sees her. The woman she noticed earlier, in the wallet photograph. Estelle picks up the frame. 'This one?' she asks.

'Katya. My late wife,' he says. Late. As though she has missed a dinner engagement and might be arriving at any moment. His eyes glance outside, involuntarily, away from the picture and from Estelle's enquiring face; the sky is clouding over and is giving out a dull, heavy light that reminds him now of the past. That colourless, oppressive air had been such a memorable feature of the days following Katya's death that, even now, he cannot bear to feel it too closely about him. He walks to the door, his tone brisk: 'Could I ask you to accompany me to the kitchen?' he says, with an exaggerated bow. 'And is there anything you don't eat?'

'Sauerkraut,' Estelle says promptly. 'If there's one thing I can't stand it's cabbage. Especially when it's all pickled and disguised and wishing it was something else.'

'There goes my centrepiece dish,' he says.

The kitchen is large, as she had expected it would be for someone in his line of work, and it immediately gives her a sense of inadequacy. Painted wooden cupboards bestow a homely air, arranged round a vast, gleaming stove that takes up much of one wall. Above it hangs a wood and steel rack from which shining pots, pans and colanders are suspended. On metal hooks over the stove there are large cooking spoons and a number of other items: tiny frying-pans and sieves, mashers and graters, and many others whose uses she cannot even guess at. Here, she notices, there is none of the casual disarray and untidiness that always seems to creep into her own home, no matter how she tries to keep things in their proper place. There is abundance here, but also a feeling of order. With quick movements, he ties on a half-apron. 'I've been longing to be in this kitchen all morning. Thank you for giving me the opportunity.'

'You're more than welcome. I wish I had your enthusiasm for kitchens, but I don't. Which is why I always promised myself I'd marry a man who could cook.'

The opportunity he has been looking for. Some part of him has hesitated to ask her outright whether she is married. 'So your husband can cook?' he asks.

'No,' she replies, with a laugh. 'He can't.'

He weighs the tomatoes in his hand – they give a little to his touch, the deep red skin showing the faintest wrinkles of overripeness. Satisfied, he pours boiling water over them, waits a moment for the skins to split, then peels and chops. They are tossed into the pan where smashed garlic and fine-chopped onions are already frying, filling the kitchen with an aroma that makes her feel hungry at once. She watches the chunky freshness of the tomatoes collapsing in the pan, melting into the translucent onions.

'What can I do?' Estelle asks.

'You could grate the Parmesan.' He hands her a large block of cheese, rough-edged and pungent.

She smells it. 'My God, that's wonderful. And I thought it came from the cow ready grated . . .'

11

'Shame on you,' he says. 'Here.' He shaves off a piece with a knife and offers it to her. 'Taste this.'

Carefully, she takes the cheese and places it in her mouth.

He points to her wine-glass. 'Now take a sip of that over it.'

She is inordinately conscious of his hand touching hers as he passes her the glass. The cheese is rich and full, with layers of flavour that are completely unlike anything she has tried before. He turns away, as if to give her time and space to enjoy the tasting, and washes basil leaves at the sink. The wine runs smoothly over the lingering taste in her mouth, deepening and rounding it. She resists closing her eyes to concentrate her other senses and, instead, watches him tear the basil into the sauce. He pauses and holds a handful of the leaves under her nose. She smells them and smiles, an acknowledgement of the vibrancy of the herbal scent. She watches as he works, leaning over the pan, and takes another sip of wine, grateful for a moment unobserved to absorb the discoveries she feels she has been making all morning.

They begin the meal with steamed asparagus, dipped into melted butter. They eat with their fingers, cradling the stems, coaxing them into the sauce.

'I don't think I've ever met anyone who loves food as much as you do, Alexander.'

'It's just fresh, simple ingredients,' he says. 'I got used to stale food in Russia, at least some of the time, but here there is no excuse. And I was lucky. My first job in America was in my brother-in-law's grocery store. I was surrounded by food all day.'

'So you really did start with nothing?'

Less than nothing, he thinks. No money and no prospects was the least of it. A heart as dead as a blighted tree was much harder to overcome. 'Yes,' he answers.

She looks at him, a pin-sharp gaze, but he will not speak the sorrow in his eyes.

'I remember it so well, even now,' he says. 'Coming from Russia, I had never seen so much food. So much *fresh* food. So many wonderful breads and cheeses, and fruit and meat all in one place. Of course, compared to the delis and supermarkets we have now, it was nothing, but then . . . I thought we sold everything. Flour and sugar came out of big drums, into paper bags which were weighed.'

'I remember,' smiles Estelle.

'After a while, I began baking in the shop. Cakes, pies, tarts. We sold them piece by piece.'

Slowly, they had added more dishes – brown-crusted meat pies, lentil-rich soups. Shop and office workers began to stop and buy their lunches there, and Alexander would watch them from the kitchen at the back, noting a shop-girl's smile as she caught the scent of her soup, or an old man biting gratefully into a pie, unable to wait until he had left the shop.

'From there it was a natural progression to catering and canapés,' he says, with an ironic smile. He sprinkles the grated cheese into the hot pasta and carries it to the table.

'Who were your clients?' Estelle asks.

'Mostly well-to-do women. Lots of families in Beacon Hill.'

'That's where I used to live.'

'Really?'

She shakes away his interest. 'A long, long time ago.'

He watches her. Even though she has stopped speaking, he cannot help himself. There is something about her. He scans her face – the high cheekbones are clear, but their defined edges have become a little blurred with age. Her eyes are an unlikely shade of bright blue, with an animation behind them that makes them crackle, like neon. He had noticed this the first time they met. He had spent a few minutes settling her in his own office to wait for her daughter, who had remained in his boardroom where they were slowly negotiating the terms of her purchase of his company. He had liked Estelle at once: although their conversation that day did not move much beyond pleasantries, there was a quickness, an ironic undertone to some of her replies that had suggested a vibrant personality, and found a complement, a ready means of expression, in her startling eyes. Melissa's eyes are grey, perhaps after her father. He searches Estelle's face for something of her daughter's cool, veiled look but he can find nothing of it.

'What is it?'

'I was just trying to figure out if Melissa looks like you.'

Estelle shrugs. 'Not much. She has my nose, maybe, but the rest of her is her father.'

The pasta, like everything else she has tasted so far, is a revelation. The firm bite of the *penne* beneath the sweet spiciness of the tomato sauce. Then the balance of the fresh basil and the smooth, rich Parmesan. She leans back in her chair, feeling almost indecorous, overwhelmed as she is by a surfeit of pleasure. She takes another fragrant bite as Alexander asks her if she ever had a career. 'Not until my mid-twenties. I didn't need to work, I suppose. My father was well-to-do, and it wasn't the thing in those days. One just waited to get married.'

'And you did?'

'Not immediately, no.' She runs a crust of fresh bread over the sauce that remains on her plate. 'All those young Harvard boys that would come visiting.' She makes a face at the memory.

'So you began working?'

'Yes, to my father's great consternation. I just couldn't stand sitting around any more, drinking tea and preparing for dinner parties. So I got a job, though goodness knows how. I couldn't type, couldn't

14

take dictation . . . Couldn't do any of the things young women needed for work back then, although I learned pretty quickly. I worked at Boston University. As an assistant to various professors. Mostly in the English department.'

'Why the English department?' he asks quickly, and she hesitates.

'I always loved books, I guess. The smell of them, the feel of the pages, the idea that whole worlds I'd never seen or felt before were sandwiched between their covers. Every now and then I'd be typing up a paper or an article, and I'd read something completely unexpected about a book I knew. Or thought I knew. I did a lot of rereading of classic novels based on those papers.'

'When did you stop?'

'After I got married. My husband was the last professor I assisted. In the end he travelled a lot, and wanted me with him.'

'Would you have preferred to continue working?'

'Oh, no.' She laughs, and feels a warmth in her cheeks, which she hopes is not visible. 'Not then. I was so in love with him. I couldn't bear the thought of us being apart. Anyway, I still helped with his research and typing for a while . . . And then I had Melissa, and it stopped. Once she grew up, I went back to doing a little reading and typing for him, which I still do. It's been a pretty ordinary life.'

'Not really. You could have gotten married out of college to a suitably well-to-do young man. But you went to work, which, as you say, wasn't the thing to do, then ended up marrying a professor. I assume marrying for passion rather than comfort. Sounds like you didn't play by the rules at all.'

Estelle flushes. She is partly embarrassed that he is interested enough to analyse her existence in this way, and partly pleased. She has never considered her choices in the maverick light that he has cast on them.

'Tell me about your writing.'

'Oh, that,' she says, and for the first time he senses in her a shyness. 'I'm just an aspiring novelist, I guess. In search of a really interesting character.'

'I thought writers are always searching for a good plot. Or theme.'

'Oh, no,' she replies, with certainty this time. 'The themes are almost always the same, don't you think? Love, passion, death, betrayal.'

She feels a tiny pause, which for that instant makes her wonder if she has said something wrong – but then he looks up and smiles his assent.

Back in the living room, sinking deep into soft leather armchairs, with a second glass of wine beside each of them, Estelle considers how to approach the subject of his life in Russia. He has fired gentle questions at her all through lunch, but something about his look or his bearing has made her reluctant to do the same. At last she gestures to the photograph on the piano. 'Your wife was very beautiful,' she says.

'Do you think so?'

'Don't you? Such life in those eyes.'

'I have never seen anyone or anything to match her in all my life.'

He turns, conveniently, she thinks, to the dessert plate, an apricot tart, left over from the day before, warmed through.

'She looks very happy there. In the photo,' she comments.

Had she been happy? He thinks. Perhaps, some of the time. But with Katya, happiness had never been a deep-seated state of being. Rather, it had been a fleeting sensation, a series of brief respites from the world as it existed for her. 'She had quite a difficult life,' he says blandly. If his guest, the aspiring novelist, is in search of an interesting character, he feels no immediate obligation to provide it. He cuts two generous pieces of the tart.

'I suppose I should be declining politely and thinking of my figure,' Estelle says, 'but at this stage what's the point?' She thanks him and sits down again, the plate balanced on her knee. 'You were telling me about your wife?'

'Katya, yes. We grew up during the last part of Stalin's rule, you see. He died in fifty-three. There was a lot of in-fighting in the Party, people pushing for power, but by the late fifties, Khrushchev had taken over.' True statements, but vague ones, a ploy to move the focus away from the specific.

Estelle moves forward, interested. 'Tell me about Stalin's terrors. Wasn't that when all those thousands were arrested and killed?'

'By the time all the waves of arrests were done, it was millions. Tens of millions, even, when you count all the people who starved to death in the countryside. Unnecessarily, after terrible government policy decisions.'

'Why?'

Alexander shakes his head. 'That's the terrible thing. For no good reason. Paranoia, perhaps. A wish to keep control and power at any cost. Stalin was a cruel man, and he ruled with fear. You disagreed with him, you died. Very few people will argue in those circumstances.'

'But when so many die, when people are losing their families for no reason . . . didn't it inspire them to fight against it?'

Alexander considers. His eyes are almost closed with the effort of transporting himself back to that time. He had been a child then, during the worst of it. Why hadn't people fought it? How much suffering must a population go through before it revolts? Those who did revolt, and many who did not, were imprisoned, tortured, killed. One way or another. He looks away.

'Is that what happened . . .?'

'To Katya? Not directly. We were just children when Stalin was in power. Anyway, Khrushchev was a change. He still did as he pleased, but there was more accountability. You were allowed to criticise. A little.'

He stands up, under pretence of pouring more wine. Suddenly the boredom of the meeting that he has just fled seems comforting, and safe. His movements are measured and careful, designed to gain time. Time to rebalance, to bring himself back to the present, away from a place where Katya's name is arising naturally, and too often.

'Do you mind me asking when your wife died?'

'Nineteen fifty-nine,' he replies.

'Ah. That *is* a long time.'

'She was very young. We were very young.'

'Do you have any children?'

He shakes his head.

'Do you regret it?'

'No regrets. About anything.' He smiles, and she sees that the smile is merely a cover for his lie.

He sits down, recalling how he had lain next to his wife at night, coated in a darkness unrelieved by street-lamps outside, and he would imagine her child – their baby – and he had begun to love the idea of it almost as if it had actually existed.

He is concerned that she will ask him what happened. Why Katya died. Even after so many decades he has not found a way, a simplified, subtle way, to explain yet gloss over what had happened to her. It would be so much easier to be able to put forward an acceptable reason. An illness, a terrible accident. But he has still not learned what one says when it was neither.

Estelle is about to ask how he and Katya met, when she notices his quick, nervous movements, his eyes roaming away from hers. She sits back in her chair at once, sorry to have pressed the topic. It is rude of her, a guest in his house, to make him uncomfortable. She is trying to decide how to change the subject when he speaks.

'It's a funny thing,' he says. 'Even though it has been such a long time, sometimes I can still remember how I felt in those weeks after I first met Katya. The excitement, the dizziness, the agony of meeting the person you had never believed existed. It is a wonderful thing to be truly in love.' He looks up. 'That is what I remember most about my wife. How very much I adored her.'

That much is true, he thinks. All the rest, the betrayals, the nightmares, the waking horror, the guilt, he has packed away over the course of the years, packed it all tightly into one corner of his mind. No regrets. About anything.

Chapter Two

Moscow, March 1956

T H E   R O O M   I S warm and full. Most of them are young, about his own age, their chatter filling the peeling high arches that sweep across the ceiling above them. There are lights, and laughter, and glasses that touch each other musically; an unfamiliar feeling of excess and even decadence that forms a welcome illusion for certain moments during this evening. For certain moments, from certain angles, with his eyes half shut, he can see that the long, narrow room in this apartment belonging to Misha's friends has regained some of the elegance and life that perhaps filled it so often in another, pre-revolutionary lifetime.

There is a small window at his back, and when he feels a cold draught touch his jacket, he turns, and the preternatural glow of the snow lighting the gloom outside attracts him and makes him look. On the street below he sees a small boy and an old woman. Both are carrying large bundles on their backs. Both look small and frail under their loads and he watches them for a long minute until they move round the corner of the building and are lost to sight. Probably they are carrying home wood to warm their rooms. Or room. He looks at his watch. It is ten o'clock.

It is becoming hot at the party, and Alexander runs a finger round his slender neck, under his collar and tie.

'You look like a government man,' Misha had told him, with no small measure of sarcasm, when he picked him up. 'Don't you have any casual clothes? This is not one of your State Department cocktail parties, you know.'

'I came directly from work,' had been Alexander's taut reply, before he had seen Misha's teasing eyes. Then he had laughed. 'Anyway, in the end we are all government men, aren't we?'

A light haze of smoke drifts up high, drawn towards the gleaming, makeshift lights strung up in the corners, and he watches Misha, standing across from him, talking, intent on his own words, then listening to those nearby. There is a buzz of excitement in this room for the first news of Khrushchev's secret speech has been leaking out into Moscow, creeping through cracks in office windows, gusting into apartments where neighbours have been passing overheard comments through thin-walled buildings. The speech was made at a closed congress session but Alexander is pleased that their leader's forthright, shocking denouncement of his predecessor Stalin is becoming known to the people outside. The sense of openness, of freedom that has made some of them light-headed at work over the past weeks will start to infect others too. How can that be bad?

As if he has been listening to his friend's thoughts, Misha turns to him. 'And what do you think about Comrade Khrushchev's brave speech, my friend? That the "cult of personality" mustn't happen again.'

He takes a drag on his cigarette before continuing. 'That old man Stalin was a cantankerous, bloody-minded butcher all along.' Misha smiles thinly, and exhales a long stream of smoke upwards.

Alexander does not smoke. He used to, as a teenager, but as a young man the residual taste of tar, the insidious smell of ash in his clothes, bothers him. 'I think it's about time,' Alexander replies. 'People will see that things are different now. Really different.'

Misha slaps him on the back. 'Such an idealist, Sasha.' He smiles again, but the smile is forced, and when he speaks next, his voice has lowered so that only Alexander can hear him. 'You do remember that our beloved leader Nikita Sergeyevitch was around during all that terror, doing his part?' The soft tones are a precaution, one that may or may not be necessary here, but Misha, like all of them, cannot get used to any other way when talking about certain subjects.

Alexander shrugs as if to say, 'You asked me,' and Misha laughs. His eyes are smiling now, not just his mouth: he looks happy.

'Don't you feel the change, Misha? In the government, in the people, in the air? There is hope. Maybe now the Soviet system will work as it should. As it can. And whatever he might have done in the past, well, at least he is trying to change all that.'

'But can people cope with change? Most of them still worship the old man – even more since he's been dead.'

'They saw him as immortal, that's all. Even though he took away husbands and fathers and families, Stalin was a god, to be worshipped and deferred to. He set himself up that way, aloof from the destruction. Khrushchev is different, you can see that. He under-stands the people. It'll be different now,' Alexander says simply.

'Maybe. Maybe it will be. Maybe I do feel it. Hope. Freedom. Truth!' Misha raises his hands over his head and declaims the words, and a few drunk people around him applaud before going back to their glasses. He takes a breath and another drink, then looks up again. 'Oh, but I've worked hard to build up this cynical surface, Sasha. I'll be sorry to let it go, just like that. Don't make me abandon it all in one night.'

Alexander smiles at his friend. He cannot remember a time, even when they were boys together at school, when Misha did not have that cynical surface. Carefully cultivated, it had lent him an aura of sophistication in the eyes of his friends as they were growing up, and even now, in tandem with his startling good looks, it seems to ensure the attraction to him of any number of women. Alexander turns, for Misha's eyes are wandering over his shoulder. Two girls are standing behind them. He steps aside and allows his friend a free try at them, then scans the room as Misha and the girls talk.

A few couples are dancing in one corner, to the music of three men who sit cramped closely together, brows pulled into ridges of concentration, heads swaying, fingers spinning old remembered melodies from a guitar, a fiddle, a pocket flute. The music has been moving faster, gaining speed slowly as the evening progresses, and now has a rhythm that is well held and infectious. Alexander notices that, in the absence of a drum or tambourine, almost everyone in the room is tapping a foot or a finger in time to the music. As his eyes sweep back towards Misha, his gaze catches on something and he turns to look.

She is sitting with two other girls at one of the groups of wooden chairs placed haphazardly around the edges of the room. Alexander watches her intently – he is trying to decide what is it about her that has caught his attention. She is beautiful certainly, but there is something else, something in the proud set of her shoulders and head, that sets her apart from the girls around her. She is talking animatedly, telling a joke or a story, and her friends are laughing, and so is she, but her laughter is controlled – she is smiling, but also watching her audience's reaction. He strains to hear her voice, but he is a little too far away, and the people around him are noisy. He looks about him, with the air of someone who has just woken up, and he realises that he does not know how long he has been staring at her; but now a young man has gone up to her, and is talking to her, trying his luck, obscuring Alexander's view.

'Sasha! Where do you wander off to in your head? Come, let's get another drink.' Misha gives him a friendly slap on the back, then looks across the room, to see what has turned his friend into a statue. 'The blonde?' he asks, puzzled. He has never known a man less easily pleased with women than his best friend, and this girl looks like so many others whom Alexander inevitably turns down.

'No.' Alexander moves across a few steps, to see past the young man who is still standing in front of her. He pulls Misha with him, and they both look at the fine-boned, dark-haired girl. Misha's eyebrows go up, and he laughs slightly, hesitantly. 'If you're going to fall, Sasha, don't fall for that one.'

'Why not?'

Misha does not answer, and Alexander looks at him.

'You know her?'

'A little. Not so well,' replies Misha, with a shrug. 'We grew up around each other. My parents knew her parents. They were university professors. They were taken. Years ago. During the war.' Then he makes the final comment, the one he would have held inside, were it not for all the alcohol sloshing in his head. 'Khrushchev's speech came too late for them.'

Alexander's frown deepens. 'For what reason?'

Misha almost snorts with laughter. An excess of vodka is sharpening everything he feels, making him lapse into stating what they all already know. 'For what reason! The same reason as everyone else. They were declared "enemies of the people". For no damn reason. Some asshole who worked with them probably wanted their jobs, or their apartment or something, and turned them in.'

'Imprisoned?' he asks.

'No. They got their eight grams.' It has been a while since Alexander has heard that expression – the slang for the bullet in the head, the reference being to the weight of that bullet. Misha takes a

25

last drag at the remains of his cigarette and shifts his weight, as though he is suddenly restless.

Alexander is looking back to the chairs where she is sitting. It seems that the young man has been sent away, sauntering with poorly hidden embarrassment back to his laughing friends, and the girl is now listening to the music, watching the guitar player with intent eyes. The musician has fingers that move lightly, flowing like warm water over the rippling strings. Alexander turns back to Misha because a thought has occurred to him. 'Do you . . . I mean, are you . . .?'

Misha waves his hand, which holds an empty glass.

'No, no, not at all. She's pretty, but a handful. Not for me. You go ahead. If you must.'

Alexander pulls his tie back up to his collar and starts off across the room, stepping through the whirling dancers like a man who has plunged into a stormy lake and is determined to make it to the other side.

'Her name is Katya,' Misha calls after him, but there is no acknowledgement from Alexander, who is crossing the room with the solid, blind steps of a sleepwalker.

He is half-way to her when he catches sight of himself in a large, badly tarnished mirror that was once imposing, and that is mounted on the wall to his side. He does not stop, but is taken aback at the sight of the smart, confident-looking young man who looks back at him. His hair is short and neat, his eyes large, with long lashes. His chin shadowed and strong. The poised, purposeful reflection is unrecognisable to him, because inwardly his heart is pumping so loudly that he can no longer hear much of the music, and he can feel the dry taste of nervousness in his mouth. Then he is standing before her, and she is looking up at him, with the same intent, evaluating stare that she gave to the guitar player a few moments ago. Alexander says nothing, and she waits for him to speak, but after a short, stiff bow, he offers her only his hand. He is faintly aware that her companions are giggling, made nervous by his intensity, and at once he feels ridiculous, just standing there, holding out his hand and waiting, especially when he realises that she is not going to take it. In the same instant that he begins to withdraw, however, she reaches out. He looks down, watches her slender fingers lying lightly on his palm, and closes his own over them. The moment feels absurdly romantic to him, but when he glances at her face for recognition of this, her dark eyes hold only an amused, aloof look, and he feels immediately chastened. But he lifts his hand, gently, and she acquiesces and walks with him to the middle of the room where the dancing is, and there they move together, easily. He can hardly feel her against him – she is as light and insubstantial as a shadow – and he looks at her and realises that this is because she is moving with such unconscious elegance, such unconsidered grace, that he has to prevent himself stopping to watch. He can feel the heat of her against his palm, and he tries to partner her well, to keep up, although he is not quite sure how since he can hardly hear the music through the pounding of his heart in his ears.

When the music dies away, it is she who pulls him aside. They have remained together there for some moments after the music has finished, and she waits for him to lead her away from the dancers, but the silent, solemn young man seems unaware that the song has ended. She bites her lower lip, uncertain of what to do next. He has said not one word to her yet, which strikes her as odd; and although something about his boldness and resolution has attracted her this far, now she feels her customary sense of caution returning. 'Thank you,' she tells him politely, with a hint of dismissal in her voice that seems to jolt him into speech.

'Have a drink with me?' he says.

She glances back to the group she has just left. She does not feel like returning to their jokes and giggles and gossip – not just yet. She looks at Alexander and nods. Then, taking his hand once more, she steers him back towards the long tables at Misha's end of the room that serve as a bar. They pass Misha on the way, and Katya smiles at him in recognition, but does not stop to talk for she is preoccupied and sees him only vaguely, as though he were a familiar painting that she is passing while walking quickly through a gallery. When they reach the table, she asks the girl who is watching over the bottles to pour two drinks.

She hands Alexander a glass and picks up the other. 'You are the strangest person I have ever met. And yet . . .' She hesitates.

'And yet?'

'There is something about you that is almost familiar.'

She frowns and raises the glass, as though she has just made a toast, and she drinks down the cool liquid. He offers her his own full glass, but she refuses it.

'Why am I strange?' he asks.

'Because those are practically the first words you have spoken to me.'

'And what is familiar about me?' he asks.

'I don't know.'

'My smell, perhaps?'

She looks suspicious. 'What do you mean?'

'I mean that smells and scents have strong evocations for people, and usually, when you cannot place what is making you comfortable with someone or some place, it is often their smell.'

It is the longest sentence he has spoken to her, and she likes the sound and timbre of his voice. It is reassuring and gentle. 'Are you trying to get me to smell you?'

'No.' He laughs. 'Only if you want to.'

'No, thank you. Some things should be kept for the future.'

She cannot think why she has said that. About the future. Without any thought, it just tumbled out of her mouth, and now he is smiling, he looks happy, as though he is hoping to see her again. Suddenly she smiles too. After all, something has drawn her to this man – perhaps his eyes, which are open and honest and intelligent. 'How old are you?' she asks.

'Do you want to guess?'

'No,' she replies, rolling her eyes. 'I just want to know. I can't tell from the look of you whether you are eighteen or thirty.'

'I am twenty-five.'

'Like me.' She nods, as though this satisfies her in some way, and then she closes her eyes. Etched into the skin between those eyes is a furrow of concentration. Alexander watches her, then asks the girl to pour two more drinks.

When Katya opens her eyes, she sees the young man standing before her with his own eyes tightly shut, and a look of absorption on his face. She laughs. 'What are you doing?'

'I'm trying to see what you were concentrating on so suddenly.'

'And? What was it?'

'The music?' he ventures, and she smiles her affirmation. The musicians are playing more quietly now, and are almost drowned by the rising of voices made freer with alcohol and laughter, but the music is there, behind everything, and it is soft and emotive. An older man has joined them and, with his balalaika, is wafting a mournful tune that twines out over the heads of the crowd like a long curl of blue-tinged smoke.

'I love this song,' Katya says, so quietly that Alexander can barely hear her.

'So do I. Doesn't it remind you of your childhood?'

'Yes. That's exactly it.' She looks away from him. 'My grandmother used to sing it. She'd make my father play the piano to accompany her, and she'd sing it to my brother and me before we went to sleep.'

'Is she still alive?'

Katya shakes her head but offers nothing more, and Alexander looks around at the deaf crowd, then back at the opaque eyes of the girl before him. 'Nobody can hear it except for us, I think.'

'Perhaps he is only playing it for us,' she suggests.

'Yes, perhaps,' he says, and asks her to dance again, for she seems to be on the verge of tears, as she stands there, alone, listening.

His question wakes her from some faraway reverie, from unbidden, unwanted memories – no, they are not even memories, she thinks. It's just a feeling that has enveloped her without warning: that feeling of being a child and being warm, with everything as it should be, nothing complicated or difficult. The smell of onions and fried potatoes still lingering from dinner, and sitting close between Yuri and her mother, and watching her father and grandmother play and sing, and feeling safe and just happy.

'Would you like to dance?' he asks again.

She shakes herself, and refuses, politely, for she feels that if she continues to focus on that song, even by dancing to it, she will start crying. I must speak, she thinks, say something funny or witty or intelligent to this kind-faced young man. Ask him what he does, where he lives, what he thinks, feels, knows. That's what I am supposed to be doing. He is not what I expected to meet here tonight.

She opens her mouth to address him, and he leans forward a little to catch the coming words, but they don't arrive. The perfect bow of her upper lip remains open for a second, but no words come out.

I cannot speak, she realises. I cannot say one word without crying. It must be the drinks. What is in them? Her head turns to the bar table, and she sees the second round of glasses sitting there, brimful, their wet bases leaching colour out of the red paper that covers the table. A hand comes into her line of vision, and she sees long fingers and square nails closing round one glass and raising it up to offer to her. 'Another? Or have you had enough?' Misha is smiling grimly. Beside him, Alexander stands, attentive, polite. 'I think you know each other?' he offers.

Misha nods, his eyes, reddened with too much alcohol, still upon Katya. 'She's like my kid sister,' he tells Alexander, 'which is why I warn her off men like you.'

Alexander laughs. 'Am I so bad?'

'You're too good, my friend. Too good by a long way.'

Katya takes the glass and downs the drink, while Misha watches her. She is restless, annoyed with Misha for interrupting, for breaking the delicate web of memory she had spun here alone with this young man. Now they will be forced to banter with each other, to laugh at stupid jokes that are funny only when you have drunk enough vodka.

'How do you both know each other?' Katya asks.

'We were in the same class at school,' Misha tells her. 'I was the handsome, brilliant, popular one, and he wasn't.'

'Then why were you friends with him?'

'I took pity on him.'

'Are you sure it wasn't the other way round?' Her voice is clipped, with no hint of laughter, and Misha grins to cover his displeasure.

She looks at Alexander. He is smiling at his friend indulgently, but there is also a hint of distance in his eyes that suggests he, too, is finding this conversation tedious.

Misha glances from one to the other, and through the clouds of vodka that have gathered in his head, he sees that both of them are immune, for the moment, to his charm. He takes a deep breath that neither can detect. Never mind, he thinks, I'll deal with this later. Now is not the best time. Without another word, he squeezes

31

Alexander's shoulder, and leans to kiss Katya's cheek. And then, as suddenly as he joined them, he is gone, and they are left alone again among the crowd.

Alexander hands her another drink, and she takes it, then winces and coughs at the burning of the pure liquid snaking down her throat. He rubs the top of her back to ease her discomfort, and she leans in to him, and lays her head on his shoulder. Almost as soon as he has absorbed that she really is leaning against him, that he can feel her whole body beneath his hand on her back, she straightens with an abruptness that surprises him. 'What is it?'

'I hardly know you.'

He cannot contradict this so he stays silent.

'I want to go home,' she says.

'Don't. Please.' He turns to follow her movement away from the bar, and when she looks at him, his eyes are concerned and alert.

'Why not, if I am tired?' She looks much stronger now, less fragile. Misha's interruption has given her time to gather herself together, and he knows that her petulant question is only her way of reasserting herself after the lapse of allowing herself to lean against a strange man. She knows it too. She does not really want to go back to the faded, cold apartment where she lives with her friend Maya and Maya's mother.

'Can I accompany you home?'

She shakes her head. 'Thank you, but there's no need. My roommate is over there. We'll go together.' He turns to see the blonde-haired young woman who had been sitting with her earlier.

'And you won't stay just a few more minutes?'

'I'm tired,' she says, but her tone is softer now – she is physically tired, but also mentally weary of fighting her attraction to this man, just because it is unexpected and unsettling.

'If you are tired, you should go,' he replies. 'I only wanted you to stay because I would like to talk to you, and to see you.' He swallows and makes himself continue. 'But that can wait for another time, perhaps?'

The waiting: the waiting for her to answer, as the crowd of drinkers clustered at the bar around them grows louder and louder. He sees the bulbous eyes and reddened cheeks of the mass of people around him; he watches them shout for the attention of whoever is pouring the vodka, watches them toast each other and drink, and he frowns and fixes his eyes on Katya's face, on her mouth, so that if her reply is drowned in the noise, he will still read it.

'Come to see me,' she tells him, raising her voice above the others around them.

He nods, and waits again.

'At my home. Tomorrow,' she says, and tells him the address.

He repeats it after her, grateful for her trust in him, and she walks away at once, darting among drinkers and dancers. He takes a step as if to follow, but then stops, because he senses that for now his time with her is over. He only wishes he could have left her with some memorable, romantic parting words, and not with the desperate, loudly spoken repetition of her address. He turns back to the bar tables and sees Misha watching him, Alexander feels, and Misha looks away, wrinkling his nose, as if he has just smelt something unpleasant, then orders three more drinks.

He had been planning to take them back to share with the girls he has just left, but by the time they are poured, he somehow thinks better of his plan and he drinks them all down himself.

Chapter Three

Boston, December 2000

A FEW WEEKS AFTER their lunch, he receives a postcard
from Estelle. It arrives at the office, a picture of a sun-drenched
boulevard and palm trees, sitting jauntily and unexpectedly atop the
rest of the more mundane mail of his desk. 'Lots of sun and lots of
facelifts (not mine) here in LA,' it reads. 'Having a break in the sun
while Frank gives a paper at a literary-theory conference. Thanks so
much for lunch. Back on 22nd, for Xmas. Expect you for tea some
time? Estelle.'

Today is the twenty-second. He is pleased to have heard from her
for he had enjoyed their afternoon together, even though by the end
of it he had also been a little disconcerted: with her smiling eyes and
quiet questions, she had stirred the settled surface of his interior past
life. There had been moments during that lunch when he had felt
the carefully filtered, clear, still pool of his memories being shaken,
the clarity slightly sullied by a swirl of dust unexpectedly disturbed.

He props the card against his computer screen, with the written
side facing outwards, then walks out and into the glassed-in conference room. His vice-presidents are already there, as is Melissa
Johnson's small team. Day after day, her people arrive in full, formal

business dress, although Alexander and his employees tend to dress more casually. His company headquarters is a relaxed environment in which to work. People have pictures of or paintings by their children pinned to the walls. There are armchairs and sofas among the desks where informal meetings are frequently held. Outside the row of conference rooms is a large kitchen station that looks like a coffee bar. From there, drinks, snacks and samples of new recipes can be collected throughout the day by any employee. From time to time during longer meetings, an assistant comes in with fresh cakes or muffins.

It immediately irritates him that everyone present already has their laptop flipped open, humming, expectant. It seems to him a false show of eagerness. This deal should have been – could have been – completed in principle several days ago. But he has been finding Melissa intractable on certain key points. As soon as the problems arose, he removed himself from the negotiations for two full weeks, a tactic designed to worry her into compromising – but Melissa appears to have nerves strung like steel wires and has stuck with him every step of the way. In retrospect, he realises that anyone who has come so far so young in the business world as Melissa Johnson is likely to be a far stronger negotiator than he. In fact, what he has been seeing with considerable clarity during the past several meetings is that for the last decades, during all the time he has built up his business, he has been largely protected. He has always had the majority stake in his own firm, he has always been able to run it as he chooses, and he has tended to surround himself with like-minded people. He has never bought or sold a company until now, has never had to play the ruthless games in which others like him are so well schooled. These past weeks have made him feel like something of a gentleman amateur who has wandered into a kind of financial Olympics where all the other players are highly trained and motivated in a single-minded way with which he cannot quite empathise.

He sits down, and pours himself some coffee from the pot that sits on the corner of the table. 'Good morning,' he says to the room, and there is a ripple of greeting in reply. 'Where's Melissa?'

'She's in the bathroom, Mr Ivanov. She'll just be a second.'

He nods, and turns to looks out of the window while they wait.

Melissa Johnson leans her head against the cool glass of the long washroom mirror and closes her eyes against the overhead lights. The oppressive ache in the centre of her forehead, which has been with her since the early hours of the morning, has spread now to the left side of her head, and is building into a deep, throbbing sensation. She knows that, left unattended, it will mutate into a migraine within an hour or two. Not now, she thinks, please not now. She can hardly leave everyone waiting while she rushes out for medication. It would be unprofessional and, even worse, they would all know she was feeling rough. They would certainly sense an advantage. Alexander Ivanov, she feels, is just waiting to sight a weakness so he can up the deal. She rolls her shoulders, a poor attempt to loosen clenched muscles, and tries to recall the last time she had a migraine. She remembers suddenly, and in some detail – she was closing the telecom deal: they'd worked the whole night, and she had forgotten to eat dinner or breakfast. Her blood sugar had dropped. But that was at least two years ago. Since then she has stayed off red wine and red meat, and cut out chocolate and most carbohydrates. She works out each morning and, most useful of all, she has a set of relaxation exercises her trainer taught her, which are unobtrusive enough to use even during business meetings.

She opens her eyes and leans back again. Splashes some water on to her face, then stands gripping the sides of the basin. Today, when she is so near to closing this deal with Alexander, she is tense enough, apprehensive enough, to give herself a migraine, and she hates this. It does not speak well of her inner strength, or her confidence, and she is someone who prides herself on possessing both in copious quantities. She takes a deep breath, then lets it out through her nose in a series of short, sharp, noisy bursts.

Behind her a lavatory flushes, and she starts. Melissa watches in the mirror as the stall door opens and a young woman emerges. Dark hair and eyes, pretty. Tailored trousers, a soft shirt unbuttoned to show some kind of trendy leather necklace round her throat. No jacket. Around thirty years old, Melissa thinks, a few years younger than she. Top-level assistant, possibly very low level management. Probably on about sixty thousand a year.

'Hi,' says the woman. 'You okay?'

'Fine, thanks.'

'Sounded like you were having trouble breathing there.'

Melissa clears her throat. 'No. That was a cleansing breath. It's a yoga thing.'

'Ah.' The woman washes her hands, using enough soap to make a lather that drips messily over the side of the basin. Melissa waits for her to leave, but she dries her hands, then takes out a small washbag. 'What are you cleansing?' she asks.

The question focuses Melissa on the pulsing pain in her temples. She puts a hand to her head as unobtrusively as she can. 'I have the mother of all headaches,' she says.

'Tension?'

Melissa nods.

'Want me to get you something for it?'

Melissa feels elated with relief. 'I'd be grateful,' she says.

The young woman leaves her bag on the sink and disappears. She is back within thirty seconds, and deposits two foil-wrapped tablets in Melissa's hand.

'Thank you,' Melissa says. She looks at the tablets. '*Aspirin?*'

'Yes.'

Melissa shuts her eyes again. 'Thanks.' She almost breathes the word, for all her energy is divided between the disappointment and the effort of pulling herself together. With nothing further than a quick nod to the woman, she turns and leaves.

'How do you want to proceed, Mr Ivanov?' Melissa asks. The directness is typical of her style of work: in a meeting such as this, pleasantries take too much time in relation to their value.

'Let's just get this done,' he replies, matching her tone. 'I'm sure everyone here would like to finish up before Christmas.'

'The holidays have never been important to me,' she replies. 'I think the main thing is to achieve a win-win deal for both sides. And if that means working through Christmas, we'll do it.'

Alexander nods, trying to look tough, when really he feels tired. This is not where he wanted to be three days before Christmas. What he had wanted was to be browsing in delis and supermarkets with nothing more to think about than what to cook for the next meal. And Lauren will be arriving soon to spend the holidays with him. The idea of spices and fruit and roasting has been slowly insinuating itself into his mind, imbuing him with a feeling of festivity. But that feeling is melting away all too quickly under the searing focus of Melissa's laser-like gaze.

There is a knock on the glass door, and it opens to reveal the young woman from the bathroom. Melissa glances at her hand, half hoping that she has searched her out to supply her with a more useful medication, something to kill her headache; but before she can even finish this thought, she is watching Alexander almost leap up from his chair and throw his arms round the woman, who hugs him back. 'I didn't expect you till tomorrow,' he tells her, his face flushed, excited.

'I was able to get away earlier. Sorry to interrupt . . . Betty said I could put my head in . . .' She glances around, conscious of the room full of people watching them. 'Anyway, I didn't have the house keys, so I stopped here.'

'This is Lauren Grinkov, my niece,' he explains, for the visitors' benefit; most of his own team have met her previously.

Melissa computes the name. 'Shareholder,' she says. 'Forty-nine per cent.'

Lauren cannot help but stare. Melissa's gaze is direct, her posture in her chair upright yet also very much at ease, as though the company is somehow already hers. Except for her perfectly high-lighted dark blonde hair and clear grey eyes, she seems an entirely different person from the tense but polite individual of five minutes ago. There has been no greeting, not even a glance of acknowledge-ment. Instead, with four words, Lauren feels she has been stripped of all human traits and reduced to the essence of what she represents here and now, in this boardroom, for the purposes of this meeting. She puts down her handbag and holds out her hand. She will force a modicum of courtesy into this exchange if she has to. 'And you are?'

'Melissa Johnson.'

'Ah. The potential purchaser.'

'Yes.'

'Nice to meet you.' The comment is more than a little pointed. She pauses, looks more closely at Melissa. 'You okay?'

Melissa appears somewhat less comfortable in her seat now. 'Fine, thank you.'

Lauren looks at her uncle. Alexander is giving her a glance of query, an invitation to stay for the meeting. She takes a place to his right-hand side and settles quietly into her chair, accepting with a smile the coffee that he places before her.

'We're stalled right now,' says Alexander, 'and I was telling Melissa that I'd like for us both to be open to compromising a little, if we can.'

'For instance?' Melissa's eyes are intent upon him.

In response, an assistant hands Alexander a printout, several items of which are typed in red ink. His eyes pass down the list and return to the first item. 'The homeless initiative. This was one of the things agreed by your company at the start of negotiations – that you would continue the facilities we have set up to get the homeless off the streets.'

'We're agreed to keep at least fifty per cent of the current shelters. If we can do more, we will.'

'They're not just shelters,' says Lauren quickly. She had planned to say nothing during this meeting, mainly because her understanding of her uncle's business has always been limited. She has always loved his passion for food, the recipe creation, but the intricacies of management, growth and company structuring have never held much interest for her. This point, however, is not about numbers: she knows something about this side of the company. She also knows that she is needled by Melissa Johnson, and she is impelled to prod at her a little, to see what sort of woman lies beneath the crisp, brisk exterior. Melissa turns to her now, waiting. She is composed; there are no signs of headaches or cleansing breaths or anything else that might suggest vulnerability.

'People can go to those facilities, get cleaned up, get fresh clothes and live while they try to find work,' Lauren continues. 'They're given help with the interview process, and when they do find jobs, they can stay till they can afford to pay rent. They're not just places

SHAMIM SARIF

to sleep. They help people into homes of their own. If anything, we need more of them.'

'With all due respect, I'm looking to run a business, not a charity foundation,' replies Melissa.

'So are we,' says Lauren, crisply. 'Isn't that why you're buying us?'

'These are minor issues,' Melissa says, to the table in general. She seems to be trying to avoid Lauren, to slide out from beneath her haughty gaze.

'Not to the people being helped.'

For the first time, Alexander sees Melissa falter, and he is surprised. Certainly Lauren's earnest argument is the kind she would have shredded to pieces with a few pointed rebuffs if he had voiced it. He looks at his niece. Her head is up, her dark eyes fierce. Melissa takes a moment before replying – she is experienced enough in boardroom tactics to know that snapping back now will only allow Lauren to retain the upper hand.

'You're right, you have a very good business,' Melissa says at last. 'And it is entirely your prerogative to give away as much of your profits as you like to charitable causes. But it's equally my prerogative, assuming I buy the company, to give nothing if I choose. I respect your choices, even admire them, but they're your choices. Not mine.'

It is a logical response, and it forces Lauren to nod in acknowledgement.

Alexander clears his throat. 'The philanthropic side of things has always been a very major part of our business, Melissa. It's a huge part of who we are as a company,' he says. 'More to the point, I believe I stated at the start that it's very important that they are continued by whoever takes over. What chance is there that you can continue everything as is?'

'Everything?'

42

'The homeless initiatives, the arts foundation, the micro-financing for immigrant start-up businesses . . .'

'At a cost of eight million dollars a year? It's unlikely.'

'But not impossible?' Lauren smiles at her encouragingly, radiantly.

Melissa blinks, tapping her pen. She reminds herself that this woman probably doesn't even know a cash-flow from a bank statement. 'I'm afraid it is impossible. Maybe we should move on.'

Although this is doubtless part of the ebb and flow of working out a business deal, Lauren cannot help but feel this response as a personal affront. More concerning to her is that she can see her uncle wavering. Surely it cannot be so easy for all that he has worked for and believed in to be lost? She can see that Melissa's headache is back, or at least on its way. She holds her gaze for a long moment, then turns to her uncle.

Alexander has already outlined in his mind a contingency plan. A situation in which one of his subsidiary companies would retain control of the charity initiatives in exchange for an increased purchase price up front, and perhaps a small percentage of sales ongoing. He is considering whether to suggest this to Melissa now, when he catches his niece's eye. What he reads there surprises him, but also reassures him in some way – because he finds that he is in agreement. There is a pause as he examines his pen thoughtfully. Nobody is moving, no coffee cups touch the table, the shifting of pressed cotton shirts against the leather chairs has stopped. Only the background drone of the computers fills the space. He looks at Melissa. 'I'm sorry. Without the initiatives, there's no deal to be made here.'

With considerable dramatic flair, Lauren zips up her handbag, finishes the last gulp of her coffee and edges back her chair.

Melissa looks from one to the other calmly, giving not the slightest hint of her internal impulse, which is to lay her pounding head against the table and close her eyes in resignation. 'Fine,' she says, and before anyone else can speak, she excuses herself and is gone.

There is a lively, light feel to the large house now that Lauren is there. From the kitchen, he can hear a jazz CD playing above him, the upbeat sound bouncing down to him. He wipes his hands and makes his way upstairs. The bathroom door is open, and the bathroom empty, but it is still hung about with moisture, steam and scent. The music is coming from the suite of rooms that he has always kept for Lauren; here, too, the door is ajar. He walks towards it slowly and quietly, wanting to savour this moment, when his niece is home earlier than he had hoped. And some other, smaller part of him is already lost in dreams as he stands on the landing, imagining a world where he always comes home to find someone who lives with him, and waits for him and expects to hear his step in the doorway. It is a pleasurable feeling, one that suffuses his whole being and confuses him, the way the gentle waking from a wonderous dream overwhelms and unbalances.

He stops just before the open door. Through the crack of the hinges, he can see her. While the music jumps and dips all around her, Lauren is lying on the bed, motionless except for the occasional blinking of her eyes. He knocks at the open door, loudly, and she sits up at once.

'You look thoughtful,' he says.

She waves away the comment, and swings her legs off the bed. 'It's good to be here. Feels like home.'

'Good. This is your house, you know. I wish you'd live here.'

'I'd drive you crazy.' She smiles.

'You mean, I'd drive *you* crazy,' he replies. 'Don't say anything. I know. Your "fastidious uncle".'

'You always throw that back at me, Uncle Alex,' she said. 'I meant it in a nice way. Anyway, I might stay a while, if it's okay with you.'

She is avoiding his look and he at once infers why. 'And Carol? How is she?'

She turns away a little and takes a long time to fasten her leather-strapped watch on to a fragile-looking wrist.

'I don't know,' she says, still looking down. 'I haven't seen her in a few weeks.'

He waits, but she does not elaborate. 'I'm sorry,' he says at last.

'Don't be. It hasn't been working out for a while now. It's for the best. I guess I was just surprised by how much I missed her. When she left.'

There is a weight in her voice that lends it an unnaturally low tone and tells him she is only a step away from tears. 'So it's definitely over?'

'Yeah, but it's fine.' She looks up at him now. 'You know me. Easy come, easy go.'

She regrets saying this as soon as the words are uttered. It is the kind of blithe, throwaway comment that she might be able to get away with among people who don't know her so well, but her uncle's kind eyes see directly through her. Earlier that day he had read her meaning in the meeting, and he can read her now, although he is, of course, too considerate to say anything. 'Anyway, I thought an extended time away from New York might not be a bad thing.'

'I would love it,' he tells her, and takes her hand encouragingly. 'And if your performance this morning was anything to go by, you can help me complete the sale.'

'What sale? I thought I blew it.'

Alexander shakes his head. 'I think you may have saved it. Let's wait and see.'

'I hope so. Last thing I wanted to do was ruin your deal.'

'Our deal,' he corrects. 'And I made the decision.'

It is typical of him to try to remove the responsibility from her shoulders for what might turn out to have been a bad mistake. 'Let's go get something to eat,' she says. 'I'm starving.'

Downstairs, she rummages in her bag and hands him a bottle of wine, which he holds at arm's length to read the label without searching for his glasses.

'Lauren!' It is an excellent wine and an excellent vintage. He knows she must have spent a fortune on it.

'Well, I wanted to bring you something nice. I have another – a Burgundy this time – for Christmas dinner.'

'You shouldn't be spending your money like this.'

'Stop. I do well with my painting.' She shrugs. 'I'm getting a lot of private work now. Everybody wants to see themselves up on a wall. Apparently there was an article, in *Vanity Fair* or the *New Yorker* or somewhere, recommending it. So now I'm in great demand. I've been spending my time in the houses of some of New York's finest. I could tell you some tales.'

'Here, have a glass of wine, and let's talk.'

She laughs, a deep, happy sound, and takes his hand, the affectionate grasp of a mother telling off an errant child. 'I have to respect client confidentiality, you know.'

'Really? We'll test that after the wine.'

She watches him decant the contents of the bottle, slowly and respectfully. Then he loosens a pâté of *foie gras* from its tin and slices fresh bread while directing her to wash salad leaves at the sink.

'Dressing?' she asks.

'I have homemade vinaigrette from last night. Or shall I make fresh?'

'That *is* fresh. You'd die if you saw the bottled stuff I throw over my salad.'

They transport their meal into the living room, spreading every-thing over a table that sits between the armchairs, and then they discuss the details of the sale.

'Uncle Alex, are you sure you're ready to sell?'

He has thought about this continuously during the last few weeks. He sips the wine appreciatively. 'You know that after Katya this work, building this company, became everything to me. But for the last few years I haven't felt driven. Not the way I used to. Maybe I'm just getting old, but at my age I don't want to spend even another month doing something I'm not excited about. I don't have to.'

'So what are you excited about now?'

'For now I'll be happy just cooking, and taking it easy. I'm tired, Lauren. Maybe you can teach me more about art too. How long have we been meaning to go round all the museums and galleries together?'

Lauren nods in acknowledgement. The warmth of the fire and the wine have seeped into her muscles, loosening and soothing them, and her head feels heavy. To shake off the sensation, she stands and walks about the room. Her gaze catches, as always, on the photograph of Katya that sits on the piano. Her aunt. The younger sister of Lauren's father, Yuri. Lauren was a late and completely unexpected arrival for her parents, at a time when they had long assumed that they could not have children. Her mother was thirty-seven, her father already fifty when she was born. As a small girl in a crowded, slowly decaying area of south Boston, her father would tell her stories about his old life in the Soviet Union; and often these stories were built round his memories of, and longings for, his own parents and his sister Katya. In these tales, she had come to know her aunt as a lively, spirited young girl who always outwitted her more pedestrian older brother. Through her father's stories, Lauren had found in Katya a vivid character for the imagination, to be cheered on in their childhood escapades in the quiet side-streets of a Moscow suburb. She was a heroic, colourful figure in an exotic setting, made up of those qualities that mattered so much to the young Lauren – daring, defiance, laughter, and sophistication of a sort.

It had been a considerable time later that the deeper, more mature knowledge of her aunt had come from Alexander. She remembered only a little of her aunt's husband from her childhood – he had been a quiet, kind presence, but one without much impact in her life until her parents' deaths. In quick succession, Yuri had suffered a heart-attack, then her mother died of cancer, and when she found herself flailing in the ensuing void, she had found that Alexander was there, holding out a hand and emotional sustenance, and she had gratefully allowed him to step in, and confide in her, trust her and love her.

She had understood that at least some of his initial interest in her teenage self had stemmed from her strong blood link with his great love. But it took little time for him to come to know her on her own terms: their relationship had deepened quickly, and he came to love her as if she were his own child. If the line of her chin, or the colour of her eyes, or the tilt of her head offered him an occasional, fleeting, aching suggestion of his late wife, then that was only to be expected and understood. Lauren has never felt that she bore a great resemblance to her aunt, but her hair and eyes are dark, very dark. These features, combined with the simple fact that Katya died young, at around the age Lauren is now, probably continues to make noticeable the occasional passing similarity.

Alexander was aware that the mystery and tragic elements of Katya's story might have lent it a kind of glamour in his niece's eyes, for she was distanced enough from the events and emotions of that time for them to seem dramatically unreal. And Katya had lived her brief life with an intense passion and conviction that would be irresistible to any young woman. It was with slow inevitability, then, that Lauren moved away from her uncle's reticence in excavating the past, and towards a trip to Russia to explore the places where he and Katya had lived and grown up. It had been a momentous journey for her, a revisiting of roots that was accompanied by all the romance and excitement of a new city and a wholly different culture. She had visited the usual museums and galleries and the Kremlin, but what she remembers best, what she still savours inside when she recalls that trip, are the small, quiet moments. She remembers standing on a street corner outside the building where Alexander and Katya had once lived. She had imagined them returning there, weary after work. She imagined them walking out together along the snow-crusted river. She rode the metro that her aunt might have taken on her way to work. Or to so many other, secret places. She had sought out archives that might shed more light on her death and her life, but found only a sparse, clinical summary that added nothing to what they already knew. She had even looked, without much hope, for their old friend Misha. Someone who might give her a more intense taste of their lives then, of why things had turned out as they had. She had asked Alexander to accompany her, but he had made his excuses and declined. Without wishing fully to consider his own reasons for refusing, he had simply attributed her fascination to her artistic, romantic temperament, and left it at that.

'I wish you could have met her,' says Alexander, softly, as he watches Lauren looking at Katya's photograph.

'I would have liked that.'

Alexander runs a hand over his head. He is weary and an air of melancholy, of unfulfilled longing, has taken him over.

She returns to the fireside, where they sit in silence for a few minutes, and when she glances at him, she sees that he has fallen asleep. Quietly, she removes their plates; when she comes back he has nodded awake again.

'You fell asleep,' she says.

'I was just resting my eyes,' he tells her, and his smile lets them both know that he is lying. 'What shall we do now?'

'I'm going to read a bit,' she tells him. 'And you're going to bed.'

He protests, but she is adamant and knows how to handle his insistence; with an effort that he tries to hide, he gets up from the chair.

'Are you sure?'

'A good book, a glass of wine and a roaring fire. I'm in heaven,' she tells him.

She walks with him to the staircase, the panelled hallway cool after the warmth of the flames, and he leaves her with a kiss. She watches him walk upstairs, then returns to the living room. Half-way back to her chair she stops with an abrupt turn, and moves to the piano. She sits down on the cracked leather stool and lets her hands move over the keys: the ivory is soft, almost powdery to the touch, and her fingers recall their character at once, remembering that they need only the most delicate pressure to coax out the full tone and nuance of each note. She plays for perhaps twenty minutes, a series of melancholy pieces that leave her somehow indulged and depressed. She sits back and looks at Katya's picture again. She gives it a close, detailed stare that now contains no emotion, only the cool precision of the artist's eye. She is evaluating angles, shade, light, expression. She remains absorbed in this way for several minutes, until at last she steps back with a small sigh, a sound that encompasses both satisfaction and regret.

Chapter Four

Moscow, March 1956

THE MORNING AFTER the party there is not enough water in the whole of Moscow to slake Misha's thirst. His throat burns as he drinks another cupful. This insatiable thirst always takes hold of him after he has drunk too much – that, and the sensation that his stomach is hollow, burned clean, as though scoured with acid. He glances down at his flat abdomen, lean and keenly muscled like the rest of his tall, lithe body. He looks fit and healthy – he is healthy, for the most part, even though on mornings like this it can take a little time for his body to remember that. But six or seven long draughts of cold water, some strong tea and black bread go a long way to bringing him back to himself, after which he will bathe, and wash his curly cropped hair in the sink, allowing himself to enjoy the soft oiliness of the soap lather around his ears and forehead.

Twenty minutes later he is dressed. Dark trousers and a black roll-neck sweater that fits his slim contours closely. Over these he shrugs on a long, thin overcoat. He does not bother with a hat. He spends all day at the Aviation Institute, becoming warmer and warmer under the over-zealous heating, and he likes the grasping rush of the cold evening air that plays over his head when he walks out at the end of the working day. Anyway, he is not prone to colds, has never been a sickly man, and if you treat the Russian winter like an enemy who has power over you, you will be caught out by it every time.

She is waiting for him at a bar just a few blocks from her apartment. Misha sees her inside, drinking a glass of tea, and he slows down as he approaches. This evening the inside of the bar is illuminated and has an unreal quality, as though it is a festive stage set, placed in the middle of the fading, dank, slush-lined streets that surround it. And in the centre of the lights and warmth and smoke Katya sits alone at a small table. He watches her keenly as he approaches, then smiles when she looks up and catches sight of him. He goes straight to the bar and orders two vodkas, then kisses her cheek.

'I don't want a vodka,' she says. 'I had too much last night.'

'I know,' he says, easily, with mild sarcasm.

She waits for him to explain himself.

'I've never seen you behave like that with anyone.'

She presumes that he is referring to Alexander, and is momentarily pricked by his directness, then irritated. What concern is it of his how she acts at a party? A taut reply rises to her lips, but she holds it back: she realises now that he must have mentioned Alexander for a reason.

Misha wastes no time in explaining. 'He's government,' he says. 'Nice position too. Couldn't you tell?'

A pause. 'Ah, yes,' she says. 'Of course . . .'

Beneath the even tone of her voice, Katya is shocked. Shocked that the man whom she found so appealing and attractive, so unexpectedly, is working directly for the system she so despises. And she is even more surprised that she did not pick this up straight away. Now that she considers it, the signs were there: the neat blue suit; the sense of uniformity, a bland correctness, in his manner, his dress, even the shine on his shoes. All these things should have alerted her. It should not have been difficult to spot. In the end those political pigs are all the same, on the surface and deep down.

'I told you I drank too much,' she says, and her ironic tone is a cover for the small pang of disappointment that she also feels in her stomach. She had really liked him, for a while. 'He's so young,' she says.

'I know. Nice, too. A little boring, but nice.'

He has already drunk both vodkas. He stands up and pays the bill, and Katya puts on her coat. She understands that the rest of this conversation is best held outside. 'Are you using him?' she asks, her voice altered in the vast dampness of the outdoor air.

Misha smiles. 'Alexander is not easily used. He is a man of integrity. And he would have suspected me if I'd tried for information. Besides, only now is he in a really useful position.'

The pause that follows seems to her to be a test. He is waiting for her reply, for the right reply, and it should not be so hard for her to give it. Perhaps it only seems a little difficult because she had liked Alexander. She swallows the last taste of disappointment that remains in her mouth and speaks: 'Seems like a good opportunity,' she says.

He turns with a half-smile and examines her face. 'It is. Could be. If you can keep your head. If you're not attracted to him.'

'You know me, Misha.'

'Yes, I do.' He stops walking and holds her gaze. 'That's why I was surprised. Last night. I've never seen you like that with anyone.'

She sighs. 'I liked him. But if he's government, he's everything I work against. It's not a dilemma for me. It's black and white.'

'Good.'

'But he's coming tonight. To see me. I told him he could,' she adds, with as much nonchalance as she can manage.

'You don't waste any time, do you?'

'I don't think that's something you should be concerned about.'

He raises an eyebrow but lets the comment go, and they walk on side by side in silence. Beneath her ribs, deep inside her empty stomach, Katya feels the teasing itch of fear and the flickering of excitement. This could be an opportunity for her, a chance to make a difference. To tap her own source, not just pass out information from others.

'Listen,' Misha says, and he is all briskness, all business now. 'If you can do it, it would be wonderful. Just imagine. But it's not easy to become involved with someone purely to betray them. You have to be emotionally strong. Clear. Clean. Business is business.'

'I know.'

'I hope so.' She resists the urge to turn away. Evidently she must reassure him a little more if she is to be trusted with this job. 'Misha, he's sweet. Like a puppy. But now that I know who he is, I *can't* fall for him. It's impossible, it would be a denial of everything I am. If you want me to do it, I will.'

He finds himself momentarily irritated at her admission that she felt some attraction, any attraction, to Alexander. When it comes to women, he has within him a certain expectation, born of arrogance, which means that he is always slightly surprised by their awareness of anyone other than himself. But her earnest, decisive tone now pleases him, and she can see that. He is not the type to express himself openly: he prefers to play games with people, to keep his responses neutral and unreadable wherever possible. But she knows him well enough to read the quickening of his step and the bright animation of his manner as he instructs her: 'Very good. For the next few months, you captivate him. Get to know him, allow him to know a little of you, enough for him to fall in love – and, above all, get him to trust you. He's a good man, and he hasn't yet had disappointments in life. He's young, like us,' he adds, his voice lower, perhaps even hesitant. 'He trusts easily.'

They are at the crossroads behind her apartment, and he has stopped. 'I'll leave you here,' he says. 'Think about it a little. Start seeing him, and think about it. You must be sure.'

'I am sure.'

He smiles. The pleasurable tension of a new avenue, a new contact; the arousal of a new game. A pulse of energy moves through him. He will go out tonight and celebrate. Drink a little and find a girl with pretty eyes to flirt with and make love to. 'Then good luck,' he says. 'Let me know how it goes. Keep me updated every step of the way.'

She nods, accepts the touch of his cold lips on her cheek, and turns to cross the road, her mind still reeling with the shift that has occurred. Within the space of a few minutes the focus of her evening, and perhaps even her life's work, has changed. The heady excitement of attraction and potential romance has brewed into a bitter but real possibility of stolen government secrets, the possibility of making herself useful at first hand, not just as a go-between. This, after all, is what she has always struggled for. Let the real work begin now, Katya, she thinks. You can do it. Let the work begin.

One month later

Katya squints into the bright morning. She can hardly see her way to school through the snow that flurries around her. There is no hint of a blizzard in this springtime snow: there is barely any wind, and the fall itself is not heavy, but her head is light, and the glare of the whiteness that has already coated the streets is dizzying her further.

She walks along in the right direction; after all, she knows the way to her own place of work. But all around her fat flakes of frosted water land gently on the ground, on her head and on her arms; one or two alight upon her eyelashes. She narrows her eyes to close down her field of vision. The snow dances lightly around; when she tries to watch, and follow the descent of some few, particular flakes, she finds them eddying about her, disconcerting and teasing her, following a balletic path, spiralling downwards, and whirling back up, pausing to whisper kisses of cold moisture against the exposed tips of her ears.

She thinks briefly of Alexander. It has been four weeks since the night they met and she has seen him a few times. Fewer meetings than he would have liked, which is how she feels it should be: she is teasing out his eagerness. He came to see her again last night, and she talked to him. That, she knew, was the way to begin. To reveal something of herself, not to probe him, not just yet. And although she has asked him a little about himself, he has been uninterested in replying at any length – in that respect he seems unlike most other people she knows. Instead, he has been full of questions to her – her work, her daily life, her thoughts and hopes and fears. She told him about the first two. I am a school administrator. I run the school. And I get up at this time, and eat that for lunch, and do this in the afternoon, and sleep at around this time. The rest could come later, or not at all. He will wait for her tonight, this time at his apartment. She smiles to herself. Although she told him little of real depth, she felt a liberation of some kind in speaking to him. Any kind of self-revelation is so rare for her that the mere fact of spending several hours with one human being who is focused solely on her, interested only in what interests her, has given her an unfamiliar sense of release. Of light-headedness. What will happen if she does not find her way back through this shower of snow? What if these pattering, dancing, floating flakes blind her and unhinge her and mislead her, and whisk her far away into the immutable, unending whiteness of the desert, and what if she never makes it home again? The long, pure vista of snow that she sees stretching out before her will continue for ever and ever, she feels, and her head is almost spinning with the seductive pain of being surrounded only by whiteness and cold, no humans, no life, no end to it.

At the street corner she stops, disconcerted, and finds that she is standing next to other people. Coated, hatted, bundled black shapes, blurry against the ice. She is back in the city, back on the street that she knows by heart, and has been removed from the snowbound Siberian plain of her imagination. So, she thinks, as she crosses the street with the other shapes, I will continue to live in this new world of mine, I will see him tonight, and he will see me, and we will carry on this game of getting to know each other a little better.

Five minutes later, she is inside the echoing concrete hallway of the school. Her everyday mind is returning as, bit by bit, the brilliant white of her imagination is painted over with the various greys of the building. The stairs, the floor, the thick metal doors. The grey cabinets and chairs, and her own metal desk. Her grey metal typewriter. The grey skin of some of the teachers. The grey hair of the head teacher, who asks Katya, every few months, if she would not like to teach instead. If she would not like to be out of the administration offices and in front of a class of minds eager for knowledge.

Not for the knowledge I would be forced to teach them, she thinks, as she refuses again, politely. The children would love you, the head teacher tells her; they already do. Her heavy squat body and square rustic face nod to the young woman in hopeless encouragement. Yes, Katya thinks, but children are innocent and superficial. They like me because I am prettier than most of their teachers, and because I am young. They would have crushes on me, the small girls and the small boys. They don't care about anything else. Do they?

She has seen their eyes, the little children who come to that school, and she has seen in them a thirst and an adoration that shocks her. Such naked emotion in the eyes of those children. Smile at them, and they smile. Shout and they withdraw. Hit them and they cower. Such raw power those greying teachers hold. She wants no part of it, not directly. She does what she has to do behind the scenes. Curricula, timetables, state funds. As good a job as any other to earn a wage and fill her days. But she would rather not face that dependence and devotion, that innocence, which has already had its new, sharp edges roughed away by state and parents.

She hates herself when she thinks like this, but she does not often think any other way. She herself has cowered, and longed for love from too many different aunts and uncles and friends with whom she spent her own childhood and adolescence. Much of the time she was even separated from her only brother. No one wanted to take in two orphans. Two extra mouths to share the thin soups and occasional meat at the table. Two more pairs of feet to buy decent shoes for. In her loneliness, craving the love of her parents and the companionship of her older brother, she learned to turn in to her own mind and heart for the satisfaction she sought. Hours spent learning how to unfurl her imagination, teaching herself to fight through to the furthest reaches of her mind to remove herself from the lonely, terrifying world she now inhabited. Nights spent holding herself in, learning to be content with her own company, to push away the longing for others, and to trust only herself. A good training, as it turned out, but not the easiest way to live. Alexander is already trying to find a way into her interior life. She shakes her head at the idea. She walks into the office, and smiles a hello at Svetlana, who shifts self-consciously in her seat. At her desk Katya begins to sort out the stack of letters and memos that has piled up since yesterday afternoon.

For once the day is passing swiftly, and Katya types away, fingers dancing over the clattering keys.

'I can do those for you,' Svetlana says.

'I've given you more than enough for one day,' Katya replies. Besides, she likes the feel of the keys, and to watch the words being formed on the paper before her. She works with a soothing rhythm that is slowly freeing her unconscious mind, and she is finding that her thoughts are drawn repeatedly to Alexander.

With a start she looks up. At her open door, two round blue eyes are staring at her out of an oval face, and they are welling with tears. The boy must be five or six, and his knee is bleeding. She stands and goes to him, kneels down beside him. 'Did you fall?' she asks.

He nods, and the tears pool out and edge down his cheeks. She touches his head affectionately, then stands and briskly gets out a box of tape and bandages.

'Shall I take him to the nurse?' Svetlana asks, half rising from her chair.

'I'll manage,' Katya replies.

'But all injuries are supposed to be reported to the nurse . . .'

Svetlana's voice trails away, silenced by Katya's look of disbelief. 'It's not a sin to do things differently now and then, Svetlana,' she says, with a laugh in her voice. Svetlana subsides, her full lips pursed hard against the mockery.

Katya cuts a small piece of tape, and applies it to the bandaged knee. 'There you are. Is that better?'

The boy glances down, uncertain.

'You're a brave young man, aren't you?' she says.

He eyes her, suspiciously. Her amiable, kind tone is unexpected, and he turns suddenly and runs away. Katya watches him go with a small pain in her heart, and anger flashing in her eyes. Not at the boy, but at everything that has made him push her away. She is almost sitting down at her desk again when she stands instead, and the abrupt scraping of her chair, together with the metallic slam of the office door, which Katya throws open, make Svetlana look up, wide-eyed. But Katya is already gone, her chair having fallen to the floor.

She is running down the hallway. It is silent and deserted, for the children have started their final lesson. But as she flies down the corridor and round a corner, she sees her little boy, the one with the cut knee: he is almost back at his classroom. He stares at the woman bearing down on him, and she stops, and they watch each other. She considers. Another kind word and he will probably run again. 'Come here,' Katya tells him, with authority, although she is suddenly unsure what she is doing, following this unknown child.

He frowns, then slowly walks down the corridor towards her. He stands before her, and she looks down at the top of his head, her arms folded. 'Please,' she says. 'Please don't run from me like that,' she says, her voice low and kind now.

Quickly, she passes her fingers through his hair, caressing it, tidying it, and then she walks back down the corridor. She can hear the echoing of her own footfalls clamouring at her from the hollow walls, but nothing else. She turns again, and the boy is standing there, watching her still. His soft eyes are too large, too tentatively adoring, too thrilled. She closes her own against them. 'Go back to your lesson,' she says, pushing a tone of command into her voice, and he runs from her, back to the classroom.

*

'Where did you go to?' Svetlana's timid voice makes Katya want to snap back a reply.

'Bathroom,' she says.

'Oh.'

Katya suspects very strongly that her secretary's main purpose in life, or at least here at school, is to watch her. Either she is one of those people whose lives are so dull and mean that she keeps herself from boredom by spying on everyone around her, or she has a definite instruction from someone somewhere to keep an eye on Katya. This would not be unusual, given that Katya's parents were executed under Stalin as enemies of the state; and her brother Yuri's subsequent escape to the United States did nothing to help the situation. But, then, Katya has always relished a challenge, and had begun her campaign for acceptance and credibility in the Party long ago as a young Pioneer. In her smart uniform – a red hat and scarf over a white shirt, which were some of the best pieces of clothing she owned – she had stood in an orderly row and sworn solemnly to uphold the ideals of Lenin, Stalin, the Party, the country. She still remembers the thundering sound of hundreds of childish voices around her, echoing through the hall in which they stood. Soon after that she had calmly signed a denouncement of her parents, requested of her at the age of thirteen as her civic duty. That had won her some points for 'heroism' in the Party records. Even then, at that age, with no idea of how she could ever effect revenge for her parents' deaths, she was clear in her own mind that she wanted to do so. It was always a question of how not whether she should.

She glances once more at Svetlana. Her light brown eyes hold streaks of gold, and they are superficially striking, but they are always darting, watching; and her delicate mouse-like ears are always twitching. There is plenty of use for unassuming, steady people like her: the local residents' associations, the work councils, the police – they all use observations from people like that all the time.

The school bell rings, and a dulled scraping of chairs in thirty rooms above and around them penetrates the thick, solid blocks of the office walls. Katya looks at her co-worker and smiles. The girl is pleased, and smiles back coyly, but not without a desperation behind her light eyes that makes Katya shiver inwardly. She looks back to her own desk, and listens. Outside the office door, hundreds of pairs of feet hustle through the corridor. There is no stampede for the door – even getting out of this place cannot inspire these children with enthusiasm, Katya thinks. She tries to settle down to her work. These last hours of the day are always the longest for her, after most of the children have gone home. Some of them stay late to attend music or sports clubs. Either these children have a talent to cultivate, or they need somewhere to wait until one or other of their parents is back from work. There is an incomplete feel to the buildings at this time, as though the quiet heart of it has been sucked out. She looks down, and tries to work.

'Did you get rid of the books?' Katya asks some time later.

'Yes.' Svetlana looks depressed. 'I know orders are orders but . . .' She stops as if she is about to reveal something shameful.

'What?' asks Katya.

'I think it's terrible,' Svetlana blurts out. 'To throw out good text books because they praise Comrade Stalin too much!'

Katya reins in her contempt and amusement, but her eyes retain a disingenuous gleam. 'You wouldn't think it was possible, would you?' she says to Svetlana.

'Exactly. I know Comrade Khrushchev does not want to exalt him, but Stalin was a truly great man.'

Katya glances at the clock on the wall behind her. It is nearly six o'clock, and she begins to pack up her things.

'It's only five minutes to,' Svetlana points out helpfully.

'I can read a clock,' Katya tells her. 'I am going home.'

Svetlana watches Katya's swift, easy movements. Her admiration of her beautiful superior, with her tall, slim figure and her ink-black hair and eyes, has turned to envy over the past year, and even dislike. Svetlana, too, is pretty in her way, and as helpful as she can be, and she has tried to make Katya like her, but she will not.

''Bye, Svetlana,' Katya says.

''Bye, Katya.' There is a pause – enough to mark a change of subject but not enough to allow Katya to escape.

'Doing anything tonight?' Svetlana asks, and her sugary friendliness makes Katya's skin crawl.

'No.' She is seeing Alexander. She will go to his apartment, where he wants to cook dinner for her. But that is something private. Even when it has nothing to do with her clandestine work, Katya has never been one to speak of her internal life, of thoughts and feelings, even to her few friends.

'No,' she repeats. 'You?' she asks politely, although she does not really care.

'I am rereading Comrade Stalin's speeches. A little every evening,' Svetlana replies.

That should be a stimulating night, thinks Katya, but her eyes lose nothing of their polite smile. 'They are very interesting,' she says. 'Very good.'

'I know. They—'

'I have to go.'

'Going home, Katya?' she asks.

'I already said so,' is the curt reply.

'Oh.' Svetlana looks down at her account books once again. 'It's just . . . you don't always go straight home after work. Do you?'

Katya resists the impulsive response, which is to stare sharply at the girl, to evaluate the meaning of her words. Instead, she keeps her eyes down and begins searching for her hat. When she finds it, she pulls it out, looks at Svetlana with a sigh and says, 'Don't you have anything else to worry about?'

She takes a step or two forward, so that she is standing even nearer to the girl in the oppressive office that they share, then puts on the hat, and dons her coat and gloves, slowly and methodically, pulling the woollen casing over each slender finger. Her eyes are softer now, dancing, with a hint of flirtation in them, and they are fixed upon the girl's own. It is a dirty trick, and Katya knows it, but she holds the look anyway, watches the other glance away, then the darting eyes becoming inexorably drawn back. Svetlana is confused: something about Katya makes her heart beat heavily and her stomach feel weak.

'See you tomorrow, Svetlana,' she says, as she walks out at last.

'See you tomorrow.' The voice is whispery, hopeful.

Why do you play such games? Katya asks herself. If she is dangerous she will only become more so if you tease her like that. But she does not stop to think about it any more. When she steps outside, the snow is still falling and, with a feeling of pleasure, she steps into the tumbling flakes, thinking briefly of the boy in the corridor, and the evening still to come.

His apartment building is new, of course, high and wide, and it overlooks the river. It is no more than twenty years old, and was constructed specifically to house government employees; particularly the privileged ones. His own rooms are bright, and very warm; the over-heated air feels stolen from some distant tropical place. The space is brilliantly illuminated with lamps, candles, wall-mounted lights. She walks in from the early-evening gloom, and immediately she has entered another, more welcoming, more pleasurable world. She places her coat in his waiting hands, and catches the clean, soapy scent of his hair when he leans to kiss her cheek. While he goes to pour them each a glass of vodka, she looks around. What must it cost for the electricity to light this building? And the gas to heat it? Yet who would not want to live here always?

'What are you thinking about?' he asks, handing her a glass.

'How light it is in here.'

'A privilege that I enjoy to the fullest,' he tells her. 'I hate the dark.'

'Like a little boy?' She smiles.

'Well, not the darkness, really. I mean the dreary grey light of winter. The dusk at any time. That sort of thing.'

'Yes,' she says. 'I know what you mean. It can be oppressive.'

In the kitchen she stands watching him. He has a chicken. Whole and uncut, and it is roasting in the black oven with potatoes. She watches him cut up winter vegetables and toss them in a dressing of vinegar, with a little oil and salt. She offers to help him, but he refuses. 'I love doing this.'

She can see that he does. His fingers move with grace, weighing the knife, scooping up the strips of carrot, cabbage and beetroot, stirring the simmering pots.

'You look very happy.'

He stops stirring to look at her, and his large brown eyes are serious and kind. 'I am happy,' he says. 'I am happy that we met. And that you are here now.'

'Thank you.' She is embarrassed by his openness. It is not what she is used to, and she walks away a little, under pretence of looking into the oven. She pulls open the door, and glances in at the roasting bird.

*

65

As they eat, he tells her that he works as a first secretary to a minister, a good, trustworthy position. She shows little interest; she does not want to think about this now. Her first task is to get to know him, let him feel he knows her, and let him begin to love her. There will be time later for finding out these practical things. For now, she remains wholly absorbed in her plate. The flesh of the chicken is soft and melting; it possesses a texture and taste she has never before encountered and that bears no resemblance to the stringy specimens of fowl she has eaten before. 'This is an incredible meal,' she says. He thanks her.

'Who do you work for, Alexander?' she asks, and her eyes have a glow in them, as though she is sharing a joke with herself.

'A government minister,' he repeats.

'From the quality of this chicken, I think it must be Khrushchev himself,' she jokes.

He laughs. 'The chicken was not a privilege. At least, not directly. You know Misha?'

'Yes, of course,' she replies. 'We were friends growing up. Not that close, but we saw each other occasionally.'

'We were best friends when we were boys. He was a genius with physics and mathematics. All the subjects I hated. He'd help me with my science homework, and I'd help him with history and literature. He's still one of my closest friends. The closest, probably.'

She says nothing to this, and he has to draw himself away from the dark beauty of her eyes, watching him.

'Anyway, his grandmother is part of a small *kolkhoz*, out in the country. She raises all her own chickens and a few pigs and goats. His father was coming into the city a few days ago, so I gave him the cash for her best chicken, and he carried it with him on the train. Under his jacket. Flapping away, no doubt. And here it is.'

66

She smiles at the story. 'Do you always go to so much trouble for food?'

'This was an exceptional occasion,' he tells her, 'but yes, I enjoy good food – when one can get it. Life can be full of small pleasures, if you take some time now and then to enjoy them.'

'Most people don't,' she says, which is the closest she can get to saying anything about herself.

'Why do you say that?' he asks, not because he disagrees, but because he would like to hear her thoughts, to draw her out of her reserve.

She takes a drink and considers. 'People are too used to thinking about the past or the future. There is no consideration for the present. It is taken for granted.'

'Perhaps that is because many people are unhappy with their lot in life. They are hoping for a better future. That is the promise this country has made them.'

She is surprised at his sympathy for people less well off than himself, but also irritated at his politician's talk of promises. 'Those promises have been made for many years,' she says.

'What do you suggest?'

She has already noted four places where bugs may be in this government apartment and, anyway, her true thoughts do not concern him. 'At least the worst is over,' she says.

'Yes. The worst is over. Now, after the long winter, comes *ottepel*.' The snow melt. Khrushchev's famous 'thaw', after the stiff, frozen years of Stalin's rule. He carves more meat and, with a smile of thanks, she holds up her plate to accept it.

He does not, that evening, specify which minister he works for, but Misha has already told her. She feels edgy, suddenly – nervous, irritable. She takes a few deep, controlled breaths, breaths that he will not notice, and she tries to think. What is troubling her? She considers. If she is to be honest with herself, she has found that she likes Alexander more than she can remember ever liking anyone. In the tiredness of the late evening, she wishes that the calculation and evaluation and consideration of how to steal his secrets would not play constantly inside her head, even though she knows that to put them aside, even for a moment, would leave her exposed. They are walking outside now, a walk after dinner, in the wide, snowy streets. She has been trying to do this only for a few weeks, and she is already having trouble with it. He is arousing unexpected, unusual feelings in her. He seems to be inspiring respect and gentleness, perhaps because he demonstrates those qualities himself.

'I like my work,' he says, when she asks him.

'Passionately?'

'No. How can you be passionate about something you have not chosen to do?'

'Then why not do something else?' she asks.

'Is that how things work in the Soviet Union?' he says, his voice lower. He offers her his hand as they climb over a snow bank to get closer to the softly iced expanse of the river. His grip is firm, and he does not try to hold on for longer than is necessary. They stop under a street-light and she looks out over the cool blue-white of the frozen water on one side and the gracious, expansive street on the other, where the buildings are tinted yellow from the lights and the snow. It is how she imagines a deserted Parisian boulevard must look and feel.

He follows her gaze, trying to see what she sees.

'It's beautiful,' she tells him.

'Yes.'

And a world away from the Moscow I live in, and that most people know, she thinks.

They have walked as far as the square, near the Kremlin. There

68

has been a new, light snowfall since the early evening, which lies largely undisturbed. The purity of the crisp, white carpet gives a magical quality to the square and it decorates like fine sugar the tops of distant, golden Kremlin domes and spires that rise up from the walls that close them in. He takes her hand as they absorb the beauty before them, and she feels warm now, even out here in the cold. Quickly, she glances up, as she always does, at the building that towers over the street ahead. It is a habit of hers, a reminder, and she feels suddenly she needs it more than ever.

'You like that building?' he asks her, noticing.

'No. Do you know about it?'

He knows that on either side of the grey monolith of the main structure, the wings of the building are designed in slightly differing styles. It looks unbalanced and confused, despite its solidity.

'The architect who designed it submitted two different plans to Stalin,' she tells him, 'and they were both signed off. Or perhaps neither were. Something like that – I forget the details. Anyway, the man was too terrified to ask which design Comrade Stalin actually wanted. So he built half one way, and the other half the other way.'

'Is that true?' he asks her.

She shrugs and smiles, but without pleasure. 'I think so. It *could* be true, anyway, and that's what is important.'

He has nothing to say to her in response, so he stays silent, and they keep walking, footsteps crisp on the frosted pavement.

'Tell me about the school. I want to know more,' he says.

Of course, she thinks. You cannot say much about your work. Not to someone you don't know and trust. Not yet.

'No,' she replies. '*I* want to know. How did you get where you are? You are so young, and so . . .'

'So what?'

'Nice.' She laughs. 'Tell me, please.'

'All right, I will,' he says. 'Come back for some tea, and I will tell you.'

An image of his father swims into Alexander's head from the far edges of his mind, where it usually sits. An image of him excited, angered, passionate, brimming with ideas and with confidence. He was, still is, a good man, honest and with compassion. At the time of the revolution, he was very young, the son of a merchant who had inherited a good business from his own father. When the revolution occurred his inherent idealism was overwhelmed with the possibilities laid out by Lenin and his group. He joined the Party at that time, giving up the comfort and security with which he had been brought up, happily and without pride in his actions. He saw no use in arguing for a better, more equal Russia if he himself was not prepared to take the first step. He worked hard and long, moving up through the ranks of the local Komsommol, before taking the next steps into central government. When he came upon corruption and injustice, he explained it away as an inevitable part of any human endeavour. It would not last long, could not last long, in the new Soviet Union.

Stalin had been his undoing. Not in any physical sense. He was not fired, or sent into exile, or killed. But towards the end his mind and heart began silently to doubt what they had believed in for so many years as Stalin's methods of rule became unmistakable, and inexplicable. The pervasive fear that you could sniff in the air, like hanging smoke, the terror, the petty-minded spying on one's own family and friends became too widespread to be passed over or explained away. It became apparent to him that almost everyone he knew, from colleagues to friends, was acting from the wrong motives. They spoke only the words that were expected or required; their work was inspired by fear, not belief. It nearly broke him, Alexander told her. He continued to work, but his passion was dying away, like a marching song that fades as the parade moves out of sight. And then when Stalin died, and the political manoeuvrings of his rivals were over, the ascendance of Khrushchev had given him some small relief. He had used his remaining contacts, and had started Alexander at once on his career in government service. 'He told me that he had hoped to make a difference during his own lifetime, but that now he placed his hopes in me.'

'And is he pleased with your work?'

'I think so.'

'But you don't have the passion that drove him.'

'No. That is a rare thing, and everyone must find it where they can.'

Katya opens her mouth to reply, but thinks better of it. Why should I be concerned about this young man and his family? And yet she cannot help herself.

'Tell me,' he says, for he is watching her hesitate. 'Whatever it is, tell me.'

'How will you find *your* passion in life if you are following your father's dream?'

Later, alone in the kitchen while he makes some strong tea to warm them after their walk, he hears her ask that question again. He could not answer at the time and, if he is to be honest with himself, he was shocked at her words, at her talk of passions and dreams and following paths. It was so different from anything he had ever considered before, yet he sensed some part of his mind shifting, something falling into place, although he cannot pin down what exactly. As he thinks over their conversation out there in the glow of the snowy streets, he is caught between embarrassment and elation at her incisive, clear mind, and at the way she got the measure of him in minutes, showing him things he had preferred to hide even

71

from himself. For his part, his questions, encouragement and interest in her life have brought him hardly any closer to knowing her than he had been when they first met.

As she sips her tea, he mentions her parents, a gentle query, and she shakes her head. 'They are both dead.'

He nods and waits, so she will understand that he already knows this, but it seems she does not wish to elaborate. He asks something else, to change the focus. 'Any brothers or sisters?'

'One brother,' she says, in barely more than a whisper. 'Yuri. He left here. Four years ago.'

Alexander is inwardly shocked again. It is rare for anyone to be able to get out, to escape, for that is what she means. There is no leaving this country: one can only escape, and that is rarely successful. He is about to ask how and why, but her eyes are dark and he does not want to upset her. Her brother's leaving must have made her life harder – not only that he is now lost to her, but that suspicion would have been transferred automatically to her, like a rough blanket she must always carry around.

She takes a small taste from the customary saucer of jam that he has placed alongside her tea glass, and holds it on her tongue while she drinks. Only then does she look up at him again. 'You know they were taken?' Her voice is matter-of-fact, but her eyes are sad. But, then, they often are, he thinks. 'My parents, I mean.'

'Yes. How old were you?'

'Twelve.'

'Just a little girl,' he says quietly, and in her mind she curses him, for she is feeling again the strange wave of emotion that overcame her at the party on the night of their first meeting. The feeling that she cannot possibly hold everything together any longer, that she is about to scream or cry, or both. It must be him, she thinks. He is the common factor here. It must be him. With a snap, her eyes focus on his face, and, with an undetectable effort of will she speaks, coolly: 'They were anti-Stalinists, and they were quite open about it. They knew the risk they were taking.'

He is disbelieving. 'But they were your parents. And it is not wrong to have an opinion . . .'

'It is. It was then. And they knew it. And they still kept their opinions, and made them known.'

'Didn't you think the same way as them?'

'No. Not really. I was a child when they were taken away. I didn't think much about anything, except playing and school.'

'And it didn't turn you against the state? Or its systems? Afterwards?'

Is he testing her? Checking her credentials? Her suspicion splashes over her like a burst of freezing water, and it wakes her out of the warm, relaxed state into which he has lulled her. Lured her. It is easier now that she suspects him a little. Now she knows once more where she stands and who she is. 'No. It didn't turn me against the State. My beliefs came to me as an adult, and I have thought them through, and know them to be rational and true.'

'And so you remain a good Communist to this day?'

She shrugs. 'Of course. The crimes or mistakes that one man may have made does not negate a whole ideology, does it?' And I have striven to be the perfect Communist, she thinks, to avoid the taint of my parents' beliefs and my brother's actions. And if they must watch me a little more closely, and if that makes my work harder, it also makes it more satisfying.

'No, but they were your parents! Can you be so rational when your own mother has been taken from you? Katya?'

Why does he say her name like that? She closes her eyes and, despite herself, feels the moist hotness of tears searing the edges of the lids.

He watches her for a moment, sorry that he has failed to see through her calm, logical bravado. Then he is on his knees by her side, and he touches her hair and finally puts a sure arm round her shoulders. 'I'm sorry,' he whispers to her, again and again. 'I'm sorry.'

She puts his arm away, firmly but kindly. 'It's over,' she tells him, and when she looks at him her eyes are clear and calm, and her voice is steady.

'It's over, Sasha.' It is the first time that she has addressed him by his informal name. 'I hardly think of it any more.'

She does not allow him to escort her all the way to her apartment. Instead, at the metro station, she insists that he leaves her and turns back. He is reluctant – he would like to see her safely home, but is also eager for more time with her, even twenty minutes on a train. But she has been shaken by certain feelings that have bubbled up within her while she has been sitting in his apartment. There was a moment towards the end of their long evening together when she felt herself relax, when she felt unexpectedly that she would be happy never to leave, that she would be content just to stay there with him, this young man who is still little more than a stranger to her. She had noticed this weakness within herself at once, and within five minutes she had come up with a convincing reason why she needed to leave immediately, and she had pulled on her coat and left, with Alexander almost running beside her, at least as far as the station.

She needs time to think, and as she sits limp and tired in the underground carriage, her body swaying with the rocking of the train, she asks herself what she will do next. He likes her, she would have to be blind not to see it, and this is exactly as she would have wished. The more he likes her, the more he will learn to trust her. It will take time, of course, and subtlety and caution, but she can do it.

The train slows inside the blackness of a tunnel, and she blinks away the sudden darkness. The key is to think of him as a means to an end, not as a person. She nods to herself as the carriage emerges into the light of her station. She stands and waits by the door. Forget his kindness, and his handsome eyes, and his open smile. He is a means towards an end, an important end; he is not a person. She steps off the train and runs quickly up the staircase. At the station exit, the freezing night air is waiting for her; the cold pulls her back to herself and, with a deep breath, she walks briskly back to her home.

Chapter Five

Boston, December 2000

ON CHRISTMAS EVE they walk down to Newbury Street. The morning sky is dim, cloud-filled, with a feeling of late afternoon. Alexander is grateful for the lights of the shop windows, the coloured bulbs strung over balconies and railings, the mocha-tinged steam that escapes into the chill air from the coffee shops. He leaves Lauren at a small gallery and goes to buy his last gifts.

When at last they meet in Copley Square for lunch, she is radiant, glowing – there is excitement in her face, and the frost has quickened her blood so that energy and warmth pulsate through her, despite the sheets of cold that beat down from the steel sky. He watches her walk across the paving stones, glad that she is with him for the holidays, happy to share her liveliness, and delighting in the pleasure that shows in her eyes when she recognises him standing outside the restaurant, muffled up in a yellow cashmere scarf. In moments they are inside, overtaken by dry warmth, talking over the Christmas music, drinking a small whiskey each. The alcohol curls through him, reaching thin tendrils of heat through his chest and stomach. With a contented sigh he puts down his glass. 'How were the galleries?'

'Oh, fine.'

He sees that she is hiding something, suppressing it without much success beneath eyes and a mouth that are conspiring to give her away. 'What are you up to, young lady?'

'Nothing. I'm having the finishing touches put on your present. It'll be ready after lunch.'

'Oh, good,' he says. 'I'm sure it's huge, I'll help you carry it.'

'Uh-uh. You're going home. I'll collect it and we'll meet back at the house.'

'Are we opening things tonight or tomorrow?'

'Whatever you want.'

'It *is* Christmas Eve.'

'Tonight it is, then. After dinner.'

Lauren struggles into the house, swaying a little under the weight of the parcel. Now, as she carries it over the threshold of her uncle's house, she has her first sense of misgiving. Arms aching, she pauses in the hallway and props the present against a wall. It is large, wound with an outsized ribbon and bow. In the gallery she had thought the bow a festive, bright touch, but here in the warm darkness of Alexander's home, and considered in the light of her new uncertainty, the gold ribbon appears garish. She reaches over and tugs at it, but the knot is firm and does not unravel at a touch. She pulls off her gloves and scarf, her lip caught between her teeth as she considers.

'Lauren?' He is calling – from the kitchen, of course. She can hear pots sliding on the stove and the tap running.

'Coming!'

But he is already in the hall, a blue apron round his waist, and a towel between his hands. She turns and sees him with her artist's perception, for she is still in that other space in her mind, and his age shocks her. Not that he looks any older than he did the day before, or even six months ago, but now she notices him as an older man – his silvery hair, still holding the pattern of his comb, his veined, slightly crooked hands, the light spots that run under the grey hair of his forearms. She greets him and glances at her own hand as it touches his shoulder; she notices the planes of the bones and the flicker of muscle and vein. She feels like drawing it.

'Is that for me?'

'Of course,' she says.

'Shall I open it now?' he says, feigning impatience, when in reality she knows his small excitement in unwrapping it will only be enhanced by a period of anticipation.

'After dinner,' she says, and leads him back into the kitchen.

An hour before their meal she is upstairs, immersed in a hot bath, from which he knows she will not emerge for at least thirty minutes. He thinks with pleasure of the new candles he had thought to scatter around her bathroom, and he knows she will be lying there with every one lit. Since there will be only the two of them, he has decided to serve beef rather than turkey, and the joint is almost done, its savoury juices melting slowly into the pan where the potatoes are crisping. The wine is decanted, and he has the remaining vegetables browning, bubbling or roasting, according to their needs.

When the telephone rings, he considers leaving it, but the bell is persistent. Finally he scoops up the handset and flicks it on.

'Merry Christmas.'

He recognises Estelle's voice at once. 'And to you. How was California? Did you succumb to a facelift?'

'Are you implying I need one?' she returns.

'Of course not. I was thinking of your postcard, that's all.'

'I have to say, LA has nothing going for it except maybe silicone implants and orange juice. How are you? Melissa told me the deal is probably off.'

He notes the word 'probably'. Perhaps there is a chance to complete this sale after all. 'Yes, it is. But it happens. Perhaps it just wasn't the right fit.'

'That's too bad.' She sounds unconcerned. 'Listen, I wanted to see if you're free to come over for tea tomorrow. And your niece, if she'd like to.'

Alexander accepts, trying not to sound over-eager. He is pleased to hear from her. He had liked her relaxed tone, her forthrightness, the lack of formality, during their lunch – as he gets older, he has little patience for the careful treading that most new friendships require. 'How did you know Lauren was here?'

'Melissa mentioned it. In one of her few moments of conversation.'

'She's with you for Christmas?' he asks.

'Yes. Right now she's at one end of the apartment typing away on a laptop as thin as a wafer,' Estelle continues, 'while at the other end, her father is scratching out literary criticism with a fountain pen that looks like something Dickens might have used . . .'

He smiles at the image, then risks a more intimate remark. 'Sounds lonely for you.'

She hesitates. 'I'm used to it.'

His perception has unbalanced her, and he feels at once that the easy tone of the conversation has been lost. Without remaining on the line for much longer, she confirms the time for their visit and hangs up.

After dinner they sit in the living room, almost stupefied by the food.

'I can't believe I ate that much. I can't move,' Lauren tells him.

He offers her a chocolate truffle. 'Are you trying to kill me?' she asks.

'Certainly not. I want my present first.'

She struggles up with exaggerated anguish, but refuses his offer of assistance. With difficulty she slides the package into the living room. He comes to where she holds it upright, and glances to her for permission to open it. An edge of anxiety scores into her as she watches him pick at the tape.

'Just rip it open, Uncle Alex. It's a portrait,' she admits, unable to wait. 'I finished it a couple of weeks ago. I brought it here rolled up in my suitcase.'

'A portrait of whom?'

They continue unwrapping together, leaving curls of gold paper all over the floor. He is about to ask the question again, but now enough strips of paper have been removed so that what was initially a swathe of textured paint now reveals itself as a white blouse, a neck, a throat . . . then a chin and a mouth – a familiar mouth. The smile freezes on her face as she sees his watching eyes change from anticipation to shock. Or is it horror?

'Uncle Alex?' she says, taking his hand. She has stopped peeling away the wrapping, but his free hand reaches up and pulls it loose, an impatient, urgent movement. He must see the rest of it at once. He gasps for air, an alarming sound, for in its shock his body has forgotten to breathe. Lauren's hand is on his forehead, stroking, panicking.

'I'm fine,' he whispers.

'Are you sure?'

He does not reply. He is engrossed in the painting. He now realises that he had forgotten what Katya looked like, how she really was. The shape of her nose, the tilt of her chin, the lines on her forehead. Those details that get blurred in memory after months and years, that you find you can recall only by staring at the two photographs that you came away with, and that return only for sweet, ephemeral moments when the beloved's face comes unsummoned into dreams or recollections. He feels he might cry if he speaks so he says nothing, and Lauren knows him well enough to wait in silence while they both look at the portrait. He forces himself to focus on the work involved, on Lauren's achievement, as a way out of the labyrinth of emotion that has claimed him. His niece, Katya's niece, has captured her aunt with such vivid clarity and life that he has to remind himself that she never met her.

'Was it the wrong thing to do?' she asks.

He shakes his head to buy time, though he finds that part of him is almost resentful of what his niece has done. How she has forced before his eyes, with unrelenting candour, the vision of his lost wife. His lost love. She waits, sensing that he is displeased in some way – she watches him biting his lip. Perhaps he is trying to regain some control. Then he speaks, as quietly and calmly as he is able. 'Tell me about it,' he says.

Still gripping his hand, she explains slowly, carefully, how she worked from the two pictures he has, and from a couple of Yuri's photographs, taken when Katya was a teenager. Her features and facial structure were the same, of course, and gave Lauren different angles and expressions to work from.

'And the eyes?' He looks at her for the first time.

'Are they good?' she asks gently.

They are exact: so true. They look directly at him while revealing so little. Katya always had a hint of haughtiness about her, and Lauren had captured that too, but also a fierce intelligence and an infinite sadness.

'When I was thinking about this piece, and how to do it, I went through everything I knew about her, and I realised that, basically, there were two Katyas. One was my father's. You know Yuri's stories,' she smiles, 'the laughing, clever kid sister who was always leading him a dance and getting him in trouble with their parents. And then I knew your Katya. Or, at least, your stories of her,' she adds, to qualify any presumption.

He waits for her to go on. Tell me, Lauren, what she was like, let me try and feel it again, even though you cannot possibly understand it all.

'That was the Katya I wanted to capture. The bold, strong, vulnerable, angry woman who chose to—'

A quick movement of his head catches her eye and stops her.

'Anyway, that's what I was trying for,' she finishes mildly.

'You're a genius, Lauren. It's almost hard to look at.'

'I'm sorry. The last thing I wanted was to hurt you . . . It's funny, I was excited all the time I was painting it, varnishing, even framing just today. It was only when I got it home this afternoon that I had my first panic-attack, wondering if I was doing the right thing. It must make you miss her all over again.'

They are quiet together for a minute or two.

'It does,' he says. 'I mean, it sharpens what I've felt for the last forty years, but that's not necessarily a bad thing.'

'As long as you're okay with it. I can always take it away.'

'No, no. It was a shock, that's all. I just need some time.'

He sounds more like himself and she is immeasurably relieved. The self-control, the rationality are back, and she is no longer fearful that she has made a terrible mistake. She leads him back to his chair and pokes at the fire, which has settled down into small, melting flames that curl round the last luminous log. 'I'll get some tea,' she tells him. 'Camomile?'

'You're having some?'

'Yes.'

He watches as she goes out to the kitchen, leaving him alone. He glances at the fire for comfort, but the logs, too dry, are spitting and hissing, putting out a violent heat that causes him to move back his chair a little. Closing his eyes intensifies his awareness of the canvas looming behind him. With conscious, almost ostentatious calm, he turns in his chair, and looks at it, at her, once more. She is watching him with an expression that is half smile, half frown, an expression that perhaps she never had in life but which captures her character perfectly. He feels a stab of guilt and swallows, but his mouth is dry. He looks for water, but there is only the remains of their wine. Lauren will come soon with the tea, he reminds himself. In the meantime, Katya is regarding him evenly, without accusation or blame. He has always known that she would never have blamed him for what happened – his own pain and guilt have been punishment enough. But that knowledge has only ever reinforced the sense of how much he lost when she died.

Chapter Six

Moscow, May 1956

THERE IS A low, disbelieving whistle from the man standing beside her. She watches the sound escape from his lips, which form a question that hovers in the air before them. 'So, it's going exactly as we'd hoped?'

She nods, leans over the bridge and looks out on to the river. If she narrows her gaze, the surface of the water sparkles like a field of diamonds under the early evening sunshine.

'And he is in love with you?'

'Who knows?' she replies.

'Well, you should know. You *must* know. Or it's no good.'

His eyes remain on her and a last outline of amusement leaves her features. In the face of his expectant silence, she gives a shrug: a conceding gesture, a reluctant acknowledgement.

Misha sighs. 'Good work, Katyushka. It must be hard, but you've done well.'

Her eyes are downcast and she appears in no hurry to answer. 'Thank you,' she says at last.

He drops his voice, matching her tone. 'It's not easy, is it?'

She looks up. Of course, it must be difficult for him too. Much more so than for her. She hardly knows Alexander, while Misha has been friends with him for fifteen years or more.

'But, in the end, Katya,' he continues, 'you have to make choices in life. Especially in this life of ours. To sacrifice your personal loyalties for a greater cause. Alexander represents everything I despise, and even though he's my friend, I can't live with myself if I'm not doing everything I can to fight the system I hate.'

She is not as reassured by this argument as she feels she should be, not least because to her ears it sounds too carefully concise and rehearsed. It is not that she disagrees with Misha. They have all come out of years of terror and horror, years of becoming used to those crippling moments when your mouth turns dusty with fear, when you hear that someone else you know has been spirited away, when you are glanced at with a guilty look by someone you work with or live next to or, worse, when you are avoided altogether. Where personal loyalty between friends, colleagues, even family is forgotten in the name of the greater good. Denounce your cousin if he is an enemy of the people. Turn in your neighbour for crimes against the state. Or for anything at all. They might be thinking thoughts that could threaten the Soviet people. She had lost her parents because of this ethos, taken to extremes.

But then, perhaps, this choice he is talking of making is not so relevant to her. She is not betraying her best friend, she is only cultivating a source.

'Katya?'

'Yes?'

'Do you care for him?'

Misha watches her carefully, picking through her expressions and movements for signs, but she looks up and meets his gaze without hesitation, her eyes unreadable.

'We are different, the two of us, aren't we?' he asks.

She waits for him to explain.

'I mean, we are friends, too. Even if we don't see each other much.'

So I can tell you how I really feel? she thinks. Would it be a relief, a pleasure, even, to confide in someone when she has never confided in a soul through her entire adult life? She pictures the scene. Sitting with Misha over a glass of vodka, or some tea, perhaps, the way other people do, trying to explain, faltering, confused and perhaps a little shy, that she has been unexpectedly moved by Alexander. No, not moved, exactly, that is too strong a word, maybe touched. Or disconcerted. She smiles at Misha. She cannot conceive of sharing her deepest thoughts with him. Especially thoughts that are in need of clarity and certainty and definition. No, Misha. Not even you, whom I've known since we were barely teenagers.

He sees the cold steel behind the look that she gives him now, and he starts to say something, but her face contracts into a frown of concentration. Her eyes are no longer with him but focused on a building several hundred yards away. His glance shifts sideways, and they both watch as a large man carrying a shopping bag emerges from the entrance. The man looks about, up at the blue sky, and walks away briskly.

'It's not him,' says Katya.

'No.' Misha glances at his watch. 'It's not time yet. Good. All we need is another one who doesn't stick to his routine.'

They face each other again, two friends strolling and lounging out on the bridge on a day that holds the promise of summer – a day that has drawn out young couples all over the city, and will tempt more once the day's work is over. Katya is facing the apartment block and as she talks to Misha her eyes flicker constantly back and forth, between his face and the building. He finds it distracting to talk to her in this way, when her attention is diverted,

but there is no help for it – they are here for a reason. But he smiles
to himself as he thinks that, even were their positions reversed and
he was the one watching the building, her eyes would never rest. It
is a habit of hers – a nervous habit, probably – and he cannot
remember a time when she was not like this, darting, sparkling,
always moving.

Misha examines his fingers, thinking. He knows little of Katya's
private life, but it has always appeared to him that she has never
really had one. He doubts that many men have come and gone
during her young life. Perhaps one or two, nothing serious certainly.
She is an introverted girl, the type to hold herself in and probably
deny any sexuality or passion. Some women, he thinks, are just not
capable. Certainly he has never felt able to make any kind of overture
towards her, even before he recruited her and they began working
together. He glances at her again. She is a beauty, but an inaccessible
one – and he is not a man who finds women intimidating. On the
contrary, he has always had as many women as he pleases, and he has
enjoyed the fact that he can attract them with only a slight, pleasant
type of exertion – of his looks, his conversation, his personality. But
Katya has always been just outside his grasp, even though over the
years he has reached for her, in his own way – that is, without
seeming to do so: to give the appearance of trying too hard, or caring
too much, would go against everything he has brought himself up to
be.

'I think you're falling in love with him,' Misha says.

'And you would know best.'

'Aren't you?' he demands.

Katya laughs, and raises an eyebrow, but her eyes never leave the
building. 'I thought that was how it's supposed to be.'

'Not in this situation.'

She turns away. 'I know who I am, and what I believe in, Misha, and no one can ever change that.' She is sincere, and he nods, to calm the passion that has risen up in her.

'He is nice to be with,' she offers, as an attempt to reassure Misha that she is not hiding things from him. 'Easy. I don't have to fight so hard all the time when I am with him.'

'He is exactly what you are supposed to be fighting.'

'I know.' He catches the irritation in her voice. She is often dismissive to avoid being emotional.

When Misha speaks again, he keeps his voice neutral – he is probing, but moving around her words carefully: he is a man handling a live grenade that cannot be shaken or dropped without consequences. 'You really do care about him, don't you?' he says.

'A little. But that makes it easier. Imagine being involved with someone who repulses you. Don't worry, Misha, I know what I'm getting into.'

Her eyes are scanning people around them, looking for anyone who may be looking for them. 'Are you sure he won't suspect me?' she says suddenly. It is a deep pool that she is about to plunge into with Alexander, and she cannot help but look for reassurance, even if it can only be superficial.

'No, he won't. Not if you're always aware. Always. And not if he cares for you the way he seems to. Not if you wait for the right time. When you have his love and his trust, completely.'

In Misha's eyes she sees the recognition of her dilemma, even though it is one she will not voice. It is not what she expected, nor how she would prefer to work.

'Fighting an enemy without a face, using strangers, those things are easy. It's not so easy compromising someone you love,' he says. It is a gentle probe and his voice is warm, safe, relaxed, so that she might not even notice what he has just implied with his last three words.

'He's not like anyone I've ever met,' she says, 'but I don't love him.'

He smiles. She is intelligent and quick. Perhaps she will pull it off after all. There is one sure way to find out, but before he can lead into it, she turns, so that she can watch more easily, and Misha catches the scent of her, the cool, clean smell that is always hers. She lacks the sweet, flowery, feline perfume, the heavy dabs of standard Soviet scent worn by many of the women he knows, but her fragrance is honest and real. He looks at her sideways, at her distant eyes and long lashes, at her exotic black hair and finely drawn lips. Standing in the sunlight, against the cool stone, she looks like an idealised sculpture of a woman, with no feature ungainly or imperfect. Sasha, he thinks, you may get what you want, but she will be a handful, my friend. Even without the added complications. 'So he thinks you're a card-carrying Communist?'

'I am.'

He just laughs.

'Idiot,' she says, and touches his nose, then his curly dark hair.

'I'm not the idiot.'

'Yes, you are. Look at you. Your nose is all red, and it's not even winter. What kind of Russian are you?'

'I'm not,' he says facetiously. 'I came here from Italy last year. I felt like freezing to death and being grey, and never having anything good to eat. I got tired of all the sun, the sea, the delicious food and the dark-haired women.'

'Yes,' she says. 'The women I can believe. Have you ever had one who wasn't blonde?'

'Only kissed.'

'Who?' she asks.

'You, of course!'

'Oh, Misha. *That*. A teenager's peck – this is what you count?'

'There he is,' Misha says, with no change of tone or expression.

He lounges back against the bridge and smiles at Katya. She takes his hand to glance at his watch. He is intensely aware of the feel of her fingers on his arm – they are light yet strong against the inside of his wrists.

'Good. Seven o'clock again. What do you think?'

'I think he's stayed away for an hour every day this week.'

She watches their man, short, grey-haired, plump, walking away from them down the sun-streaked street, where shadows are falling with the lowering sky.

'Okay,' she says.

He looks at her. 'Okay what?'

'Okay, I'll go in now.'

They linger by the bridge for five more minutes, talking with suppressed excitement. They are both nervous, but now Katya takes two deep breaths and smiles. Misha straightens the collar of her blouse.

'Where does Alexander think you are now? He must know that school is over.'

'Yes, but the school administrator sometimes works late, to catch up,' she says, and her smile has changed a little: he imagines he sees the bright determination slipping out of her slightly, so he focuses her mind once more on the job in hand.

'You'd better start,' he says.

'Okay.'

They walk together towards the building and, as they near the front steps, he calls goodbye and leans and kisses her on the cheek, an affectionate parting from her friend or brother or lover – who would be able to tell which? Then he strolls away down the street, relaxed, unconcerned.

She watches him go: Misha, who has always been considered something of a subversive, with his daring views and his *bitniki* clothes, the American-influenced jeans and sweaters that give the suggestion of a disaffected rebel, but in a way that offers no real threat. He often plays the role of the doubting intellectual in public, and among friends he is usually free with his criticism of the Soviet system; but his anger is carefully controlled for effect, and is never pushed too far. It gives him an edgy persona: he is the maverick employed in one of the state's most trusted positions in aviation research. In many ways, it is the best cover he could ever have concocted, the kind of double bluff that is the direct opposite of her own strategy of modelling herself as the perfect, non-questioning Communist. There is also a large part of him that enjoys the subterfuge and thrives on the danger of the work that they do. Part of him, she feels, is like a small boy who has been given the toys and tools to play spy games, and consequently is always filled with excitement and self-importance.

She runs up into the building. Immediately she has good luck. An old man is coming out, and holds open the heavy front door for her. She wishes him 'Good afternoon,' and starts up the stairs. Above the ringing of the cold cement under her feet, she hears the old man call after her. She stops. A nosy one, probably. One of those who know everyone in the building.

'Who are you here for?' he asks, his voice shaky.

'Sasha,' she replies, and is shocked that Alexander's pet name is the first name that comes to her, that she has already dragged him into this part of her life. Usually she replies with any male first name – something different each time, of course. Using the diminutive makes them think she is on intimate terms with whomever she's visiting and, with luck, makes them hesitate as to whom she means. She smiles at the old man, and continues up the stairs, showing no hesitation. She is relieved when she hears the acknowledgement and the slam of the door.

It does not take her long to open the inner door. She has knocked first, of course, just in case, but she can sense that the apartment is empty. She walks down the short hallway and into the bedroom. There is a chest of drawers and, on the mattress, the sheet is caught up in one corner, as though the bed has been lifted. Sure enough, in an improvised pocket beneath the springs, she finds the code sheets. Some cable transcripts, too, which look old and pointless. They may be hidden as a decoy. She takes it to the small table, and lays the code pad down, avoiding moist rings of tea spills. From her inside pocket she extracts a camera, and leans down to fit the whole page into the viewfinder. She snaps, winds, then lifts the top sheet, snaps the one below. She gets into a rhythm at once: click, wind, lift, click, wind, lift. Kneeling down, she stuffs them back into the mattress pocket.

She stands quietly in the middle of the room and frowns. It has been almost too easy, and she still has plenty of time. She runs a finger over the shelf of books above the bed. Nothing stands out. Then she goes through the drawers, and the desk, and his books. Then the bathroom. The floor and basin are dirty and marked, and tiny chest hairs are curled into every corner, but the mirror is surprisingly clean. Vanity? she wonders, and stops to examine her face. It appears gaunt and closed off, distrustful. She is startled, as though she has caught an unknown woman standing behind her, and then unsettled, for this is not how she sees herself in her own mind. She wonders if this is the face that Alexander sees. As she thinks of him, her features soften, and this change is so clear on the unrelenting surface of the mirror that she turns away quickly.

She has what she came for, so she removes the film and tucks it inside her shirt, places the camera in her handbag. Quietly she moves across the floor, and closes the front door behind her. By the time she emerges on to the street, the sunlight is receding, and it feels cooler than before.

She cannot see Misha anywhere. She slows down, but does not look behind, not at first, but then she can sense him walking up behind her and, without thinking, she turns to look. He is not there. As she looks ahead again she bumps into him.

'Katya!' he says, for there are many people around now, leaving work. 'How are you? What a surprise.'

'Yes, isn't it?'

He laughs. 'What did you think you were doing?'

She swallows. 'Sorry. I thought I felt you behind me.'

'Even worse. Don't ever look for me, and don't ever wait for me. If they get one of us, they mustn't get the other.'

'I know.'

'Don't ever wait for me, Katya.'

'I know. I'm sorry.'

Her step becomes a little faster, as though she is trying to pull away from the conversation. Misha keeps up.

'Did you get everything?' he asks.

'All under the bed.'

'Again?'

'Will these people never learn?' she asks drily.

'They would,' he says, walking her in the direction of her apartment, 'but they think it'll never happen to them. More paranoia – that's what they need.'

'You don't think they have enough? They rule with it.'

'Maybe they need to bring some into their own homes. They're making your job too easy.'

She pushes her hands deeper into the pockets of her long cardigan. 'Don't worry, it will never be too easy.'

They walk quietly until he broaches the thing he has been considering all afternoon. 'It's time you took something from Alexander.'

She seems startled. 'Already?'

He nods. 'Just once. Just a test run. See how it works.'

He wants to see how *she* works, to test her, she is sure of it. He is concerned that she has lost control of her emotions, that she will begin to like Sasha so much that she will no longer want to betray him.

'It's not the right time. He'll suspect. I don't want to ruin it before we've even started.'

'I think it's time,' Misha repeats. His tone now is authoritative. He has slipped into his role as the senior one in this partnership. She is his recruit, his responsibility, his agent. In the end, she must follow orders.

'Fine,' she replies. 'What do you want me to do?'

'You see him in the evenings, don't you? Does he bring work home?'

'Sometimes.'

'Anything interesting?'

'I don't know, I haven't looked yet. I was trying to be careful.'

'Take whatever he brings next time,' Misha says, and his tone is the same, firm, leaving no room for argument. 'Photograph it, copy it, remember it if you have to – you decide.'

'Give me a week or two.'

'Sure.'

They have reached the corner of the street she lives on. The light summer green of the trees casts little pools of shade on to the uneven paving stones, and in the fading sunlight, the yellowing concrete of the apartment blocks looks warm and burnished. Misha stops here, and kisses her goodbye, and as he grasps her hand fondly she slips the camera film into his palm. From here he will turn back on to the main street and walk down to the metro. No other words are exchanged between them, and she is glad of it, for he has ended the day in a way that she had not anticipated and she is feeling more than a little perturbed. He is already walking away, and she watches him disappear round the corner. She stands, lonely on the quiet street, and waits until she can no longer hear his footsteps.

Chapter Seven

Boston, December 2000

'SO TELL ME about this person we're having tea with.'
'Her name is Estelle.' Alexander watches Lauren butter her fourth piece of toast. 'How do you have the appetite for breakfast after last night?' he asks.

She bites into it with relish. 'Want some?'

He declines. Perhaps when he was younger, and his digestion a little better than it is now, he would have been able to eat like that. Though he has always been satiated by a little food of excellent quality, rather than quantity for its own sake. It is a fastidious tendency that has served him well through all the years of building a business based on food.

'And she's the mother of the awful Melissa?' Lauren asks. 'How did you meet?'

She continues eating while he tells her, giving the impression that she is more caught up in her breakfast than in the details of her uncle's story. She has sensed something interesting here, an attraction on his part, but she wants him to speak freely without noticing that she is probing deeper feelings.

'Anyway, Melissa wouldn't leave the meeting to have lunch with her, so I brought her home. I liked her.'

'How come?'

She dusts toast crumbs from her hands as he talks; he mentions Estelle's wit, her quick mind, her unnaturally blue eyes. The romantic slant of this last observation is not lost on Lauren. 'So, are you going to ask her out?'

'Of course not. She's married.'

'Happily?'

He stands up to pour more coffee. 'What's that supposed to mean?'

'I don't know. I guess . . . if she's unhappily married, would that be less of an obstacle for you? In pursuing her?'

He is taken aback. Not because the wish that Estelle was single has not crossed his mind but because he is disconcerted that his innermost thoughts, which strike him as ignoble, have been uncovered by his niece.

'You know me,' he tells her tersely. 'I wouldn't even think like that.'

'I know. But passion has been known to drive people to madness.'

'It's hardly passion. We just met. It's a friendship, barely. A possible friendship.'

The city is as quiet as Lauren has ever known it, the thick grey light adding to the sense of isolation and desolation. They walk together without speaking, glancing in at the window displays of the closed shops. Then, deliberately, they turn off the main road and stroll through silent back streets. Cooking smells slip into the air around them as they walk past the brownstones that loom up on one side. Across the broad, deserted street, through the stark winter trees, the vast river lies cloudy and still.

A few windows have coloured lights or candles in them, but the decorations in this street of academics and students are largely subdued or absent. Few residents remain here during university holidays, and it shows. Only one house on the corner sports a garish display on its small front patio. A large plastic Santa Claus, streaked with soil and snow melt, stands forlornly in a flower-bed; behind him, a plastic reindeer lies on its side in the earth, staring up at the sky.

'That's a nice look,' Lauren comments. 'Take a tip for next year.'

They walk back up the street, purposefully now, scanning the door numbers until they find Estelle's entrance. There are lights in the second-floor windows and Estelle's voice floats over the intercom, altered and indecipherable as the door clicks open and they walk in.

She is waiting on the landing, and Alexander stands aside for his niece to precede him. It is innate courtesy on his part, but he is also grateful for the buffer, for someone to shield the unlooked-for nervousness he now feels. Before they reach the top of the stairs he hands to Lauren the bouquet of roses he carries. Estelle receives them from her with a smile, but is awkward, he feels, and fusses for a while over the flowers as she leads them into a long, narrow hallway, lit with lamps that cast a delicate light on to pure white walls. Before they have managed more than a few steps, a voice thunders out from a darkened hallway to their left: 'Christmas Day. It must be Santa Claus.'

In the dimness of the unlit passageway stands a tall man whom Alexander assumes must be the husband, the professor. The balance of his large body looks strangely precarious, as though a mere breeze, or a gentle push, might cause him to list to one side. He is holding in one large hand an even larger cup from which steam rises.

'Not even the tooth fairy, I'm afraid,' Alexander replies.

Estelle smiles. 'This is Lauren, Frank. She's an artist. And Mr Ivanov, her uncle. It's his company that Melissa was trying to buy.'

'Ah. Ivanov, you say?'

The professor raises eyebrows that are unkempt and expressive. 'Are you of Russian extraction?' he asks.

'Yes, I am.'

'You know, you share your name with a play written by your compatriot, Chekhov?'

'Ivanov. Yes, that's right.'

'Do you know it?'

'A little.' Alexander smiles, and so does the professor.

'A rather dull play, is it not?'

'It has never been one of my favourites.'

'And tell me, is your Christian name also Mikhail, like the character?'

For a brief moment he feels like a schoolboy, standing there, being given a sneaky test by the teacher. Perhaps Professor Johnson knows no other way of communicating. 'My name is Alexander,' he replies. 'Not Nikolai, as I believe the other Ivanov was called.'

There is a barking noise from the hall, which Alexander takes to be a laugh, because Estelle smiles also. Perhaps he is imagining it, but he sees a trace of pleasure in her eyes – perhaps she is pleased he has kept up with her difficult husband. In the meantime, the professor turns and walks away from them. Lauren's eyebrows are raised; she is beginning to understand from where Melissa must have learned, or inherited, her somewhat deficient communication skills. She glances at her uncle, her lips curved in a half-smile.

'You will excuse me if I take my tea in my study, Mr Ivanov,' Professor Johnson calls, over his shoulder.

'Of course.'

A door clicks shut, and he is gone. Estelle sighs.

She doesn't remember the last time she was able to enjoy his banter, his sharp brand of humour, even though she likes to laugh.

She has always been an easygoing counterfoil to the foibles and moods of her husband, the more serious professor. An outgoing character to balance his deep introversion. She has a wisecracking, dry, quick sense of humour that he had liked when they first met, which was so long ago that on the odd occasions when she recalls those memories, it seems to her that they play themselves out in black-and-white. He, too, was ironic at times – is still ironic, but in a less pleasant way than he used to be. His intellectual strength has made him impatient, or even contemptuous sometimes, of people who try to engage with him. She does not remember him being like this before, though she is willing to admit to herself that it may be nothing more than a trick of nostalgia, the inevitable filtering out of the hard pieces of grit through the fine mesh of memory. What she remembers is watching, sly-eyed, through his study door at the university as she typed in the reception area outside. He would leave it ajar during the summer months, when the sweltering Boston heat rose moistly up the red-brick building and slipped in through the windows.

She remembers watching him teach his students. A tall, imposing presence, he seemed to her, lowered into a wooden captain's chair, listening intently while different boys and girls, by turns nervous and bold, read aloud their essay for the week. He listened well, and without self-consciousness, so that she felt sure he was not aware that she half observed him. Later, when they were together, he would laugh, a gruff sound that seemed to match perfectly the rough-hewn contours of his features, and he would tell her that he had always known she was watching him. She would listen to him, intrigued, absorbing into her own mind the lush overflow of words, of poetry and prose and criticism, that issued from that room. In her mind the inside of his office always looked summery – she could not remember it dark or cold, although it must have been so for many months at a time. But whenever she put her mind to it, she could still summon up the smell of old books and dust that pervaded it, no matter how bright the light that washed the walls. It was the smell of scholarship and absentmindedness, and it brought to her the sensation that she was stepping into one of the Victorian novels she loved so well. She would often put her head into the empty room before she left at the end of the workday, just to get a last lungful of that air, a sense of understanding and kinship with the professor, and with the contents of those age-speckled books, something to take home with her; an unusual need that she could never explain to anyone.

'Come on in. He doesn't mean to be sarcastic,' she says, leading her guests into a kitchen that blazes with light and seems the direct antithesis of the dark hallway behind them. 'It's just his way. I think too many years shut up with only his books have left him not knowing how to speak to people. Even to say hello.'

The kitchen is large, for an apartment, and about half of it is taken up with a well-used wooden table and chairs. The table is already set with cream-coloured china, the perfect delicacy of the plates and cups at odds with the lived-in, almost faded feel of the rest of the kitchen furnishings. There are only three settings, Alexander notes. Evidently she has not expected her husband to join them, or her daughter.

At first she talks mainly to Lauren and Alexander watches them, his eyes drawn particularly to Estelle, for Lauren's earlier observations are still playing on his mind. He tries to be casual in his examination of her, but when Estelle looks at him, politely, during the course of the conversation, she is instantly disconcerted. He transfers his attention at once to the slices of cake that sit on the table before them. Lauren has already tasted a piece: 'This is amazing . . .'

Alexander tries it and asks at once for the recipe. 'It's kind of an old family secret.'

'Everyone has a price, Estelle,' he says. 'And when it comes to food, I can usually find it.'

'Really? Now I see the no-nonsense businessman.' She frowns and pours cups of aromatic tea.

'Well, since you do love your food so much . . . it's an autumn cake. You have to wait till fall – preferably late fall.'

He sits a little forward in his chair, intrigued.

'You need to dress up warmly,' she continues, nodding at Lauren. 'And then . . . do you know Fisher's Pond? Where all the berries grow?'

Alexander nods.

'You walk over there. When you get to the north-east corner, where most of the fruit bushes are, turn left down the pathway.'

'And then?' he asks.

'And then when you get to Marion's Bakery Stall, you go in and buy as many as you want from the counter. She makes them fresh every day except Monday.' The women look at each other and laugh.

'Come on, Uncle Alex, didn't you see that coming?'

'I had you going, didn't I?' Estelle adds, with satisfaction.

'You have a naughty streak, Estelle.'

'Sorry I couldn't oblige you with a new dessert recipe. What will you do now?'

He tastes his tea. 'Maybe I'll suggest that whoever eventually buys our company contacts Marion as a potential new supplier.'

'Of course.' Estelle says. 'And before you know it Marion will be a conglomerate, and her cakes will taste like plastic.'

The strong tone of her words leaves a pause hanging between them for a moment, until Alexander puts down his cup. 'First, have you considered that Marion, whoever she is, might not want to go on baking only ten cakes a day for the rest of her life? And second, that not all big business means poor quality.'

'Maybe, but you have to agree that companies like yours are the exception rather than the rule. And,' she adds, with a note of triumph, 'even you are on the point of selling out. You know things won't stay the same. The home-made touch that you're so famous for will probably disappear.'

'I'm "selling out" because I'm getting old and I want to do other things with my life.'

'I know. I'm not accusing you of taking the money and running. But no matter what your reasons, the outcome will be the same.'

Her eyes dance: she seems impassioned by this exchange. Lauren is noting the change in her electric blue eyes and the colour in her cheeks.

'And Melissa?' Alexander asks. 'Do you include her as part of those impersonal business machines that you seem to hate so much?' He stops short, realising that his niece is giving him a warning look.

But Estelle does not seem insulted so much as eager to explain. 'Melissa and I don't see eye to eye on many things. And definitely not big business.'

'Well,' Alexander tells her, 'I'd like another piece of the cake that's causing all the trouble. And since I don't want you to throw it at me I'm retiring from the debate.'

He holds her glance a little longer than is necessary, a way of making amends for the altercation. She understands and is grateful that he has been generous enough to shift the focus of the conversation. For her part, she turns to Lauren: 'I can't tell you how much I loved your work. The two abstracts in your uncle's house – they left me with such a feeling . . . I don't know why, or rather how, they had such an effect.'

Lauren is flattered. She had almost forgotten those paintings, but Estelle's remarks bring back a momentary sense of what she had felt when she produced them several years ago. 'Thanks. They're pretty old pieces, though. I do portraits mainly now.'

'I'd love to see them. Whose?'

'Oh, some socialites. Some old money, some new. A lot of your favourite corporate types. More and more. They're mostly the same. They like to see themselves in suits, tailored but relaxed. The arms are usually folded, and the expression – that has to be strong yet benevolent, tough with just a hint of condescension.'

'Sounds like you have it down to a formula.' Estelle smiles, but Lauren does not smile in return. She finds she cannot. Her own flippant description of her work is still ringing in her head, and Estelle's remark has distilled it, has had upon it the unforgiving effect of a fluorescent light being snapped on in a pitch-dark room. For that instant, Lauren has a perfectly clear vision of her work – and she is horrified by what she sees. A formula.

During the ensuing silence Estelle clears her throat – she is unsure of anything at this moment except that she seems to be upsetting one or other of her guests every time she opens her mouth.

'I have to tell you, my Christmas present is anything but formulaic.' Alexander is polite, intent, desperate to alleviate the distress he can read in his niece's face.

With alacrity, Estelle grasps the line that has been thrown. 'Really? What was it?'

There is the slightest hesitation from Alexander as he realises that his quiet gallantry has led him to a point where he will have to mention things he had no wish to talk about. 'A portrait,' he says. 'Of Katya.'

Estelle appears intrigued. 'I'd love to see it,' she suggests, and Lauren nods.

'You must.'

She is too considerate and polished to allow this unexpected realisation about her work to keep everyone off-balance and floundering. She will simply store it up in the back of her mind to think over later, if she dares.

'What about tomorrow?' Alexander suggests. He is almost surprised to hear himself say it. Although he would like very much to see Estelle again, the focus on Katya and Russia does not come easily to him. But Lauren has already made the offer, and it would be rude to ignore it.

'I'd love to,' Estelle says. 'I'd like to look at your other work again too.'

She feels recovered now from the previous, edgy exchanges, and eager to ask him something about himself, and about Russia in particular, but she feels a little apprehensive of those soft brown eyes watching her unwaveringly, as though daring her to probe the secrets they guard so politely. She decides against skirting round the subject since he seems so adept at side-stepping. 'Tell me about Russia when you were there. Or the Soviet Union, rather. It's fascinating to someone like me, born and brought up here.'

He regards her kindly but without openness. 'What do you want to know?'

'Everything. How was it back then? Did you have to fight for a loaf of bread? How did you get from Russia to America? When did you leave? *Why* did you leave?'

There is a pause. Lauren drinks the last of her tea, even though it is cold.

'Gathering material for your novel?' Alexander says, and he is instantly sorry. The comment seemed just to slip out of him, unconsidered, and he had meant it lightly, to divert away from those questions of hers, questions that he has courted but which have already thrown him off-balance. Instead he feels he has been unkind, and accusatory.

'No.' She offers no further explanation or justification – her denial is vehement enough without them.

'I'm sorry. You must think I have the worst manners . . .'

'You met my husband,' she replies, with a smile. He shakes his head as if to assure her that he will not be made to feel better so easily.

'I left there just before Katya died,' he says. 'Nineteen fifty-nine. I was twenty-eight.'

'How old was she?'

'The same age as me.'

Estelle winces. In the expectant silence that follows, he senses more questions about Katya's death, and he moves on: 'It was hard back then,' he tells her. 'I can hardly remember it sometimes, and at other times I can think of nothing else. My wife has always remained the most real thing about Russia for me. But we didn't struggle the way many people did. My father did well in the civil service . . .'

'A good Communist?'

'Yes. He came from a well-to-do family. At least, they had money before the revolution. But he believed in the fight for equality, for a better life for everyone. It was a real belief for him, and he gave up everything he had to follow Lenin. Then, he rose in the Party ranks, during the early years of Stalin's government, and he got back some of the privileges he had had before – a better home, better food.'

'But surely that wasn't the Communist ideal . . .'

'Exactly. But it is hard to keep completely aware of ideals when you are hungry and cold and have a wife and baby.'

'And did you follow the same path?'

'There was no other path to follow in the Soviet Union. If you were given the opportunities I was given, you didn't turn them down. But I began to see many things that did not make sense. People were brainwashed.' He pauses, considering.

'Perhaps that's not quite right. We were simply brought up not to think for ourselves. Because thinking might cause you to question things, and if you questioned the Communist Party, then you were a threat, a loose cannon. They wanted everyone to conform – to think and work the same way, for the common good, supposedly. Katya made me see these things more clearly. She always thought for herself and, believe me, that was incredibly unusual in Soviet Russia, especially during Stalin's time and just after. It seems normal to us now, in the West, but it was so different then. It was like suggesting the world was square. But I carried on with my work because there was nothing else to do. Maybe I thought I could make a change from within the government. I don't know. And I was always reassured by the beliefs of my father because he was a good man. I was too much reassured.'

Estelle waits, hoping for more. She is intrigued, but the effort of revealing this much seems to have been enough for Alexander.

'You worked for the government?'

'Yes.'

'Interesting.'

'Not especially. I had a decent apartment and a good enough life with Katya.'

'And she changed your way of thinking?'

'She enlarged it and shaped it and refined it. She was a long, long way ahead of me on that score. She even found ways to challenge things—' He breaks off and takes a sip of tea.

'How?' Estelle asks. He can feel her watching him carefully. Lauren shifts a little in her seat. He is suddenly defensive, tired of speaking after his unaccustomed openness; and then, with a timing he could not have wished for, the kitchen door opens and he is spared. Melissa

Johnson stands just inside the doorway, where she concentrates on pulling off her charcoal grey gloves.

'Hello, my darling. I didn't realise you'd be back so early,' Estelle says.

Melissa blinks. 'I'm not back – I just forgot some papers. Where's Dad?'

'You really have to ask?'

Melissa realises only then, with considerable surprise, that Alexander Ivanov is sitting in her mother's kitchen. Even more discomfiting, his niece is with him, watching her with an amused look in her black eyes. Alexander stands, uncertain of whether to offer a handshake or a kiss, but Melissa leans forward for the latter.

'We were just talking about you, earlier,' Alexander tells her.

'Really?' Melissa leans over to shake Lauren's hand, and gives her mother a wry look. 'All good things, I'm sure.'

Estelle smiles. 'We were discussing big business.'

'And I suppose I was cast as the big bad wolf?'

'Of course.'

Just visibly, Melissa takes a breath, although she keeps the sound of it packed down inside herself. Her eyes look tired, Lauren notices, and she chooses not to take up this line of conversation; but in any event, Estelle has already moved on.

'Lauren is a portrait painter and I thought you might commission a portrait one of these days.'

'Of myself? I don't think so.' Melissa lays her gloves on the counter but keeps her coat on. She takes the empty seat beside Lauren. 'Do you do other things than portraits?' she asks.

'Sure.' At least, I used to, she thinks. 'But I don't like my potential clients to be beaten into commissioning anything by their mothers.'

'Don't worry about that,' Melissa says. 'I won't do anything I don't want to. I'd love to see your work, though.'

Lauren opens her mouth to speak, then glances at Alexander, a glance of query.

'Why don't you both come over to our place tomorrow?' he tells her. 'Your husband, too, if he'd like to. We can see some of Lauren's pieces, and then, Melissa, you and I can talk business. Or not, if you prefer.'

It is an elegant way to reopen the negotiation, and Melissa takes advantage of it with good grace. 'Sounds good. I have a few suggestions I'd like to go over with you. I tried you at the office yesterday and today, but you weren't around.'

A sigh from Estelle.

'It's Christmas,' Lauren says easily.

Melissa looks at her. Her grey eyes seem less austere. 'And you all think I'm the grinch.'

'Never too late to change,' Lauren says.

Melissa holds her look. 'I can try, I guess. What time do you want us tomorrow?'

'About eleven.'

'So time to stop in at the office first.'

'Or just to stay in bed,' suggests Lauren.

'Possibly,' Melissa says, and smiles.

Alexander coughs. He is somewhat surprised to see his feisty niece charming the woman she so recently dismissed as 'awful'. Melissa's eyes take in the table, lingering with feigned disinterest on the cake.

'Would you like a piece of this?' Lauren asks, offering her the plate.

'Is it carb-free?'

'No, but then it's not taste-free either.'

Melissa refuses. 'Please, don't try and break all my rules in one day. It may be Christmas, but my goodwill to all men extends only

110

so far.' She stands up, reaches for her gloves, and is ready to leave almost as abruptly as she arrived. Lauren watches her, bemused. 'I have to get going,' she says. 'I guess I'll see you all tomorrow.'

Chapter Eight

Moscow, July 1956

IF SHE CAN get to the Metro just after six, when her working day is over, it is usually not overcrowded, and the ride is easier, quicker than the bus. But today she has had work after her school-administration job is over: she has had to carry a message and some documents and she has had to lie. She has helped to set in motion a train of events that will undermine, delay and irritate the people and the system she hates. The usual necessary work, but it is occasionally distasteful none the less. And now it is late, seven o'clock, and she steps off the train with a hundred other people. She lands lightly on the platform. Before her feet lies an expanse of polished marble blocks. She watches the shoes of her fellow passengers tap and scrape across them. The walls rise high with the smooth, veined marble too, except where they end in pale grey stonework, carved firmly into imposing images of Stalin, Lenin and other heroes of the Party. Above her head hang glass chandeliers, wide bowls of glittering glass that blaze light into the subterranean cavern. The height, the space, the dramatic beauty – these have become an everyday phenomenon to the commuters who use the metro, to people whose homes have ceilings which hang low and walls thin enough for a forceful fist to punch through. Katya pauses and blinks – she is standing suddenly in a ballroom, in another, pre-revolutionary world, where at any moment a flock of white-necked women will be escorted to dance by tall men in ties and long jackets and waxed whiskers. Something she has read of in Tolstoy perhaps. Someone bumps into her shoulder and she spins round. An old woman disappears across the station without any word of apology. Katya rubs her shoulder, and follows the rest of them out and upwards, away from the subway station, away from this 'people's palace' built by Stalin.

What use is a station that looks like a ballroom when people are still struggling for meat and milk?

Out on the street the air is fresher, and she walks quickly into her apartment block, for Sasha will be coming soon, and she wants to bathe and change out of these clothes that she feels are soiled from the places they have just been. It is a strange idea of hers, but she cannot rid herself of it. Whenever she finishes such work, her real work, she changes all her clothes from her sweater to her underwear and washes them, no matter how clean. She thinks it is her way of separating the strands of her life, or maybe, she laughs to herself, she believes the ideas of the people she deals with will rub off on her like a germ.

She is ready twenty minutes early, and she waits as the minutes drip by, glancing to the open window for any sign of him. She hears a firm footfall on the road below, and there is a hollowness in her chest, a pleasant emptiness that she knows is a strange type of anticipation. She stands casually, with her face up against the grimy window-pane and peers down, but it is not him. She breathes in to slow the sprinting of her heartbeat. This is all new to her, and all wrong, she thinks, very, very wrong. She should not be waiting like this, like a hopeful puppy, looking from windows. She has to try to be more rational about the situation. It is just one more step on the path you want to take through life, Katya.

Of course, it would be much easier if he was petulant, or unkind, or hungry for power, or even just ugly or inconsiderate. But there is time for her to uncover these things about him. No one is without their bad points: she just needs to look harder to find them. And then she can work to subdue these unlooked-for feelings, these slow droplets of escaped emotion that are slowly filling her inside. It will be easier when she finds out what a bastard he really is.

She knows he will probably come slightly before the appointed hour, for he has trouble keeping away from her, and sure enough, he is fifteen minutes early. He has taken the metro to her area, and has tried without much success to use up the extra time by walking slowly for much of the way. Now that he is before her building, though, within a hundred paces of her, it is easier to slow down, to savour the anticipation of seeing her. Her block is uniform, indistinguishable from the others around it except for the numbers on the front. A sigh escapes his lips. The apartments are depressing. Prefabricated, hastily thrown up by Khrushchev to help solve the housing problems of the city – there are a million more people living in Moscow now than there were only ten years ago. They have served their purpose well, these apartment blocks, but the people who live in them call them *khrushchoby*, a joke that combines their leader's name with the word *trushchoby* – slum. They are better than slums, certainly, but are not comparable to the stone and brick buildings in which Alexander has grown up. He moves quickly through the dank, gloomy stairwell. She lives on the top floor, the fifth. These blocks are rarely higher, for they dispense with the luxury of lifts also. Her door is thrown open before he reaches the top, and she is looking out for him.

'Katya,' is all he says, as he reaches her, lifts her up in a hug, spins her round and kisses her. His briefcase and two parcels are dropped on to the floor. She pushes the door shut behind him, and he glances around. 'Where's Maya?'

'Gone out. She's eating with her workmates. And her mother's staying with her sister in the country for a week.'

He smiles, kisses her again.

'Will we always be this excited to see each other, Sasha?'

'Always, my love.'

'Even when we are ancient?' She has asked the question from her heart, without thinking, but as soon as the words are spoken she feels a weight in her stomach, a weight which makes her feel sick. This suggestion of hers that they will be together until they die, when she knows that she is only with him, for one reason. It is difficult to remember sometimes. To stay aware, in the way Misha said she should always be aware. But if she tries to be aloof with him, or distant, or if she holds herself back in any way he will feel it. The relationship will not progress, and the game will be over. She has to let herself go, to immerse herself in the role of a woman in love, even when the acting comes too easily, and she no longer has to think so hard about her lines.

'Especially when we're ancient.' He pulls back from her and looks at her eyes and mouth and face. 'You will never be old in my eyes, Katyushka,' he says gallantly, and with honesty.

'Are you sure?'

'Completely. Are you hungry?'

She nods. She has not eaten since her lunchtime meal of meatballs and soup from the school canteen.

'I brought bread and some fish,' he tells her. He holds up his prized packages with a flourish. She cannot help but notice that his briefcase, perhaps full of papers from work, is still lying on the floor behind him. Perhaps he sees her glance at it, for he reaches to pick it up. Should she offer to take it, to put it in the bedroom with his jacket, or will that be too obvious? In fact, she is saved from the decision, because he passes her the food parcels, turns and strides into her bedroom himself, depositing the rest of his things there.

'Where did you get fish, Sasha?' she asks, as he walks past her again, into the tiny area of the living room that passes for her kitchen.

'Never mind.'

She feels a quick burn of anger in her stomach. He will not say, but she knows he has ready access to special shops, to the types of food that most people will never see or afford. He senses her feelings, and regrets that he dismissed her question. 'I know I have privileges,' he tells her, 'but I just wanted you to have it. The fish, I mean. I wanted you to enjoy it.'

He is caught between repentance and the wish to give her everything in the world, and she sees his uncertainty, this dilemma.

'Is there any dessert?' he asks.

She pushes away the remnants of her anger, and stops at the entrance to the kitchen. She holds out her arms, offering herself. Her eyes are teasing, but her movement is awkward, for she does not quite know how to be so relaxed and affectionate with another person: she is still learning to open out her natural insularity. He puts his arms round her, pulling her close to him, willing her uncertainty to crumble away. Then he kisses her hair, loosens his tie, and rolls up his shirtsleeves, for he has no intention of letting her cook for him.

First, he reaches into the kitchen drawer for a match, which he applies with caution to the back of the oven. She feels the slow heat rising at once, catches the tangy smell of the gas.

He tosses the parcel of fish up behind his back and it drops on to the small plywood counter in front of him. Katya is laughing – at

SHAMIM SARIF

the fish, at his playfulness, at the fact of him being there. She gives
him a knife and watches him slit open the layers of paper.

She shrieks.

'What?' he asks.

'It looks alive!'

'I promise you it's not,' he replies.

He slams the handle of the knife down smartly on the chipped
countertop and stamps his foot. A flourish to start the cutting of the
fish. He picks up the blade, and holds it to his face, so that he is
looking down its silvery length at Katya's expectant eyes. 'Ready?' he
asks, voice solemn.

She nods. 'Ready.'

'And so.' He grabs it by the tail and turns it over with a slap,
merely for effect, and then, in a flash of strokes with the blade, he
has decapitated it, and removed its tail. These parts are deftly and
swiftly wrapped in the old, oily paper, and pushed to one side.

'Better?' he asks her.

'Yes. What's next?'

'Gutting,' he says.

'Let me watch, then.'

He begins work with the knife, and she moves closer, near to his
moving arm. He is concentrating now, enjoying the attention to detail
required of him, and she sees the tip of the knife caressing the soft
belly of the fish, watches the gentle strokes with which he scrapes away
the scales. He handles the knife with respect, as though it were an ally,
working with him to subdue and prepare this clear-eyed creature.

Again, his wrists and fingers move so quickly once the fish is cut
that she barely sees a glimpse of the soft, red, spilling insides before
they are also gone.

He turns his head to look sideways at her, and, enquiringly, she
meets his glance. 'Does the smell trouble you?' he wants to know.

118

'No. It is a fresh fish.'

'Yes, but still . . .'

She is mesmerised by his hands. The long bones of the fingers, visibly lined with gentle muscles. Their lithe, light touches, the patient, repetitive movement, the firm strokes of his fingertips, the careful caress of his palms. In too short a time, he is finished with his task and wiping his hands, and she sighs slightly that it is over.

'What is it, my Katyushka?' he says. His mouth is near to hers, his warm breath on her nose. She stands very still, not yet able to lift her lips to his, but not wanting the sensations of this moment to end – there are times when his easy intimacy seems wondrous to her.

'I could watch you cook all day,' she tells him, and he laughs, his mouth still close to hers, but not touching.

He does not know why, but he feels he must leap across a chasm that lies hidden within her to reach their next kiss. 'Is that what you want me for? To cook for you all day?'

'Yes,' she tells him. 'That is exactly it.'

Their flavourings are few: some salt, dried herbs, vinegar. He wraps the fish and puts it into the oven.

'What did you do today?'

'At work?' she asks.

'Yes. Why did you have to work late?'

'It's time for the school reports – again,' she adds wryly. 'So much typing. It gets boring.' She frowns at the memory of her afternoon's overtime work, trapped in the office of the school administrator, a fictional hour that for this moment, is completely real in her mind. In fact, with Svetlana's help, she had finished typing the reports by lunchtime.

'I can imagine. Aren't you tempted to rewrite the bad reports as you go along?' Alexander laughs, but she is serious when she replies.

119

'Sometimes. Sometimes I have . . . rephrased them. So they are less harsh. They are so uncaring, Sasha. They call the children stupid and dull and useless.'

'I am glad that you rewrite them, then.'

'I don't change them completely, just . . .'

'I know. But I'm glad.'

'And yours, how was your work today?' she asks. They sit down together on the small sofa. She likes the warmth of his leg touching hers, feels a stir of desire, but will not or cannot show it.

'I don't know.' His eyes are troubled. 'It's not the same since . . .'

'Since what?'

'You make me look at things in a different way, Katya.'

'But I'm proud of you. And your work. Why am I ruining it for you? Because I told you it was your father's path?'

He looks at her for a long time, thinking about the answer. His eyes are still considering when he leans over and kisses her throat. She closes her eyes against the pleasurable touch of his lips on her skin and, looking up at her, he catches that moment of release.

'No. Not just that,' he continues. 'I don't know how to explain. Everything looks new since I met you. It's as though I was sleep-walking through the world until now. You have sharpened all the blurred pictures that I had in my mind, and now I feel that I see things – or begin to see things – more clearly. I'm not really helping people, Katya. All I can do—'

'All they *let* you do,' she says fiercely, and he shrugs.

'All I can do is push paper from one side of my desk to the other, and try to argue a small point or two in meetings, or watch and wait and hope that things will improve. I begin to see it in a different way. A very different way.' His voice is low, and she moves even closer to him, allowing his arm to press her to him, so that when they speak they can whisper. Just in case.

120

'How did you see it before?'

'You know. I like Khrushchev.'

'He followed Stalin around like a puppy,' she says, with an ironic smile. 'His little *liubimchik*.'

'Look. Everyone believed in Stalin unless they figured out what he was really about. And if you figured that out, you were trapped anyway. Khrushchev did what he needed to in order to survive. I think some of these new ideas of his are good. Not all of them will work, but he has been sweeping away that hero-worship people had for Stalin, and the fear, that terrible, terrible fear. I think he's really trying to help now. It's just . . . there are no controls. He overrides Bulganin, Malenkov, all of them. And they're all watching their own backs, trying to keep their positions. Sometimes at the expense of doing good work. But it is changing,' he says, almost to himself. 'At least now they're trying to control people by giving them something, not by threatening them.'

'But they are still trying to control people?'

'I don't know. I think so. Possibly.' He gives a wry, desperate smile. 'You see, with one question you open up a new way of looking at things for me. I see things differently now. And once you do that, you cannot go back to the old way of thinking, can you? Can you, Katya?'

His last question is softly spoken, almost a plea. She hears it, but her eyes are focused on some faraway point, somewhere that he cannot see. 'No,' she tells him. 'You can never go back.'

He swallows a sigh. 'Come on,' he says, pointing at the stove. 'It must be ready. Let's eat.'

While he is filleting the fish and slicing bread, she has excused herself and disappeared into her bedroom. She quickly applies a little lipstick, for that is what she has ostensibly come here to do. In the mirror she eyes the briefcase. There is no time to consider, she must simply do it. She walks over to the bed in her bare feet, as silently as she can, and flips open the catch. It makes a sound and she glances at the door to see if he has heard, but he is busy outside, and the background throb of the cooling oven is probably all he can hear. Inside is a notebook, full of clean paper, and one folder containing five sheets of paper. She scans them. They seem to be minutes of a meeting, something to do with defence research. They are in his handwriting. She reads two of the pages within a minute, memorising what she thinks are the key names and points. She will write them down later, when he is gone.

'Katya,' he calls.

She slips the folder back into his bag – she can hear him coming to find her. Quickly she twists the catch closed again, and she is up and at the door of the bedroom, kissing him as he crosses the threshold. She stays in the kiss for a long time, to his surprise and pleasure, for she needs a few moments to recover herself, to slow the adrenaline that is coursing through her and making her hands tingle. Unexpectedly, she is also racked by guilt. She is consumed by it, without any warning, without even having to think through what she has just done. She leans her head against Alexander's shoulder, positioning herself so that her face is hidden from his gaze. You've done what you were told to do, she reminds herself, as he holds her. You've done what you've always wanted to do, and it will be all right when you get used to it.

Later, she lies back on her bed with one arm crossed protectively over her stomach and chest. Often, these days, she misses him when he leaves but tonight she is grateful to be alone. With her other hand she rubs her temples, as though soothing a headache. There is no pain, but there is confusion, and she does not like it. She has been

DESPITE THE FALLING SNOW

unhappy since she opened his briefcase. It is the kind of thing she has had to do many times before, but today's assignment, with Alexander, was the most difficult to execute. Partly because he knows her so well and is sensitive enough to read her every look and expression; and partly because for the first time in her experience, she did not want to do what had been asked of her. She knows this move was made too early, and that Misha only wanted to put her to the test, but she knows also that something more is at play. She is worried that stealing secrets from Alexander and abusing his trust and love will not become easier as time goes by.

All her life has been a struggle against confusion, a wish to keep things clear. Ambivalence and uncertainty are of no help to someone who has chosen the path she has taken. You must believe in what you do and why you do it, even more so than any Communist leader who sentences millions of *kulaks* to death with the stroke of a pen must be certain that he is acting for the greater good, or at least for his own good.

'I do believe in it,' she says, in a whisper. That is not the problem. She will fight until she dies the system that made her an orphan, that killed her parents and everyone else's with such brutality. But now she is falling in love – she can barely allow herself even to think the phrase in her head, much less admit it aloud – with a man who represents that system and is deeply involved in it. What does that make her? A traitor to everything she has lived for, probably. A traitor to the cause of making amends for what happened to her parents. A traitor to the anti-Communists, to the Americans for whom she works indirectly.

She thinks about Alexander, running through her conversations with him in her mind. She is sure that he is a good man, and this makes her think of the others she works against, steals secrets from, lies to. Are they good and just working in a system that she considers bad? She rarely knows these adversaries well enough to judge, but it is possible, probable, even, that the majority are good but unthinking. Unquestioning. And in a state where questioning and thinking can cost you your life or your freedom, can they be blamed?

But Alexander has told her that she has made him think. Or start to think. His boss is not Stalin, it is Khrushchev. Would his questioning cost him his life now? Perhaps not, but his career certainly. He would be left with nothing if anyone found out the thoughts that are winding their way into his head. Or that he was falling in love with Katya. No, that would not cost him anything, not yet, because nobody knows what she really is. What she really does. But they might find out – she lives with that awareness at all times. And then what would happen to him?

She laughs to herself, a laugh of sarcasm at her own thoughts running in that direction, imagining this life with Alexander, and the potential consequences for him. As if his future should be of any concern to her. She should want to know him only to access his information. Khrushchev may not be the same breed of monster as Stalin, but the system is the same and it still stinks. His crazy agricultural 'reforms' are leaving people starving. And Misha has just told of the latest disaster for his father and grandmother out in the country. Their co-operative farm, their small *kolkhoz*, is being forced to buy all its old tractors and equipment from the government outright and at inflated prices, leaving them with huge debts that they can never hope to pay off. And here in the city, who you are and whom you know are still the only certain way to progress. Alexander is where he is today because of his father. These, Katya, are the kinds of things you must keep in your mind.

But, for the first time, she is discovering that the head and the heart can have two different wishes, different motives, different objectives. To Katya her heart is a frightening organ. She neither trusts nor understands it. When she was twelve, and she watched her mother and father being hustled out of their apartment with guns pressed to their heads, leaving half-finished plates of food behind them, her heart broke. Where it had been, there remained only a hollow into which she swallowed her tears of terror at what they might do to her parents, and the desperate fear that she could not speak, the crude fear of a child being left all alone. Those roughly hurt emotions left raw, open wounds that no one but she could try slowly to soothe. And since then her heart has been sitting quietly within her, untroubled by much more than the effort of pumping blood through her veins. There is nothing more that she wants of it, for she knows that it is a fearsome, ruthless animal that can rise up and rip out the rest of her organs in a second.

'Katya? You awake?'

She jumps. She has been so absorbed in her thoughts that she has not even heard Maya return. 'Yes. How was your dinner?'

'Good.' Maya stumbles to her bed, a few feet across from Katya's, and Katya can smell the faintly acrid, smoky smell of a bar on her friend. 'I drank too much, of course. I'll have a hell of a headache in the morning. How was your date?'

Katya gives a half-smile in the dark. My date. 'Fine. He's nice.'

'About time you showed some interest in someone. Men are not all pigs, you know.' Maya is unbuttoning her clothes, pulling on a nightdress. She wanders to the dressing-table they share, where brushes, towels and soap are all kept so that they will not be taken from the bathroom out in the hallway that they share with the two daughters from the apartment upstairs.

'I didn't think they were,' replies Katya. 'I'm just . . .'

'Picky,' finishes Maya.

Katya laughs. 'Perhaps.'

Maya disappears to the bathroom, and Katya lies looking at the pattern that the moonlight makes on the corner of the ceiling as it plays through the small, high window of their room. When she returns, Katya whispers to her, 'I like him, Maya.'

But the drink, or exhaustion or both have made Maya deaf. Katya listens as the girl clambers into her bed, giving a small moan of relief or pleasure at lying down between cool sheets after a warm, tiring evening.

'Goodnight,' Katya calls.

But Maya is already asleep.

Chapter Nine

Boston, December 2000

ALEXANDER CANNOT WALK home fast enough, and Lauren is having to work hard to keep up with him, to enclose him fully beneath the capacious umbrella she carries.

Courteously, he tries to slow down, and smiles at her briefly, but his face reflects a series of indefinite emotions – irritation, nervousness, depression. His thoughts are black-edged with melancholy. Around them the settling evening darkness is made weightier by the relentless drizzle, and they are both grateful for the lights of home that come into sight when they turn into their street at last. The two hours at Estelle's apartment have unsettled him, have left him unmoored and feeling exposed. He tries to pin down which aspects of the afternoon have led to his present mood, but he senses something more insidious at work, something that has crept into his mind and now lies curled up and threatening inside his head. He glances sideways at his niece. He had seen pained surprise, yet such clarity of vision in her face earlier, when Estelle's comment about her portraits had stung her. The idea of such unexpected awareness, such illumination is strangely attractive to him. If he had been as clear about certain things in his life – in his younger life especially – would he have taken a different path?

'So what do you think?' Lauren asks, as he unlocks the front door.

He is embarrassed to realise that he hasn't heard anything she has been saying. With a look of apology he shrugs off his coat, then takes hers. 'I've been miles away. Sorry.'

She follows him into the living room, where he paces about, switching on lamps, lighting the fire and putting on music. He keeps moving, diligently, but it does not help – wherever he goes he feels that he is followed by the eyes of Katya's portrait. Finally he looks at it, a hungry, desolate look, until he becomes aware that Lauren is watching him, and he smiles at the picture, as though taking pleasure in it, as he would with any present.

'I just thought it might be a good project,' Lauren continues, 'sketching, then painting the two of you.'

He looks at her, not understanding.

'You and Estelle.'

'Are you serious?'

'Absolutely.' She remains standing, even after he has sunk into his armchair. 'I've been thinking about a series. Sort of based around the Seven Ages of Man.'

Her choice of title makes him smile. 'I don't suppose I would be number six, would I?'

'What?'

'Of the seven ages of man.'

'I haven't decided yet. Maybe not.'

'You know how to hit an old man where it hurts.'

'But, Uncle Alex, you have such character in your face, such romance in your eyes . . .'

'Please. You should be ashamed of yourself, trying to charm a man of my age.'

Despite his banter, he is distracted, she can see that, so she decides to leave aside her idea for a while, even though she is keen to discuss it. She has deliberately chosen a theme, an underlying idea that she can think about and work on to try to bring some emotional and intellectual depth to the next portraits she does. She wants to discuss with him what Estelle had said earlier about her work sounding formulaic. She had felt a cool prickling of fear at the realisation, so sudden and yet so clear, that Estelle was right – what she has been doing for the past few years has lost any edge, any philosophy. Her work is now steady and comfortable and plentiful and, if she is to be brutally honest with herself, meaningless. She is living the kind of easy, uninspired existence that is precisely what she has always despised in others and dreaded for herself. She has always assumed that being an artist of any kind somehow implied a sense of integrity in your work – the kind of integrity not so easily found in other fields. Like business, for instance. But then she sees the fervour with which her uncle has built his company from the seeds of his passion. And now it occurs to her to wonder whether Melissa Johnson's devotion to her work might represent a passion also. Perhaps it is harder for Lauren to recognise because it is rooted in the day-to-day work of deal-making and consulting, rather than in a desire to make a life's work out of an art or a single love like Alexander's for food and cooking. She glances at her uncle once more, hoping to talk through some of this; she is astute and sensitive enough, however, to tell that he is in one of those rare moods when he has no wish for company. She kisses his cheek and tells him she wants to have a bath.

A sigh escapes him – it has risen from deep within, on the tide of memories and feelings that have been stirred up by Estelle and her questions. He smothers the sound under a smile and, just before his niece leaves the room, he calls her back. 'And Estelle? Where does she fit into the Ages of Man?'

'I guess she'd be number six. Of the seven. She has a great face – such life and movement in her eyes. What do you think?'

Whether she means to ask his opinion of her as the sixth, or of her eyes, he is unsure, but he nods mildly, and gives away nothing of his pleasure that Lauren's new idea might throw Estelle and himself together more frequently.

He sits prodding at the fire, a pointless gesture since the logs are burning well. He is missing Katya. Not in the vague, intermittent way that he has fallen into over the years, but in a deep, urgent, aching way that he fears will give him no respite. He puts down the poker and buries his face in his hands, trying to stop himself turning to look at the portrait that leans against the wall behind him. He does not feel his age, despite the ache in his knee, and the silvering of the hairs on his arms. He feels young, very young, and as though he has just lost her. The memory of the intense, pure pain that her death inflicted on him is easily summoned. He remembers that at first he had been shocked and disbelieving, desperate for answers. He had focused on trying to get them, to find a way to see her, to look at her poor dead body for himself, to see that it was true that she could have been removed from the world so quickly and brutally. He had not been able to do so, of course, and then he could no longer resist the feeling that he was slipping, that his hands were grasping a sharp ledge of life, and that below him there was the comfort of an abyss, an infinite drop into oblivion. The taste of that drop, the sensation of falling, was so sweet that there were many times when he had nearly let go. It was so simple, the work of a moment, to lift away a hand and plunge downwards. To continue to cling to the brutal roughness of life seemed the harder course but he followed it doggedly: a young, grief-torn attempt to make himself suffer just a little of what she had suffered.

'I'm so sorry, Katyushka,' he whispers to the portrait. He wants to touch her, to hold her close, to bury his face in her soft black hair, to feel comforted by a pair of arms round him, without having to speak, or ask, or explain.

He also knows that when he left Estelle's apartment no more than an hour ago, he had wanted to touch her as well. It is a hard truth for him to admit to himself – that he wanted to feel some human warmth and, in particular, *her* warmth. The touch of her hand on his own. But Estelle is married. To a man he wishes to believe is uncaring and cold, but who may be a very different person when he shuts his books at night. And Katya is dead, long dead and disappeared, and all that remains of her are a few tiny grains of memory, many of which he suspects are more and more embellished in his own mind as time passes, and those few grains will themselves dance away into thin air, as though blown by a breeze, as soon as his own life is over, leaving nothing more of her, anywhere, ever. Except for a portrait, an arresting, accurate portrait, which will be of a woman of whom no one knows anything.

His rational instinct is to try to break out of this mood, and his thoughts move almost automatically to his kitchen and to what he might cook. But he has no appetite after the tea and cake they have just had and, besides, his fingers are stiff from the cold. He stands and glances through the bookshelves on his left. The familiar titles jump out at him in a familiar order, and he pulls down an old novel. His eyes trace the lines in a purposeful, direct manner, for he is eager to be pulled into some other world and is prepared to work hard to manage it. But it seems to him that the book is not helping him. He tries again, selecting poetry this time, but this does little except

SHAMIM SARIF

indulge his mood. He is almost relieved to look up and find that the fire has burned down. He walks upstairs, takes a hot shower, calls goodnight to Lauren and goes to bed.

The next morning he sleeps until nine, which is unusually late for him and throws off his sense of the day to come. But the early part of the night was seared with dreams of Katya, and one in particular had hung about his memory for several wakeful hours in the night. It had seemed unrelentingly long, and he was relieved when he awoke, but also disturbed. In the dream, he had got out of bed and gone to the window, except that it did not look like his bedroom window, but was divided into several smaller, wooden-framed panes of glass. He had the sense that he was inside a *dacha* somewhere outside Moscow – there was a grand entrance hall, and wicker chairs on a wooden veranda, and a feeling of sunlight in the house, that reminded him of a *dacha* for government officials where he and Katya had once stayed during a summer holiday. And in the dream it was summer: he knew somehow that it was windy but warm outside, and he had got out of bed because he had heard a woman laughing. He wiped the dusty glass and saw Katya outside the window. He felt that she must be a ghost, because she was moving in strange ways. At first she seemed to be at a great distance, and he could see her bare feet and the swirling hem of her summer dress. But there were moments, too, when she seemed to be right next to him, when he could feel her touch on his arm, could breathe the scent of her neck. These sensations lifted him into a kind of tormented ecstasy – for somewhere in the back of his mind he understood that she was not real. He was grateful to wake up after falling into a final, fitful sleep in the early hours, and pleased to remember that Estelle and Melissa will be visiting in a couple of hours.

*

132

Estelle's desk, in contrast to her husband's, sits under a window in their living room, where the sunlight floods it in the mornings. She cannot bear the artificial light under which he labours in his study, but he tells her that he prefers it – his books and papers are lit in the same way at midnight and midday, and there is nothing to distract him from his thoughts. She sits down with a trace of self-consciousness, although she is alone in the room, for she feels a definite sense of purpose today, something different from the usual vague possibilities that lead her to her desk. She pushes back the leather penholder, the box of white letter paper and envelopes, the untidy stack of bills that usually claims her attention when she sits here. She wants space today, clarity and openness, and when she has made a good empty area round her computer, she begins. A new document, a blank page. She writes: 'The snow has blurred the outline of the woman standing outside; to Alexander, she appears as something ghostly.'

Of course, names will have to change, particularly since most of this will be fiction. She types in a little more, then highlights the whole piece and taps the delete button. Her fingers are ill at ease on the keyboard today. Letters are flying up to her touch in the wrong order, and the keys are conspiring against her. She opens a drawer, and pulls out a handwritten paper of her husband's. The sort of thing she usually types up in minutes, with no problems. She attempts to copy it on to the computer. 'Undoubtedly, the extreme deference with which the writer approaches his subject provides a sense of . . .'

She has no trouble typing this. With impatience, and a sudden decisiveness, she thrusts the paper back into the drawer, and pushes the computer screen further back on the desk. Now she checks her fountain pen, and looks around for a pad of paper. She will write this thing in longhand if she has to. One lies beneath the sheaf of bills, and she reaches for it, noticing as she does so that the electricity payment was due last week.

Twenty minutes later, she is still writing cheques when Melissa knocks at the open door. 'Does genius burn?' she asks.

It is a quiet reference to *Good Wives*. It is what Jo March's family asks her when she is writing. Estelle looks at her over the top of half-moon glasses. 'I'd forgotten about that,' she says. 'How long is it since we read that book?'

It is not a question, but a recognition of a time long past, of the shared history of mother and daughter; but Melissa has an answer: 'I was twelve,' she says. 'I remember because you read it to me every night the week before I went to summer camp.'

Estelle nods, recognising Melissa's deeply held emotion simply by the precision and detail of her recollection. 'I liked reading to you,' she tells her.

'I liked listening.'

'Come here.'

Melissa goes and stands before her mother's chair. Estelle's arms are up, outstretched, and Melissa leans down to accept the embrace with something like relief.

'I miss you,' Estelle says quietly.

Melissa wonders at how such a short, hackneyed phrase can have such a reassuring effect. Perhaps it is the feel of her mother's arms round her, after too long an absence. 'Thanks,' she says. 'Listen. We have to go in a little while.'

Estelle puts away the untouched pad. 'I'll get ready.'

'Good,' Melissa replies. 'I don't want to be late.'

On her way to answer the doorbell, Lauren glances at the paintings that hang on the walls of the entrance hall. They are the two abstracts that Estelle had mentioned, pieces that she worked on perhaps six or seven years ago, and that catch her attention for a second because they are good. She has a vague recollection, little more than the kind of transportation of mind that a certain scent or taste can effect, a hint of the ideas she was working out when she painted them. That hyper-awareness, the sensation that a moment of grace was close to being grasped. The bell rings again, long, insistent, this time, and she hurries forward and throws open the door. Estelle and Melissa stand on the doorstep.

'You know, patience is a great virtue,' she says to Melissa.

'So they say, if you're sure that what you're waiting for is going to show up.'

'I was on my way.' She stands aside to let them in.

'But I didn't know that for sure. It's a big house. You might not have heard the bell. We could have been waiting there for ever.'

Lauren rubs her forehead.

'Am I giving you a headache?' Melissa smiles.

'Yes. And don't try to alleviate your guilt with a lousy aspirin either. I'll expect a shoulder massage.'

'If that's what you want.'

Estelle takes in this exchange with some surprise; Melissa's reply, its directness, has caused Lauren to flush. She walks briskly ahead of them, showing them into the living room, and immediately Estelle sees the portrait of Katya. She stands close before it.

'She is quite stunning. The painting is stunning.'

'I can't decide whether it was the best present I've ever given him or the worst.'

'Has it brought it all back?'

'I think so. Though he's trying to put a brave face on it.'

Estelle turns back to the portrait. She is finding herself increasingly intrigued by this woman and her story – whatever it might be. She seems enclosed in mystery, and that mystery reeks of danger, of undiscovered secrets and hidden passions. Katya's portrait looks back at her, with unknowable dark eyes, and Estelle feels momentarily effaced, lost under the gaze of this immortalised young woman.

Alexander pushes open the door with his foot because he is carrying in a large platter covered with canapés. He wishes them all good morning, and holds the door for a middle-aged woman in a white apron, whom he introduces as his housekeeper. She carries a bottle of champagne and a tray of gleaming glasses. It occurs to Estelle that if she spends more than a little time with this man she will end up as big as a house.

'Your husband wasn't able to come?' Alexander asks.

'He's with another woman right now,' Estelle says. 'I asked him to join us, but he won't leave her.'

There is a stifled sound of exasperation from Melissa. 'Dad's an English professor. The "other woman" is George Eliot.'

'For now,' adds Estelle. 'But next week, it'll be someone else.'

Alexander smiles, but Estelle feels her daughter watching her keenly, almost clinically. This kind of ultimately inconsequential talk is so alien to Melissa that Estelle does her best to repress it when they are together, but occasionally it will declare itself. While Alexander pours drinks, she turns back to the portrait.

'It makes you want to know more about your aunt,' she says, 'and yet you feel you already know her, or at least part of her character, just from the expression and the eyes. Actually, you resemble her quite a bit, don't you think?'

'Maybe just the colouring. Eyes and hair.'

'I think there's something more,' suggests Melissa.

They all consider the painting again.

'I love the way she's standing, with her arms folded,' says Estelle. 'There's something relaxed and almost haughty about her, but also the hands grip the elbows just a little too tightly, and doesn't that suggest defensiveness?' Estelle steps back from her analysis and imagining, and looks uncertainly at Lauren. 'Or am I way off base?'

But Lauren is elated. 'That's exactly it,' she says. 'Those are the kinds of complexities that made my aunt such an irresistible subject for me. It's hard to put a portrait into words, but that's a great description.'

'Estelle writes,' Alexander says, partly to interrupt Lauren.

'It shows,' says Lauren. 'What do you write?'

Estelle ponders, as if trying to choose between her many styles and forms is a great burden. 'Sum total of my output to date? Five short stories, and half of a novel that's so bad it makes me cringe, but it cost such an effort that I can't actually bear to throw it away.'

'One of my art teachers told me once that those old canvases which have taken the longest time but are going nowhere – they're the ones to paint over first.'

'You mean a brand new novel?'

'Sure. Any ideas?'

Alexander is watching her, Estelle knows, and she turns to meet his look for a second.

'A few.'

'Care to share them?' Alexander asks, handing her a glass.

'Not just yet,' says Estelle. 'Genius can't be rushed, you know.'

Chapter Ten

Moscow, August 1956

THE RESTAURANT HAS been loud and smoky and filled with talk, laughter and dancing. It is a Georgian restaurant, on the ground floor of an apartment block near her own. The food is rich with tomatoes, nuts and spices, the atmosphere carefree, somehow reflective of that southern heritage. They finish their meal – a chicken *satsivi* and some fried aubergine, and they watch two soldiers dancing with three women in the centre of the room. They are stamping their feet and swinging around – the people at the tables closest to them are having to be careful of their drinks. But everyone is smiling: their enthusiasm and excitement are contagious. Alexander watches Katya watching the dancers.

It is the end of the week, and both of them have had a busy time at work. Alexander is happy to be with her, but he can't help feeling tired and subdued, eroded by a poor week of meetings and discussions that he feels have led only backwards. She is smiling as she watches the dancing, but her eyes are not part of the smile. She has been lively this evening, and he has hardly been able to take his gaze from her, but something is making him uneasy. She seems to be behaving with him as she sometimes does with other people whom she does not know so well – not falsely, but not altogether relaxed. There is an air of effort about her convivial conversation and her laughter.

He drinks his last mouthful of sweet Georgian wine, and fills her glass with what remains in the bottle.

'You look so young with your haircut,' she says, reaching across to ruffle his hair.

He puts a hand defensively to his head. 'Do I look like a boy?' he asks.

She smiles and shakes her head. Then she leans across the table and kisses him, a light brush of the lips that lingers on his mouth, becoming slowly deeper, until he can taste her tongue running lightly over his own, can feel her mouth pulling at his. After a minute, she moves away, leaving him dizzy. Then she turns back to watch the dancing as though nothing else is of interest to her just now. The shadows that play about her face tonight are textured and thick, accentuated by the array of lamps and candles that light the restaurant.

He passes her another piece of the *khachapuri* bread which she likes, rich with cheese and eggs, and she breaks off a bite and washes it down with the last of her wine.

They walk back to her apartment, holding hands, not speaking. The late-night air is cool even here, where the narrow streets are bound by high grey buildings, and he is happy. Even his fatigue is pleasurable when it is relieved by her company. When they reach her apartment, he walks behind her up the stairs. The concrete walls and tiny stairwells are oppressive, and he is relieved to get away from them, even into her small, dark living space. As usual, Maya is still out. Maya's mother is asleep in her tiny cupboard of a room, the door tightly shut.

They go into the bedroom and Alexander sits on the foot of her bed, draws her to him and kisses her. 'Happy anniversary,' he says.

It is not a particularly significant day, but while they have been strolling home, he has been calculating in his mind and has come to the conclusion that today they have been together for five months exactly. Katya looks up with a jerk, almost as though he has reached over and slapped her. She stares at him coolly.

'What is it?' he asks, as a mild panic grips him.

'What are *you* talking about?' she replies. Her tone is harsh.

'I was just thinking . . . I was just thinking that we have been together exactly five months. Today. An anniversary.'

'Oh.' She stands up abruptly, upset still, and embarrassed. As she knew would happen, he is on his feet in a moment, and has moved to hold her, but it is hard for him to do so for she has the palms of her hands pressed over her eyes. He holds her from behind, cradling her in his arms, and kissing her neck.

'What is it, Katyushka? What is it, my love?' he asks and, despite herself, she feels the tears fall.

He holds her more tightly. 'Is it so bad to be with me?'

She laughs, briefly, as she weeps, and he kisses her hair. He can smell in it the metallic, inky odour of the school.

'Tell me. What are you thinking about?' He pauses. 'What anniversary?'

Almost at once the sobbing stops, and her body has stiffened beneath his hands.

'Come here,' he says. He pulls her down on to the thin mattress, and lies next to her, precariously close to the edge of the narrow bed, shifting closer so that her head is against his shoulder, and his arms are round her. She has stopped crying, and he waits, rubbing her back gently, as if soothing a child, and he listens to the breath entering and leaving her, rhythmic and slowing. 'Tell me,' he says, and, for the first time, she does.

'Fourteen years ago today,' she says, as though beginning a bedtime story, 'I was sitting at the table in my parents' house. Having dinner.' She stops to take a deep, ragged breath, and then she smiles.

'I loved that table. It was a big wooden thing that my grandfather brought on the back of a cart from his *dacha* years ago. We all had our own places at it, and our parents let each of us carve our names into the underside, at the places where we sat. It was easy, the wood was soft.' She stops and looks at Alexander. He is thinking whether to ask her where the table is now, but decides against it.

'They were quite strict, my parents. They never let us do anything like that usually. But, anyway, we were all there, at dinner, both of them, my brother and myself. They were laughing a lot, my mother and father. There had been some joke at the university, some piece of research that had crossed into both of their fields – I forget exactly what – and they were explaining it to us, and they were excited and happy that the unthinkable had happened, and they would have to work together for a while.'

'Go on,' says Alexander, with trepidation, for he knows how the story must end, even if he has waited this long to hear from her how it started.

'We were sitting there, having dinner. I was twelve, Yuri quite a bit older. I was the afterthought, the baby they didn't expect. They were so shocked when they found my mother was pregnant,' she adds, with a quick laugh. She is telling him things now that he already knows, delaying the moment when she must put into words the thing she has never spoken of before. He touches his lips to her forehead and waits.

'We had finished the meal, almost, and we were about to have dessert – I remember, because we rarely had any, not during the war anyway, and I was looking forward to it – when there was a knock at the door. The knock that for the last ten years people had always waited for but never really believed would happen to them. People are so stupid sometimes. We were stupid. Maybe to survive. Better to blind yourself to the danger than have a heart attack every time someone knocks at the door. Anyway, no one was nervous. No one thought twice about opening that door, although I suppose it would have made no difference if we had tried not to. We all knew that Stalin was arresting people all over again. Jumpy from the war. Looking for collaborators, more enemies of the people, as though any could have been left after the thirties. But that knock was supposed to come at three in the morning, not nine at night. That gave us a false sense of security, I suppose, even though we already knew someone who had been interrogated, or who had been imprisoned or killed. Especially my parents. They knew lots of so-called intelligentsia. That was what they were, after all. And noncon-formist intelligentsia at that. The worst sort of people.'

He is stroking her hair, but she seems oblivious now, her voice brittle, still carrying the residual sound of tears. She is staring up at the ceiling, watching the whole scene again.

'So we opened the door – Yuri did, I remember, because my parents were still at the table, still talking, one eye and ear on the door, waiting to see who had come to visit. And then they were inside, pushing Yuri to one side – poor Yuri, he blamed himself after that for opening the door, as if it would have changed anything. And they showed some papers – some kind of stupid identification – and they grabbed my father by both arms, shouting that they were arresting him for crimes against the state, and then my mother, too. They pulled her up, and her chair fell over, and my father was shouting at them not to hurt her, and we were watching, just shocked, I think. There seemed to be so many of them but, you know, there were only three men. They just seemed so powerful. They *were* so powerful. They had my parents out of our apartment in a matter of seconds. Seconds. They did not even have time to look back at us or say anything to us. By the time I ran forwards, crying for my mother, she was gone. There was no trace of her or my father. We never saw them again.'

Her eyes are bright but she is not crying, and he holds her, his own tears dropping unnoticed into her thick black hair.

'I felt so helpless,' she is saying. 'So helpless and lost. I miss them so much, Sasha. I miss my mother so much.'

In his short life, Alexander has rarely encountered situations when he does not know how to respond, or what action to try. He has never been faced with such raw emotional trauma in someone he loves, the kind of primeval pain that no one outside can heal. He watches the narrow shadows thrown about the room by the street-light outside. Her back and shoulders shake with sobs that she cannot control, and he tries to hold her even more closely. Then, after a few minutes, she sits up on the bed, and glances at him, her face tear-streaked and red, and she pushes back her hair and stands up. He reaches out to hold on to her still, but she is back to herself now. She touches his face gratefully and releases herself from his hands.

'Yuri looked everywhere for them, the Lubyanka, the Butyrka prison, the police stations. It was as though they had vanished into thin air. How did he get away with that for so long?' she whispers.

'Fear,' Alexander says. 'He ruled with fear. We were all relieved when it was over.' Then he regrets what he has said, for while his dislike of Stalin is mainly intellectual, hers comes from an emotional pain he can barely imagine.

'Not all. Not even most, Sasha. Everyone was distraught when he died. Even your father.'

'Not in the same way.'

She lets it go, but he knows what she means. His father, who was so disenchanted by Stalin, was still devastated by his death. Millions of Soviets, most people, were. The emotional reliance on their leader had been so deeply rooted, the respect that grew from fear was so ingrained, his insidious charm so great that it was difficult for people to imagine how the country would cope without him. Or even how it would exist without him.

But since Stalin's death, Alexander muses, his father has allowed himself to think about things in a more balanced manner, less emotionally, perhaps. He has allowed himself to deconstruct the source of his disillusionment and disgust. Khrushchev's early, far-reaching movement towards deStalinisation helped to shock him and others like him into reconsidering the years that had gone before – to face the fact that the torturous methods of terror were a direct result of Stalin's orders and way of governing. And even now when Khrushchev panics that he is losing control of his reforms, and takes steps back into stiff, harsh governance, such reversals only throw into relief the inconsistencies and injustice of the system that they had become used to. His father, Alexander thinks, has become a man who sees that his life is not built on a series of solid, upright bricks, as he had once thought, but on a set of rubber, shifting blocks that are showing ever-increasing holes.

'When did you discover what had happened to them?'

Katya can do no more than whisper now. 'Maybe six months later. We were lucky to find out, I suppose. Apparently they were taken straight to a state farm owned by the KGB or the NKVP as they were then. At Kommunarka, just outside the city. No one knew that it was one of the places they sent people to be killed. They refused to sign confessions that they were enemies of the people. But then there was a report that Yuri saw – he bribed an official. It said my father had stated for the record that he had been wrongly arrested, that it was Stalin who was the enemy of the people.' A twisted smile passes briefly over her face. 'I'm sure it was true, that he said it. My father always had a good sense of irony.'

'And so they shot them. My father was a historian, a good one, and therefore an intellectual terrorist, and my mother . . . well, my mother's mistake was to be his wife. To support him. Those six months, waiting to find out if they were dead or alive, were the worst. I had such dreams. That someone was holding my father over a balcony. I would watch, wait, on a knife edge, praying they would pull him back. But always, with the lightest movement, the hand would let go of him, and he would fall to his death. I would wake up crying, I was so sick with sadness.' She clears her throat. 'Don't make me think about it any more.'

She walks out, away, into the hallway, then into the tiny damp bathroom, and looks at herself in the mirror. 'Sasha?'

'Yes?'

As she suspected, he has followed her and is waiting outside, in the dank hallway. Above him, in the corners of the low ceiling, he can see patches of damp and the white bloom of mildew beginning to take hold.

'What are you doing with me? Misha told me once that he tried to warn you away from me the first time we met. At the dance.'

'I didn't hear him,' Alexander replies. 'I was a man possessed.'

He sees the outline of her head among the shadows in the bathroom, as she watches herself in the mirror.

'Ah, but possessed of what, now?' she asks, without humour, and she leans down to splash icy water on her face. She feels sorry for him: even though he is the same age as she, she can feel his childlike helplessness in the face of her grief and anger. She runs a hand over her burning eyes, and thinks that she will go in, lie down next to him and let him hold her, let his warmth and love enclose her so that she does not have to see or hear anything else ever again. That will help her, and it will help him also. But for now she remains standing there, fiddling with her hair, for she is thinking. She looks at her eyes in the mirror, and knows they are the same as her mother's, and from this starting point she tries to reconstruct her mother's face as she recalls it – the rough dark hair, the high, broad forehead and long nose, uneven from some childhood mishap. The face appears to her – a face, any face, really, not truly as it was. She is trying too hard to see it, and it has been too long, and Katya herself was too young. All these circumstances conspire against the retaining of the perfect memory, and she sighs. She comes out to the hallway and together they walk back to her room.

'I can't even remember what my mother looked like,' she tells him, and he walks her back to the bed. His body is warm, compared to the cold air of the apartment, and she closes her eyes, places her mouth and nose almost flat against his chest and breathes his smell and listens to the blood pulsing inside him. Now she will begin once more the process of forgetting it, the terrible thing that happened so many years ago. And what a hard process it is, whenever she recalls it, to then tame it and push all of it back into the furthest, unlit recesses of her memory where it will never stay willingly but lies waiting, like a sly, hungry animal, ready for her guard to drop, for her shell to crack open and let it back in.

She feels safer with Alexander's arms round her, and his sensitive, kind eyes watching over her, but she also feels brittle and cold inside. She had made notes on the information she had gleaned from his papers that night, several weeks ago, and passed them to Misha the next day. He had been satisfied in some way and, since then, she has not had to do anything similar. But since that evening she has begun to dislike herself, and the feeling of self-disgust is especially strong at times like this, when Alexander is showing her more care and adoration than she has ever received in her life. She sighs. Perhaps she will not think so hard about it for a while. Just for a few weeks. She is too confused to consider anything properly now. Perhaps she will just relax a little, and enjoy her time with him, and then, when Misha wants her to begin work, she can decide what to do. She feels tears prick at her eyes again, and tries biting her lip to hold them back, but they will not be held. They are tears of anger at what happened to her parents, tears of self-pity for the lost child she remembers being, and tears of frustration at the dilemma she now feels, because she is not at all sure that there is any decision to be made by her about Alexander; she is almost certain that there is no way out.

Chapter Eleven

Boston, January 2001

Estelle opens her front door. She is dressed entirely in black – trousers, a turtleneck and a scarf that swathes softly over her shoulders. The effect is elegant, effortless. A faint smile of approval passes over Lauren's lips as Estelle shows her in, guiding her to a drawing room, which Lauren takes in with a precise glance. The original floorboards are exposed, sanded and varnished to a warm brown colour that matches the outside of the fireplace. On top of the mantel is a photograph of Melissa as a child, sitting on her father's shoulders. There is an air of the dashing, the Byronesque, about Professor Johnson in the photograph. His face shows a casual pride as he holds his child. Melissa is smiling, the kind of fully released expression that is so much more common in children than adults. Lauren looks away, to a couple of old rugs placed beneath leather sofas. The soft grain and folds of the leather might make an interesting background, she thinks, and she suggests that Estelle take a seat there. Tinged with self-consciousness, Estelle takes a few moments to find a comfortable position, but Lauren is busy unfolding her easel and setting out her pencils.

'Just give me a bowl of fruit,' Estelle says. 'I can pose as a still-life.'

'I see you as anything but a still-life,' says Lauren. 'Just relax. The point of sketching someone at home is to have them be comfortable.'

'In their native habitat,' comments Estelle.

'Exactly.'

Lauren refuses the offer of a drink or breakfast: she has a nervous tension in her stomach and in her hands that, if harnessed correctly, can be helpful to her work. She begins to draw, talking to Estelle as she does so, inconsequential chatter, the kind that she can manage easily to keep her subject relaxed and interested. They talk about her husband's work, and then her daughter's.

'Melissa can be a little short sometimes,' Estelle says suddenly. 'She doesn't even realise she's being less than gracious. Her mind is always moving at a hundred miles an hour, always thinking about the next thing, and words or communicating just take up precious time.'

'Is that how your husband is?' Lauren asks.

'Yes. But he means well, mostly.'

'And if it's too much bother for either of them to communicate, who does that leave for you to talk to?'

'I don't know,' says Estelle wryly. 'Maybe I should get a therapist.'

'Too expensive. How about talking to me? Tell me about your story ideas.'

'For my great novel, you mean?'

'Uh-huh.'

'Don't laugh,' Estelle instructs.

'I won't.'

'Alexander and Katya.'

Lauren laughs.

'I'm serious,' says Estelle. 'Your uncle is an intriguing person, and Katya – well, there seems to be a ton of drama and mystery hanging around her.'

'It's not that mysterious,' Lauren replies. 'He just doesn't like to talk about it much.'

'Why not? Can the wounds be that raw after so many years?'

Lauren stops drawing. 'I don't think it's that. He feels somehow responsible, and therefore guilty, for what happened to her. He had to make some hard choices before he left Russia. And she was the love of his life. I guess, in the end, he's not a heart-on-his-sleeve kind of guy. He'd rather keep it all in.'

'Which doesn't make my job any easier. Anyway, I just want to use them as a starting point. For a fictional piece. Unless he authorises me to write the official version.'

'I'd love to see that,' Lauren says, and Estelle looks at her, unsure if she detects a note of sarcasm, but Lauren gives her a glance of confirmation.

'No, I really would. You see, for a long time now, I've thought there was a lot more to the story than even Uncle Alex knows. He was out of the loop of what was happening. And there are loose ends that just don't tie up. I don't think he was as responsible as he thinks.'

'You're forgetting – I still don't know what happened. Only that your aunt died. Care to fill me in?'

Lauren rubs at her eyes with her hand. 'I'd love to. But I think we should clear it with your lead character first, don't you?'

'I suppose.'

Lauren looks at her closely. 'You have the eyes of a naughty child, Estelle. I need to find a way to capture that.'

Estelle gives a half-smile, but does not reply. She is involved in the idea of this story. Of Katya. A different era, an intensity of life so far removed from her own. Aware that she has fallen silent, she looks at Lauren, but she, too, is absorbed, her attention moving more fully to the paper before her, to the lines of charcoal darting over the page. Estelle watches the young woman working, and she can feel that she

151

is rapt, excited, interested. Everything that Estelle is afraid to allow in herself when she sits at her desk. She is overtaken by the desire to be there now, with the glow from the high sun on the wall behind her, and her pen flowing across the lined sheets. When Lauren leaves, she decides, she will write. Anything. She will describe the portrait of Katya, then Katya herself or, rather, the character she wants to begin sketching.

'So you wouldn't mind me using your story as a starting point?'

Alexander has only been in Estelle's apartment for ten minutes, but he is already ambivalent about having come. At first he had been secretly disappointed that Lauren preferred to sketch Estelle in her own home rather than having her come to their house. He would have liked constant proximity to his new friend without having to contrive reasons for it. But he has resolved simply to acknowledge that he would like to see Estelle more so has offered to come and walk his niece home when she has completed her morning's work. For Estelle, Alexander's arrival seems the perfect opportunity to ask the question that has been in her mind all morning.

'You're planning a whole novel?' Alexander asks.

Her eagerness and enthusiasm are clear to him, and she seems different, more vibrant, when she talks about working.

'I've already started researching. Books and the Internet. The big impression I've found so far is that Khrushchev made a huge difference, just in attitude and atmosphere, after the dictatorship of Stalin. There was less suspicion, more openness.'

Alexander nods. 'Yes, it was like that, mostly. Khrushchev was not infallible – he made many mistakes, often because he was rushing through changes to avoid opposition, but he was a big step forward. They called it the "thaw", that period. That was when I was working in the government.'

'It must have been an exciting time.'

Alexander studies his hands, thinking. It has been so long since he has thought of that time and place as anything other than threatening and choking. Had he thought it exciting once, when he first started? Probably. But that was before Katya. Before the institutions he had been reared to respect and serve began to threaten what he loved most. He blinks away the thoughts.

'You seem happy,' is all he says to Estelle, and the directness of his comment makes her look away for a second.

'I guess I am,' she says. 'But I know these things are hard for you to talk about and, contrary to the impression I may have given up till now, I hate to be a pushy broad.'

'I can't pretend that I relish going over things that I haven't considered for many, many years . . .'

'Maybe it's time you considered them again,' Lauren says.

He is irritated. 'I've kept them at arm's length all this time for a reason. They are painful subjects for me.'

'I know, but the more I've looked into my aunt's life, the more discrepancies there seem to be.'

Alexander rubs his chin. 'Can anything be changed by all of this?'

'Maybe,' Lauren says. Her face shows determination and life – the same qualities he recognises in himself, though perhaps not as frequently any more.

'Katya is dead,' he says. He is getting tired of saying it, and of thinking it. 'Nothing is going to resurrect her. Estelle, I want you to write, more than anything. I think it's wonderful, and if I can help by providing your starting point, or even with telling you what I know about Katya's life and death, I guess I'll do so. But I won't have a whole investigation reopened. Nothing can be served by all this rehashing and probing.'

His hand hits the table for emphasis, and although he has meant the gesture merely to emphasise his point, to his embarrassment the teacups shake visibly.

'That's not in the spirit of study and enlightenment, Mr Ivanov.'

He turns to see a looming outline in the doorway.

'Professor Johnson.' Alexander stands and shakes his hand. 'Enlightenment can never be achieved in this case. It is always a good thing to know when to leave something be.'

'Stop, stop,' the professor replies, a note of delight in his low voice. 'You're opening up too many wonderful debates all at once. The nature of enlightenment, the nature of achievement itself . . . Ah, we could talk for hours.'

Alexander sits down again. 'With respect, I don't want to open up debates. I want to close them.'

Professor Johnson does not comment further, only nods, then makes his way to the fridge. Estelle is up already, bringing him a glass, into which he pours the contents of a can of tonic water. He takes a sip and looks at the company at the table. 'Excellent protection against malaria,' he informs them.

Lauren laughs, and his eyes fix on her. They are fierce, and bird-like, giving the impression of continual movement and extreme concentration at the same time. 'You remind me somewhat of my wife,' he tells her. 'Though not superficially, you understand. Something in the eyes. "All the wild summer was in her gaze . . ." '

Estelle busies herself with scooping tea leaves into a pot.

'Thank you,' says Lauren.

'William Butler Yeats,' continues the professor. 'The quotation, just now.'

He is a big man, broad in the chest and shoulders, yet somehow he contrives to look lanky. He walks slowly to the kitchen door, placing his legs gingerly, as though they have not been tested away from the confines of his desk for some time. He shakes his head when Lauren asks him if he will join them. 'I don't take afternoon tea,' he tells her. 'I have to save something to look forward to in my old age.'

Alexander can see Lauren examining his face and frame, placing him against an empty canvas even as she smiles at his joke. And then something happens, something Alexander would give much to be able to undo. He reaches for his teacup, but Estelle is still pouring milk into it, and their hands brush. Without thinking, he reaches out to steady hers. The touch is brief, intimate, and he feels it in every fibre of his body, and a second after the nervous, pleasurable tension has faded, he is appalled that the professor might have seen and sensed what has happened. Estelle glances up at her husband as she fills Lauren's cup, but he is not looking at either of them. Alexander cannot help but feel, however, that the professor does not miss a trick.

Estelle's voice is bright when she breaks the pause. 'I'm stealing Lauren's research on Russia for my own purposes.'

There is a slight snort from her husband, a residual response to what he has just seen, perhaps. 'Not another book attempt, my dear?' he says.

Estelle is silent, compact, pulled in. Like an animal on alert. Professor Johnson smiles at once. 'You know, you mustn't feel badly about appropriating Lauren's research. After all, much of academia rests on the study of stolen books and papers.'

Perhaps he feels badly for having denigrated her attempted work, or perhaps, Alexander thinks, he just feels badly that he did so in front of their guests. But Estelle's glance at her husband is kind, if cautious.

'Never mind, Frank,' she says, and he seems to take this as absolution. With a cough, he moves out of the kitchen and walks back down the hallway.

*

155

It takes almost two hours for them to go over the history of Alexander's life with Katya as he remembers it. His discoveries, her decisions, and then her death: the central issue, as overpowering as a poisonous gas to the rest of the conversation. It is here that he has always been at a disadvantage when faced with Lauren's probing and questions – for what he knows is hearsay. He was not there before, during or afterwards, and he cannot therefore know precisely what happened and when. That is Lauren's point, one that seems to make sense to Estelle also. It is now, for the first time, that Alexander recognises something of Melissa in her mother's clear eyes, a reflection of the careful sifting going on in her mind.

'I think there's a lot more that we could try to find out. Especially now,' Lauren tells him.

'Why now?' asks Alexander.

'Because I found out that Misha is alive,' she says gently. 'Their best friend in Russia,' she adds, for Estelle's benefit.

Why this should hit him as a physical shock, he has no idea. It is not as though he had known or believed that Misha was dead. But for all the years since he has left Russia, his thoughts of Misha have been, like those of Katya, rooted in the past. In some ways, it was as though they had died together. He had rarely thought of the possibility that he still existed, and he had always told himself that this was because it would have been too difficult and too dangerous for them to have kept in touch for the first decades. That was true enough, but if he is to be honest with himself, that close friendship with Misha was also the strongest remaining reminder of Katya, and Alexander had found in the aftermath of her death that he wanted a clean break, a pure, deep cut that would sever him from their country, and from everyone and everything in it, with the exception, perhaps, of his parents.

The women watch him expectantly, but he is at a loss. He has been feeling his grip on the afternoon, on the whole situation, loosening for some time, and now his head feels light and as though it is filled with cotton wool or the meringues of which he is so fond. Everything is soft, there is nothing solid to grasp, and he hates the feeling. It is how he has imagined the onset of senility might feel, and the very idea makes him want to shiver. 'How long have you been keeping all this from me?'

'I wasn't hiding it. I didn't know if we'd find him, and I didn't want to bother you with it unless we did. It started when I went to Moscow last year. I couldn't find him then so I hired a private agency – a detective, really – to look for him.'

'And?'

'They found him. A couple of weeks ago. Still living in Moscow. I've been trying to find a good time to tell you.'

Alexander feels the last thread unravel in his mind. He can no longer think or feel. He touches his forehead, and Estelle hands him a glass of water.

'He was in Moscow when Katya died. He was her best friend, and yours. He must have tried to learn something about her death. And since you were never able to speak to him, you don't know what he might have found out.'

'You want to see him?'

'Don't you?' Lauren's hand is on his shoulder. Estelle is sitting forward in her chair.

'I think we should,' Lauren continues. 'I think a trip out there would help a lot. I could help you figure out the full story, and Estelle says she'd love to join us – it would be a great chance for her to do some research. It would be good for all of us.'

He does not reply. His throat is still dry, despite the sips of water.

'Uncle Alex? All I'm trying to say is that there are all these missing pieces, and maybe it won't change anything, but don't you want to know the whole story, once and for all? You might even find out that you weren't as responsible as you feel. That's what I'm hoping,' she adds, her voice dropping.

He is listening, she knows, but he makes no sign, he is just leaning forward, eyes staring at the floor. When she looks up at Estelle, the blue eyes are thoughtful, and concerned. Estelle shakes her head slightly, and Lauren nods, knowing she has taken things as far as she can for the moment.

Lauren has an image of her own mind as a canvas, spattered with wildly coloured paints, colours that are random, without any coherence, colours that are bleeding into each other, forming a coagulated mass that is confusion and uncertainty. This bewilderment has been with her since she began having doubts about her work. But now the revisiting of Katya's story is also seeping into the mess. She has not previously had any doubts about looking for Misha and going to meet him – she has been more and more convinced that the unknown parts of Katya's story should be discovered. How can partial information be a good thing when the full story is potentially available? How can ignorance be better than knowledge? But her uncle's distress is causing her to reconsider.

She is reading a memoir about Africa when the telephone rings. She is still surrounded by dunes and desert as she answers, so it takes her a moment to realise that it is Melissa, but when she does recognise the voice, the book drops and she sits up. After the standard pleasantries, she offers to bring Alexander to the phone, but Melissa refuses. 'I'm calling for you, actually.'

'Really?'

'I've just been given two front-row seats to the ballet, for to-night, and I wondered if you'd be interested to join me. It's *The Nutcracker*.'

'I'd love to.' Lauren feels the confusion in her mind spreading again, although now the feeling is a pleasant, heady one. As soon as she has accepted, it occurs to her that perhaps she should be checking with her uncle first regarding the etiquette of the impending business deal. They arrange to meet at the theatre, and only when she hangs up the phone does it occur to Lauren that perhaps this invitation is part of closing that deal, as far as Melissa is concerned.

The theatre is warm and dark, the lights of the stage reflected softly back on to the entranced faces of the audience. Without moving her head, Melissa takes a sidelong glance at Lauren. She seems engrossed in the dancing, her eyes following the light movement of the leads, her mouth upturned, happy. Melissa looks back at the stage. The music is dramatic and moving, but she does not know enough about ballet to be able to tell whether the dancers are superlative or merely good. She will ask Lauren later what she thinks. In the meantime, she is a little restless. There is still another hour to go, and Melissa can think of a number of things she could do in that precious amount of time – she could be working, or working out; she could be catching up with the news on TV, or even taking a long soak in the bath, a luxury she rarely has time for. But she is here, with a guest, and she makes an effort to relax about the wasted time. When did life become so frantic that to sit still, listening to music that she cannot even imagine having the brilliance to write, becomes something she has to remind herself she enjoys? Clearly Lauren does not see it that way, neither do most of the people sitting around her. With cool analysis, Melissa wonders if she is slowly losing whatever capacity she once had for pure pleasure, for learning, for art, for spending her time outside work in a way that might not be the most efficient but that might be the most enlightening. She resolves to enjoy the rest of the performance. Then, later, she will make an effort to schedule in some down time, perhaps an art gallery. Something she can ask Lauren to show her.

Later, over dinner, Lauren questions her about her parents. Melissa's conversation is terse and to the point, but with an undercurrent of dry humour that Lauren finds particularly amusing when she talks about her father's lack of awareness of anything outside his books. After a few moments, though, Melissa's tone changes, becoming more subdued. 'You know, the last two times I had dinner with them, my mother's been talking non-stop about Russia. And my dad answers all her questions, but it never once occurs to him to ask why she's interested. He has a kind of purity in his thought process, which I admire, but I guess it can blind you when you're in a close relationship.'

From Melissa's slight shifting, and the movement away of her eyes, Lauren senses that this is her hesitant way of explaining something of herself, but she decides not to pursue the point. 'I think she's developing quite a fascination with your uncle and with Katya,' Melissa continues. 'Everyone seems taken with this woman, whom none of us has ever met.'

'I guess when I was younger Katya seemed like a comic-book heroine to me. Exotic and exciting, leading a double life. Spying, the Cold War, all that stuff.'

'But you still admire her, don't you?'

'Sure. I mean, she lost both her parents very young in the most horrible way, yet found a way to be so strong, so sure of herself and what she believed in. Even when believing it meant defying everyone and everything around her. She lived with passion and I aspire to that.'

Melissa smiles. 'She sounds a little like you. Losing your parents, living with passion. I mean, you don't become an artist to get a regular income. You do it because you love it, right?'

Lauren has not considered herself in the same light as her aunt since she was a teenager, and is even less inclined to do so now. 'I think I have a long way to go before I'm anything like Katya,' she replies. 'She really knew what she wanted in life. She had a purpose.'

'And you don't?'

Lauren hesitates. 'I love painting. I'm just tired of portraits. I've been playing it safe for too long. Taking commissions that don't stretch me intellectually or technically. I'm not learning anything new.'

'That's a problem,' says Melissa. 'You don't ever stay still in life. If you're not stepping forward, you're falling behind.'

'Did you get that from a desk calendar?'

Melissa sighs. 'You love thinking of me as a corporate robot, don't you? I might not be able to express myself poetically, or through art or whatever, but I know what I believe. Sorry if it sounds trite.'

Not for the first time, Lauren finds herself cursing her own quick tongue. 'No, I'm sorry,' she says. 'I really am. I've been giving you my artist's superiority complex from day one, and you don't deserve it.'

Melissa smiles and refills their wine glasses. 'You have been pretty feisty. But nothing I can't handle.'

'Oh, really?'

'Yes, really.'

There is a pause, and Lauren looks at the dessert menu noting that Melissa has pushed hers to one side. 'I don't suppose you'll split a chocolate cheesecake with me?'

'Too many carbs. And the fat grams . . .'

'If you do, I'll take you around the Museum of Fine Art, and show you a few things. If you want to.'

Melissa frowns. 'So, let me get this right. I have to eat a dessert I don't want in order to win a trip round a museum that I haven't asked for?'

Lauren shrugs.

'You're a hell of a negotiator. For an artist.'

'Do we have a deal?'

Melissa smiles. 'I love cheesecake. And I'm pretty sure I can learn to love art. I'm going home to New York for a few days. But maybe when I get back?'

Lauren sits back in her seat and smiles. 'I'll hold you to it.'

Chapter Twelve

Moscow, October 1956

ON HIS BED, she lies naked and trembling. He cannot see her shaking in the cool darkness, but his hand can feel the tiny tremors in her muscles as it passes gently over her stomach. He has pulled back from her kisses, the kisses that she sometimes uses to shield her face from his eyes, because she knows that when he is so close to her he cannot watch her. The desire that had overwhelmed him a few moments ago has receded slightly, a conscious, monumental effort on his part, because he wants to see her now and know what is passing through her mind or heart, leaving a shivering imprint on every fibre of her body.

He sits alongside, and when she tries to pull him down towards her, he carefully takes possession of the hand that grasps his shoulder and brings it to his mouth. With his eyes closed, he kisses her fingers, every joint of every one, slowly, slowly. Then her palm, warm and salty. He holds it pressed against his face, and with his other hand touches her chest, between her breasts. Her breath comes shallow and fast, and the trembling is there still.

'Sasha,' she whispers, and he brings her palm down to his own chest, holding it against his heart, and looks at her.

'What is it, Katyushka?' he asks, his voice low.

She turns her head away from him, towards the window, and in the thin moonlight or street-light that penetrates the curtain, he sees tears gleaming on her cheeks and eyelashes. Without taking even a moment to undress, he lies down alongside her. Although he cannot see her averted face, he can hold her, and his arms encircle her whole body, his hands caress and stroke her wherever they rest – her waist, her hip, her thigh. Her shaking becomes stronger. He can feel her ribs against him, the soft down of her back against his arm, her thin shoulders, all shivering. 'What is it, my love?'

A shift of her head towards him. She brings up a hand to try to wipe her face, but he is holding her so tightly that she cannot reach. He guides her towards him and, willingly now, she turns over so that her head is against his neck, and he can feel the wetness of her eyes and nose on his skin.

'What's wrong?'

But she says nothing, and a sound comes from her that is like a laugh, but it rises from so deep within, and is laden with such raw emotion, that he cannot be sure what it is or what it means.

'I'm so happy with you, Sasha.'

It is the first time she has ever told him anything like that. Even during their most intimate, tender love-making, she has been unable to bring herself to respond to his quiet speaking of his love.

He feels dizzy with pleasure, with a deep, uncontrolled joy, and he closes his eyes and kisses her forehead and eyes. He wants never to move from here, or let her go, or get up from this bed, ever again. In a little while it occurs to him to ask her again what he had asked her a few days ago. 'Katyushka, will you marry me, please?' She had not answered, had been withdrawn and confused beneath her insistence that she needed time to make a decision. He had felt sick with despair, for how could anyone need time to answer this question, unless the answer was really no? But here, now, he knows that she loves him. But he does not ask: the moment is too precious to break and, besides, she will answer when she is ready.

The trembling of her limbs has ceased. She lies quiet and peaceful against him, her breathing even and deeper. He lies still, wondering if she has fallen asleep. But there is a slight tension in her legs, which she is deliberately holding fast against his own that tells him she is awake.

'Sasha,' she whispers. 'I will marry you.' And then, in a tiny, quiet voice: 'I love you.'

He kisses her head as a reply. Nothing will induce him to release his hold of her right now – and she does not try to look up or kiss him. They lie there, complete, silent, and eventually he feels her arms relax and her hand fall away from his leg. She is sleeping.

She can somehow tell when she falls away from consciousness and into sleep that she is about to have the dream again. The knowledge comes to her like a sixth sense, and she always struggles to pull back to wakefulness, but it is a useless attempt, like trying to sprint out of quicksand. It is terrible and inevitable, but she is fully trapped now in the swirling current of her slumber, and there is no way for her to rise to the surface, to pull away from the dream and burst up into the fresh air. He feels her limbs twitch against him, and he smiles that she has slept so quickly and easily. Another sound comes from her throat, a moan, and he kisses her and rubs her back.

She sees her mother in a cell, windowless, airless. The smell of faeces and urine soaked into the walls. Her father is there somewhere, too, in another part of the jail, but she never sees him in this dream. Only her mother. And her face is so clear, so well remembered, it gives her a pinprick of pleasure in the midst of her anguish. Her mother is sitting in a corner of the cell, which is garishly lit to prevent her sleeping; and she seems strangely calm, but the calmness comes from resignation or despair, something that hurts Katya more than seeing her mother's panic or anger would. She knows her mother has refused to sign a piece of paper, her fabricated confession to her crimes against the state, and from somewhere outside the cell, Katya can hear herself begging her mother just to sign it, don't let them hurt you, just sign it.

'But then they will shoot me anyway, Katyushka, if I confess,' her mother says. Just like that, coolly, without recognising her daughter's fear and anguish. She knows it is an effect of the dream that makes her mother so distant and unaware, but it pains her anyway. Doesn't she care that she will never see Katya again, or hold her or kiss her?

Then she is beaten. This is a terrible part of the dream for Katya, but she knows that it is only the start. She feels a primal yell rising in her throat, as two of the guards go in on her mother, jabbing with rifle butts, swinging with black boots. They are heavy men; she sees one of them is short, with a thick neck and shoulders, and the sound of his gun thudding against the prone body on the ground is sickening. There is a wetness, a squelching to the sound, when they have been hitting for long enough. Then she can hear her mother gurgling, blood filling her mouth and throat and eyes. Then comes the worst part of the dream. Another man unbuttons his trousers, he is a guard, she thinks, and the heavy man is still there, laughing now, and her mother is being pulled out of her corner, being uncurled, her limbs pushed apart, and now she hears her mother sobbing. The guard drops down on top of her with quick brutality. There is a savage, relentless grunting from his slack, open mouth as he rapes her, an obscene groan of pleasure as he thrashes about on top of her, his hands groping her dress, grasping at her breasts.

'Just sign it,' Katya begs. 'Just sign it.'

She signs it. In the end. And then she is taken out of the cell, and Katya watches her being walked outside, and her mother's knees are buckling and her face is unrecognisable now, a bloody pulp; her dress is stained and streaked, and she has a cigarette burn on her neck. And when they get her outside, they will put her against a wall, with a few others, and shoot her. But she never sees that part. Which is why the rape is always the worst.

He has been shaking her very gently for a few minutes now, since the screams began, tiny, strangled sounds, as though she is trying to shout and gasp for air at the same time. He is hesitant to wake her suddenly from such a deep sleep. But then her breathing slows and the noises stop. A tear escapes from one eye, and her mouth is contorted in pain or sadness. He rubs her back and strokes her head, whispering to her that she is fine, nothing can hurt her. And her face slowly relaxes, and within a few minutes she is awake. 'You were having a bad dream,' he tells her.

She wipes a hand over her eyes and face; she is panting for breath. She turns over, and looks away from him, up at the ceiling. Suddenly she does not want to feel his hands on her. She shifts again, so that the warmth of his body is held away from her. Now the coolness of the air can reach her hot limbs and she is grateful for it.

'Katya? Do you remember what it was?'

'What?' she asks, her voice hoarse.

'Your dream. You were so unhappy. Do you remember it?'

Her breathing is wild, barely controlled. All that she can do is shake her head.

'Are you sure?' he wants to know. 'Are you okay?'

She draws in a long breath and then she can turn to look at him, clear-eyed. 'No, I don't remember any of it,' she says. 'Nothing at all.'

She closes her eyes and pretends to sleep. She is still holding herself a little away from him, and he can sense that, and she knows he is hurt by it, but he shifts away from her anyway to give her the space she is now craving. Then she hears him get up, quietly, and go into the bathroom. The sound of the water running in a thin stream into the bath. He will be a while. She opens her eyes and takes an audible gulp of air. The dream is fading from her mind, much more quickly than usual, because on waking she remembered that she has agreed to marry him. She blinks hard and wipes away a light sheen of sweat from her cheeks and nose. She has been in a state of suppressed panic for days, since he first asked her, considering whether she should marry him for his information or whether she should refuse him because she would only be using him. She wonders what she was thinking just now when she said yes; and then she realises she was not thinking at all, was not being rational, controlled, sensible. She agreed to marry him because she loves him, and that was all she could feel and think and know. She turns over on to her back and looks at the ceiling. What on earth is she going to tell Misha? How will he ever understand?

Chapter Thirteen

Boston, February 2000

THE EVENING SHADOWS are stretching fingers of dusk into the kitchen. Lauren stands before the stove and notices the reflection of the weak late-winter sunshine slipping down the walls of the room. It is a warm colour that slides away, and it leaves a solemn darkness in its place. It is the kind of twilight she loves, that has an atmosphere of early spring about it, and she glances at Alexander. He is busy whisking together eggs and milk, and has not yet noticed the fading light. She is glad of it. In this house she can rarely indulge her appetite for the quiet dusk, or the velvet cover of night-time. A surfeit of lights and lamps and candles chase away these tones whenever Alexander is near.

'When do you plan to leave?' he asks her, grinding salt and pepper into his eggs.

'I was hoping *we* would leave next week.'

With a deliberately cavalier gesture, Alexander cuts a large knob of butter and puts it into a saucepan.

'I wanted scrambled eggs, not a heart attack,' Lauren comments.

'You wanted to learn to make *my* scrambled eggs,' he says, 'and I'm not running a health farm. Wait till the butter is just foaming.'

Obediently, she watches it melt.

'I'm not going on this trip,' Alexander says suddenly. 'I told you that from the start, and nothing has changed. If you really think you can find something, then fine. Come back and let me know what it is.'

Lauren tips the eggs into the pan.

'Keep stirring,' Alexander instructs.

'So you do want to know more?'

'No!'

She is startled by the harsh decisiveness of the reply, but she will not look up from the stove. She moves her wooden spoon back and forth among the gently setting eggs. Watches them intently, giving herself time to harness her instinct to yell back at him, and giving him time to gather himself. She can feel that he has taken a step back and is standing awkwardly beside her. He takes out his handkerchief and wipes his face. A long minute or two passes, during which he dare not guide her about the eggs, even though he is longing to take over. Instinctively, she lets go of the spoon and turns the handle of the pan so that it is within his reach. Then she looks up.

'Well, maybe you should start wanting to know, Uncle Alex. Or stop pretending that you don't. No,' she cuts him off before he can utter a sound in defence, 'and don't think of trying that tone again with me. It might work in business meetings but I'm your family.'

'Keep stirring, Lauren,' is all he says.

She takes up the spoon again. 'Looks like they're nearly done.'

He sets two places at the kitchen table, and puts bread into the toaster. She brings the saucepan over to him and he checks the eggs, nods approval. She divides the contents between their plates and waits for him to sit down.

'Now, listen to me, Uncle Alex. The reason I've been pursuing this is because I think you've been wrong all these years. Wrong about blaming yourself for what happened to Katya, and wrong not to have checked it out before now. I think someone else was involved.'

'That much is obvious. But what does it matter? I started the ball rolling. I started the investigation.'

'But someone else finished it. Brutally. No arrest, no trial. That wasn't Khrushchev's new way of working, was it?'

'It could have been,' he says. 'We've been through this before. Things don't change overnight in any government. Khrushchev made big strides towards transparency and accountability, but old ways die hard. And the KGB dies the hardest. To them, what Katya and I did was treason.'

'And what about Misha?' she asks quietly.

The telephone rings and, gratefully, he reaches over and picks it up. There is a gruff, unfamiliar voice at the other end. 'Is this Mr Ivanov?'

'Yes, it is.'

'President of the Chekhov Appreciation Society?' A brief bark of a laugh follows. The professor. Alexander feels a faint throb of headache invade his temples. 'Is everything all right, Professor Johnson?'

'Ah, that's the thing, you see. I'm not quite sure.'

Alexander is not in the mood for games, and he waits, silently, for an explanation.

'I would love to meet you, if you've time,' Frank Johnson offers at last. 'There are some things I would like to discuss with you.'

'Such as?'

'I would like us to meet face to face.'

'Very well.'

'Good,' he says. 'Can you come tomorrow?'

'Where?'

'To my office. At the university. English department, in the Grayston Building on . . .'

'I know it.'

'Ten o'clock.' It is a statement, not a question.

'Noon would be better for me,' Alexander replies, as politely as he can. In truth, the time is of no great relevance, but he feels an impulse to bridle against the professor's presumption. He hears some pages turn and, above the noise of paper, a sigh of irritation.

'I have a tutorial at twelve. How about eleven?'

'Sounds fine. I'll see you tomorrow.'

Lauren is watching him, confused. 'What's going on?'

Alexander takes a small mouthful of his eggs, then pushes away the plate and rubs his aching head. 'The professor wants a duel,' he says.

The following day dawns with the kind of pure, hard sunlight that suggests coldness, and Alexander is up early, sitting at his study desk, high on the top floor of his house, under the sloping eaves, watching the blue of the sky turn from a deep azure to a pale, icy sheen. He pads into the kitchen in his robe and slippers and prepares bacon and pancakes for breakfast, leaving the door wide open in the hope that the scent will drift up the stairs and wake Lauren.

Within a few minutes, she appears, hair wet from the shower, and sits down at the table with her head leaning tiredly on her hand.

'You smell lovely,' he says. 'Very clean.'

'I am very clean. What have you been cooking?'

He fills a plate and deposits it in front of her.

'My God. I'm going to weigh three hundred pounds by the time I leave here.'

'Do you want me to take it away?' he asks, and her arms move protectively round the plate. He watches her, pleased that something has healed between them.

'What is it?'

'I've been thinking about what you said yesterday.' He sits down and, in the next few minutes, tries to explain to her about Misha. How they had been in the same class at school since the age of eight, how the ties of friendship that had bound them were far too strong to be pulled apart even by small differences in ideologies or political loyalties.

'But you did differ?'

'Not much. At university, we both questioned the government a lot – quietly, though. We talked for hours about the changes we wanted to see, how we would make a difference from within. You see, he was in the system, like I was. He had a good research job in an exciting field – aviation and space exploration. Remember, the Soviets launched the world's first satellite in 'fifty-seven. It was a great time for him, but he couldn't discuss it much – so much was new and secret. I remember, we had such a celebration when he got the job. My first serious hangover.' Alexander smiles at the recollection.

'I was so proud of him, and yet I was anxious too – eager to find my place in life, to start working as he had. He graduated from the Institute of Aviation. He'd always wanted to fly. He was as disillusioned as Katya and I after the years of Stalin. But, though he hated to admit it, I think he felt there were possibilities for change under Khrushchev.'

'Why did he hate to admit it?'

Alexander shrugs. 'That was Misha. He had this cynical, devil-may-care attitude, and that meant not appearing to give much respect to anything or anyone.'

'He sounds like a character,' she tells him. Then, more softly, she adds, 'And I look forward to meeting him.'

Alexander stands up from his chair as though she has thrown her hot tea in his lap. Then he pauses, trying to cover the sharpness of the movement. 'I'd better get ready,' he says, and goes upstairs.

Under the soothing pulse of a very long, very hot shower, he tries to argue down his internal resistance to Lauren's and Estelle's planned trip to Russia. Either they will find something or they won't. If they do not, which is the likely outcome, nothing will have changed. If they do, would he not want to know any other detail, any other small crumb of information about Katya that they could bring back to him? Only when he starts dressing does he remember the professor, and he consciously takes a little extra time in choosing what to wear. It is strange that after the turmoil of the past few weeks, and despite the anger and headaches he feels more alive and invigorated than he has for months. Perhaps because there are challenges to face once more. A part of him is longing for the pain of Katya's loss to be fully understood, then buried for ever. And instinctively he wants Estelle to help with that process. And yet perhaps all that has happened is that he has begun to acknowledge something he has pushed aside for too many years – that he has dealt badly with the aftermath of his wife's death; that he has taken the easier route away from it, a route of disassociation, not involvement. He used his grief and horror as a good enough excuse not to return to that worst of times, but forty years later it is becoming apparent to him that he has been naïve to think he has ever had a choice in the matter. Perhaps all he has managed to do over the course of his life is to delay the moment of confrontation he has been trying so quietly to erase.

When he comes back downstairs Lauren is still in the kitchen. She has a fresh pot of tea and a newspaper before her, and has waited here to try to win him back, to smooth over once again the roughness that keeps edging between them. Her eyes look him up and down over the edge of the broadsheet. 'It doesn't matter how spiffy you look, he's going to hate you. Probably more so.'

Alexander laughs. 'Should I wear my oldest clothes and forget to brush my teeth?'

She wrinkles her nose. 'Maybe not. Whatever you do, you'll never compete with his rumpled professor look. Better to stick with what you know.' She stands and kisses his cheek.

'You look very handsome,' she says. 'Good luck.'

With the aid of various signposts, he makes his way to the English department. Inside, the brick building is dark and poky, though impressively panelled in wood, and in the gloomy lobby he sees the back of a woman typing and speaking on the telephone. After a few moments' wait, he looks in at her door.

'Professor Johnson?' he whispers.

She places a hand over the receiver. 'Up the stairs – third door on the left.'

'Thank you.'

His name is written in rolling script on a small card insecurely attached to his door. There is an air of impermanence about the sign, which adds to the desolate feel of the place. Alexander removes his hat, and knocks firmly. There is a rustling of papers, a gruff 'Come,' and he enters.

Frank Johnson's thick, iron-coloured hair is swept back over a craggy forehead and disjointed nose, but several locks have escaped and hang limply over his brow. He is closely shaven but has cut himself recently, low on the chin. He stands to shake Alexander's hand and seems even taller than before, perhaps more so in the confines of this small room.

175

'Good of you to come. Sit down, sit down.' He points vaguely behind Alexander. There is an old wooden chair, which holds a tall pile of books, including a complete works of Shakespeare. Professor Johnson reaches over and tries ineffectually to push away the books, but his action is surprisingly frail. Alexander turns to help, and together they clear the books on to the floor, and he sits down.

'Something to drink?' the professor asks.

'No, thank you.'

'I'll open a window. It can get stuffy in here, and I tend not to notice, you know.'

Alexander acquiesces gratefully – the room is more than a little oppressive. While he waits, he looks at the bookshelves that surround them. As he would somehow expect in an English professor's room, they are stacked to overflowing, with books placed horizontally wherever there is the slightest bit of space. Further tall stacks lie on the tops of the bookcases. As he glances at titles and authors, he can see that they had once been laid out in some kind of chronological and regional order but that the thread has been lost somewhere along the way. Directly in front of him is a case devoted entirely, it seems, to Irish works.

The professor is watching him when Alexander turns back. 'I like books.'

'I noticed. Irish literature?'

'A fondness of mine, if not truly a speciality. The Irish have a certain . . .' He sighs, and places his enormous hands behind his head while he selects the right words. 'A certain . . . wildness, a certain desperate enjoyment of life that often overlies a certain darkness and blackness of soul. Which reminds me not a little,' he says, with a sideways glance at his guest, 'of the Russian temperament.'

Alexander is at a loss. The comment sounds innocuously general, but is clearly aimed at him.

'You don't agree?' Professor Johnson asks.

'On the contrary, I think there is a lot of truth in what you say. But I also believe one has to be wary of generalisations.'

'Indeed. Let's choose some specifics, then.'

'Very well.'

'I wish to know a little more about you, Mr Ivanov.'

'Please, call me Alexander.'

'Thank you. I wish to know more about you, Alexander.'

'May I ask why?'

'You may. How can I put this?' His fingers tap along the paper on his desk and he glances about, as though searching for a book that will perhaps help to explain his meaning. 'I'm a man of routine. I am at home almost all of the time, and then two days in the week I come here, to this esteemed institution of learning, in order to tease out some semblance of a coherent thought process from the young minds entrusted to me.'

'You don't work full time?'

'I work all the time. But not here. At home.'

'I see.'

'Wherever I'm working, I am home every evening, and I have dinner there with my wife.'

Alexander catches the first gleam of suggestion in the professor's eye. He nods in a noncommittal way, and waits for him to continue.

'Every evening we talk a little. About various things. Our daughter. My work, even, now and then, though I blame myself for not being as open and articulate as I might be on that subject. We talk about music sometimes. Sometimes,' he says, staring off at a point somewhere behind Alexander, 'we don't speak much at all. Anyway, what I'm trying to say is, we don't speak about Russia.'

Alexander wonders if the professor rambles so much in his tutorials. 'You don't discuss Russia?' he repeats.

177

'Ah,' the professor says, lifting a finger triumphantly, as though Alexander has somehow proved a point for him. 'We never *used* to. We never used to. And then, out of the blue one day, we were eating dinner, and Estelle begins talking to me about Russia, and Stalin, and Khrushchev. Asking me questions, you know.'

Alexander shifts slightly in the chair, which is uncomfortable.

'I thought nothing of it at the time,' Professor Johnson continues, 'and I answered her questions as best I could, which is to say, I answered them rather poorly. Russian history is not my best subject.'

'I'm sure you know a lot . . .'

He raises a hand. 'Anyway, I discussed various things with her, and then she mentioned you, and how you had met, and so on, and that was the end of that. Or so I thought. And then,' he says, 'we met, you and I, over tea, a couple of times. And now it's happening again.' He sits back with some satisfaction, as though his explanation is now complete.

'What's happening again?' Alexander asks, puzzled.

'The Russia questions. Again and again. And again. And do you know something? Every last one of those conversations ends up being about you.'

'Oh.'

'I am not a brilliant man when it comes to emotional or psychological affairs,' he says, 'but it would take a dunce not to draw the obvious conclusion.'

Alexander's stomach drops. 'I see,' he says, hoping that the aforementioned conclusion is so obvious that there will be no further need to articulate it.

'My wife has found something in you.' He makes it sound distasteful, as though it might be ringworm or a virus.

'What do you mean?' Alexander asks.

'*Something*,' Professor Johnson replies, as if unsure. He pauses,

178

and looks out of the window. 'Something that attracts her. Something she does not find in me. Attention, perhaps, excitement, understanding. I have no definite idea.'

Alexander sits forward in his seat, and assures Frank Johnson that he is a man of some integrity at least, and that he is certain that his conduct has not been inappropriate.

The professor laughs, heartily, but the pressure of sound cannot quite cover the tone of concern beneath. '*Inappropriate*,' he repeats. 'I'm sure it hasn't. I am not, after all, accusing you of a sordid affair, or of any type of affair whatsoever.'

Alexander holds his look. 'What *are* you accusing me of?'

The answer takes such a long time to come that Alexander begins to think that the question has been forgotten. Professor Johnson swings round in his chair, and looks out of the window again. And all that can be heard in the tiny room is his laboured breathing, and Alexander's own quiet shiftings on the chair. When, ever so slowly, that chair of the profesor's creaks back round again, Alexander feels his limbs stiffen in anticipation.

'I accuse you,' the professor says, rubbing at his huge forehead, 'of endearing yourself to my wife. Of conversing with her in a way that pleases her much more than my way. Of giving her something to look forward to each day. Of making her happier, but also more dissatisfied. In short, I accuse you of coming between us.'

'We are friends, nothing more.'

'Please . . .' he says, raising a hand. 'You are taking her to Moscow.'

Alexander stands up. 'It seems to me that this is something you should be discussing with your wife. I don't make her decisions for her.'

'That's the easier way of looking at it. You have certainly influenced her.'

'What would you have me do? Stop seeing her?' Alexander wants to know what his view of the situation is. He does not, as yet, feel compelled to let the professor know that Estelle will be travelling to Russia without him. There is a principle at stake.

'There's the thing,' Frank Johnson says. A slow smile spreads over his granite face. His teeth are a little crooked, Alexander notices. 'Logically I cannot see a reason why you should. As you say, you are friends, nothing more.'

'But?'

There is no further comment.

'Then what is your reservation?' Alexander asks.

The professor looks down, with a sigh, and waves a hand as if to close off this particular line of conversation. When he glances up again, his dark, heavy eyes seem infinitely tired. 'You confuse me, Alexander.'

'Imagine how I feel.'

A brief smile at this. 'You see, I can't decide what your inner response has been to our discussion,' the professor says. 'It seems to me there are two general possibilities. That as a man of integrity, as you call yourself, you feel your conduct has been, and will continue to be, nothing less than honourable, and therefore there is no need to stop . . . socialising with my wife. Or second,' he continues, 'that your intentions towards her are in some way inappropriate – be they romantic or otherwise – and that, as a man of integrity, you think that perhaps you should stop seeing her.'

Alexander sits silently: he feels he is being pushed to agree to the latter suggestion. 'At least in both scenarios I have integrity,' is all he says. 'You know, Professor, feelings rarely conform to the "general possibilities" that you speak of.' He is buying time.

'True, but that is very rare,' comes the reply. 'I believe, Alexander, that feelings are not quite as complex as people like to give them

180

credit for. Usually one main force drives you in any given situation – jealousy, anger, compassion, even honesty – and this will condition your responses. Time and again, the same responses occur to the same situations. All part of the human condition that people are so fond of invoking.' He turns again to the window. 'You see it in history, in science and, of course, in literature. Very little changes in novels over the years,' he says with a sigh. 'Style, primarily, and the method of writing, but the rest of it, well . . .' He swivels his chair so that he is facing Alexander once more. 'What sort of man are you?' he asks.

'Modest,' Alexander replies.

'Ha!' he barks. 'Amusing, but you don't get away that easily.'

'Why are you concerned with my character?'

'I may not take a minute interest in the day-to-day details of my wife's life,' he says, 'but I am interested in what makes you interesting to her.'

'I am honest, and direct, and reasonably kind. I love learning, and I love life – I find it exhilarating most of the time.'

'Good qualities, all. What else?'

'I can cook.'

A shout of laughter. 'I know. Ever since I can remember my wife has been telling me that she always wanted a man who could cook. And now she has the "King of Catering".'

The silence that follows is awkward, unwieldy, and Alexander does not know how to grasp and subdue it. The professor watches his own large fingers as he laces them in and out of each other. In his mind, Alexander curses *Business World* for that circus-like headline. 'Perhaps you're making too many assumptions about what she wants,' he offers at last. 'If it's any consolation to you, I can tell you that it seems to me your wife already has what she wants. And who.' He tries to stop there, graciously, but finds he cannot.

'Except perhaps for a little encouragement regarding other things she is interested in – like writing or travelling. Whether she is able to write brilliantly is irrelevant. And subjective. The point is she wants to try. And the encouragement to do so may be all she lacks.'

'Perhaps,' Frank Johnson replies abruptly, frowning. 'But from what I have read of her work, which I admit is not much, she is not a great writer. She may improve, but the chances are that, at the end of the day, she will contribute nothing to the world by typing prose into a computer. Even I don't attempt it. Because it's difficult for me to encourage mediocrity. It goes against everything I stand for. I know it's harsh in one respect, but there it is. Can you understand that?'

Alexander nods. 'Yes. It's a view I try to uphold too. But I don't think you're giving her a fair chance. She's hardly begun. And when she does, who sets the standard that decides whether her writing is worthwhile or not?'

The professor frowns, but does not reply. Then he reaches a big hand across his desk to the shelves of Irish literature, like a child reaching for a worn, loved blanket, and he extracts a small paperback book, whose title Alexander cannot read. 'Joyce,' he says, raising the book. ' "The Dead". A fine short story. Do you know it?'

'I've read it. But it has been a good while. I don't remember much.'

'Good. May I?'

Alexander acquiesces, and watches as he leafs quickly through the pages. They fall open easily at certain places, those he particularly likes, he presumes. Why the professor has decided to read to him, he cannot say. Perhaps he feels, as Alexander does, that they have exhausted whatever they have to say to each other. It takes him only seconds to find the place he is looking for, but as he lifts the book to read, there is a knock at the door. 'Two minutes,' he shouts, and there is a muffled reply. 'My twelve o'clock tutorial,' he says. 'A good boy, but a feverish imagination. Now, where was I?' He looks back at the book, and after a short pause to indicate the end of conversation and the start of the reading, he begins: ' "The air of the room chilled his shoulders. He stretched himself cautiously along under the sheets and lay down beside his wife. One by one they were all becoming shades. Better pass boldly into that other world, in the full glory of some passion, than fade and wither dismally with age. He thought of how she who lay beside him had locked in her heart for so many years that image of her lover's eyes when he had told her that he did not wish to live." '

He looks up. 'Have you ever loved a woman so much that you felt unable to live without her? I haven't.'

Alexander is deeply saddened by this admission. He would have been better pleased if Estelle was married to someone utterly devoted. 'Yes,' he replies. 'My wife, Katya.'

'But you *have* managed to live without her.'

'I have had little choice.'

Professor Johnson shrugs, a gesture of dismissiveness, and Alexander feels he could easily hit him, with his ironic tone and his air of superiority. 'My life with and without my wife is something you will never know anything about.' He stands up to leave.

The professor stands, also, quickly. 'Wait a minute. You're right. I push things too far sometimes to no real purpose. It was bad of me. I apologise. Please don't go.'

Alexander is burning, with anger, with sorrow, with confusion again, but he remains there. He forces himself to read the titles of a row of books behind the professor's head. Then he takes a breath. 'Your tutorial is waiting,' he says.

'He will wait.'

'I'm sure, but I must go.'

183

'Do you like it?' Johnson asks, pointing at the book.

A pause. 'Very much.'

'Good. I had a feeling that you might. Please,' he says. 'Please.'

The pleading tone sends a shiver through Alexander's core, and he feels both contemptuous and pitying. He does not sit down, but neither does he make a move to leave, and at once the professor continues: 'I like this piece, that's all. I think it is a fine, melancholy piece of writing. And I'm trying – in some sense – to learn what it means.' His voice softens at this last sentence. He looks up. 'May I continue a little?'

'Yes.'

' "Generous tears filled Gabriel's eyes. He had never felt like that himself towards any woman but he knew that such a feeling must be love. The tears gathered more thickly in his eyes and in the partial darkness he imagined he saw the form of a young man standing under a dripping tree. Other forms were near. His soul had approached that region where dwell the vast hosts of the dead." ' "He was conscious of, but could not apprehend, their wayward and flickering existence. His own identity was fading out into a grey impalpable world: the solid world itself which these dead had one time reared and lived in was dissolving and dwindling." '

The book closes with a snap.

Alexander cannot speak. He would like to – he would like to tell Frank Johnson that he reads beautifully, for his anger has left, to be replaced by something deeper and sadder, but his throat is dry, a sensation that is becoming too familiar these days.

'I wanted to know if you would see in it what I do,' Professor Johnson says. 'Purely selfish motives. One is always looking for understanding.'

As he speaks, he makes his way to the door and opens it. Outside, a blond-haired young man scrambles to his feet from the floor where he has been sitting and, at a signal from the professor, comes inside the room as Alexander leaves. The windowless hallway is dark and cold, and Alexander turns briefly to look back at that tiny room where only a desk lamp makes an impression on the shadows of the winter's afternoon.

'I thank you for coming,' Professor Johnson says.

Alexander nods briefly, then places his hat on his head and walks quickly away.

Chapter Fourteen

Moscow, November 1956

MISHA TOLD HIM that he was naïve to think that his wedding day would be the happiest day of his life. 'The most *nervous* day, my friend,' he had said, 'or the most frightening. But happy? You won't have *time* to feel happy.'

Alexander buttons his newly pressed shirt, and carefully tucks it into his trousers. He feels his chin and cheeks, shaved just two hours ago at the barber shop in the courtyard of his building. They are smooth, but in his current fastidious mood he fancies that there is a fine stubble there already, and he goes back into the bathroom to shave once more. He leans well forward over the basin, his feet too far back because he does not want to splash any water or soap on to his clean shirt. He loves clean clothes, and so does Katya. Some evenings, when they meet at her apartment, he has noticed her walk in and throw down everything she is wearing in a pile to be washed.

He rinses his razor in the bowl and dries it, aware that there is barely any difference in the state of his chin, the shadow being either imagined or too slight to be gripped by the blade. It matters little, however – half the pleasure for him is in the preparation, the quiet anticipation. He pats his face dry, and goes out to the mirror that stands on the dressing table. The table that he will now clear of his things, ready for Katya to use. He looks at his face. It is a handsome face, so he has been told, all the years of growing up as the only child of his parents. It is also a serious face in the mouth and the eyes, although those eyes have a latent sparkle, and show a personality that appreciates irony. He wonders how his face would look diluted into the features of a baby, and then he shakes his head, because what he really wants is a baby that looks like Katya. He imagines a tiny body held close to his chest, imagines breathing in that baby fragrance of sweetened milk. He buttons his starched collar, and smiles at himself in the mirror. Misha was wrong, he thinks. This really is the happiest day of my life. The only cloud on his horizon is that he must face another two hours without Katya, two hours that they must spend apart, each of them getting dressed up and ready so that they can finally spend the rest of their lives together.

He is at the Wedding Palace, with Misha, nearly an hour early. They both stop together at the entrance; ornate, gilded and imposing. This particular building is primarily for the marriages of government officials.

Misha lets out a whistle as they walk in.

'Very nice,' he comments sarcastically. 'Maybe just a little bigger and flashier than the places where the rest of us get married . . .'

'My grandparents were married in a church,' Alexander says, ignoring the tone, and Misha nods.

'Mine too. Even my parents were.'

It has been many years now since the majority of churches were converted for other uses, or vandalised, or destroyed. The clergy and those faithful who had tried to continue the practice of their faith were sent away to the camps. Or shot. So many were found dead in those early days that, after a little while, people became numbed, immune to the shock. Alexander does not remember the incident himself, but he remembers his mother telling him, one evening, in a voice choked with urgency and tears, that their own priest had been arrested and taken away. They had never heard of him again.

The entrance hall is magnificent. A converted palace, the place is used as a registry of public records as well as for weddings. Alexander looks up at the domed, soaring ceiling, the high moulded windows. Here they will have a full ceremony, complete with Mendelssohn's *Wedding March* – except that the blessing to their union will be given by the State. Would a church be more atmospheric perhaps? He imagines a smell of incense, a glow of stained glass, a cross over an altar. It is a romanticised vision and, anyway, he has no real belief in God, and certainly no belief in religion as such. Both he and Misha were taught that religion was nothing more than a means of controlling the minds of the population; something that Alexander, after much argument and consideration, still believes to be true. It is beyond his comprehension how anyone can subscribe to a school of thought based on a book or a self-enclosed set of teachings from an ancient era. To have faith in such things, blind faith, appears to him a convenient way of excusing people from any thought or reasoning. But then he remembers how he and Misha laughed ironically that instead of icons of the Virgin, they were all now given overblown pictures and statues of Stalin to worship. One cult had replaced another. But while he senses from Misha no existential questioning, no philosophical uncertainty, Alexander remains quietly unsure, and unsettled. He has a sense sometimes, deep in the night, of revelation, a realisation of his own infinite smallness, and he feels the world itself getting smaller and smaller, subsumed into some vastness that creeps in on him from the shifting edges of consciousness. He cannot say what it means, and this alone is what troubles him.

They speak to the girl at the counter, and explain that they are here for a wedding. With a smile she winks at Misha and sends them up two flights of stairs.

'Why do women always react that way to you?' Alexander asks him.

Misha is almost forced to shout over the ringing sound of their footsteps, climbing the polished stairs in unison. 'They can't help it, my friend,' he says. 'They just can't help it.'

Katya's uncle has arrived even before them. One of her few relatives, and perhaps the only one she has any contact with, he is old and infirm now, but he hurries to stand up when he sees the two young men approaching down the hallway. He was once a priest, back in the twenties, but now he works at the railway station, selling tickets. Misha and Alexander quicken their pace, and Misha puts a hand on the old man's shoulder to guide him back into his seat. He is smiling, and mumbles some words, which they have to strain to catch. He has spent seven years in the camps and his face was beaten so much that now his speech is barely intelligible as such.

'Thank you for coming, Dimitri Petroyavich,' says Alexander.

He catches Alexander in a handshake that he holds for a long moment. The vein-ridged hand has a permanent tremble now, but it seems in that one grasp to convey congratulations, gratitude and blessing all in one, and it brings a feeling of tears to Alexander's eyes.

'I need the bathroom,' Dimitri says. The two men stand again and Alexander walks him down the corridor to the toilet, then returns to Misha.

'They have wrecked him,' he says.

'They wreck everybody. Sometimes it is better just to be killed quickly than to go through what they go through.'

Misha's slow, ironic voice is harsh and hard, and Alexander touches his friend's shoulder, disturbed by the depth of anger he sees in his eyes.

Misha reaches for his cigarettes. 'They wiped out the clergy,' he continues, striking a match with vehemence. 'Wiped them out, Sasha!'

'I know.'

'And then, our great comrade changes his mind – he thinks bringing back the Church will help to bring the country back together, after he ripped it apart during the stinking war, so he says, "Okay, tortured priests, come back. Come on back to your churches that I spat on. Practise again the things I killed you for yesterday." ' Misha keeps the anger low in his voice, a habit they have all assimilated from their anxious parents since they could talk; now he gestures in disgust.

'If I were that priest, if I had endured what he had, and seen what he'd seen, I'd have the shakes too.' He pauses. 'And then the rules of the game only change all over again.'

Misha begins restlessly to prowl, smoking his cigarette. Alexander stands too, and explores the hallway from the other side. His stomach is clutched by a sick feeling, one that passes over him often when he thinks of this world about him and the many changes that still must be made. From the corner of his eye he watches his friend, sees the deep inhaling and exhaling, sees him calming down a little. Alexander reads a few general notices pinned on to a board, then glances at his watch. When will she be here? Misha is at his shoulder.

'My best man,' Alexander tells Misha. 'The best man.'

'*You* are the best man, my friend. As far as Katya is concerned. You are the best man.'

'Really?' His tone is earnest and the question too quick.

'Really. She adores you, Sasha. Even she can't cover that up.'

Alexander thinks of her – she must be almost ready, preparing to leave. Attending her this morning are her flatmate Maya, and Maya's sister-in-law. Uncle Dimitri will take the place of Katya's father and brother. She is missing Yuri today, he knows. She misses him often, but will rarely admit it, as if to do so would be somehow to dishonour his decision to escape. It has made life hard for her, especially now that she is marrying a government official. She has perhaps been under surveillance from the KGB, and so has he, her background checked and rechecked. It is probably only because her record for the Party is exemplary that they have been able to come this far undisturbed.

The two young men wait together, marking off the minutes silently. Alexander is just thinking to check on Dimitri when the old man emerges. He moves slowly down the hallway, and continues past the bench where they sit, motioning to Alexander to follow him. He does so, walking with him until they reach the other end of the corridor. 'My son, how are you today?'

Now that Alexander's own dark head is bent down to Dimitri's white one, he can better understand what he says. 'I am fine, Uncle. Very happy,' he adds honestly, but not without a trace of self-consciousness. He waits for the old man to speak, and sees a swollen mouth, the skin and lips bruised and twisted into a shape that is unnatural and harsh. The eyes that meet his own are dark and dulled with age. Alexander watches Dimitri weighing his words. His brown suit smells musty and faintly damp, as though it has been hanging unused in an old cupboard for years.

'You are sure you wish to marry?'

'Yes, Uncle.'

'Katya. You will look after her?'

'Yes, Uncle. I love her.'

Dimitri's face is stern, his mouth set into a downturn, and

192

Alexander feels a sense of forbidding. The old man seems displeased, unconvinced about something. 'What's wrong?' he asks.

The grainy eyes turn to him, surprised. 'Nothing. I am very happy she found you. That you found each other.'

Alexander nods, and swallows. Nothing else in the old man's face has changed, and he realises now that he has been smiling all this time. But the attempted grin has been foiled by the palsied, frozen mass of skin around his mouth. For a moment, Alexander cannot take his eyes off the lower part of Dimitri's face: in his mind he visualises the kind of brutal beating and cutting that might have led to such a gruesome countenance.

'Her parents were very dear to me. Atheists, you know – intellectuals often are.' Dimitri gives a chuckle, which ends in a wheeze that comes up from the bottom of his chest. 'But they were good people. They helped me to hide, for a while. When the trouble came. And then they themselves . . .' He does not finish the sentence for the wheeze has turned into an unhealthy cough, and Alexander smiles to indicate that he understands, and at the same time he tries to pull back a little from the hacking breath that is invading his own.

'Good luck to you, my son,' he sputters, dabbing at his eyes with the handkerchief Alexander has given him from his own top pocket. He raises his trembling hand and pats Alexander on the back, then together they walk back to the velvet-covered chairs that line the waiting area.

People are arriving. Only a few, here and there, but, then, there will not be so many people at the wedding anyway. More will come afterwards, to his parents' apartment for the celebration lunch. The Director of the Wedding Palace has arrived, and is showing Misha the main hall where the marriage will take place. He also begins to guide the men and women to their customary separate anterooms, where they will wait until the ceremony is ready to begin.

When Alexander turns from greeting people, he sees that his parents have come. He hurries to meet them, watching his mother quieting his father, who is apt to talk too loudly when he gets excited.

'My son,' says his father, embracing him heartily. His mother's congratulations are more delicate, less effusive. She is conscious of her makeup and her clothes, concerned that they should not become creased. They sit down with him for a moment to wait, for he has no idea of where they should go, he has no experience with the formalities and protocol of a wedding. He watches his mother trying to reclaim parts of her own seat over which his father has somehow spread himself, watches her fidgeting, and his expansiveness, and he smiles. It is not how he sees himself with Katya in thirty years' time, but his parents' movements are familiar to him, and they are reassuring on this day, in this unfamiliar place, where suddenly he feels very much alone.

He turns and looks about. Several young men of his own age – his work colleagues and a few friends – come up to shake his hand and he accepts their congratulations, happily and without speaking much. His mind is filled with her now; with the thrilling fact of his impending marriage and he is finding it hard to articulate anything else. He looks at his watch, and is surprised to see that she should be here within five minutes, and when he looks up, with the astonishment still upon his face, he sees Misha, and Misha laughs.

'What happened to your handkerchief, my fastidious friend?'

'Dimitri Petroyavich needed it more than I did.'

'Here,' Misha says, tucking his own handkerchief into Alexander's top pocket.

'Thank you, Misha.'

'You are welcome, my friend.'

*

Twenty minutes have passed, and Alexander has felt them like twenty lashes on his back. He stands in the central hall now, with the Director, and alongside him he can feel Dimitri, with his trembling hand and beaten mouth. In the ante-rooms beyond, the guests talk in low tones among themselves, and now and then a concerned face peers into the hall to see what is happening.

She has not come. He feels Misha tug at his arm, a firm pull, and is relieved to have some diversion, someone to look at, someone who can tell him what to do. He has never been good at acting, at pushing his own raw emotions down so that they do not crack the façade of his expression. Misha can do it, many men he knows can – but he has never learned the trick.

'What is it?' he asks.

'Come and sit down with me,' says Misha. 'Let's sit down till she comes.'

Alexander obeys placidly. His heart is so heavy that he can feel it resting like a leaden mass in the base of his stomach. She has not come. He looks at Misha. His face is a picture of reassurance.

'No way, my friend. She's coming. Trust me.'

Misha is not at all sure that she is coming. He is concerned that she has had a change of heart. That despite all the encouragement he has given her, she has been unable to reconcile this marriage, which he knows has become a love marriage, with her work. Misha is momentarily annoyed. He has invested a lot of time recently in making her see that this is the best way she has to make a difference, to help kill the system that killed her parents. And it has not been easy because she is emotionally aware of all his psychological tricks, and because she is intelligent and, worst of all, has a stubborn integrity that she is now focusing on the wrong things.

Misha sighs and puffs his cheeks. Perhaps, he thinks, this way will be better for them both in the long run. It will certainly save Alexander possible heartbreak. But the opportunities we will miss, Katya . . . Misha shakes himself inwardly and tries to remember that today he is the best man. He glances at Alexander; his friend's eyes are fixed on the floor beneath his feet.

Alexander is deeply wrapped in the misery of betrayal, in a cold mist of sorrow that envelops him like a shroud. Then, to his right, he feels a movement, and a sideways glance reveals that Misha is standing up. He pats Alexander on the back and leans down to whisper in his ear. 'I'm going to find her. Give me a few minutes. I'll be back.'

The assembled company watches quietly from the ante-rooms. The men are on the left, the women on the right, and Misha walks easily down the centre corridor between them and outside, leaving the huge carved door to slam behind him.

Running down the front steps of the building, Misha looks around. He has no idea where Katya might be – at home, having changed her mind, for all he knows. He turns left on to the street, and almost knocks over Katya's flatmate, who is coming along the pavement from the opposite direction. He stops and she stares at him, her breath short from her hurried walk, pooling into the cold air in clouds. He waits silently, for her name has escaped him at this moment.

'She wants to see Sasha,' she offers.

'Where is she?'

'Down there, by the metro.'

Misha moves aside for the girl to pass him, then walks down the street and round the corner. He can see Katya standing outside the metro-station entrance, her eyes already looking for Alexander. When she sees him she gives a rueful smile, but also takes a small, unconscious step back. She has not expected to see me out here,

196

Misha thinks, and she would probably prefer not to. He gives an easy laugh when he reaches her.

'They don't perform weddings at metro stations,' he says.

She makes a good attempt at a smile. Her dark hair is pulled back from her clear-skinned face and her haughty cheekbones. Her eyes look too moist, and they are slightly red at the edges, but he cannot tell whether this is from crying or sleeplessness or the cold. She glances at his watch, and rubs at her temples. Misha tries to maintain a semblance of sympathy in his expression, when in truth he is already losing patience. He will not speak and help her. Let her think, and then say what is bothering her.

'I don't think I can do it,' she says, finally.

'Your fiancé is not going to be happy,' he observes, but she shakes her head, and a sense of misgiving hits him in the gut.

She is gazing at her feet when she speaks again. 'No, not the wedding, Misha. The rest of it.' Now she looks up at him, unflinching. 'The work. I don't want to do it any more.'

He puts a hand over his eyes – he feels tired suddenly, and this is not at all what he was expecting to deal with. Never in all the time he has known her has he seriously suspected that she would want to stop working against the government. Not completely. Not for some man. It has always been too deeply a part of who she is. It has been all that she is.

'You're not thinking straight,' he tells her. 'You're emotional and confused.'

She gives a short laugh. 'Yes, I am, but it's more than that, Misha. Please try to understand. I can't explain it to anyone else. I love him. And I can't lie to him. It doesn't feel like the right thing to do any more.'

With a considerable effort, Misha bites back a sarcastic response, but it hardly matters because she knows him well enough to guess what he is thinking. He takes her by the shoulders, pinning her down with a firm gaze. 'I thought this was your life's work?'

'It is.'

'You mean it *was*.'

Her eyes look pained, as though he has forced a realisation on her. He waits, certain that he has pulled her back.

'Yes,' she says, 'I mean, it *was*.'

'My God, what has happened to you?' He sighs, unsure of what tack to try next. Then he has an idea. Perhaps honesty will work. For a moment, he tries to focus hard on what he is really feeling. 'You know, Katya, I'm surprised. For me, this work has always been important, always meaningful, but I do it for reasons that are intellectual. Well considered reasons. To be simplistic about it, I have political convictions and passing whatever secrets I learn at work out to the other side is the best way I know, the most efficient way, to fight for those convictions.'

She is listening.

'But you. You have a drive that even I don't have. For you it's personal. They took a gun and shot your mother and your father through the head, for nothing. Never mind that they had young children crying for them at home. Never mind that they were honest, decent people. Never mind that they were probably sick and crying with fear. They shot them anyway. And left you with no one. Now, that's a basis for conviction.' He shrugs, paces a little. 'I'm surprised at you, that's all.'

He has touched nerves with his brutal, obvious depiction, he is sure of that, because she will not meet his eye.

'Misha,' she says, 'I'm just not sure it's the right thing to do. Not like this. You see, I always thought I would end up with someone like myself. Or like you, who is on our side, against the government. Not someone inside the government, who I can't say anything to,

198

and who can't help me, or understand. It's ironic, I know. Believe me, nobody has laughed and cried more about this than I have. But in the end I love him. There is something very good and decent about him. He represents this terrible system, but he is not an evil man. I have a feeling there is another way to fight this battle . . .'

'Really?' he says, with exaggerated interest. 'And tell me, what is that way?'

'I don't know yet.'

'Ah. Well, then.'

She looks at him angrily. 'I don't want to hurt him, Misha. I won't hurt him.'

'Of course you won't. He'll never know . . .'

She shakes off his wheedling, and he stops short, then tries again. 'Don't lie to him, Katya. I've told you already, you have nothing to do for two years. Two years. I don't want you to do anything except run your school. Nothing else.'

'We only agreed that to avoid suspicion. So he doesn't find me out at once.'

'Yes, whatever. But you have two years, and in that time you don't have to lie to him. Then, when the two years are up, we'll talk. See how you feel then.'

'I know how I'll feel then. I won't want to do it, and you'll try to make me . . .'

Misha smiles, his look almost indulgent. Oh, no, Katya, you don't know how you'll feel. You imagine you will feel just as you do now. But in two years, Katyushka, the delicate bloom will be off your new love. You will be used to each other, and you will be irritated by his fastidious ways, and tired of having someone with you all the time. You, who are so jealous of your privacy, of your solitude, have chosen a man who is passionate and probably obsessive. He will drive you mad. Yes, in two years it will be so different. He will probably have moved up in the world, and his information will be all the more valuable, and you will be tired of him, Katya, you will be ready to remember who and what you are. My recruit, my agent, my source.

'Fine,' he says, his tone reasonable. 'Just marry him. You love him, he loves you, it's all beautiful. Marry him now, and we'll talk again in a couple of years, and we'll decide then. If you don't want to, you don't want to. Okay?'

Alexander tries to slow down as he approaches the metro station, to give himself a few moments to think, but he sees her standing there, with Misha, neither speaking, and he finds himself by her side in a second. Around them people hurry up and down the metro stairs, or walk purposefully along the street. He sees all the moving bodies around him dimly, as scattered blurs, and as Katya takes his hand and looks at him, their stillness amid the bustle gives him the feeling that their private world has stopped and time with it. From outside his consciousness, Misha puts a hand on his shoulder and squeezes reassuringly.

'I'll leave you two now. See you inside,' he says, and is gone, absorbed into a body of people who have just spilled out from the exit.

Alexander takes her hand and waits.

'I'm sorry, Sasha,' she says. 'I knew you must be waiting for me, but it didn't seem real. It felt so peaceful and isolated out here. I almost couldn't move.' She hears her own words and laughs quickly. 'I mean, the street is not peaceful, and there are people all around, but . . .'

'It doesn't matter,' he tells her. 'You don't have to explain.'

But she owes him something, they both know, for being late, for making him come to see her on the street when by now they should already have been married. 'I just had to see you,' is all she can say, and her fingers tighten round his, a desperate grasp, like that of a scared child.

'You would have seen me in there. I was waiting for you.' He has only wanted to be understanding and kind, and he is disappointed at the petulance he hears in his voice.

She looks down, ashamed. 'I know. I wanted to see you alone, though, not in front of all those people.'

'You've changed your mind?'

'No.'

He is momentarily grateful, but forces himself to focus on the fact that she has still not explained herself. 'You don't seem certain about this,' he says. 'It's better to call it off if you . . .'

He trails off, inviting her to fill in the rest for he cannot fathom what troubles her. But she says nothing, just stands watching him blankly. In her mind there is a series of sentences, phrases and unconnected words that are telling him things about herself that she has never spoken before. She takes a breath, lets her lips part slightly. If she exhales without thinking, will any of those words or explanations begin to emerge from her mouth so that he can hear them? She waits. Nothing comes. He is looking at her and his eyes are probing, trying to read thoughts that he cannot guess at. She presses her lips together, then smiles at him. It will be all right. She has told Misha her view of it, and he knows she is serious. The confusion in her mind about her work, her life, her parents – there will be time to consider all of this. After they are married. She takes his hand and puts it to her face then turns her mouth into his palm to kiss it. The love she feels for him is wondrous, amazing to her. She cannot believe that leaving it behind would be better than embracing it. Embracing him. 'What is it?' he whispers.

'Can we go and get married?' she says.

He watches her still. It is not enough for him.

'I am so sure of you,' she tells him, her face serious, earnest. 'I love you so much.'

'Then why are you out here?'

'I was worried. There is so much you don't know about me. So much I haven't let you know.'

She can hardly believe that she has spoken the words. That she has brought herself so close to the point where she will have to reveal her secrets. The idea elates her, then drops her again. For he will never marry her if she tells him.

'I want to know everything about you, Katya. And there will be time for that. Our whole lives are for that.'

He has not pressed the point, probably because he does not understand it; instead, he is giving her a way out and, hastily, she takes it. 'Yes, you're right. I think I'm just too emotional. No one has ever come as close to me as you have, Sasha, not in my whole life. It's wonderful, but there are times when I'm afraid.'

'Of what?'

'That you're not real. That what we have found together is too good to be real.'

He lifts her hand, raises it to his lips and holds it there. His lashes close, and brush against the warm skin, and he holds his eyes shut against the noise about him, and concentrates on the scent of her and the taste of her. She reaches out to stroke his head, but he does not move at all. In the pause that follows she can hear the low rumble of a train arriving under the ground beneath them. A gust of wind whirls up and into the street. His head is warm against her hand and, inside the recesses of her mind, she hears again that childhood tune, played by the balalaika that they heard at the dance on the first night that they met.

After a few moments, she tugs at his hand and, as he looks up, she starts walking towards the Wedding Palace, pulling him with her.

'Wait, Katya. Are you sure you will be happy with me?' he says.

She stops, turns, and looks at him. He has not asked if she is sure she wants to get married. Rather, he is concerned whether she will be happy. It is typical of him to do this, to look a step beyond to what really matters.

'If you want the truth, I was once sure that I could never love anyone enough to want to be married.' Her eyes are clear, the emotions laid bare within them as she speaks. 'But I want to marry you, now. Because, yes, I'm sure I will be happy with you, and you with me. Despite everything, I am sure.'

She begins walking again, and the question is in his mouth, so close to being uttered – 'Despite what, Katya, despite what?' – but she is ahead of him now, and he hesitates to keep pressing, to break the fragile beauty of this moment, so he follows after her, catching her hand in his own, and consciously pushing his worry out of his mind. He smiles when she turns to kiss him as they go.

Chapter Fifteen

Boston, February 2001

MELISSA HAS THOUGHT a lot about Alexander Ivanov on the flight from New York. He remains something of a cipher to her. A brilliant businessman who behaves like an old-school gentleman. A philanthropist who donates large portions of his wealth to others – probably to alleviate the remains of his old Communist guilt. A man devoted to his work, but not at the expense of those around him. There is much to admire in him, and perhaps something to learn – and his company is not in bad shape either, so she is pleased that he has given her another try at the deal. His telephone call two days ago had been brief and he had focused only on arranging a time for her to come back and discuss the sale – he had made no mention of the terms he might be looking for but she has schooled herself well enough in the strategy and psychology of deal-making to know when to hold back questions, and she agreed to fly in. She can look for all the answers she wants when they are face to face.

He shows her into his office. There are two walls of books, mostly related to food and wine, and a slim laptop sits on his wide desk. His paperwork is stacked neatly on assorted trays; only the centre of the

desk, right before his chair, is a confusion of paper, pens and
correspondence.

'Good to see you again,' he tells her.

'You too,' she says. 'I hope we can work this out.'

When he had first met Melissa he had thought her cold. The
impression had been a function of the brusque tone of her words,
and their concise content, but he had changed his mind before
that first meeting was over. Even though she has often stretched his
patience, and made this sale impossible so far, at times he has
enjoyed working alongside her, and he feels that sense of satisfaction
again now, as they talk about the details of the business. She is
wholly focused when she works, always absorbing and learning
from him everything she can. He notes that her mind seizes
instantly on whatever he says and refines it, looking at an issue
from every side to see how it can be improved, or streamlined or
both. He is learning a lot from her through her precision of
thought. He is precise also, but often his business mind is clouded
by his creative process, the part of him that produces new recipes
and ideas. Hers is not, and that seems to provide her with a
permanent clarity of vision.

'We can discuss details all day,' he says, 'but I have to ask you if
your position has changed on the charitable initiatives?'

'How much are you willing to negotiate?'

'Not at all. I want to sell but I don't need to. And I have interest
from other buyers.'

She sits back in her seat and closes her notebook. 'Can I ask you
something, Alexander?'

'Sure.'

'When you lived in Russia, did you believe in Communism?'

He would never have predicted such a question from Melissa,
who so rarely crosses the personal with the professional. He wonders

if there is a ploy here, a trap to lure him into some counter-argument.

'Yes, I did,' he says. 'There was nothing else to believe in. Why do you ask?'

'I'm interested. You're the model of capitalism and free enterprise now. How do you move so easily from one extreme mindset to another?'

'It wasn't easy. And yet it wasn't hard either. The first belief – in Communism – had been drummed into me from childhood. I knew nothing else, and was convinced, for a while anyway, that such a state was the fairest way for everyone to have something. But I had changed my mind even before I left Russia. I still thought that everyone should have opportunities, but I was less convinced that this was the way to achieve it. I knew the system was flawed, but I began to wonder if the base ideas were flawed too…There was too much cost in individual expression, individual thought, and no mercy for those who rebelled—'

He stops short, and she is quite sure that this last sentence has reminded him of his wife. There is a look of utter desolation in his eyes. Then he blinks hard, noticeably, and he is back with her.

'Then I lived here, worked hard. Rose on my merits, as they say. But it still troubles me that most people in the world are born without any opportunity to start a business, to feed themselves, to take advantage of the positive things that capitalism and democracy can bring. I believe very strongly – and so does Lauren – that we have a responsibility to use well the wealth that we have.'

'Does everybody have the same responsibility?'

'I think so, but I can only control what I own. Which is why I am refusing to sell if you, or anyone else, compromises the philanthropy.'

Melissa says nothing, and he glances at his watch. He has a six o'clock conference call, which is due to begin in five minutes. He excuses himself, and closes the meeting without suggesting a further one. She will contact him, if she wants to, once she has considered what they have discussed.

The apartment is too dark and too quiet. She can tell at once that her mother is not at home. She puts down her suitcase and looks down the side hallway at her father's closed door. The carpet leading towards it is old and worn out in a line just to the left of the middle, which is her father's accustomed route out of his study. It is his habit to touch the wall as he walks along, so the pile of the centre strip of carpet looks clean and thick by comparison. She wonders if her mother walks down there – has reason to walk down there – more than once or twice a month.

'Dad?' she says, in a voice too small for him to hear.

She goes into the kitchen and switches on lights. Scans the fridge for food. There is Parmesan, a platter of raw meat, the sight of which turns her stomach, some fruit and yoghurt. Then she turns, walks determinedly down the unwelcoming hallway and stops outside her father's study door. She knocks and opens it. 'Hey,' she says.

With a single push of his foot, he allows the swivel action of his chair to bring him slowly round to face her. 'Hey,' he replies. 'When did you get back?'

'This afternoon.'

'Business?'

She nods. He blinks, trying to disengage from the literary world of the nineteenth century that has absorbed his brain without release for the past few hours.

'Where's Mom?' she asks. A simple question to help ease him back to the world of the apartment, the world of his family.

'In the kitchen, I think.'

'She's not home,' she tells him, a reminder.

He frowns, remembers. 'She's at the movies. She'll be back by eight, she said.'

'Did you ask her what she's seeing?' She gives him a half-smile, a way to soften the accusation that underlies her question. She knows that usually he would not think to ask.

'*Doctor Zhivago*,' he says, and his voice is a curious mixture of triumph and regret. 'She's in a Russian phase, you know. She's set on going over there next week. Lauren asked her.'

'My mother's scoring better than me.'

He grins. He loves the utter dryness of her wit, the complete unexpectedness with which it darts from her serious face. He indicates the chair beside him. On its seat are open books, and its back carries various outer garments, which Frank Johnson alternately wears and discards throughout the day, according to his mood and temperature. It is a chair that has not been sat on for some considerable time. She gathers the items strewn on it and places them on the floor, then sits down.

'Why don't you go to Russia?' he asks. 'Very interesting place, you know.'

'I know.'

A pause. 'You like this girl?'

Melissa gives a short laugh. 'What makes you ask?'

'Oh, I pick things up. Your mother and I discuss you quite a bit, you know.' He waits, giving her time to reply, but she says nothing. He watches her with a frown, then goes back to his papers, reads the last sentence he wrote, scratches out a word and replaces it with another. Then he turns to her.

She looks at him, a little amused but mostly irritated. 'What?' she asks.

'Try,' he says. 'Try, and see what happens.'

'Maybe,' Melissa says. 'Maybe I'll ask them. I need a vacation.'

Her father's back is to her now, and his pen is working up and down on the paper once more. She stands up and puts the books, cardigans and scarves back on the chair.

'Just get another ticket,' he says suddenly, just as she reaches the door. 'Or, better yet, persuade your mother to stay here with me.'

Melissa waits silently, hoping that he will turn round and that she will be able to read in his eyes the full meaning of his last words. But he does not look up from his work. She closes the door behind her, and goes back to the kitchen. From there she will call Lauren and ask if she will come out for dinner.

Estelle is trying to locate within herself what she imagines Alexander must feel when he cooks. She moves about her kitchen purposefully, trying to shake off the heady languor of the cinema, the sense of loss she felt as the vivid screen darkened, taking with it that other world of Russia, revolution, passion and snow. She is preparing steaks and pasta, and she tries to look at and handle each ingredient as Alexander might. Initially this only makes her conscious that her pasta is not Italian-made, and often turns out a little soggy. And that she has forgotten to buy fresh basil to tear into her tomato sauce. She opens the fridge and pulls out her new purchase of fresh Parmesan. A whole piece of real cheese, not the ready-grated imitation strands she usually scatters. She serves the pasta while the steaks lie warm in the pan, and she grates the cheese over the hot sauce. It smells wonderful, but still she cannot build up quite the enthusiasm or the delicacy of handling that Alexander shows. The steaks land with a slap in their allotted positions on the plates, and she wipes her hands and walks out to the hallway.

'Frank!' she calls. 'Dinner!'

She has said those two words in exactly the same way for as long as she can remember. Sometimes she has an impulse to vary the phrase. Occasionally she does so. She will shout, 'Dinner's ready,' or 'Shall we eat?' But usually it's the same. Why this should bother her now, she does not know. Except that most things about her usual routine have felt restrictive over the last few days. She listens for a grunt of recognition, which is generally the signal that he will take another five minutes or so to emerge from his study, but instead the door is flung open immediately and he is walking down the hall towards her.

'Smells good,' he says.

She precedes him into the kitchen.

'Fresh Parmesan.'

They sit down in their accustomed places and, with one of their worn, blunt knives, Frank Johnson saws at the meat on his plate.

'Parmigiano Reggiano,' he says, in an exaggerated Italian accent. 'The king of cheeses.' He leaves a pause, and then: 'Tell me, do we owe our initiation into the king of cheeses to the King of Catering?'

Estelle feels a jolt at her husband's acuity – occasionally, she mistakes his absorption in his work, and his inattention to any detail outside the walls of his study, for a lack of perception. And then she is invariably caught out. 'Why? Do you prefer ready-grated?' she asks.

He gives a grin at her sidestepping, and lets her know he has recognised it by not bothering to answer. For a few minutes they continue to eat in silence. He is conscious of the high, metallic scratch of her fork on her plate; she is trying not to listen to the liquid sound of his chewing.

'What's that?' he asks. With his knife he points to a book that lies on the counter behind her.

She glances round, playing for time, even though she knows what he is gesturing at. 'It's a book,' she says.

'Ah, so it's going to be one of those evenings, is it? If you want me to stay quiet, just say so.'

She looks up at him, repentant. She did not mean to be dismissive but is not sure she has the courage to carry through the conversation that will result from a proper reply. 'Sorry.'

'It's all right.'

'It's a book about the Cold War.' She takes a breath, steeling herself a little. 'I'm reading it as research for my novel.'

He makes no comment, while he chews another piece of meat. He always eats the contents of his plate one item at a time – he will first eat all of the steak, then the pasta. 'For pity's sake, Estelle,' he says, when he has finished. 'Not the writing lark again.'

Now it is her turn to concentrate on her food, although the last thing she feels she can do is swallow it. But she attends to the strands of spaghetti winding round her fork as though there is nothing else of interest to her, for she cannot bear to look up and let him guess how much he has hurt her. When the fork is loaded with pasta, she cannot raise it to her mouth so she lays it down next to the remains of her steak. 'Yes, the "writing lark" again.' She picks up her plate and takes it to the sink, feeling the anger rising through her body. 'Is it so terrible that I have something I enjoy doing and want to do?'

'No,' he replies evenly. 'But it must be done well.'

'By whose standards?' She turns on him, and comes straight back to the table, standing with her arms crossed. But he does not reply. He looks down at his plate where the Parmesan-coated pasta lies untouched. 'Are you the divine authority on all literary matters, Frank?'

'I have trained and read a lot. Literary criticism is my life's work.'

'Believe me, I know that! If anyone knows it, I do.' She picks up the volume on Soviet Russia and moves away as if to leave the room, but something holds her back. If she walks out now, there will be an end to it, there will be an impasse between them, the same impasse that has never yet been crossed. She wants him to understand her for once. If he can. If she can explain. She sits down at the table, holding the book against her chest like a heavy talisman. 'Listen, Frank. We always argue about the same thing, and in the end it's beside the point.'

'I don't agree,' he begins, but she cuts him off.

'Just listen to me for a minute, can you? It doesn't matter if I write like Shakespeare, or if I turn out the worst sort of badly written romantic trash. Because I'm happy doing it. And I am your wife.'

'So our relationship should excuse poor writing?'

'No. Our relationship means you should support me, and be happy that I'm happy in whatever I'm doing. And then, if you feel I need help, then help me to improve. Not by being sarcastic and dismissive, but by showing me how to change, helping me with what to read, how to phrase things. You do it with your students, for goodness' sake. Be kind, Frank. That's all I'm asking.'

'Be blind, you mean.'

'Goddamn it!'

He cannot resist the impulse to be facetious, but there are moments when she feels he must try. She gets up, wanting to bring the book down on to the table with a crash, to vent her frustration, to jolt him from his sanctimonious attitude. She is at the door when he almost shouts, which is unnecessary, since she is no more than two feet away from him. 'Estelle, wait!' He reaches for her hand, but it is clutching the book, and she will not give it up to him.

'I'm sorry. That was a stupid thing to say.' A pause. 'Don't go away to Russia.'

'I want to.'

'To be with him?'

She is taken aback, had not considered that he would probably assume Alexander was going too.

'To research,' she replies. And then, although she does not feel he deserves the comfort, she adds, 'He's not even going.'

He looks up at her, his hair dishevelled and his eyes pouchy with exhaustion. 'Then why didn't he say that yesterday?'

Estelle takes a step back into the room. 'What do you mean?'

Her husband pushes away his plate. 'He came to see me yesterday. At the university. I asked him to come.'

'Why?'

'I'm not sure.'

'Why didn't you tell me?'

He waves a hand. 'I didn't want to make a song and dance about nothing.'

'Well, you are.'

As if he has not heard her, he continues, 'It's strange. I really liked him. He kept me at a distance – very proper and correct, and reserved. But I liked him, even as I tried to dislike him because he is attractive to you.'

A long pause hangs there, as if waiting, hoping for her denial. She says nothing, and he speaks again: 'Under that polished veneer, in his eyes, I could see that he has a gentleness to him, and also great passion about many things. A passionate man. Attentive, kind.'

'He is.'

'And I am not, of course.'

For a man of such advanced age and intelligence, he reminds her too frequently of a wheedling child.

'You're a good man, Frank,' she says quietly. 'But attentive? Kind? Passionate, except maybe about your books? No.' They are the harshest words she has ever spoken to him, and she feels sorry for him, but relieved, as though something shameful has finally been revealed.

He is watching her, unflinching. 'You knew who I was when you married me. And you have known for the last thirty years. Why are you only complaining now?'

She looks down. 'Maybe I've changed. People can, you know. Sometimes it's a desirable thing, to progress as a person. Maybe the ideal thing would have been for us to change together.'

'Spare me the popular psychology.'

But she hardly hears him. 'Is there a statute of limitations on complaining? If you've put up with something for thirty years, is it too late to put in a request for a change?'

'Now you're being facetious.'

She takes a breath, which manifests itself as a long sigh. When she speaks again, her tone is calmer and less harsh. 'The truth is, what I just said hurt you, and maybe that's why it's taken me so long. It's not an easy thing to say.'

She puts the book down, and touches his shoulder. There is no response so she walks back round the table and sits down opposite him.

'Frank . . .' she says, but she can get no further before he stands up and walks out of the kitchen, down the dark hallway. She looks at the doorway where she seems still to see the large outline of his frame and, stunned, listens to the thud of his study door, the turn of the key in the lock.

Chapter Sixteen

Moscow, January 1959

KATYA HURRIES INTO the apartment, throwing off her coat and walking straight into the kitchen. 'I have to hurry,' she says, kissing Alexander on the back of his neck. 'I have to leave again in half an hour.'

He is retrieving some butter from their new refrigerator. He taps the solid block unhappily, then looks at the temperature dial. 'This refrigerator won't just cool things,' he complains, 'it insists on freezing them.'

He leans towards her, butter in hand, waiting for her to kiss him again, on the mouth. She does so, smiling.

'At least it works,' she tells him. 'What did Irina leave?' She lifts the lid on a pot of food that sits waiting on the stove.

'Stew,' he replies. 'She says we are keeping the place too clean, and that she didn't have to work the full four hours so she gave back some money.'

Katya is taking down two plates, and gathering cutlery. 'The last honest woman in Russia,' she says.

'I told her to keep it,' says Alexander.

'And the last philanthropist,' she comments, hoisting the pot to the centre of the table.

He comes over to her, carrying several slices of dark brown bread and two opened bottles of equally dark beer. They sit and spoon out the stew, bowls full of steaming, scented sauce and small pieces of meat.

'Where are you going in such a hurry?' Alexander asks. He loosens his tie, and watches his slim, ravenous wife dipping her bread into her bowl.

'The school play, remember?'

'Ah, yes. And tell me, what does the school administrator have to do with the children's play?'

She sighs. She knows this light, bantering tone of his, but cannot enjoy it tonight, does not want to cope with the request for attention that underlies it. 'The school administrator has everything to do with it,' she says. 'All the staff have to be there. To meet the parents, and applaud the children. You know how it is.' She looks up. 'How was your day at work?'

'Bad.'

'The same problem still?' Katya asks, concerned.

'We are losing a lot of valuable information. They have been watching all of us for weeks now, but I know it's someone from outside.'

'Are you sure? Who else but an insider would have been able to get so much information to Washington for so long?'

He shakes his head. 'I don't know. It doesn't make sense. But they must be found. The atmosphere is becoming more and more paranoid. None of us trusts each other any more.'

'So you've told Oleg?'

'I've told everyone. At every level. They're worried.'

'Ah,' says Katya.

'What is it, my love?'

'So the man who came to check the wiring in the building this morning, he was putting in more listening devices?'

Alexander shrugs. 'Probably.'

'When they find whoever it is they'll kill them, you know.'

'Perhaps,' he says, without satisfaction. 'Can I come with you?' he asks.

She rolls her eyes. 'I'd love it, but I couldn't let you sit through yet another version of *Peter and the Wolf*.'

He says nothing, and she continues, 'They're primary-school kids. You'll be bored. Won't you?'

'Yes.'

They eat, and she feels guilty that she has been so unequivocal in her refusal. After a few moments, he looks up at her and smiles, so that she should know he is not upset.

'Do you really want to come?' she asks gently.

'I really don't,' he tells her. 'But I will miss you, that's all.'

'I know. So will I.' She touches his hand across the table. 'It won't be long. I should be back by nine at the latest.'

'Okay.'

When they finish, they rise with their plates, but Alexander takes Katya's from her. 'Go and get ready,' he says. 'You have to leave.'

Five minutes later she is back in the kitchen doorway, watching him wash the dishes. 'Why don't you leave them for Irina?'

'I don't like the mess. And I don't mind doing it.'

'Thank you,' she says.

'For what?'

'For doing that. And for being here.'

'Where else would I be?' He goes over to her, drying his hands, and kisses her. 'Go on. You'll be late.'

She nods and turns in the hallway, and tells him goodbye.

He frowns. 'Are you going to be on the stage?' he asks, and she laughs, her head back and her delicate throat exposed.

'Certainly not. I'm not an actress.'

She opens the door. He is turning to go back to the kitchen when something makes him stop and look again. She is still standing in the doorway, framed there, smiling at him, and now she makes a sweeping, *faux*-actress curtsy, then blows him a kiss. He laughs, and she is gone.

He is lying on the bed, reading through the reports he has brought home with him, when the telephone rings. It is his mother. They want his help with a young man who works at the bank. The young man, it seems, is too talented to be working as a mere clerk and they have asked Alexander to see if he can find a place for him somewhere as an assistant. 'He's here now,' says his mother. 'If you are not busy, come over with Katya and speak to him. Tell us what you think.'

He is pleased to have something to occupy his time, for this evening has already dragged without her. He tells his mother that he will come, and that he will bring Katya, if he can pick her up when he goes past the school.

He puts down the solid black receiver, then picks it up again. He dials the number of the school where his wife works. There is no reply. 'Of course,' he tells himself. 'They are all watching the play.' He cuts off the call and while he considers what to do, he tries the number again. This time a man's voice answers.

'Is that the school?' Alexander asks, frowning.

'Yes.'

'Who are you?'

'I'm the caretaker. Who are you?'

'I am Alexander Ivanov. I am looking for my wife Katya. The administrator?'

There is a grunt that, from its tone, Alexander assumes to be one of recognition. 'Is she there?' he asks.

'No, she's not here. Nobody is here. It is nearly eight thirty at night, comrade. Nobody is here.'

The man sounds genuine. 'What about the play?' asks Alexander, his stomach dropping.

'What play?'

'The school play. *Peter and the Wolf.*'

'They did that last month.'

Alexander pauses. 'Are they doing it somewhere else, perhaps?'

He can almost see the man shrug. 'Where else would they do it?' he asks reasonably.

Alexander does not remember thanking the caretaker, or saying goodbye, or any of the formalities that he knows he must have completed before putting down the receiver. His heart is filled with a mixture of misgiving, fear and anger. If she is not at the school, where is she? Is she safe? Why did she lie to him? The question that recurs most often in his head. Why did she lie?

There is something about what has just happened that, deep down, does not shock him quite as it should. Something in his wife's personality or nature that has made him almost expect something like this. There has always been a tiny kernel, a hidden part of her, that he feels he has never seen. The certainty of this feeling has, however, been worn away over the months and years of their marriage by Katya herself. She has told him time and again that he is not logical, that he is insecure for no reason, and when she asks him what she has done to make him feel as he does, he cannot point to any one thing. And he, knowing that she does love him, and knowing also that she would not hurt him, has slowly come to disbelieve his own gut feelings.

But now he sits forward in his chair, then gets up and goes and lies, fully clothed, on his side of the bed. He is feeling sick with anger now. She must be with somebody. He thinks back to all the times he has felt uncertain about her, and those feelings are gradually refined and magnified until they are all that he is aware of. By the time the hallway clock chimes half past nine, he is so sad and angry that he is again sitting up. He pulls out the new *Literaturnaya Moskva* magazine – he likes to look through the poetry and commentary, now that censorship has eased a little – but he cannot make sense of the firm lines of print through the blood pounding in his temples. The telephone rings, and he snatches it up. He hears his father's voice and, dispirited, Alexander tells him he has a bad headache and cannot come over. His sentences are terse and tense, and the conversation is over in seconds, after which he walks helplessly round the apartment, looking out of every window, waiting, waiting for her to come back.

It is ten o'clock now, and he has checked his watch more than ten times. Still there is no sign of her. She is never late. He goes to the window and looks out at the street, but there is only the night guard. No Katya walking up the road, no muffled sound of the outside door closing, no footsteps flying lightly up the stairs. For the first time he begins to be afraid. The anger settles down within him so that the burning in his stomach is now like faintly glowing coals, not the licking flames of the last hour. He paces up and down, hoping she is all right, and wanting her to come in so that she can tell him the reason for the lie, for there must, he realises now, be a reason: a simple, logical reason.

At almost eleven o'clock, he is slumped in the armchair, listless. For a few minutes he has ceased waiting on a knife edge so when the muffled slam of the downstairs door comes, he is surprised and sits up, wondering whether he has heard it correctly. He has, for there are footsteps on the stairs, and they are hers. Before she can place her key in the lock, he has opened the door. His manner is cool and distant, but is belied by his appearance – reddened eyes, unkempt hair, creases in his shirt where he has turned back and forth on the sofa, trying not to worry about her. She takes him in while she stands there on the threshold. She says nothing, but neither does she walk in. Something momentous has occurred or is taking place. A turning point, and she must read it and assimilate it and understand how to deal with it before she opens her mouth to speak.

'Where were you?' he asks.

She steps inside and kisses his cheek, and she can feel that he has resisted the impulse to turn away from that kiss, and that he suspects something.

'I'm so sorry, Sasha,' she tells him, her voice normal, neutral. She is speaking more to the listening devices that she is sure are in their apartment than to him directly. 'The play finished at nine, and then Elena was ill. Svetlana and I stayed with her until her husband came. He took her straight to a friend of theirs who is working at the hospital. He's a doctor. The friend.'

'I called the school.' His voice sounds sad, the harshness falling away despite his intentions. She is so plausible, so believable, she loves him, she would surely not lie – not with such detail.

'My school?'

He nods. Of course.

She smiles. 'It wasn't there. It was at the sixth district school. A joint production. We did it last month for Christmas. They did it now for New Year. Here.' She is holding out a yellow leaflet, printed with the school names, and a picture of Peter trapping the wolf, and the date and the time and the place.

He takes it and scans the information. He feels suddenly ridiculous, standing before her with his wild eyes and accusing manner.

'I should have explained properly. I was in such a hurry, I'm sorry.'

'What was wrong with her?'

223

'Who? Elena?'

'Yes.'

'I'm not sure. Seemed like food poisoning to me. She ate some meat at dinner that was a few days old. She got it with rations, but it was the last piece, someone brought it out from the back for her. They'd probably had it in the shop for a week. It happens.'

He runs his hands over his head, brushing down his hair with his fingers, and then retucks his shirt. She has not yet taken off her coat or gloves. She holds her hat in one hand. 'Are you tired?' she asks him.

'No.'

'Shall we go for a walk? It'll relax you.'

He feels angry again, let down in some way. Irritated that she wants him to relax when it is her late return that has so troubled him. But before he can say anything, she pulls off a glove and places a hand over his lips. The fingers stay there, and when she knows he will not speak, they trace the line of his mouth, and her own lips go up to meet his.

'Come on,' she says, and he gets his coat and hat.

Outside, snow is falling, very lightly, a few, delicate, downy flakes that are barely felt when they touch the skin. When she looks up at the deep grey of the night sky, she sees the white flecks tumbling down, their light weight making their descent seem too slow, a pace that seems out of tune with the laws of gravity, and she feels dizzy, nauseous.

Why is she out here with him, when they should be in the warmth of their home, getting ready to sleep? What does she want to tell him? When she had first walked into the apartment, under the weight of his suspicion and anger, she had been concerned, perhaps even hopeful, that she would need to tell him things, to admit certain truths. But now she has told him the surface facts, about the play, and about Elena falling sick, and she can perhaps still wriggle away from his deeper uncertainties without too much effort. So why has she brought him outside? What does she *want* to tell him?

'I thought you had lied to me about the play,' he says. 'What could I think? Especially when you were so late.'

She has not lied about the play. She needs a good, true alibi for whatever she does. A lie about a play or about a woman going to a hospital would be too easily found out and exposed. No, she has been at the play, she has sat through *Peter and the Wolf* again, and she did lay a comforting hand on the deputy head teacher's back as the other woman vomited into the stark white toilet of the school cloakroom. She tells him this again.

'Why did you doubt me, Sasha?' she asks. She is so much in love with him that she can hardly keep her rational mind working. Her impulse is to throw her arms about his neck and beg him to forgive her for feeding his doubts, for she has been lying to him, for the last three months she has been lying. Or, at least, not telling him everything – about where she has been, what she does, whom she meets. For three months, after the two-year break that Misha insisted was necessary to avoid suspicion, she has started working again, her real work, stealing his thoughts and papers and transposing them, passing them on to the people who will use them to fight his government. His employer. His life. Even now, on the way home from the school play, she has dropped off a camera film containing snapshots of documents. Her husband's documents, private papers from his workplace.

She has felt every minute of the past three months creeping slowly by because she has hated every second of them. She had known that once the two-year grace period was over Misha would try to play on her doubts, on the fact that she had once sworn to dedicate her whole life to fighting the Communist system. As she had expected, he had teased and pushed and wheedled and manipulated, but still she had held firm, and even though in her mind she found some of his arguments persuasive, she would not betray her husband – she had come to believe that she must live with integrity in her own house before attempting to do so out in the world.

But then Misha had played his trump card. 'Remember, Katyushka,' he had said, with a cool smile, 'you already betrayed him once. Before you were married. Imagine how devastated your husband would be if he found out that the love of his life had married him only for his information.'

At that moment she had hated Misha. She had seen at once, at last, that he had made her steal from Alexander that first time not as a test of her resolve but to have something to hold over her if the plan went wrong, if she fell in love. She knows it is that kind of foresight and ruthlessness that makes him such a good agent, but she never expected he would use such tactics to blackmail her. She had felt trapped, confused, desperate, so she had agreed to start spying on Alexander – anything to avoid him learning that she had betrayed him already. But instead, with each passing day, with each completed theft of his information, she has become increasingly tangled in the net, increasingly unable to find a way out of her dilemma. Until the weight of guilt has built up to such a level that part of her is now willing her husband, her victim, to find her out so that she can confess at last and put an end to this waking nightmare, however terrible the consequences may be.

Alexander is no longer angry, but neither does he seem embarrassed nor sorry for having accused her. Something still troubles him, she can tell, and she now realises that it is his new awareness that has made her bring him out on to the wide, silent, snowy street, away from ears and eyes that should not observe them.

'Why did I doubt you, Katya? I don't know.'

'You know I love you?'

He stops and looks at her. 'Yes. But when I phoned the school, and the caretaker said there was no play, I felt terrible, and yet a small part of me was . . .' He touches the snow that sits on a black railing behind them with the tip of his gloved finger. 'I was not surprised. And I can't think why that should be.'

His eyes are searching hers for an answer. He has not used the diminutive of her name since she returned, and there is a new coolness to him which she hates. She is the one who keeps certain aspects of herself aloof, not him. And now, a few short months later, she cannot even manage that. What has she become? she wonders. Something better, or something worse?

'I have something to tell you,' she says quickly. Although she is far from decided about what she wants to say, she must put out a sentence that will make it more difficult for her to stop. He waits for her to continue, and he looks small against the broad background of the snow. She gestures to a bench, and together they walk to it, brush off the crisp ice that has settled upon it and sit down to talk.

With innate politeness, he waits for her to sit first. He is filled with misgiving. She has something to tell him. It cannot be good, that much he knows. Is she having an affair? Is she in love with someone else? He examines his gloves and waits for her to speak. She touches the back of his neck with such affection that he cannot imagine she does not love him any more. Then she speaks.

'I have been lying to you, Sasha,' is her first sentence. 'Or, at least, I have not been honest with you. Since we met. Since before we were married.'

He cannot say a word. His large brown eyes meet hers, mute with dread.

'Sasha, you know how the murder of my parents has affected me?'

Perhaps it is cowardly of her to approach it in this way, round-about, giving the justifications first, but she cannot just come out with it. He nods. It is the first time she has spoken of it as murder, rather than 'loss' or 'death' and he senses that there is a reason for the new directness.

'Well, I became a Pioneer after that, in my third year at school, just like you, a good young Party member, and no one could fault me. I denounced my parents in writing, just like they asked me to, and I followed the road that one takes in order to get along. And then, when Yuri escaped to America, suspicion was thrown on me again, and I worked even harder to prove myself a model Com-munist. I succeeded quite well.'

She takes her hand from his neck and presses her stiff fingers between her knees. Snowflakes settle on her coat, then melt into the woollen fibres where they will sit, slowly making her wetter and colder.

'I did all that for a reason. And the reason was not a love of Communism, or the government. Quite the opposite. You know I look at things differently from most people, but I have never told you how differently. I hated Stalin. I hated his government. I hated his paranoia, which infected the whole country so that it became everyone's paranoia. Not to be suspicious, not to be sneaky, not to be fearful would have meant not to be alive. To survive, your neighbour had to reveal five names of traitors, whether he knew them or not. You never knew who was watching you, or who was being beaten into giving your name as an enemy of the state, just because they had to give someone's name. I hated the so-called Communist ideal that could allow a government toad like Beria to rape as many young girls as he wanted, and that let Khrushchev and Molotov and all the rest of them live in huge houses and eat well while the working people starved. I hate the fact that, even now, we have a "proletarian aristocracy". I know, because I married into it.' She cannot help but laugh bitterly.

'Is that what Communism is supposed to be about? That, with you, I can live in a beautiful apartment overlooking the river, while with Maya I had to live in a cold cell of a room while her mother slept in a cupboard?'

He doesn't reply, but his eyes are fixed on her with surprise and sympathy. 'You're right,' he says. 'But things can be changed, slowly . . .'

'No. I don't hate the Communist system because it has been abused, Sasha, I hate it because it cannot work, even when there isn't a dictator in charge. It stifles people, it kills freedom of thought and expression – everyone and everything must be the same, uniform. Well, people are not the same. There is no room here for artists, writers, poets. Look what they just did to Pasternak. The whole world is praising his book – he won this prize, the Nobel Prize. And here, in his homeland, he is driven to despair. Treated like a criminal. It is unforgivable, Sasha. And it's not just writers. If anyone, a farmer, a clerk, a train driver, wants to work extra hard and try to make something of himself, or if he wants to invent something, or try to do something he enjoys or loves, is that so wrong? Or if someone has a good business idea – why should that person not be able to do as he pleases, and even make money and live in the big house that now only a politician can live in? At least he would be there on merit. That's how it is in America.'

Alexander cannot speak: he is caught between shock and amazement at her words. He is trying to take it all in, trying to absorb her passionate defence of the enemy, of capitalism, and he is absorbing it easily because her words are seductive, because they are rational. And behind it all he is waiting, still waiting for her to explain how

SHAMIM SARIF

she has been dishonest to him, for he cannot yet see what point she is moving towards.

'Anyway,' she continues, a little more calmly now, 'from the age of thirteen I knew what I wanted to do with my life. Most people don't, ever. Especially here, where there is no room for wanting. We just do what we're told, don't we?'

His head is light, reeling from her words. *I knew what I wanted to do with my life*. It seems so simple and clear, but so alien. How did she learn even to think in such a way? He is full of admiration for her swift mind, her unconventional thinking, even as he is apprehensive of what it has led to. She is talking again, and he looks at her closely, to listen better, to allow not a word or nuance to escape him.

'I wanted to fight the system that had caused my parents, two kind, intelligent, *innocent* people to be brutally killed. I wanted to avenge the pain they put me through. Taking my own mother away from me. And from Yuri. And millions of other children. Shame on them, Sasha.' Her voice breaks, the tears bubbling under the cracked surface of her sentences. 'Shame on them. How did we let them get away with it for so long? Why do we still?'

He puts a hand on her shoulder, which is shaking now from weeping, and waits as long as he can before asking: 'How did you fight it, Katya? Tell me . . .'

She takes a gulping breath and looks up. Her gloves wipe the edges of her eyes. 'I'm an agent,' she says, in a whisper. 'I work for the Americans. I have done for years now.'

'What?'

She knows he has heard, so she shrugs and says nothing else. Takes more breaths of the moist, cold air. A flake of snow dances into her mouth, burning away instantly on the heat of her tongue.

What she has just revealed seems meaningless to him, almost beyond comprehension, yet it makes perfect sense.

'You had no idea?' she asks. He shakes his head. And then a thought forms that he can hardly articulate. But he must try. He looks at her, jaw slack, eyes anguished, and tries to form the words. Nothing comes out, but she hears them as clearly as if she has just been inside his mind.

'No, no, no,' she says, and she grasps his gloved hand, pulls it to her breast. 'That is not why I married you, Sasha. It's why I almost didn't. It's why I said I had to think about it when you first asked me, when every part of me was crying yes.' She touches his head. 'Do you remember on our wedding day, when you came to meet me at the metro? Well, I nearly told you then. But I was too weak,' she says, with a trace of bitterness. 'I told myself I was just being careful but, really, I was weak. And, anyway, I had agreed not to work for two years, to avoid suspicion, and I was sure I would never start again. But I did. A few months ago. It has been killing me, Sasha, and I can't do it any more. I wanted you to know.' She is crying again, but there is no sobbing, no change in her voice, only tears which slide down her cheekbones, gaunt and starkly shadowed in the half-darkness.

He cannot move. He just stares at her, shocked. 'How could you have lied to me, Katya? All this time? And *spied* on me?'

She is unable to speak. He feels anger tingling in his throat and hands. The sheer purity of the emotion is making his voice constrict, and his head spin. He looks away. 'How could you betray me?'

'I couldn't. I hadn't worked for them since I married you. And now I've started again only because they blackmailed me into it. They said if I didn't do it, they would tell you anyway. And I was scared to lose you. But I can't lie about it any more, Sasha, I can't . . .'

She finds that she is calling after him because he is walking away from her now, almost stumbling through the snow in an effort to distance himself from her quickly, as quickly as he can. He cannot look at her, or hear her pleading voice, not now, not when he does not know if he can ever again trust a single word that comes from her mouth.

He does not return home for five hours. It is very early in the morning, the small hours, the hours that feel diminished to her, in the way that her whole life feels suddenly reduced and meaningless now that he hates her. In those five lost hours, she has passed through fear, and sorrow, and self-loathing, and dread, and now she sits at the kitchen table in the dark, drained of feeling and of thought.

He has walked for five hours, with numb feet and a cold heart, and during the last hour of anguish, as he walked past the restaurant they went to on their first wedding anniversary, and past the bridge that they have so often crossed together on their way to visit his parents, he has remembered something of their old life, the one they had before tonight, and he has also started to attribute some meaning to the fact that it was Katya herself who confessed her betrayal.

He walks into the house, switches on all the lights and comes into the kitchen. There she sits, squinting in the sudden glare like a newborn animal. She has been crying a lot, he can see that, and despite himself his heart goes out to her. He takes his frozen hands from his coat pockets, and picks up the coat she has left draped across the table. He hands it to her and, almost automatically, she rises, puts it on and follows him out of the front door, down the stairs, into the deserted street. He turns and looks at her, eyes stern.

'I can't lie to you any more,' she whispers. 'Even if it means it's over between us. I love you.'

He believes it, and he is tired of anger, and of pushing her away, and he cannot bring himself to ignore her pain. His fury and his hurt are subsumed now by his heart. Uncertain of what to do, he puts his arms round her, and although the action is mechanical, it stimulates something within him, his love, his care, and he finds himself feeling relieved that she has said what she wanted to say, even if he has no idea what to do with her words just yet. He kisses her forehead, inhales her, the cold skin where it meets the warmer scalp, and holds her to him.

'You don't hate me?'

'I don't know you,' he says.

'I'm sorry,' she whispers. 'I said nothing because I was so afraid of losing you, and instead I just made it all worse.'

He glances round. Suddenly even the quiet glow of the snow seems threatening to him. He has spent the last several weeks alerting his department to the fact that there is a mole, or a leak of some kind, never suspecting that the leak was himself. Through Katya. The realisation that she may be caught at any moment, that she may be wrested from him and into prison, ignites a fear within him that for the time being overwhelms his sense of betrayal.

'What have I done?' he asks. 'Because of me, they're looking for you. What have I done?'

'You did your job. You did the right thing.' Her voice is muffled against his damp collar, but it is as though he does not hear her at all.

'What are we going to do? We can't stay here. They'll find you.' He cannot think properly, he needs time, and he needs his rationality back. Then, in the midst of his confusion, an idea comes to him. 'I'll cancel America,' he says.

He means the diplomatic delegation that he is travelling with the following week. It is an honour to be chosen for the trip, part of the group accompanying Deputy Premier Mikoyan to Washington, New York, Chicago, even Los Angeles – part of the new diplomatic openness between the two countries. It will be Alexander's first time out of the Soviet Union and he has been proud and excited about it, eager to go and see and explore this other culture, this other world, for himself. But now it seems faintly ridiculous to him, this schoolboy enthusiasm, when all this time his wife has been connected so deeply with the United States, has been involved with organisations that make a mockery of the surface diplomacy he represents. And on a practical level this trip is also something that will keep him away from her for a week just when he must be with her. He must find a way to understand everything that is happening, and make a plan, protect her – and himself. But how?

'You can't cancel it. Nothing could be more suspicious . . .' Even as she speaks, she has raised her head and is now staring at him, with eyes that are wild, almost prophetic, filled with revelation. 'No. You must go. You must. Don't you see? Then you will be out of here at least. We will be out. I'll join you, they'll help me get out. If I offer them your information . . . Sasha, we could do it. We could leave here.'

'Leave?' He is still stupefied. 'How can we leave?'

'You have a ticket already. I will follow you.'

'Katya, this is insane. Stop talking this way.'

'Think about it. What choice do we have? Jail, or worse.'

'It will never work . . .'

'Can we stay?' she asks. 'Can we stay?'

He stares at her for a few minutes while he thinks about her question. He is trying to consider all the options, looking at possibilities, probabilities, ideas. The hurdles they face are hard, perhaps insurmountable, but dealing with them is infinitely soothing to him for it involves thinking, deciding, practicality. Her lying, her betrayal, her pain, her reasons – all of these things are too overwhelming for him to think of at this moment, and the focus on immediate, practical issues is strangely calming.

'Let's go,' she pleads. 'I'm so tired of it here. We can't even talk to each other in private except in the street. Let's go. Please. Maybe there we could really make a difference. We could tell people how things are here. The terrible things that have happened.'

His mind is staggering under the weight of her idea. Let's go. As if they can just stroll out of this country with no difficulty and no consequences. Let's go. As if they have no life, no responsibilities, no ties here. They are of this place, born here, raised here. And she, especially, has been scarred here. And, he realises, they are not welcome here any more. They are not accepted, or acceptable. She is a traitor to the government, and he is too, because he loves her and because he trusts her so much that he is willing to listen to what she believes in and to try to understand it if he can. In the end, she is all that is important to him. So they are both traitors. And they live in a place where there is no real dissension without terrible consequences.

'Sasha,' she says again, 'can we really stay here any longer?'

He considers for a while, then shakes his head, for he is beginning to admit to himself that, despite everything, he does not see how they can.

Chapter Seventeen

Boston, February 2001

T<small>HEY LOSE EACH</small> other in the confusion of the airport for a few minutes, until Lauren finds Melissa gazing in the window of an electronics store. 'I was just looking for you,' she says. Her laptop case is slung over her shoulder, and she holds a cappuccino in one hand.

'Oh, really?' Lauren asks. 'And did I come with a DVD and a one-year warranty?'

Melissa smiles. 'I just glanced in there as I was going past . . .'

'Sure.'

'Got this for you.' She holds up the coffee.

Lauren thanks her and takes the cup. As they walk to the lounge to wait for their flight, she asks Melissa about Estelle. 'I can't believe your mother dropped out of this,' Lauren says. 'It's not like her.'

'As far as you know,' Melissa replies.

Lauren has found that the easiest way to entice Melissa to talk more is to meet her short comments with an expectant silence. She checks them into the lounge while she waits, watching Melissa's darting eyes take in the people around them.

'My mother has this feisty, fun thing going on,' Melissa offers at last, 'but when it comes to the crunch – well, she's always taken the easy route out.'

'Meaning?'

'Meaning she doesn't have the guts to follow anything through. My father only has to have a moment of drama and she drops everything. I mean, look at him. He's had the passion and drive to follow his love of literature all his life – even when it's been at our expense. I've always wanted a career in business, and I've built one. But she's never really followed through on anything. Sometimes I wonder how much she really wants to be a writer. If you haven't got started by her age, when will you?'

The collecting of bottles of water from the bar gives Lauren time to gather herself, so that she will not have to embark on a week's trip by losing her temper. 'Don't you think that's a little harsh?' she asks, when she returns to their table.

'No, but you do.' The grey eyes smile.

'Yes, I do. Maybe it would help her if your father and even you were encouraging about her writing. No drama, no sarcasm, just some positive feedback.'

'Maybe. But at the end of the day she shouldn't need it. Either she really wants to write, or she doesn't.'

'Oh, to live in your world, where everything is so black and white. Must be great. No trouble figuring out work, family, relationships . . .'

'I didn't say it was easy,' Melissa returns. 'I've found a way to get through the mess of everyday life, that's all. At least with work and family.'

Lauren hesitates only a moment before asking the next question. 'And relationships?' she says.

'Haven't had one for a while,' Melissa says. 'When you've had your heart broken, you don't necessarily feel like jumping back into the fray right away.' She shifts in her chair and pours more water for them both. 'Anyway,' she says briskly. 'Explain it to me. About my mother.'

'I just think that she might not have the confidence to write. Especially if your father is busy judging her all the time. And also it's understandable that she might not want to upset him. Or her marriage. Seems to me like she gets the burden of keeping things together in your family.'

Melissa waits.

'Think about it. You and your father are busy doing exactly as you like, no matter what the cost to your relationships. So who keeps you all together?'

Melissa checks a monitor that hangs above them. She points at the screen. 'They're calling our flight . . . Now you've made me feel guilty, maybe we can call my mom and check in on her before we leave.'

Estelle hangs up the telephone, sits at her desk and starts crying. For the duration of the call from Melissa and Lauren she has managed to convey brightness and excitement for them and their trip. But as soon as the receiver is back in its cradle, she cannot hold back the tears. There is nowhere else she wanted to be on this day than boarding that flight to Moscow with them. She has pictured it all in her mind ever since Lauren suggested it, has hoarded to herself the anticipation that she felt in the dark hours of the night when she would wake up, bubbling over with excitement. After a couple of minutes, she stops crying, wipes her eyes and nose. Leaning back in her chair, she looks out at the hallway. She can see one half of her husband's door at the far end, closed to the world and to her. But behind that door, he is happy, or comfortable at least, pleased to know that she is in the apartment with him.

'You old fool,' she says to herself. The desk before her is clear, and the computer is switched on. There are no emails, and no bills waiting to be paid, and no reason for her not to try to type out a chapter, or a few pages at least. Except that she has decided, at last, that she will not bother any more. She opens a fresh document, and watches the cursor blink. With a sudden, decisive movement, she picks up the telephone and dials Alexander's number.

'Alexander Ivanov.'

'Alexander? It's me.'

'Estelle! I was worried about you. Lauren told me you weren't going to Moscow, and I called you, but you never called back.'

'I'm sorry about that. It's been a crazy few days.'

'Are you well?'

She feels like crying again. She realises that she is rarely asked that question, and the awareness strengthens her brand-new resolve.

'Yes, I'm fine, thanks. Listen, Alexander, I was wondering. *My Fair Lady* is playing at the Colonial Theatre. Frank doesn't want to see it so I wondered if you'd be interested?'

'I'd love to. When were you thinking of?'

'How about tomorrow? There's a matinée at three.'

'Sounds good. I'll pick you up at twelve.'

'That's early,' she says.

'Well, maybe we can make a day of it?'

'Okay,' she says. 'But don't pick me up. How about if I come to you?'

'If you prefer,' he says. 'I'll see you tomorrow.'

*

The following day when he opens his front door to her, he greets her with a handshake, a formality that seems incongruous now that they know each other so well, but one that he almost cannot help. Since his meeting with Frank Johnson he has been on edge, questioning his own motives in pursuing a friendship with Estelle.

She looks at his hand for a moment, and then takes it.

'*Enchanté*,' she says, with a half-curtsy. When they look up, her eyes hold a familiar half-laugh.

Alexander leans to kiss her on the cheek. 'Is that better?'

'Yes indeed,' she replies.

'Shall we?'

'Sure,' she says. 'Do you mind if we walk? Or take the T? I feel like seeing the city a little.'

They stroll to the nearest station, to catch an underground train to Beacon Hill. Across from them, as they walk down to the platform from the busy Saturday-afternoon street, they can see the overland station. She recalls waiting at different Boston stations for her husband to come home. He would travel round the country on lecture tours, and once they had Melissa, Estelle rarely joined him. He loved to take the train. He always hated the individual concentration on the mechanical, the reliance on the ability and goodwill of others, that came with driving. Trains, he liked to say, were much more civilised. Someone else worrying about steering and braking. A night on a train could leave you with a new novel read and absorbed, a good dinner eaten and digested, and time for a sleep. A night in a car got you to a destination with nothing else accomplished.

She sees herself down there on the platforms, waiting, waiting for his train, walking down with it, watching for the doors to open. After the first couple of times, she knew that he would never be among the few eager young men hanging out of the windows. He was always busy inside, in the shaded carriage, putting away books and papers, shrugging on a jacket, waiting by the door. He was not a hanger-out of windows. She never stopped looking up at them,

241

though, for she liked to see the joyous faces of those boys, the breeze shifting through their hair, their tanned arms waving. Her husband was not boyish. She had met him when he was thirty-six, but even in the few photographs that he possessed of himself as a teenager, he had a dark, heavy look that precluded any sense of youth. He had loved her, but there was never any trace of puppy-dog adoration or young, eager passion about his love. It was mature and reasonable, with a depth that showed itself now and again when he was caught off-guard.

Alexander walks on beside her in silence, for a glance at her face has revealed that she is far away. When at last she looks back at him, he smiles and gives her a querying look.

'I was thinking about my husband,' she says.

'I see.'

A few minutes later they are walking through Beacon Hill. The tall, imposing houses of rich red brick, the ornate street-lights, the quaintly cobbled streets – all of these form the backdrop of distant memories for both of them. Estelle walks a half-pace ahead of him, her eyes clouding with recollection. Without speaking, he follows her through the narrow streets and into a broad, cobblestone road; the type of street he remembers well from his early days in Boston, delivering food in those first months and years, building his catering business from his brother-in-law's kitchen.

'It's here,' she says, and she turns to him with a smile of delight.

'What is?' he asks, looking round.

'Our house. My father's house. They'd moved here by the time I finished college, and I lived with them for two years. It was a fun time, let me tell you. My parents loved people. They were always entertaining. The parties! And dinners.'

'Sounds like a lot of cooking.'

She does not answer. Her eyes frown and she continues walking up the street towards her old home.

'What is it?'

'Nothing. We had a full-time cook,' she says. She stares at Alexander for a moment, with a look of concentration on her face, and then she shakes her head, as though throwing off a wild idea. As she stands before her old front door, she begins to tell him stories of her father and mother.

She is remembering those Beacon Hill dinner parties. The light, the abundance, the enjoyment. She realises now how much she misses the bustle of guests, the casual, lively inflow of people into the house for tea or drinks or dinner. Her mother did not cook. Few people did, when entertaining. They had a cook, or a house-keeper at least. And then, from time to time, her mother would engage a caterer. Someone she had found whose food was incredible, or so she told them. Estelle does not remember who it was, or even when it was, but a moment steals into her mind as Alexander asks her those questions. A moment of memory that she feels may not be real after all, may perhaps be an imaginative extension of what she has learned about Alexander's early work here. She sees in her mind the quiet excitement of the early evening, just before one particular party. She sees herself in a pale blue satin dress (can her memory be that good?), walking into the kitchen where Perpetua stands at the stove, stirring and arranging. Picking up a canapé. She remembers that, and complimenting Perpetua on it.

'Not me, Miss Estelle,' she can hear the cook saying. 'That gentleman there.'

She had looked at the back door, which hung open to the night, a block of black in the white, light wall of the kitchen, and she had seen the smudged, soft silhouette of a young man. That was all. She had not looked into his eyes, or seen his face, or spoken to him, and he was gone in a moment, leaving her with a polite smile on her face, before she turned to go back to their arriving guests.

It crosses his mind, briefly, that he may once have catered a party at her parents' house, until she tells him that they had had a cook. In truth, he cannot remember a single doorway or alley that he walked through all those years ago. Many of the houses look familiar in some respects, but many are similar to others, and the details have long been lost to him.

'We should go, Alexander. We'll be late for the show.'

He offers her his arm, and she takes it, as he points upwards. From the heavy, late-afternoon sky, soft curls of snow are tumbling down. She blinks against them, but the change in weather gives her a sense of satisfaction. The snow adds a new dimension to the quiet streets, dulling their footfalls and the sounds of traffic below, and gives a feeling of intimacy, as if they are the only people left in the world. Together they walk down the street, where the thin lamps are spreading fingers of diffuse yellow light above their heads, catching the soft swirl of snow in their beams, until they find a taxi. He holds open the door for her, listens to her voice giving the driver the theatre name. As he walks round to the other side of the car, something makes him stop and look back, up the winding street at the tall brick houses but, still, no clear memory comes back to him.

After the show they have to wait a few minutes for a table for supper, and Estelle pulls out her mobile phone and calls home, as Alexander tries valiantly not to listen.

'No, we're just having some supper, Frank. Won't be long. There are cold cuts in the fridge and fresh bread on the counter.' A pause. 'On the counter. No, the other one. By the stove.' She smiles thinly at Alexander. 'Okay. See you later.'

They are shown to their table, and as he waits for her to sit down, Alexander asks the question that has been in his mind all day. 'Does he know you're with me?'

'Yes.'

'And he doesn't mind?'

'Oh, I'm sure he does.' She smiles at him. 'You look confused.'

'Do you blame me?'

His eyes are clear and warm as they watch her; the soft lights thrown by candles and wall-lamps suit their deep brown colour and the firm contours of his face.

'Let me ask you something. Why didn't you go to Moscow?'

She sighs. 'Don't get all logical on me. I don't know what I'm doing any more, or why. If you really want to know, all I can tell you is that a few days ago we had a blow-up, Frank and I. No broken plates or anything . . .' She pauses, conscious that she is rambling. This depth of revelation about her marriage does not come easily to her. 'Anyway, he was upset about my writing ambitions, and about the trip to Russia, even though I told him you weren't going. And most of all, he was upset about you.'

He waits for her to continue.

'So, ever the understanding wife, I told him I wasn't sure I really cared about writing the damned novel. Not enough to fight with him all the time. Or have him carping and criticising over my shoulder. And that if he really begrudged me the trip to Moscow, I'd rather cancel it. And I told him that you had never been planning to go with us anyway.'

'And how much of all that is true?'

She laughs, but without humour. 'Just the last bit. That you were never part of the trip. And here's the funny thing. I think that's the only part he didn't believe. Because you didn't mention it to him when you met, and he sees you as an honest man.'

245

Alexander nods. 'Ah, yes. We met at his office last week.'

'Yes, thanks for getting round to telling me. He only mentioned it in passing, almost by mistake. Quite a secretive couple, the two of you. Anyway, the irony of the thing was that he liked you. A lot. Meaning, I think, that he could see why I like you. He thinks you're a passionate man. He's just concerned that you're becoming passionate about me.'

She can hardly believe she has said it, but those last words hang in the warm air between them like echoes. She sees him swallow, follows the constriction of his throat as he decides what to say. A waiter has approached them, has introduced himself, and is waiting for a response that does not come, for Alexander cannot look away from her. She glances up at the waiter and says something, she is not sure what, and he goes away. And then Alexander's hand is reaching across the table for hers, and she sees it as though she is watching the whole scene happening in a movie. Perhaps a script she has written, or would wish to write. His fingers are reassuring and tentative at the same time, and she holds them for just a few moments. And then she pulls away her hand. He takes his back, too, and picks up his menu.

'So, if you agreed to stop writing, and cancel Moscow, why are you sitting here with me?' His tone is curt. 'Surely cutting off our friendship was part of the deal too?'

'It was, in an unspoken kind of way. But then, having made all those concessions . . .'

'Sacrifices.'

She raises an eyebrow in acknowledgement, and continues. 'Anyway, as soon as I'd said all that, in fact, even while I was saying it, I realised it was all lies. I still wanted to write. I sure as hell wanted to go to Moscow. And I didn't want to lose you. As a friend.'

He feels tossed about, rocked emotionally, like a man struggling to control a small boat on a rough sea. A moment of bliss is followed by a fall from grace, and the pattern is repeated. Over dinner they have talked about other things – the play, the theatre in general; it is his way of trying to get back on an even keel, but it seems that nothing can restore his equanimity tonight. He is not happy with the food either. The scallops are overcooked, and too much seasoning has killed their inherent sweetness. He toys with them, as she finishes her meal.

'Will Lauren call you from Russia?' she asks.

He is not sure about this. Usually she would keep in touch, but she knows of his antipathy to the trip, and she may take that as a signal to lie low for a week.

'You know, she really just wants to help you. To maybe help you see that you were not the cause of Katya's death.'

'Lauren is a very kind person. She loves me, and hates to think of me suffering, and I think that has clouded her thinking up to now. The facts are that I defected, and left Katya there in mortal danger.'

'Did you have a choice?'

'I could have stayed with her.'

'But I thought they would have caught you both?'

He shrugs. 'Probably. But it was such a long shot, to try to get out the way we did. I was swept along, I never had time to think things through. She was so excited, and so desperate to leave, and I couldn't see another way. Neither of us could.' He finishes his wine, and refills their glasses. 'I remember feeling confused during that whole time. I was struggling – not only with the dangers we were facing, but with the fact that she had been betraying me, that the woman I trusted and loved had concealed a double life from me.'

'Were you angry?'

'Of course I was. But, you know, I never felt uncertain that she loved me. She went through a huge change to marry me. She had to find a way to balance her beliefs and her love for me. She was a brilliant, fearless woman. She questioned everything.'

'In what way?'

'In every way. She questioned the way things were run, the way people thought – and in the Soviet Union anyone who questioned anything was a potential traitor. Because they were thinking outside the usual parameters. And those parameters were hard to escape. We were so cut off from the outside world. From different countries, different cultures and beliefs. It's hard to imagine such insularity now. But Katya thought for herself. That's why she was always evolving, even at her young age. And that ability to think, to ask, to consider, is one of the great gifts she gave me.' He takes a drink of water. 'And in return, I left her there to perish.' He knows this is harsh, but he is melancholy and angry, and in the mood to be brutally flippant.

'That could hardly have been the case,' Estelle says.

'It's not far off,' he replies. 'What I did was unforgivable. A high-profile, total embarrassment for the government. And they wanted to punish me in the worst way, but I had asylum and they had no way of touching me. Except one.'

His eyes look older now, watery, and profoundly sad. Estelle does not know anything she can say to relieve him. 'They ruined your life,' she says softly.

'They did for a long while. It was hard to let go of it.'

'Have you managed yet?'

He looks up at her, uncertain of her meaning.

'To let go? Of Katya?'

'Does it matter?'

'Maybe. Maybe not. It may have stopped you moving on. It may still be stopping you,' she adds.

Once again, the lurch of emotion in his stomach. Is she trying to tell him something?

'What do you mean, Estelle?'

'I mean that it may be stopping you moving on with your life.'

He hears her, and hesitates, then decides he must ask the question, that he must know her meaning, or her desire, once and for all. 'You mean . . .' he says gently, 'with you?'

'With me?' she replies, and the negative tone of her voice is an icy shock to him. She shakes her head, trying to seem definite and succeeding, for he is not in control enough to read her well. In truth, his reminiscences of Katya, her brilliance, her dedication, her youth, her daring, have left Estelle feeling more than a little deficient and completely inadequate. She feels that she herself has none of those qualities, and in a life that is passing by faster with each day, she has little hope of cultivating them.

'No. I don't think so,' she says, with a firmness that is overcompensating for the uncertainty she feels inside. 'What is happening between us must find a different ending. But,' she adds, in a voice whose brightness and banality she immediately despises, 'there are plenty of fish in the sea.'

A few moments afterwards he leaves her at the table and makes his way to the bathroom. He feels unsteady, but forces himself to walk purposefully. At the mirror that is fixed over the row of frosted-glass basins, he stops and examines himself. He wishes that his pulse would not race whenever he sees her; that the intense look of her startling, intelligent eyes watching him would not make him lose his train of thought; that he could stop longing to spend more than just an hour or two in her company.

'Soap, sir?'

SHAMIM SARIF

Reflected beside him in the mirror is a young man of about Alexander's own height and weight. For an odd, head-spinning moment, he feels that he is looking at his younger self. He turns, hastily, to look behind, and the young man is there, in the flesh; no more an apparition than Alexander is. 'Excuse me?'

'Soap?' The young man indicates the basin next to him, which he has filled with warm water. He holds up the soap dispenser with an encouraging smile.

'Thank you,' Alexander says automatically, and holds out his hand. Methodically, he washes, rinses his hands and takes the small towel that the attendant now offers.

'Cologne, sir?' the young man asks.

Alexander regards him blankly.

'A splash of cologne, sir. For the ladies.'

'Ah.' Alexander looks down to see before him an array of colognes and fragrances lined up on a silver tray. The attendant waits a decent interval, then says kindly: 'My wife loves this one. Says it makes me irresistible.' He holds it up, poised to spray.

'Your wife?'

'Yes, sir,' he says, and under Alexander's keen gaze, a little colour comes up to his cheeks and his dark eyes smile.

Instinctively Alexander turns away, and leans down to the basin where he splashes his face with cold water. Quickly, correctly, the young man puts down the cologne, and hands him another towel. Alexander rubs it over his face, holding it over his eyes for a moment, because just then he does not want to look at the boy, at his flushed face and glowing looks. He can feel him waiting behind him, sensitive and aware, holding his breath, not wishing to disturb the troubled old man. Alexander removes the towel, and places it in the attendant's outstretched hand. He straightens his tie, and clears his throat. Quick as a flash, the boy picks up the scent again. Probably, Alexander

250

thinks, he feels I can use as much help as I can get. But he holds up a hand and does his best to smile. 'No, thank you. I just think . . . I think it's best just to leave everything as it is.'

'Good choice. You seem perfectly fine as you are, sir.'

'Thank you,' Alexander says. He hands the young man a five-dollar bill, and walks out.

Estelle wishes that, just once, she could arrive home to a welcoming apartment. One where the hall light is turned on, where perhaps some music is playing, where there is a comforting smell of hot toast or even flowers. A home where there is a sign of some life other than her own. She throws down her handbag, turns on the lights, deliberately walking from room to room, illuminating the whole place, except, of course, her husband's study. In the kitchen, she puts on a pot of coffee, and switches on the radio. She is irritable and restless, feeling badly for Alexander, and sorry for herself. She knows she is unlikely to see him again, and she feels deeply and surprisingly bereft, stripped of something vital.

She sits at the table without moving and waits for the coffee to brew. When she has poured herself a cup, and is flicking, unseeing, through the *Atlantic Monthly*, she hears the slow click of the door down the hall. Something within her stiffens, and she moves her head from side to side, easing a tension in her neck of which she has suddenly become aware. His steps come shuffling down the hall – for some years now, he has ceased to pick up his feet properly when walking – and then he is in the kitchen.

'Smells good,' he says. 'What is it? I'm hungry.'

'It's coffee,' she replies.

He sits down expectantly. In one hand he holds a sheaf of papers, which he does not offer her yet. She can read on his face a look of triumph and relief: it is the look that follows the satisfactory conclusion of a piece of criticism or writing he has been struggling with. Very soon, he will offer her the papers he is holding to read.

'It's nine thirty, Frank. Why didn't you eat?'

'I didn't know what to have.'

'I told you. On the phone. Cold cuts.'

A flicker of recognition. 'Ah, yes. I forgot. Just carried on working after we spoke.'

Stifling a sigh, she stands and goes to the fridge, where she takes out pickles, meat and bread, and she makes him up a plate, and pours him coffee. While she does this, he tells her what he has been doing – how he has broken through on the Joyce paper he has been working on, and how he is ready to have her read the first draft. He pushes the papers across to where she usually sits. She sees this from the corner of her eye, but does not look up. She is trying to swallow her bitterness. She does not want to pick up the paper, does not want to congratulate him, certainly does not want to struggle to read his abstruse prose right now. She almost smiles at the irony – she, who unwillingly spends eighty per cent of her time alone even when he is in the house with her, just wants to be left in peace. She places the plate before him but does not yet sit down.

'Don't you want to read it?' he asks, biting off a piece of bread.

'Maybe tomorrow.' She rubs a hand over her eyes. 'I'm tired. It's been a long day.'

This is where he could ask, if he wanted to, if it even occurred to him, what did you do, what did you eat for dinner, why are you tired? But there is nothing, of course: he is simply not used to asking, so he just nods, manfully trying to cover his disappointment.

'I'm going to bed, I think, Frank.'

He crunches into a pickle. 'I'll be in soon. I just want to tidy up the loose ends.' He slides the paper back to his side of the table and, within seconds, is absorbed in it again. She wishes him goodnight and goes out.

In the privacy of their room, she sinks down on to the bed for a few moments. Then she stands and, reaching up above the wardrobe, pulls out a worn, voluminous leather bag. Opening drawers and cupboards, she puts into it her favourite casual clothes and some spare toiletries. Then she snaps it shut and pushes it under the bed. Without undressing, she lies down on the bed and closes her eyes to think over the day that has just ended. Within a few minutes, she has fallen asleep.

Chapter Eighteen

Moscow, January 1959

KATYA HAS FELT indescribably different during the last few days. A feeling of radiance, of sheer weightlessness, has taken her over. It is as though her heavy, blood-filled organs and the solid muscle of her heart have been pulled out of her body and in their place is a suffusion of light. She has never before experienced it, and she knows it is happening because she has fully revealed herself to him: there is no longer any part of her that is cut off, sealed or contained.

In her tired grey office, she types letters for the headmistress, her fingers playing over the keys, their clatter soothing the swirl of her thoughts and tying her to the ground, to her everyday life, albeit with the slightest of threads. It is a pleasurable feeling, to be tugged down to earth now and then, for it throws into relief the freedom she feels in her heart. Svetlana is stealing more frequent glances than usual at her, for there is something irresistible about her face today, in the glowing smile that lurks within her dark eyes, and in the quick grace of her movements. When the bell rings, Katya smiles, and offers Svetlana a piece of chocolate, a treat to savour on the way home.

'Thank you.'

The girl is thrilled to receive such a gift from Katya. Since she has been married to Alexander, since she has become the wife of such a well-placed young politician, Svetlana has only admired her more. In her eyes, Katya has ascended to the highest level that any young Soviet girl can aspire to. Reverently, Svetlana takes the chocolate and holds it with her tongue against the roof of her mouth, very lightly, so that it will melt as slowly as possible.

Alexander's last hour at his desk drags, but he stays there, in his distraction, not wanting to draw attention to himself even by something as innocuous as leaving early with a headache. He massages his temples, his fingers pausing, then pulling lightly on his hair. What is he to do? With a strange irony, he has never been more sure of Katya and their relationship than he has in this past week, for he has felt at last that every crevice of her heart is wholly open to him. But he is sure of nothing else – there is not a waking moment when he is not turning over in his mind the arguments and ideas she has been sharing with him.

He, too, has disliked Stalin's regime, and the people who took part in it, although his willingness to face up to the harsh facts has increased since he met Katya. The burden of awareness has always been the problem; the sheer weight of acknowledgement – of mass starvation in the countryside, directly linked to insane collectivisation policies, of a rule of fear and terror in the cities, and of war and destruction everywhere – has often been too much for people to consider and digest. Easier to keep moving, keep working, keep concentrated on earning the next meal than to think too carefully about such nightmares and what lies behind them. But the problem for Alexander is that now there is a change: everyone can feel it. He remembers the first soft breath of it sweeping through the room at that party where he and Katya first met. The results of Khrushchev's carefully leaked speech to the closed congress. He trusts Nikita Sergeyevitch, even where he has been misguided or hurried, and even though there have been mistakes, terrible mistakes. There was the brutal, bloody Soviet response to the revolt in Hungary – a result of panic and confusion, not reasoning. And now the mass planting of corn in an attempt to emulate the cornfields of America. They all have the sense that Khrushchev's primary motivation is bravado, not necessity. Now they are struggling for bread, the people on the street, and they call him the *kukuriznik* – the maize freak. But his leader is working with a good will, even where his foresight may be lacking. Alexander feels that to be true. Books and magazines are being published now, American books and, more importantly, Russian ones. There are rumours that more are to come, books that tell of the hardships of the *gulag* and the war.

But, then, he has begun to question the whole Communist ethos. The seeds of that questioning had been within him, had been germinating through meetings and work that had been frustrating and often hopeless. But now he wonders if even a good leader and a good government can make something worthwhile of such a system. Oh, Katya, you have taught me to start thinking. And if every man starts to think for himself, and believe different things, how can such a system survive?

And yet the goals and ideas he has grown up with linger on. He always wanted to work for his country, to make a difference from within the existing framework of government. He had hoped that there would be more revolutions for the Soviet Union, but quiet ones. And things are progressing: there is more accountability, a little more respect for the individual.

'But they listen to us in our own apartment, Sasha.'

He does not recall when Katya said those words to him, but he hears them now as clearly as if she is standing in the room with him. He glances up at the imposing leather-covered double doors of his office, his head still resting on his hands, but of course no one is there. He sighs. Maybe she is right. Maybe it is time to make a difference from without. Perhaps it is the only way. Today, at work, he has found something out, some news that he has been dreading. She is in immediate danger. He rubs his head again. There is no way out of this place. And yet, if they stay, they will both end up in prison, or worse.

There is a knock on his door. It is Sergei, the departmental driver. 'Working late tonight, comrade?'

Alexander shakes his head, and gets up. 'I have a headache,' he says.

Sergei smiles, a brown-toothed smile, and puts his cap on his head. 'Then come, I'll take you home.'

In the soft cradle of the back seat, he sits quietly, mind blank, watching the mustard buildings of the central city blur past the window. The movement accentuates the throbbing in his temples so he faces forwards and watches the back of the driver's head. It is small, and fits Sergei's thin, small frame. The fragile bones and unformed muscles of a boy who grew up during the war, starved of even the most basic nutrients. There are so many like that, of a slightly unnatural height and shape. Sergei is from Leningrad, and suffered more than most in surviving the brutal German siege. He has told Alexander how his grandfather, who was already weak from old age, died within weeks of the food supplies being cut, and how his mother boiled the old man's shoes over and over again to make a soup from whatever goodness and flavour she could wring from the soaked leather. No one had much back then, but thanks to

Alexander's father's position, he got through it incomparably better than many other boys his age. When Germany attacked the Soviet Union in 1941, he and his family were evacuated with other government-related families to Kuibyshev. By the edge of the flowing Volga, Alexander lived with his parents and aunt in two small rooms. It was a strange, short interlude in his life, but they were kept safe, distanced from the worst traumas of the war. He puts away the recollections. He is tired, but the weariness is not physical.

There are long moments when he finds himself removed from the problems and issues that they are facing now, in these last days before his trip to America. Then his mind returns to Katya's betrayal, her lying. He finds himself thinking back to dinners they have had, evenings when he has waited for her to get back from the school and she has given him such detail about her day's work. At which of those times was she lying? Or omitting to tell him the things that really mattered to her? Which of his papers did she pick up from the hall table where he would leave them as he walked in some evenings? He pictures himself in the bath, and Katya outside, sliding documents from his bag, photographing them, or copying them, her eyes darting up now and then to the closed bathroom door. Her open smile when he emerges, clean and shaved. He is so regular in his routine that she must have been able to calculate to the minute the time she had for reading. For stealing.

He is staring out of the window at his own building, his eyes focused far away from it, when he realises that the car is stationary. He sits up abruptly, catching Sergei's amused look in the mirror and, taking up his neat pile of papers, he gets out. He leans down to the driver's window, which is open to the frosty evening. 'Thank you, Sergei,' he says.

The chauffeur smiles an acknowledgement, presses down on the accelerator and his tail-lights disappear into the thick, dark evening.

The main door is vast and old, and sometimes, in this cold, requires a push of the shoulder to open. Alexander slips in while it is just ajar, and continues up the stairs. He has lived in this block for nearly four years, and he has never before noticed the dark length of grain that snakes like a fine vein of feathers down the gritty, dirt-darkened wood of the banister. His hand slips along it as he walks. The whole day has been like this – he has been seeing very clearly, noticing that which he had not caught sight of before.

They will go to the Bolshoi tonight. He has had an invitation from his superiors, and they will dress up now, after work, he in a dark blue suit and tie, she in a fitted black dress. She does not wear the fur throws, overstated jewellery and overpowering scent that many of the other wives do, and by comparison she sometimes appears to the others to be underdressed or unfashionable, but to Alexander she always looks coolly elegant. After the ballet, which they will watch from the front stalls, or perhaps even from the box reserved for the Party leaders, they will have a glass of champagne with his boss and his colleagues under the brazen chandeliers of the Metropole Hotel; a drink that it would be impolite and impolitic to refuse. And so another evening will pass, another few of the precious last hours that they have together before his trip will be gone, wasted on people they do not want to see, in places where they do not wish to be.

The following night they visit his parents. They eat there, a robust meal, which Alexander helps his mother to complete. There are many dishes prepared this evening – borscht and meat and sausages and cheese – because this is a meal to celebrate Alexander's trip to America. He is leaving the following day, and his father is swelling with pride and pleasure that his son will accompany the deputy premier of the Soviet Union, will be part of such a prestigious delegation. Alexander does not know how he manages to do so but he smiles, and even laughs once or twice, and tries not to let the aching fear in his belly overcome him when his father hugs him and wishes him a safe journey there and home. *And home.*

'Well done, my son. This is everything I wished for you.' He grasps the back of Alexander's neck. 'It's everything I wished for myself too, but I am happier that it has worked out for you. Well done, Sasha, well done.'

Alexander hugs him back, feeling that he is betraying his father with every breath. If only you knew, Papa, if only you knew what I am planning to do. To walk away from all these opportunities that we are celebrating here tonight, to walk away from my work here in this government, the work that is making you so proud. He breathes in deeply, in an effort to control himself, and he takes in the smell of his father's shirt and skin. They are scents that were once familiar, but that now remind him only distantly of his boyhood. He wants to stare at his parents, to take in every last detail of their faces, their speech, their eyes – to commit them to a memory that will never fade, for after tomorrow that is all that will remain to him of these two people whom he has known longer than anyone else. His eyes fill, and he busies himself slicing more cheese and handing it round. When he reaches Katya's plate, he looks up at her, and she pauses in her chatter and smiles at him, encouragingly. The sight of her makes him feel worse, though, for he realises that spending this final night with his mother and father, attempting to hoard the details of their faces and characters for his future remembrance, is a luxury that she never had with her own parents.

'Cheer up, Sasha. America will be more fun than you can imagine.' Misha pats him on the back.

'Wish you were going, Misha?'

'Absolutely. I hear the women are—'

Katya hits his shoulder playfully, and they all laugh. Alexander is pleased that Misha has been able to join them. He has removed the burden of conversation from Alexander's shoulders and has made this a lively two hours, full of jokes and laughter. Katya is also in good spirits, has been so since the night of their talk, and Misha's laconic humour has been a good foil for her. Between them, they have entertained the Ivanovs, and kept at a distance the spectres hovering before Alexander's troubled eyes.

Now it is late, and Alexander and Katya walk home alone, spurning the two stops on the metro to have some peace and privacy among the few people who are out on the cold streets.

'You were quiet tonight,' she says, her eyes upon him, concerned. 'How is your headache?'

'Fine. Not very bad.' They walk a little further. 'Katya?'

'Yes, Sasha?'

'I'm afraid.'

'So am I. But everything will be fine, my love.'

His steps slow down and he waits for her to meet his eyes, and then, when he can see his own misgiving reflected in her anxious gaze, he speaks again. 'You don't understand. There was news at work yesterday. I haven't had time to tell you.' He pauses. 'They've caught someone.'

She takes a moment to digest this.

'Who?'

Alexander shrugs. 'No one's even supposed to know. The rumour is it's someone high up, working for the Americans.' A sorrowful laugh. 'It all seems so strange. Our lives. This catch-ing of spies. It's like one of those stories, "Red Leaves". It doesn't seem real.' He is referring to the series of articles about the outwitting and capture of American spies in the popular magazine *Ogoniek*.

'Everyone seems relieved now, but I'm worried,' he continues, with panic in his voice. 'That person will talk. Do you know anything about it, Katya?'

Misha was just at dinner with them. That is all she knows, and she breathes in the ice-laden air gratefully. There may be others who know her identity and her role – she cannot be sure – but at least it isn't Misha they've caught.

Katya shakes her head. 'I don't know what's happening.'

'It means they're getting closer.' He doesn't add 'to us'.

They hold hands, and both of them are quiet, thinking now of the practicalities of leaving. How do you plan to do the impossible? His part is undoubtedly the easier. He will leave the next day for Washington. It will be a long journey, one plane solely for the delegation. Once they arrive, he will behave well and carefully, for they will be assiduously chaperoned, and on the following evening there will be a banquet for all the diplomats and attendees. It is then that he must target someone, and quietly make known his wish to defect. He must do it then, must cross over that night, before any more time passes, for every day may bring his superiors closer to finding out who has been leaking information. In the meantime Katya will wait until the night of the banquet, then make arrangements with her contacts here to leave at once. And he will wait, with the Americans, for her to join him. And this is where his imagination goes blank. He knows she will bargain her way out by offering his information. But she has been able to tell him little else, and the timing is so important. He needs detail to feel secure, and now, in this most nerve-racking of times and hardest of decisions, he has none. Whom will she speak to, how will she escape, and when and where will they ever meet again?

'I don't think we can plan to move any more quickly than we have already,' she says, and there is a tone of query in her voice.

'No, I've just been thinking about it. I can't see how.'

'Good. Then we'll just think about the plan and wait and it'll be over with soon. So soon, Sasha. Within a few days. Less than that.' She is whispering to him now, and he tries to feel something of her optimism, or strength of purpose, but his fear is so intense at the thought of all that can go wrong that he feels himself shivering as they walk. Her hand snakes into his pocket and grasps his, through their gloves, and he squeezes it, but does not look at her. How can he leave her when he does not know what will happen to her?

Outside their building she steps on to a snow bank piled by the road. The surface is icy and brittle and her boots do not sink into it. Standing above him, her face is pink with cold, and her black eyes contain a glitter that seems to reflect the sparkling surface of the ice, refracted by yellow street-lamps. She looks different just now, like a stranger, and he feels a crisp chill clasp his heart, remembers again how deeply she has lied to him. But in America they can begin again. A life together, without threats or lies or pain.

'Will it be this cold in Washington?' she asks him.

'I don't know. Maybe not.'

'Take your galoshes and your gloves, just in case.'

'Yes.'

Inside the apartment, they shed coats, hats and gloves and she holds him, for a long few minutes, in the warm darkness of the kitchen. Then she goes to the bathroom. He hears the water running, her muttered words, perhaps complaining at the temperature, and the familiar sounds of her footsteps, and her undressing. He switches on the radio, turns it up loudly for the benefit of anyone who might be listening to them, and follows her in, having taken off his tie and belt and opened the top buttons of his shirt.

'You're bathing now?'

She steps out of her underwear, and she dips a foot into the water. 'It's late,' he says.

'I know. But I don't think I can sleep. Not right now. I feel so strange.'

She slides her body into the water and shuts her eyes. The bath is a little too small, so her knees are bent, emerging pale and bony from the warmth. He sits on the side of the bath, leans over and kisses an exposed knee. 'Why do you feel strange?' he asks.

Her eyes stay closed, but a single tear escapes on to her cheek. He leans forward to her. 'This is our last night together, for a while,' she whispers.

He is grateful for the last three words, clings to them as though they are a life-belt round his neck. He holds a hand over his eyes. He feels as though he is sinking. Outside, the radio is blaring the Soviet anthem. It must be midnight, and they have only another minute or two before the station closes down for the night.

'I can't bear it,' he whispers. 'I can't bear to leave without you.'

Her hand emerges, dripping, and takes his. His shirt cuffs get wet, and she pulls back, but he does not care about that now, and he grabs the hand again and will not let it go. Her fingers entwine with his and she sits up, so that she can grasp him properly. His head leans forward to hers and he breathes the words into her ear. 'I don't want to go. How will you manage? Can't I go with you?'

She shakes her head, a definitive movement, but her eyes hold understanding and sympathy for his anxiety. She whispers into his ear. 'You must go. It is our only hope. I'll arrange everything as soon as you've gone. Immediately.' She kisses his ear, with her cool, moist lips, and sits back in the bath.

He stands up and goes to the basin to wash. She is right, of course: they have been through it all already. She cannot arrange anything for herself until he is safely out, or he will be jeopardised.

And then, the details of her trip are uncertain, even for Katya – she does not know as yet what route she will take, where she will be hidden, how she will travel, until she has advice from those who will help her. But will they advise her well? He watches her in the small mirror, her eyes closed as she lies there in the water. Please keep safe, my Katyushka, he thinks. Please keep safe, and come to me soon.

Chapter Nineteen

Moscow, February 2001

SHEREMETYEVO AIRPORT IN Moscow has a dinginess to it that always seems to Lauren to be somehow fitting. At Passport Control, she turns to Melissa to say something, and the woman in the booth snaps at her to face forwards. Above them, a fluorescent tube casts an unforgiving light. Even this gives Lauren a small thrill. She knows it is one of the last vestiges of bureaucratic authority or state control that she will feel here in this city.

The National Hotel is one of the finest. The marble reception area and plush carpets lead up to bedrooms that lean towards opulence. Maroon velvet curtains and a view towards Red Square. Lauren looks out – electronic billboards dominate the paved square before them. Tourists mill out of the metro station below, or sit outside, drinking coffee. And beyond are proud statues, the towering onion domes and spires of St Basil's cathedral, the shapes and views that speak of the older city, the one she has always imagined and conjured from books.

When she turns back to the room, Melissa is sitting on the edge of the bed. A double bed. 'Do you want me to see if they can switch us to a twin?' Lauren asks.

'Not on my account.' Melissa holds Lauren's intent look briefly, then begins to unpack.

They eat their first dinner at the Pushkin restaurant, and the following lunch at the Central House of Writers, because Lauren has read about it in a novel, and they visit the Kremlin museums, where Lauren talks Melissa through some of the art works. She speaks shyly at first, giving only small bits of information, until Melissa asks more questions, drawing her subtly into longer explanations. Melissa finds that the golden, gilded churches, and the heavily exotic art are becoming much more fascinating to her than she would have imagined, because of Lauren's ability to illuminate them, to mix snippets of political history and social background with art history. She is also able to point out the different paints, textures or techniques used, and to tell Melissa why they were popular at the time, or what effect they were intended to achieve. It is a new world that she is slowly unlocking, a world of patient craft and devotion and inspiration, and Melissa takes it all in, her eyes intent on Lauren's face as she listens. She is experiencing a specific excitement, the kind of exhilaration she has always felt when learning something entirely new; from finding a new aspect of life opening to her. It is a pleasurable sensation, and one she has not known for some time.

The following day they meet the investigator who has taken on Lauren's brief. He appears like a throwback to another time – he has the rumpled, sleepy but sharp-eyed look of a fictional American private eye as he talks them through the hours he has worked and, at last, gives them the address he had found for Misha.

'Good luck,' says the detective. 'What do you want to learn from him?'

'We have questions about the old days. A long time ago.'

The man shrugs. 'I hope his memory is okay.' He makes a drinking motion with his hand. 'The guy looks shaky, you know?'

There is no telephone number, so they arrange for a guide who can also act as interpreter to come with them the following morning, and a stocky young man presents himself in the hotel lobby a little after ten o'clock, introducing himself as Boris.

Misha's apartment block is about half an hour from the hotel. They take the metro, Melissa marvelling at the stunning stations, carved from marble and stone, glowing with ornate chandeliers, inlaid with stained glass the colours of wine and jewels. Boris outlines the history of the stations for them.

'I thought people were starving in the thirties,' she says. 'How did the government have money to burn on this kind of thing?'

'They didn't,' Lauren replies, 'but they wanted to make a statement to the world. What amazing things socialism could achieve – the most spectacular underground system ever. Oh, and the tunnels would always come in handy as bomb shelters.'

'Dual purpose. I guess that justifies it,' says Melissa, with heavy irony.

But Lauren does not reply: she is thinking now about what she wants to ask Misha, and how she will approach the subject of Katya. She does not want to shock him, but will try to lead in gently once the greetings and catching up are over with. She is hardly aware that they have stopped before a building of sandy yellow brick. It is surrounded by others much the same, but on the ground level of this one is a restaurant. The windows of the kitchen and dining room are thrown open to the spring air, but a light haze of stale smoke hangs around the ceiling. At this time of the morning, the place looks deserted.

The guide hands Melissa the piece of paper with Misha's address on it, and starts up the stairwell.

'It should be here somewhere,' he assures them. They follow him through a dim, grey walkway that has a residual smell of old rubbish about it, and he finds the door. Lauren takes an audible breath, and Boris pauses with his hand poised to knock. 'Ready?'

She nods, and Melissa touches her back as if to reassure her. Boris taps politely, and they wait. There is nothing. He knocks again, then pounds on the wood with his fist. Now they hear someone grumbling, a shuffling on the other side of the door. It is flung open, and an old man peers at Boris. The guide asks the man his name.

'Mikhail Ardonov,' is the reply. 'Misha to my friends,' he adds. 'And to the ladies.' He speaks in Russian, and gives Melissa and Lauren a quick, appreciative glance before dissolving into a racking cough. His breath is eye-wateringly acidic, and Melissa turns her head away discreetly.

Boris has been given his instructions beforehand, and he explains that the two women are researching and wish to speak with him. After a couple of moments' conferring, they are led inside. The apartment is dark and damp-smelling, but over the staleness of the air, the tang of vodka persists, pervasive, almost antiseptic.

There are only three chairs in the living room so, somewhat gingerly, Boris sits on the floor. There is a greasiness to the carpet that has come from years of dirt and unmopped spillages, and there is one armchair that clearly belongs to Misha. It is covered in worn green velour, and the seat is caved in. The coffee-table beside it holds cigarettes, two finger-smudged vodka glasses, a newspaper and a remote control for the television.

The old man's chair faces Melissa, and it is to her that he directs his initial comments in Russian.

'Would you ask him if he speaks any English?' Melissa says to Boris. The question is relayed and Misha shakes his head.

270

'*Niet*. No. Good morning.' He adds, in a hearty bellow, 'Goodbye.'

'Very good,' comments Melissa.

'That's all he can say in English,' says Boris. 'Don't worry, that's why I'm here.'

Misha attempts to smooth back his hair, which is unruly and mostly black, though heavily and dramatically streaked with silver. He asks if the women are from England.

'No,' says Lauren. 'From America.'

Misha hums the opening bars of 'The Star-Spangled Banner'. Melissa sighs slightly.

'Where are you staying? One of the nice hotels, hey? The Metropole?' Lauren catches the trace of sarcasm in his tone.

'The National.'

Misha shrugs as if she is splitting hairs. 'It's been a long time since two such pretty women knocked at my door. What are you researching?'

Lauren clears her throat. 'I'm researching my aunt's life.'

'Your aunt? Why did you choose me to talk to?'

He looks at her, and as he does so, the end of his last sentence falters, so that Boris waits to see if there is anything else. But Misha has fallen silent, and is staring now, peering at the woman sitting to his right. He leans across and pushes the curtains further open, so that the room is brightened by the slanted sunlight. Lauren shifts a little in her chair, and watches him, taking in his yellowed skin, and gaunt cheeks. Now Misha's hand is reaching for his glass, and bringing it to his lips, but it is empty. Boris says something to him, offering water, perhaps, and Misha just holds out the glass. The guide takes it and disappears into the kitchen. When Misha opens his mouth, only a wheeze emerges.

'Are you okay, Mr Ardonov?'

Misha ignores Lauren and puts his fingers over his eyes. He seems reluctant to take them away but does so at last, for Boris is pushing a glass of water into his hand. Misha takes a sip, and speaks to the interpreter. 'She reminds me of someone. Someone I knew long ago.'

When Boris tells them this, Lauren can barely keep still. 'Who?' she asks.

Misha shakes off the question. 'Who are you?'

'I am Lauren Grinkov.'

There is a long silence. Misha sips his water, then stands up, throws the remainder of the liquid into the pot of a dying plant, and extracts a bottle of vodka from the bureau behind him. 'What do you want?'

'I want to talk about Katya. My aunt. I am her brother Yuri's daughter.'

'I don't remember anything from those days. It was a long time ago.'

Lauren glances at Melissa – this is not how she expected the meeting to progress.

'Mr Ardonov, we've come a long way,' Melissa says. 'If you could help us out, just a little?'

'You see,' adds Lauren, 'I'm very close to my uncle, Alexander. And it is him I'm concerned about.' They wait for Boris to translate.

'Sasha is alive?' Misha says, in almost a whisper.

'Yes, he is. He lives in Boston now. He was thinking about coming with us, but . . . Anyway, I have a letter for you. From him.'

She listens to the overlapping of Boris's translation, and waits expectantly, but there is no response.

'He's happy and well,' Lauren continues, 'but I feel he has never recovered from Katya's death. And a lot of that is because he does not fully know what happened to her. In fact, he blames himself for leaving her here, in danger. Not that he had much choice. From what we understand.'

Misha laughs mirthlessly. 'Everyone has choices in life. He ran off as quickly as he could.'

'So you do remember?' Melissa says. Immediately she asks Boris not to translate the remark, but Misha casts her a hostile glance – her tone is plain in any language.

Lauren speaks again, her voice even, her manner persuasive: 'The fact is that my uncle was gone, and you were Katya's best friend here. Is there anything you can tell me about the time leading up to her death? Did you see her, or talk to her?'

'I told you, I don't remember. This all happened thirty or forty years ago. And I have spent those forty years drinking too much vodka. And now the doctors tell me I don't have much time left. A few months, maybe. It kills the liver and then the brain, you know, vodka. And sometimes, if one has good luck, it kills the memory first.'

He stares off into the middle distance while Boris relays this to the women.

'I don't buy it,' says Melissa, quietly. 'He's sharp as a tack.'

'Then why would he be so difficult about talking to us?'

'Beats me. But he hasn't even looked at you since he noticed who you look like.'

Lauren indicates to Boris that she is ready for him to translate again. But before she says anything, she stands up and walks the two paces to Misha's chair. She squats down before the old man, so that he has nowhere to look except at her face. She speaks directly to Misha, and her voice is low, so that Boris has to concentrate hard to hear her.

'I know this must be difficult for you. But my aunt Katya is important to me too. I really need to know what happened to her.'

His eyes dart away, and fix down on his knees. There is a slight shake to his hand, which Lauren has not noticed until now.

'What difference does it make?' he says.

Lauren sighs. 'You sound just like my uncle. It could make all the difference in the world. Mr Ardonov – imagine being him. Imagine losing the love of your life, and then spending every day of your life blaming yourself for her death.'

He is looking straight at her now, with sharp, hollow eyes like caverns, almost devouring her features. The expression on his face shows the difficulty of the task he has set himself. Then, suddenly, a veined hand reaches up and pushes at Lauren's shoulder, almost putting her off-balance. She stands and takes a step back, shocked.

'You must leave now. I have nothing more to tell you.' His shaking hand goes to his glass again and he takes a drink. When he looks up, something in his face has hardened. 'Goodbye,' he adds harshly, in English.

Boris shrugs at Melissa and gets up, but Melissa waits for Lauren to make a move before she, too, stands. They pick up their bags and, after a moment's consideration, Lauren takes out a package and hands it to Misha. 'Here, Mr Ardonov. To say thank you for seeing us.' He does not reach for it, or even look at her, so she leaves it balanced on the edge of the table beside him. On top of the package, she lays the letter that Alexander has given her, and a card from their hotel. 'We're here for four more days. At the National. We leave on Saturday. If you decide you can remember anything.'

There is no response, so Boris thanks him and they leave.

For some time after they have gone, Misha sits motionless in his chair, watching dots of dust spiralling down through the same shaft of sunlight that revealed Katya's niece's face to him. Finally he takes another drink, and rips open the envelope. The note is short, but for a moment he leaves it on his lap where it falls, then flicks it open.

Misha—

It has been too long that we have not been in contact, and I am sorry for it. You will have met Lauren by now, and will know that she is Katya's niece. Perhaps you will have seen it in her face before she even explained. She is like a daughter to me – the daughter I wish I could have had with Katya. I know you will treat her well, but I ask you, in memory of our old, long friendship, to look after her and help her if you can in her quest to find out what happened to our Katyushka. There is not a day when I don't miss her, Misha. I know you must too. I also know you must have done all you could to help her, and I have never thanked you for that. I thank you now, my friend.

There are a couple more lines to the letter, but Misha does not read them. He crumples the note in his hand, drops it on the table beside him and puts a hand to his eyes, where tears are pooling. He cannot believe this. He can count on the fingers of one hand the times he has cried during his entire life. As if to divert his own attention, he roughly pulls open the brown paper on the package and leaves the hotel card where it falls, on the floor. The wrapping holds a frame, and when he turns it round, he finds a small brush-and-ink portrait of Katya, signed by Lauren. A tiny, animalistic sound is forced from him, almost involuntarily, for the likeness is incredible. He lets the picture drop on to his lap and covers his eyes again. His shoulders give an involuntary shake. Then, with a sudden force of emotion and energy, he picks up the frame and hurls it across the room. It bounces and lands face down on the dirty carpet, but does not break. Leaving it there, he staggers into the kitchen for more vodka.

*

The night-time darkness in the room is thick, unalleviated by any glow or shadow from outside, for the crimson velvet curtains are heavy and full. Lauren lies in bed, thankful for the blackness blanketing her. Her disappointment at the meeting with Misha is deep and the searing touch of it is only now receding. She wonders what it is about Katya that is so hard for the people who knew her to speak of. Beside her, Melissa shifts a little, and Lauren turns towards her. Her shape has become discernible now, as her eyes have adjusted to the darkness. Her back is to her, and she can see the slight rise and fall of her arm, moving with her gentle breathing.

Slowly, giving herself time to pull back if she wishes, Lauren reaches out her arm beneath the covers so that her hand lies almost flat on Melissa's back. She can feel a calm stillness in the body she is touching, so that she knows Melissa is awake and aware of her touch. Gently she lets her fingers move down her back, caressing the bare skin, feeling along the length of the spine to the hollow of her lower back. There is a shiver beneath her fingers, and she lets them rest there for a few long seconds. Then she traces a line upwards again, until she is stroking the base of Melissa's neck. Without another thought, Lauren shifts closer to her, and her lips follow the line her hand has just taken.

'Are you sure about this?' Melissa says quietly.

'Yes.'

Melissa says nothing more, and Lauren cannot trace her feelings. 'Do you want me to stop?' she asks.

Lightly, so that she will not disturb the subtle spell of this moment, Melissa turns so that her hands can reach up to enclose Lauren's face.

'No,' she says. 'Don't stop.'

*

276

For Melissa, the days have passed in a strange combination of heightened awareness and blurred confusion. Her laptop has been left untouched for the week, and her impressions of Moscow remain caught up with the sight, touch and scent of Lauren. She is perturbed by the feeling that she is slipping out of control, but there is also a new pleasure in even everyday sensations now that she does not want to give up. She takes a soothing gulp of black coffee and, through the doors of the restaurant, watches the occasional activity in the lobby. It is before seven o'clock in the morning, and too early for breakfast to be served, but she has found someone to bring her a pot of coffee. She is an early riser, always has been, and today she has been too restless to stay in bed alongside the slumbering Lauren. Their packing is almost complete, and they have several hours before their flight. She has a taste for solitude sometimes, for time alone to think things through, a trait she has inherited from her father.

The sound of talking attracts her attention as she savours the warmth of the cup in her hands. An old man is making his way past the doorman. He has been stopped because he is not well dressed; or, rather, his clothes are old and unwashed. But he is inside now, and moving towards the desk clerk. With a jolt, Melissa recognises Misha. She puts down her cup and goes out to the lobby, where she watches from a discreet distance. Misha is carrying a small, battered brown suitcase. He puts it on the counter before the disconcerted concierge, and the two men have a voluble discussion. The concierge appears reluctant to take the case, and makes Misha open it. He does so, finally, and she can make out nothing more than a small pile of clothes. The case is examined and snapped shut again. She hears Lauren's surname mentioned, and the concierge scribbles a note. Before he has finished writing, Misha is turning and walking back out through the lobby.

He has a slight limp from his hip, which makes him walk slowly, and Melissa watches him, computing, deciding. It takes only a second for her to hurry across and cut him off before he reaches the front entrance. He stares at her, then rolls his eyes as though he cannot believe his bad luck and tries to sidestep her. She is asking him to wait, saying that she must speak with him, and the doorman steps in to halt the old man. Misha stops with a frustrated gesture, looks furiously at Melissa, then barks something at her.

'He wants to know what you want with him,' the doorman obliges.

'I just want to talk to him. Will you ask him if he will have a cup of coffee with me?'

The request is forwarded, and Misha refuses vigorously.

'He says he must go. He is tired and old. You must please leave him alone.'

'I can't. Tell him I will follow him until he agrees to speak with me.'

Misha lets out a stream of bad-tempered invective that the doorman does not care to translate, and he takes a further step away from them, but Melissa has already slipped a fifty-dollar bill into the doorman's hand. With a quick, belligerent movement, he blocks the door and all but pushes Misha back inside. Melissa reaches for Misha's arm. It is thin and frail under his grimy grey jacket. 'Please,' she says. 'Just a few minutes.'

Misha sizes up the fit young man, then.

With an irritated sigh, walks towards the restaurant. Melissa follows, stopping to ask the concierge if he will translate for them. The man seems reluctant, but ventures out from behind his desk.

'Oh, and bring that suitcase with you,' Melissa says, pointing to the brown case that waits on the counter.

'It is for Miss Grinkov,' says the concierge, by way of asserting himself.

Melissa picks up the hotel phone and dials their room.

'I need you down in the restaurant. Quickly,' she says, and hangs up, anxious to ensure that Misha does not get away. But he is sitting sullenly at the first table, just inside the doors. She sits down beside him, with the concierge across from them. The suitcase has been left behind, she notes, but there will be time to deal with that later.

'Would you like coffee?' Melissa asks.

Misha glances at his watch, as though hoping he might be able to request a real drink. He waves a hand impatiently.

'What do you want?' the concierge asks Melissa on Misha's behalf.

'I want to know why you came here. What did you leave for Lauren?'

'It's there. Go and see if you want to.'

'Why didn't you ask to see Lauren?'

Misha's anger seems to seep away and his eyes hold a suggestion of sorrow, even fear. 'I just wanted to leave the case for her. That's all. I am a dying man, I had one last thing to do and now I have done it. Okay?'

His aggression has no effect whatsoever on Melissa's composure. 'Why didn't you ask to see Lauren?' she says again.

Misha looks at her, irritated, but his voice when he replies is lower this time. 'I don't want to see her face again.'

'Because she looks like Katya?'

Misha does not bother to reply. The concierge repeats the question, and he looks away.

'Why does that upset you so much? Why do you feel so terrible when you remember Katya?'

Still, Misha looks away, at the floor, but now the fierceness of his gaze is replaced with something deeper – again, that mixture of sadness and fear, Melissa feels. Behind the old man, Lauren has come into the restaurant. She has washed, and the hair round her face is damp, but her eyes still hold a haze of sleepiness. She looks at Misha in surprise. 'Mr Ardonov?'

Misha jumps in his chair. Lauren's hand goes to his back, soothing, reassuring, but her touch and her anxious gaze only seem to upset him more.

'Look at her,' Melissa says. She gestures to the concierge, who is watching in confusion, and has forgotten to translate.

Misha disregards the request. 'Tell him again,' instructs Melissa. 'Look at her. Look!'

He looks up. Lauren's face is just above his, her hand still on his shoulder, and he gazes into her eyes, takes in her nose and mouth and chin. His hand comes up and clutches at her arm. The pain and horror in his own face appalls the women as they watch.

'What is it?' Lauren asks quietly. 'What is it?'

Melissa is looking from Lauren to Misha, gauging. They are near a breakthrough of some kind, that much she can sense, but how not to let it slip away?

'You know something about her death, don't you?'

The concierge appears shocked, but she repeats the question and tells him to translate it. At last his eyes pull away from Lauren. They are watery, though whether with tears or the rheumy moistness of age and alcohol Melissa cannot tell.

'You know something.'

'Melissa . . .?'

'Trust me on this one,' Melissa says brusquely, and her eyes never leave Misha. 'She's Alexander's niece. Your best friend's niece. Don't you owe him and Katya that much?'

In the quiet of the vast room, they can hear only the clinking of plates being laid out.

'You're dying,' Melissa says softly, and he looks at her, a wounded glance, as if she has taken too low a shot at him. But she remains unfazed. 'You're dying,' she repeats. 'If you clear your conscience, what do you have to lose?'

Misha lets go of Lauren's arm. He mutters something to the concierge.

'He says he will have some coffee now.'

Melissa orders it from the waitress who is setting up tables at the other end of the room. Misha is speaking again.

'And he says you should sit down.' The concierge indicates a chair for Lauren. 'Because what he has to tell you may take a while, and now he is ready to talk.'

Chapter Twenty

Moscow, January 1959

KATYA HAS BEEN living on her nerves for the past two days. She is light-headed and a little fearful now that Alexander has left and his own anxiety is not there to balance her optimism. The café, at least, is warm, smoky and crowded, and the steam that collects on the windows to her right somehow gives her a feeling of reassurance and safety, as though the vapour is wrapping her up and enclosing her.

He will have arrived in Washington. In her mind, she has followed him through each possible hour of his day. Right now he should be at the opening banquet. It will be ending, or may already have ended, and this is when he will have made his move. A flicker of worry passes over her face, then she nods to herself. He will have already crossed over by now. He is safe and well, and waiting. That is all she must believe and remember. Now it is up to her. Across the table, Misha watches her, clear-eyed, as though reading her thoughts, and he smiles, a grin of encouragement.

She pours him more tea, and he helps himself to another spoonful of jam. Then he takes another, with a wink at her, and she laughs and pushes the saucer nearer to him. He leans forward again. 'So. Do you miss him?'

'Yes.'

'Already?' Misha laughs.

'I know, but I can't help it.'

The smile leaves his eyes and they look at each other, serious now. He is thinking about what she has told him, just now, here in this café, full of after-work drinkers. He had not seen any of it coming. That Sasha, of all people, has defected. Or is about to. That she is planning to join him, and needs help. And that this has been decided because someone has been caught, and does he know who it is? It has taken him some minutes to recover himself after the surprise of all this information, and to get his thoughts in order. He does not quite know what to do. He will have to take instructions, he will be forced to. She wants to leave now, needs to in fact, but he has explained to her that it is difficult to arrange things so quickly. And she has nodded, absently, almost without hearing him. She has that look of removal in her eyes now, as she watches him drink his tea. It is as though she has already gone, escaped. He can tell that there can be no persuading her to reconsider – she is too far gone to be brought back by any means. There is a lightness to her, an excitement, that he has never seen previously, and that makes her look more beautiful than he has ever noticed before. He puts his glass down on the tiny saucer, and reaches for her hand. It is an affectionate gesture, a touch between friends, and she will think nothing of it. He looks at the fingers lying in his palm, and he caresses them briefly with his thumb. If he holds on any longer, she will be uneasy about his touch, will feel at first that it is not quite appropriate, and then she will understand the depth of repressed emotion that lies behind it. She will pull away, embarrassed, confused, perhaps even repulsed by him. He lets go abruptly, and takes up his glass, draining the dark amber liquid. He looks at her again, and now his gaze is cooler and more distant, which is good. He is proud of himself. He has always been able to find the way to let go when he has needed to. 'I need to get things organised,' he says. 'Give me a couple of hours.'

This alarms her. 'No. The moment they know he's gone, they'll come and get me.'

'One hour, then. Meet me back here in an hour. You must prepare. You don't know how long and hard this journey is going to be.'

From beneath the table, she slides out a small brown suitcase. 'I am prepared. Here. This is everything I'm taking. I'll wait here. I feel better waiting here. If I go home, anything could happen.'

He watches her for a few moments, considering possibilities, thinking through the best strategy.

'You're right. Wait here then. I'll be as quick as I can.'

She stands up with him, and kisses his cheek.

'You should do what I'm doing, Misha. You should come with me.'

He laughs. 'Don't worry about me. I'll be fine.'

'But you must be in danger too.'

'I know how to handle myself, don't worry.'

She sighs at his bravado. 'An hour then?' she says.

He nods, and she waves as he leaves. She tries to look after him as he walks away, watching him through the window, but two men have left just after him and are blocking him from view. Anyway, the steam has risen so high on the glass that she cannot see properly. She rubs at the window with a finger and leans down to peer through it, but he is long gone now and, besides, it is snowing again. The flakes are banging against the window like demented moths, and even though she is inside she turns up her collar and shivers.

He is back in an hour, just as he promised. She stands up at once, in the smoky dankness of the café, and he offers her a drink, which she refuses, so he holds open the door for her. As they walk out on to the street, he takes her suitcase from her. Her eyes are darting, nervous, as she walks alongside him, watching him for a sign of where they are going.

'A safe-house,' he mutters. 'It will do for now.'

'And then?'

'Then I'll get you travel papers, and you can set off.'

She has a hundred other questions. Whose house is it? Which route will she take? When can she hope to make it out? But there will be time later for those questions to be asked. It is probable that Misha still needs to find the answers anyway.

Their pace is brisk, even fast, and it is hard for her to match his speed at first, especially through the slushy grey snow on the edges of the street. She aims her feet towards the centre of the pavements, where the snow is worn away. He gives her a sideways glance of encouragement, then veers off down a side road. She hurries to follow him.

'What do you have in here?' he asks, hefting the suitcase from one hand to another.

'Hardly anything. Clothes, the photograph of my parents, you know the one. And, Misha, I have to give you this.'

She pulls at his coat, forcing him to slow down. He is reluctant to do so, but her gesture is urgent – she wants to give him this while they are still alone, before they reach the safe-house. She glances around, but the street is a quiet one, on a gentle downhill slope, and there seems to be nobody about.

'What is it?' he asks.

She reaches inside her coat pocket and brings out a slim white envelope, which she holds out to him as he walks on. Alongside him, she sounds breathless. 'Here, take this, Misha.'

He takes his other hand out of his pocket and reaches for it. 'What is it?'

'A letter. For Sasha.'

Misha smiles and puts away his hand. 'Give it to him yourself.'

'In case I don't make it. In case anything goes wrong.'

For a moment, she thinks he has not heard her. He is striding onwards, his eyes intent and focused ahead, and now he turns into a smaller street. Buildings of light stone loom around them in the gloom. They both stop, glance around and up at the sky. Misha watches his breath puff out above him. 'It will all be fine,' he says at last.

'I know. But just in case,' she insists.

He looks over his shoulder, then quickly takes the letter and tucks it inside his shirt, then starts walking again. 'I don't know if I will ever see him again.'

She shrugs. 'You would get it to him eventually.'

'Would I throw up if I read it?' he asks, with a grin.

'Probably. It's just a love letter, Misha.'

They are walking more slowly now, in a thick evening darkness. They have turned again, and the alleyway where they are now has no street-lights, leaving only the surface glow of the snow to illuminate the atmosphere around them. Flakes are falling, slowly, languidly, and one catches on her eyelash. She blinks it away. 'Misha? You will be careful, won't you?'

He pauses to look at her, taking in her open, concerned face. 'You're the one who needs to be careful now, Katyushka.'

He seems nervous for her, Katya thinks. He probably knows even better than me how hard it will be to get out of here. 'You know what I mean,' she tells him. 'You're putting yourself at risk, helping me.'

Her hand is on his face, and her lips come up to kiss his cheek. There are no houses here, only a lonely patch of wasteground to one side. For a moment, she thinks she can smell the tiny wild flowers that grow there, the scent sweetening the evening air, before she remembers that it is snowing and that nothing can have grown in that cold, solid earth for months.

'Just be careful, Misha. I will be out of here, but you won't. And if they've caught someone already, they'll torture and threaten him until they make him talk.'

'I know.'

'I worry that that person will end up betraying you.' She is restless, and stamps her feet to keep warm. Then she takes a step further, as though encouraging him to start walking again, to get going. But he is not moving. He walks to the side of the alley, near a brick wall, and places her suitcase on the ground. She follows him there. 'Are we waiting here?' she asks.

He nods slightly, and takes her hand, drawing her closer to him. She can feel the warmth of him beneath his coat. She frowns: his heart is beating very quickly.

'Katya,' he says, in a hoarse whisper, 'I have to tell you something.'

His head is above hers, his face pressed down into her hair. He takes a breath, inhales her scent.

'What is it, Misha?' She tries not to pull away, but she is perturbed.

He bends his head and whispers in her ear. 'You should be careful that that person will not end up betraying you.'

She does not understand his words but, for the moment, it is as though words, and everyday signals and direct human communication are irrelevant. Something more primeval has taken her over. There is a strange sensation within her, an awareness of something terrible coming that cannot be averted, an almost preternatural sense of warning. She stands there, cold and yet warm, against Misha, and she can hardly believe the realisation that is coursing into her body. The downy hair at the nape of her neck is raised. His hand comes up, caressing her hair, and it is then that she feels the cold metallic muzzle against the side of her head. It slides against her ear and down to her chin.

'Misha?' she breathes.

He is whispering into her ear: 'I know, it's almost too ironic to be true. It was me that they got, you see, Katya? It was *me*. And now I have to help them.'

She is dizzy with shock and disbelief. This cannot be happening, not now, not today, not when she is so close to freedom, not from him. Without warning she finds herself choking on a sob. 'You *have* to, Misha?'

'Yes.'

'No, you don't. You don't.'

He moves her shoulders slightly, so that she knows to turn and look behind her. Some small distance away, a distance magnified by the snow and the darkness, she can see the smudged outlines of two men, watching them.

'They're KGB,' he says. 'My new permanent escorts.'

'How did they . . . How can you do this? You're not really going to, are you, Misha? Misha?'

There is a sound on the street that intersects the alleyway a hundred yards away. She waits, breathless, but they are young men down there, laughing and full of vodka, and they walk past. Even if anyone were to bother glancing into the alleyway, the air is too dark and the snow is falling too thickly for them to be seen. And even if they were seen . . . Misha's arm is round her waist, her body is held close to his, and anyone would think they were lovers, nothing more.

'Is Sasha out? Did they stop him?'

'He's out,' he says, with almost a sigh, and she feels relief, for his tone and voice are so familiar. 'And I wish you could have been too. Maybe you could have, if you hadn't chosen me to confide in just now.'

She is still in confusion. 'Who else could I . . .? You're the only one I know, Misha, the only one I trust. Trusted.' She makes a noise, a sound of bitterness.

'Well, they want to teach your husband a lesson. And you. They're angry, Katya. Very angry.'

She feels tears at the rims of her eyes, and they are painful. It is as though they are turning to ice before they can fall, mocking her sorrow. 'So it's me or you, isn't it?' she says. 'That's the choice they gave you.'

'I tried to keep you out of it . . . *You* came to *me*, remember?'

'Fucking bastard,' she says.

'Shut up.'

'No!' She sobs suddenly. 'I only want to get out of here and live, Misha. I don't care about the rest of it any more. About all this.'

She can hear the tears in her own voice, and her eyes are blurred with the salty water.

'Please, Misha, how can you let them win? After everything we've lived for, and believed in.' But he is pretending not to listen, she feels. Her breathing comes harder, for she is fearful that he will do it at any moment.

'Please don't kill me, Misha, please don't.' She pulls away a little, as much as he will let her. 'I don't want to smell your coat and your . . . smell, as you kill me,' she says.

This makes him stop, and she has a sense of respite. A moment to think. A second to imagine Sasha. In the back of her mind, she realises that today was one of the few days when she has not said to herself, 'Katya, you might die today. You might be killed today.' She has always been fully aware of death, and more so in recent times because of the nature of her work. Usually this thought comes to her before too much of the day has passed, and she always makes sure to focus on it, sometimes imagining possible deaths, and sometimes thinking of her misery at leaving Sasha. She hoards these thoughts consciously and regards them as talismans against the thing that has been thought of actually happening. But she does not remember having thought about her death today. She has been lax about it for many days now, swept away by her excitement and her hopes for the life they have to come. She has been so wrapped up in picturing Sasha and herself, away from here, away from the lies and deception, in love, happy and working, that she has forgotten to imagine the worst. And now look what has happened. Perhaps, she thinks, there is something to be said for superstition after all. Perhaps the fates do not like to be taken for granted. She wipes her eyes and nose on the sleeve of her coat.

'Misha, how can you betray me? And what we've been fighting for?'

'Shut up. Stop talking.'

'Why? Am I making you feel guilty?' With a swing of her fist, she hits him in the jaw, and tries to break free of him, but it is impossible. The men watching move forward, but then Misha hits her hard, on the side of her head. She staggers for a second, then straightens her thin shoulders and faces him. Her ears are ringing from the blow. He shoves her backwards, turning her so that she is facing the wall and he is standing close behind her. So that he doesn't have to see her face, she thinks. She fights a whimper that rises in her throat, because now she is truly terrified for she knows that it must happen. She tries not to panic, tries to keep an image of Alexander in her mind. He hits the top of her head, kicks the back of her knees, making her drop hard to the ground, kneeling.

'You fucking bastard. How can you, Misha? It's *me*. Please, Misha, just let me go. Please, I don't want to die like this.' This pitiful pleading will not move him, she knows, but she cannot think properly; she cannot stop herself crying.

There is no reply, but there is an inhuman sound from his mouth. Is it anguish or anger? He puts a foot on the back of her neck, and presses, with surprising control and gentleness, so that her head is pushed forward so far that beneath the wet snow she can smell the dirty tar of the alley, and the trails of old urine that have trickled down it for years.

'Let's just get this done, Katya.' It is anguish she hears in him.

'I have one thing to say,' she says, through her weeping. 'I'm pregnant, Misha.'

Why she has said it she does not know. He would never let her go because she is pregnant, but it has been in her mind all day. She has been waiting to say it to Sasha when they meet again; all afternoon she has been imagining the joy and excitement in his face when he hears it, and the words have been rolling around in the front of her mouth, waiting to be spoken aloud. And now she has spoken them.

'I thought you never wanted children.' Now his voice is harsh. He has switched off, and is pretending that it is not Katya under his boot and gun here in the filthy alley.

He is right. She had got pregnant despite her precautions, and she had always taken these for previously she had had no desire to bring a child into this world of theirs, a world in which she could see little hope. And then there was the burning mark of the loss of her parents. She has always known the risks associated with her work, of capture and death, and she has never wanted to leave her own child motherless, to put her own child through what she herself suffered.

When she had realised the reason for her nausea and her bloated stomach she had wished silently, in the late-night darkness of their bedroom, for a miscarriage. But that was before the hope of escape. Before the vision of a life with Sasha in another place, where it would be just them and their baby – no bugs, no cameras, nobody watching them, nobody for her to spy on. A place where she could fight Communism openly. She can hardly believe what is happening. She hates herself for ever wishing the baby dead, and now she is angry with herself, for she feels that she has brought this fate upon herself. It is irrational, but she feels it. Here, in this soiled, cold alley, she has been given the means for her tiny baby to die, and she has to die with it. She turns her head to the side and whispers, 'Misha, please, don't do it. You can help me. I don't want the baby to die. Come away with me. Let's make a run for it, right now, you and I. We'll go away together. You don't want to stay here working for the KGB for the rest of your life. Come with me. We'll live happily together. We can do it.'

She pauses, and he is still behind her. She can feel him wavering, she is sure of it. Something has touched a nerve. Perhaps, like her, he feels that, even if the odds are against them, he has nothing to lose by trying. Perhaps one more round of persuasion will clinch it.

'You and me?' he says softly.

She hesitates. Something strikes her as wrong, but before she can think about what it is, she speaks again, desperate to secure the advantage. 'Yes. You and me and Sasha, together. Think of it.'

He kicks her hard, this time between her shoulder-blades, and now she cannot breathe. She knows at once where she has made her mistake . . . 'and Sasha'. Now she sees with such clarity, as though a spotlight has been trained on him. He is in love with her. She sees it now, understands finally the desperate need she has sensed, but dismissed, in certain of his looks and touches. And by reminding him that she is going to Alexander, that she loves his best friend, that she is pregnant by him, she understands at once that she has just lost her last chance of evading death.

She rocks forward on her knees so that her forehead touches the dirty ground, and she waits for the spasm to pass. The kick has thoroughly winded her. Perhaps it is better if I pass out now, she thinks, before he shoots me, but instinctively her lungs fight for breath. Despite herself, she sobs. She wants to go home. She is scared of dying like this, like her parents, with a bullet that will explode through her brain, erasing her and her baby from the earth, leaving Sasha alone with the horror of it. It seems too hard that this black destiny should descend on her now, when they have come so close to the happiness they imagined together.

'Sasha,' she whispers. She pictures him in her head, which is pounding with fear. 'I love you, Sasha.'

Misha closes his finger round the trigger of the gun. This is taking too long. He is tempted, briefly, to pull her up and kiss her, to know at last how it would feel to have her lips on his, to taste her warm mouth and tongue with his own, to savour what Alexander has enjoyed for all this time without even thinking about it. But that will only make it harder than it is already. He closes his eyes and concentrates on the blackness that is revealed to him. He is blocking out sight, blocking thought, blocking all sense; but from somewhere he can hear a buzzing. His right ear is buzzing – from where Katya has hit him, probably. Misha keeps his eyes tightly shut a little longer, and pretends that the buzzing he hears is the distant sound of an aeroplane. He pictures it flying a straight course across an imaginary horizon. How he loved aeroplanes when he was a little boy. Little Misha. Keeping old newspaper cuttings of the first heroic Soviet pilots. Pictures of them in their beautiful planes, pictures of them meeting Comrade Stalin. With his classmates, he had watched them flying over Red Square on national holidays, had watched them being saluted by their leader, amid cheers. That was all he had ever wanted to do when he was young. Get into a cockpit, cheered by admiring crowds, and fly up into the grey sky, away from the city and high above the clouds where, his father had assured him, the sky was always blue.

He opens his eyes and glances down at the top of her head. His gaze is steady now, and cool, and he knows he has crossed the line in his mind, so that now she will give him no more trouble. Without another moment's thought, he pulls the trigger, twice, and stands back, dispassionate, as she slumps forward.

Chapter Twenty-one

Boston, February 2001

NEITHER OF THEM speaks much during the drive home from the airport. Throughout the long journey back they have been depressed and agitated by turns. They have talked about Misha's confession, examined his words from every angle, pieced together not only the facts of the case but the emotions of it too. Now, during the final leg of the journey home, it is as though all of that artificial nervous energy has drained from them. Lauren in particular is tense, upset. Each mile along the highway is only bringing her closer to Alexander, and she does not quite know how to tell him what they have learned.

'I feel like we've been away for months,' Melissa says.

'Missing the office?' Lauren asks.

'Sure, but that's not what I meant. I kind of got used to Moscow. Felt immersed in it, and in Katya. I think I'm still in shock.'

Lauren nods. 'I know.'

They turn off the highway and into the warren of back streets that leads directly to their neighbourhood.

'Do you want to have some dinner with us? I can pretty much guarantee that Uncle Alex will have an amazing meal waiting.'

'I'm sure he will. But it's late. And I think you'd better do this alone, don't you?'

'Yes.'

Melissa swings the car into Alexander's street and slows before the house. She gets out and helps Lauren up the front steps with her bags. As she hands her the last one, their hands touch. Melissa entwines her fingers with Lauren's and squeezes, then kisses her cheek. 'Good luck,' she says. 'Call me later and let me know how things are.'

Before she has driven away, Alexander has opened the door and is embracing his niece. He waves to Melissa, then helps Lauren into the house. 'So good to have you back. I have dinner all ready. Something light.'

'Smells great.'

She follows him into the kitchen, where he is all movement and energy.

When he looks at her, she is watching him with compassion, or is it pity? Something about her eyes causes a vague misgiving within, and when she asks him if she can have a quick shower before they eat, he is almost grateful for a few extra minutes to collect himself now that the excitement of her return is giving way to nervous tension – curiosity about what she might have found out.

'Go ahead,' he tells her. 'I need a few minutes to finish dinner anyway. And then I want to know about Moscow.'

She smiles, sensing the effort that he is making to take a distanced interest in her trip. He wipes his hands on a cloth. 'Go on. Then you can come back and tell me everything.'

'Moscow's looking more and more like downtown in any big US city,' Lauren says, as they eat. 'The ads, the coffee places, you know. At least part of it seems that way.'

'And the rest?'

'The rest of it still looks like the place of my imagination. The place I always visualised you living. Dramatic buildings, the churches you walk past where a group of people are chanting prayers, the old *babushkas* on the street corners, those solid grey Soviet buildings. The spires of the Kremlin. It's a strange combination.'

'You romanticise it too much.'

'Maybe. I can't help it.'

Alexander pushes away his plate. He has eaten less than half of the food on it, she notices. 'How are you, Uncle Alex?'

'Fine.'

'How's Estelle?'

Now his eyes avoid hers, and he stands up to load more salad into her bowl. 'I don't know. I saw her the day after you left. A week ago, nearly. We went to *My Fair Lady*. You should see it by the way.'

'Tell me. Something happened.'

He sits down, pinned there by her insight. 'Nothing, really. Without actually talking about it as such, she made it clear that she wasn't interested in pursuing any relationship with me. Not one that might trouble her husband.'

'Were you surprised?'

'No . . .' He pauses, hoping he will be excused from saying more, but she only waits. 'I guess I was somehow hoping for more from her. So I thought it best that we stop seeing each other altogether.'

'How does she feel about that?'

'I don't know. I got a note about a week ago. She said she was going out of town on her own for a few weeks. To get her bearings, think about things.'

'What things?'

'I have no idea. She wants to write, you know,' he adds, with warmth, 'but she seems somehow afraid of that man and his opinions.'

'The professor?'

Alexander nods. 'I don't think she even likes him. Maybe she loves him, from habit, or duty, but there's no passion.'

'Isn't passion a lot to expect after forty years?'

Alexander fixes her with a look that holds in it a weight of anger and sadness. 'I don't think so.'

She is silent, sorry for his distress, unsure of what to say.

'Without passion, what's the point of living?' he tells her, his tone still bristling with emotion. She nods, wanting to placate, wanting to understand.

'And Misha,' he says suddenly. 'Tell me, did you find him?'

'Yes,' she says, looking down. 'We did.'

It is nearly midnight when Lauren recounts the details of her journey over a dessert of chocolate cake, beginning with how the detective found Misha, then moving on to their first visit to his apartment. She does not hurry, for she wants time to carry her uncle slowly along with her, before the real story is thrust on him. She has no trouble managing this – despite all Alexander's previous protestations that he does not care about Russia and the details of what happened, he is hungry for facts, and descriptions, and sights, and every one of her impressions is of interest to him. He wants to know what Misha looks like, how he behaves – does he have the same sense of humour, what is his apartment like? All of these Lauren answers, obliging her uncle with her painter's eye for detail and nuance.

'So you learned nothing from him?'

Lauren catches an undertone of disappointment in his voice, and feels slightly sick. Of course, deep down, he was hoping that we would find something out; of course he has always secretly wanted every fragment of Katya that he can grasp hold of. That Lauren now has plenty to tell him does not make her feel any better. In all of her imagined outcomes, she had never dreamed that the story she discovered would be so difficult to tell.

'We learned nothing from him at first. He was very hostile to us, actually. Melissa noticed it more than me – she knew instinctively that he was hiding something under all that anger. I mean, I waltzed in there expecting to be received like a long-lost princess. His good friends' niece and all that. But instead he cut us dead. Threw us out of his apartment, practically.'

'How strange,' Alexander comments. Lauren agrees but moves on quickly, relating how she left Misha the letter and a brush-and-ink portrait of Katya – one that she had used as a study for the main portrait. At this Alexander stands up.

'Come, let's continue this in the living room. I have something to show you.'

She follows his neat, padding steps out of the kitchen – he has not bothered to clear their plates, an unusual oversight.

In the living room the curtains are still open to the blackness of the night beyond. And Katya's portrait is hanging there, on the large wall to their left. Although the size of the canvas is perfect for the space, she dominates the room, thinks Lauren.

'What do you think?'

She smiles. 'It's a good place to put it. But isn't it too much for you?'

He shakes his head. He had been worried about that – which was why it has taken him so many weeks to hang it. 'She was the most important person in my life for such a long time,' he says. 'I didn't want to be afraid of that any more.'

His simple sentence brings the threat of tears to Lauren's eyes, and she goes over to close the curtains, a task that gives her a few seconds to compose herself. She has a lot more to get through tonight.

They sit together before the empty fireplace, and she watches her uncle bend down to light the neatly built pile of kindling and logs. He is lean and economical in all of his movements. 'So you went back to see him?' Alexander asks, over his shoulder.

'No. I wasn't expecting to see him again. And then, on the day we left – this morning, in fact – a funny thing happened.'

Was it only this morning? she wonders. Her fatigue from a long day's travelling has been subsumed by the emotion and shock at the outcome of the morning's meeting with Misha. Alexander is watching her, patient, calm. He feels carried along in this whole current of events, but the feeling is not unpleasant. Not if he can keep balanced and sanguine, the way he feels now. Perhaps his relaxed air is only superficial, or perhaps it indicates a deeper peace with what Lauren has chosen to do – in any event, he is calm as he waits for her to continue. She puts her hand over his. Then she leans back and tells him how Melissa had caught Misha leaving something at the hotel for her, and how she had kept him there.

'What did he bring you?' Alexander asks.

'I'll get to that,' Lauren says.

She talks on, paying particular attention to Misha's reaction to her own resemblance to Katya. Melissa had told her that he had not wanted to see Lauren again, that he could not bear it, and that her arrival in the restaurant had been the beginning of his confession.

'Confession?' Alexander sits up, and now his surface calm has fragmented: without putting up the slightest fight, it has shattered like a barely frozen crust of ice on a puddle.

'He told us that he knew all along that Katya was working for the Americans. Because he worked with her.'

There is a pause while Alexander digests this. He is clearly stunned. 'Misha worked for the Americans?'

She nods. 'He was Katya's main contact for years. He recruited her, in fact. They worked closely together. For the most part, he used her to smuggle out research he was involved in at the Aviation Institute.'

'I can't believe this. It can't be true.'

'It is. They recruited him out of college apparently.'

She waits, allowing time for this to settle in Alexander's mind.

Her uncle is frowning, thinking, shaping ideas. 'So did he know her plans to escape? Did he try to help her?'

Lauren becomes aware that her lips are pursed, as though she is trying to avoid having to let out the next words she has to say. 'She told him. After you had left. In fact, she timed it as well as she could in the circumstances, just minutes after you had defected.'

'She knew I'd got out?'

'Not for sure. She hoped. Anyway, she didn't breathe a word to anyone until then, he says. Even him. She wanted to be as sure as she could that you were safe. But then she needed his help. And she told him that the government, or the KGB, had caught someone, and that she was worried that that person would talk and compromise Misha and herself.'

Alexander nods. 'That was why I left so quickly. The opportunity was there and we had to take it. Otherwise they would have found her.'

'Yes, they would have. They would have found both of you, Uncle Alex. You do know that, don't you?'

Her concern to reassure him and reinforce the point acts as an instant alert to his senses. His stomach sinks with misgiving at what she might be about to say. But, try as he might, he cannot weave a path through his thoughts and conjectures to prepare himself by imagining possible outcomes. He sits forwards in his chair, cradling his wine glass, waiting anxiously.

'Uncle Alex, it was him.'

'What?'

'It was Misha they'd caught.'

Now distant possibilities begin, vaguely, to jostle for position in his mind, but he cannot make sense of them. He has a small feeling of dread, like a small patch of acridity in his throat, but he cannot reason out why. 'But Misha was with us the night before I left. We had dinner with my parents, I'm sure of that. How could they have caught him?'

'They let him go.'

'Why?'

'Don't you see, Uncle Alex? He switched sides. To protect himself. He became a double agent.'

He says nothing; but his mouth is a tight line as he thinks over this revelation. 'Of course,' he says softly. 'Of course.'

She goes over to his chair and perches on the arm. Takes his wine out of his hand and places it alongside hers on the table. Her hand is on his back, and with bitterness she recalls touching Misha's bony shoulders, reassuring him in much the same way not so long ago.

Alexander can hardly speak, but he must articulate what he is thinking. 'Misha betrayed Katya?' is all he can get out, in a hoarse whisper.

She holds her uncle close, and pulls his head to her shoulder, as though trying to cocoon him, insulate him from her next words. 'Uncle Alex, he pulled the trigger.'

He is unresponsive – it is as though she has spoken in Chinese and he cannot fathom her meaning. He looks at her, his eyes wide, trusting, as if willing her to explain that what he just heard is a mistake.

Lauren is crying, she cannot help herself. 'Uncle Alex, he shot her himself.'

'No . . .' is all he can say, and then there is a moment of complete stillness in the room. All life and breath and sound and movement have ceased. And then the shoulders beneath her hands are shaking.

'Oh, God, Uncle Alex, I am so sorry. I thought you ought to know. I thought I had to tell you.'

She is holding him hard against her as he cries. She is helpless in the face of his grief, and has no idea what else to do. After a few minutes, to her relief, his shoulders stop moving and he just sits quietly, beneath her hands, composing himself. When he shifts she releases her hold on him. He is reaching into his pocket for a handkerchief. She stands and pokes the fire, and waits for him to finish wiping his face and blowing his nose behind her.

'Are you sure it's true? He told you this himself?'

She nods. 'I'm so sorry, Uncle Alex.'

'How could he?'

'I don't know,' she says. 'I don't know.'

He is sitting very still again. It is as though all life is draining from him.

'I'm sorry,' she repeats, 'sorry to tell you this.' She wants to find something to do to help him, any small thing, even though he is so far beyond relief, so she offers to fetch him some water. He acquiesces, but she hesitates, because his breath is short now, his chest moving too quickly. He nods again, and she hurries out.

In the cool darkness of the kitchen, the light of the open refrigerator door illuminates her face. As she reaches in for a cold bottle of water, she hears something. She stops, head up, listening. The noise comes again. A crash, something falling. Then another. She runs back, the bottle clutched in her hand, and throws open the living-room door.

He is standing up, almost panting now, and in his raised hand is a small vase. It appears that it is the only breakable thing in the room that is still in one piece. She throws the bottle on to the sofa, goes straight to him, takes the vase from his hand, and puts her arm round him. He sits down, covering his eyes.

'How could he? We were his best friends in the world. How could he?'

'I'm sorry, Uncle Alex.' There are shards of broken glass beneath her feet. She is a little fearful now, for she has never in her life seen him do anything remotely violent, and she does not know how to reach the part of him that is so wounded it cannot speak, only act.

'Don't be. I don't want to have another secret or another un-answered question in my life ever again.' He is shouting now. 'Do you understand? However hard it is, it's better than lies.'

She makes reassuring noises, but he cannot hear them. His eyes are everywhere, moving wildly. 'I have to kill him. I have to. For Katya's sake. And my own. I want him to know what she must have felt when he put the gun to her, the bastard. I want him to beg my forgiveness for taking her away. For taking her life from her when she was so young. How could he do it?' Tears of fury and frustration leak from his eyes. 'She had everything to live for, Lauren. We both did. He could have helped us.'

He sighs deeply, twice, and she senses that his rage is spent for now. Physically, he cannot continue without giving himself a heart attack. She sits next to him and holds him, trying to calm him. She does not know how she can go on with this story, although there is more to say. But can she really leave the next part for later?

'I miss her so much, Lauren,' he whispers. 'My poor Katyushka. What a way to die.'

She takes these last words as a sign that she must go through with the rest of it immediately. She checks that he is calmer, then leaves the room, and returns within a minute, weighted down by the small, light suitcase she is holding. She comes to where he sits and places it before him. 'Do you recognise this?'

He shakes his head.

'Misha says they gave him no choice but to kill her; and that she gave him no choice by confiding in him. But he says he's been consumed with guilt ever since . . .'

His voice is fierce. 'He could have helped her. He could have escaped with her. He was our *friend*, Lauren.'

'I know.'

'I'm glad I didn't come with you. I would have killed him myself.'

'If it's any consolation to you, he's been drinking himself to death for years now. Trying to forget what he did, I think. He's dying. He has a few months left at the most. I think that's what made him give me this.'

She picks up the case, rests it on her knees, and watches as realisation crosses his features. There is shadow over his face, as if his inner pain is somehow being reflected back darkly through his skin.

'It's not hers?' he whispers, nodding at the case.

'Yes.'

He reaches out for it, hands shaking, and she hands the case over, placing it gently on his lap. 'She had it with her when she . . . She was all packed to try to get out. He told her he was taking her to a safe-house.'

The click of the catch sounds deafening in the quiet room. Alexander slowly lifts the lid. On top of a small pile of clothes is a photograph in a tarnished silver frame. He picks it up and looks at it. Then he sets it down on the table before Lauren. 'Her parents. Your grandparents.'

She resists the impulse to take it and examine it. There will be time for that later. She looks respectfully at the photograph, then watches her uncle closely. In his hand he has a yellowed envelope that has been lying, sealed, just beneath the frame.

'She gave Misha that letter,' Lauren says, 'to give to you in case anything should happen to her. He put it away after he . . . after she died and has never looked at the case since. He says he couldn't stand to see it, and couldn't bring himself to throw it away. He said that keeping it in his house, knowing it was lying there, was his punishment these last decades.'

'There is no punishment hard enough for him,' Alexander says savagely. He holds the letter, passing his fingers over it, caressing it, a look of such seriousness and sorrow on his face that Lauren can hardly bear to watch him. Then, at last, he lifts it and hands it to her.

'Shall we keep it for later?' she asks. 'You've been through too much already tonight.'

'Please open it,' he says. She pulls open the envelope and slides out the thin paper. It crackles slightly as she unfolds it. Then she hands it back to him. 'It's in Russian,' she says redundantly.

He nods, and begins to read.

My darling Sasha
If you are reading this, I will not be with you. I may be in prison, or more probably, I will be dead. And I am full of tears, right now, just thinking of it. Believe me, Sasha, before I met you, I rarely cried. I could not, and would not. I allowed nothing to touch me so deeply, not after what happened to my parents. But now, I sit here with tears falling onto this paper, just at the thought that we might not live the rest of our lives together. What have you done to me?!

I'll tell you. You have made me real again. A real person, someone who is not afraid to be in love, to be angry, to be afraid. I am each of these things at almost every moment. But that anger is no longer my reason for living. The fear is only that you or I may not get out of here to a place where we can live together freely, and where we can tell everyone everything about what has happened in our country, loudly and without being silenced.

Which brings me to one other thing I wanted to tell you. If something has happened to me, Sasha, don't let it ruin you. Carry on well, as though we were with you. Did you read that part? 'We'. I am pregnant, my darling, and so full of hope for our little baby. I will always admire my parents, but their honesty left me an orphan – it was a hard childhood, and I am happy we are trying not to put our child through that. I am so happy we are trying to get out. I love you, and live to be with you again. But if that does not happen, I rely on you to live the life we dreamed of on my behalf.

Yours always

Katya

She thinks he has finished reading, but she cannot be sure. She is holding her breath, reluctant to make any sound or movement. The fire crackles like distant gunfire in the stillness around them. His head is still down. Something is about to happen, she can feel it, but just as she makes a move towards him, he makes a sound, an utterance that is beyond human or even animal, a noise that seems to have been ripped out of the very centre of him. The letter falls back into the suitcase, and his hands are lifting the clothes inside, lifting them up, and he is crushing them to his face, sobbing and trying to inhale the scent of his dead wife. He is rocking back and forth, still clinging to the clothes, his arms drawn up round his head and ears, as though seeking protection. The sounds he is making are new to her, and she never wants to hear them again – a distillation of sorrow, pure sadness and a deep raging that she cannot begin to reach. She sits, paralysed, on the edge of her chair. She cannot touch him or comfort him, so she just waits, helpless, and watches her uncle disintegrate before her.

Chapter Twenty-two

South Boston, 1960

THE SMELL OF fish – even the pickled fish they stock – makes Yuri's wife dizzy, she says. All that vinegar, she complains, evaporating into the air around her head. Yuri and Alexander laugh about it, and tease her. Today her complaining is defiant and loud, a challenge to her husband to listen. Yuri picks up a whole fillet of pickled herring, and chases her about the shop with it, around the central table piled with candles and cans, past the sweet counter, and behind the cheeses and meats. She runs from him, screaming and laughing, finally gaining the front door and throwing it open with such force that the shop bell rings for ten whole seconds. She disappears down the street, and will probably not come back for two hours, because they know she will keep running, and go to see her friend Lulu, who works at the hairdresser's on the next block.

Yuri comes back inside from the street where he has been watching her go and Alexander opens the big wooden barrel for him to put back the fish. 'Why do you torment her like that?' he asks.

'It's good for her. Anyway, she likes it. Women like a strong man, who gives them some trouble.'

'Chasing her with a pickled herring?'

'Whatever,' Yuri says, shrugging. 'She likes it. And it gives her an excuse to run away from her own shop, which she doesn't like, and sit and gossip with her friends.'

It is true that she prefers not to be tied to the shop. She is young and restless, and of little real help to Yuri, who seems to have recognised this long ago and has stopped trying to change her. So he is even more grateful for Alexander: his brother-in-law is conscientious and clean, and works hard. He is, Yuri thinks, always keen to prove himself an asset, and eager not to be thought a burden to them, as if such a thing would be possible in his sister's husband. His dead sister's husband. Yuri wipes down his countertops, and thinks about the day Alexander arrived at their door. Yuri had known at once that this man, whom he had never met, had loved his sister Katya well. He had understood the depth of Alexander's love because beyond his brother-in-law's polite words, and earnest tone, and uncomplicated appearance were his eyes, and when you looked into them you saw the clear, unseeing eyes of a dead man. Alexander, he realised at once, was a man for whom everything was now over.

In the months following his defection, Alexander had been investigated, interrogated and, finally, congratulated by the American government. He had his papers, and he had declined the offer, the pressure, of continuing work with the government, and he was then free to continue with his new life, except that he did not have one. Yuri had happily fed and clothed him, and he also put him to work in the shop, for if Alexander, despite his anguish, was willing to continue in the outward forms of living, Yuri decided that he would help him as much as possible. In truth he is grateful to Alexander for loving his sister. In the midst of his own grief at her death, he is relieved that she found happiness and love, even for such a short time. She had been a sensitive child, she had always felt everything deeply, and she suffered terribly after their parents' deaths. Yuri has always felt guilty for leaving her alone. He had been handed an opportunity to get out of the Soviet Union by travelling with the circus, but he had hesitated to take it because there was place for only one person, and she would have to stay. Katya, though, had encouraged him, even pushed him to go. 'In this place, Yuri,' she had told him, 'if you get a chance to do what you want, you must take it.'

He remembers leaving her at her workplace that day, after she had said this to him, and he had hurried away – he was late for work himself. He remembers he had found her gloves in his pocket as he ran, and he went back to give them to her, and he had found her crying alone, outside, over the fact of him going. She had only doubled her encouragement after that, and he had faltered, hating to leave her but in the end he had taken his chance. Now he welcomes the opportunity, which has been so unexpectedly thrown at him, to make amends to her by caring for her husband.

The two men stop talking to each other and chat to customers: there are now two in the shop. An old lady is buying bread from Yuri, complaining that the crust hurts her teeth. 'Are you sure you want it, then, Mrs Davis?' he asks, his tone teasing.

'Of course. It hurts, but it strengthens my teeth. Anything that hurts must be good for you, right?'

Not necessarily, thinks Alexander. He opens the barrel of fish for the other customer to look at. The vapours of vinegar, salt and the sea rise up and spread through the room. Your wife is right, Yuri, he thinks, while he waits for his customer to decide: the vinegar is strong. The man asks for a pound of the herring, so Alexander reaches in and pulls out the fish. Across the room, Mrs Davis is asking why they don't have cakes and pies.

'Alexander!' calls Yuri. 'Why don't we have cakes and pies?'

Alexander looks up. 'We don't make them.'

Yuri is enjoying teasing the old lady. 'Alexander! Why don't we make them?'

Alexander replaces the lid on the barrel, and puts the wrapped fish on the scales. Then he scribbles down the cost and the weight with a pencil on some waxed paper, and multiplies them, underlining twice the price that he arrives at.

'I don't know,' he says, and his tone has lost its bantering edge. Yuri looks at him. 'I don't know,' he repeats thoughtfully. 'Maybe I should try.'

'You like to cook, Sasha?' Yuri asks, placing the chosen loaf in the bag that the old lady is holding out for him.

Alexander shrugs. 'I used to. Though, what did we have there to cook with?'

'Don't remind me.' Yuri goes to the door, holds it open for the old woman and follows her out, where he stands looking at his fruit and vegetable displays, set up on trestle tables against the windows. 'These plums will have to go,' he calls in, 'after today.'

Alexander follows him out and catches the plum his brother-in-law tosses to him. They bite into the fruit, soft and overripe, and lean forward as they eat so that the juice will not fall on to their shirts or shoes.

'They are not bad,' Alexander tells him. 'Just soft.'

'They can't be sold.'

'No, but they can be cooked.'

Yuri laughs, but watches his brother-in-law closely. 'My God, were you serious?'

'Yes.'

'Another thing my wife will love you for,' smiles Yuri. Alexander waits for him to explain. 'Not only do you keep her out of the shop, now you want to keep her out of the kitchen.'

314

'She hates cooking, Yuri.'

'I know. So whatever ideas you have swimming around in that head of yours, go ahead and try them out. I won't stop you and, God knows, she won't. And if any of it is any good, we can sell it.'

'Good. Can I take them now?' Alexander asks, pointing at the plums.

'When we close, Sasha, when we close. We may still sell some, you know.'

Yuri pats him on the back, and the two men walk back inside. Wonderful, thinks Yuri, watching Alexander walk briskly ahead of him. Something else to occupy his time, and a good chance on top that we will get better food to eat.

It is two hours since they finished supper. Bowls of steaming vegetable soup and lots of thickly buttered bread. It is the first time that Alexander has gone into the kitchen to help his sister-in-law prepare the evening meal. She was disconcerted at first by his presence, but soon reconciled herself to it when he showed her how quickly and willingly he could chop the vegetables. He stirred and tasted, added salt and herbs, and persuaded her to go and wash her hair while he looked after the dinner. His soup was a great success: Yuri ate three bowls and secretly congratulated himself on his latest suggestion.

The house is quiet now. Yuri is reading beneath a weak lamp in the living room, with the wireless providing a low hum of dance music in the background. His wife has gone to bed. Alexander still sits in the kitchen, a cookbook open before him, a bowl of flour and butter by his side. He frowns as he reads, then abruptly stands up and plunges his hands into the bowl. He works the pieces of butter into the flour, lifting it high above the bowl and letting it fall. He rubs and sifts with his fingers, again and again and again, until he has before him a bowl full of fine crumbs. He consults the book

315

once more, then goes to the sink and fills a large spoon with cold water. He carries it back, carefully, to the bowl and pours it in. Again he repeats the movement, knowing he could easily take the bowl to the sink but somehow enjoying the extra steps, the effort, the concentration required to carry back the full spoon without losing a drop. Then he cracks an egg, and puts his hands once more into the bowl, turning and binding and pulling together. With some innate instinct he does not handle the dough much, but rolls it out lightly and places it in a buttered flan dish, which he fills with heavy, dried beans. Then he places it in the oven. He goes out to the living room, where Yuri looks at him over the top of his newspaper. 'Are you all right, Sasha?'

'Fine. I'm baking.'

Yuri looks back to his reading. 'He works, he cooks, he bakes. It will be a lucky woman who marries you!' Even as he finishes this last remark, he feels the pain emanating from the man standing before him. Yuri frowns. 'Sorry, Sasha, I didn't think . . .'

Alexander stops him with a raised hand, for he wishes that he did not feel such a light-hearted comment so deeply, and he hates to make himself into an object of pity. 'I have to go back to the kitchen,' he tells Yuri, his tone now deliberately ironic. 'My plums are waiting for me.'

From the refrigerator he takes another bowl, filled with the fruit, which he washes, then halves and sprinkles with sugar and a little cinnamon. He removes the pastry from the oven, pours out the beans, and places the soft fruit in the cooked case with care, piling up the layers. Over the top he lays some extra lengths of dough, in a lattice, brushes it with milk and sprinkles the whole pie with sugar. He pulls open the oven, slides it in, then stands watching the closed door as though expecting some sign. He turns his head towards the light that comes from Yuri's lamp, and it clicks off. He hears his brother-in-law rising heavily from his chair. Yuri's shadow falls into the kitchen, outlined against the soft light streaming in from the street-lamp. 'I'm going to bed.'

Alexander nods. 'Goodnight, Yuri.'

'Goodnight, Sasha. Sleep well.'

Alexander sits at the table, his chair pushed to one side, so that the streak of yellow light from the street falls next to him and not across him. He listens to the distant noises of the city night. Cars passing on the main street to the side of them, a siren fading in the distance. He hears some footfalls echoing up from the street below, and a woman's low, soothing voice, reading aloud, he thinks, in the apartment next to theirs. That voice somehow sharpens the dull ache that is always in his heart. He turns away his head, trying not to hear it, listening instead to the throb of the oven, baking the pie. But the voice is unrelenting, soft and musical, and he cannot block it out; nor does he want to now. He waits for a few minutes, listening hard, sitting with his head in his hands. The weight of his head seems huge to him now, and slowly, he lowers it on to the kitchen table so that his ear and cheek are resting on the warm grain of the wood. The pain of listening to that low, light voice is fine and excruciating, and just when he thinks he cannot bear it a moment longer, he makes himself visualise her, too, this unknown neighbour talking through the walls. He sees her, dark-haired and slim, like Katya, and in his mind she is reading a story to her baby, and the child he has invented is a miniature of her, long-lashed and beautiful, and already asleep. Now he imagines her turning out the lamp, closing the door with a click and walking softly into her own bedroom where someone she loves is waiting for her. Alexander stands up quickly: his stomach is churning and he feels he might vomit. He wants to cry, but he has cried so much in the past months that he feels all dried up inside, as though there is nothing left to weep out. A couple of lengths of pacing in the kitchen calms him, and he stops at the oven door, edges it open to look at the pie. It looks moist and delicious, and he closes the door and sits down at the table. The woman's voice is gone now, vanished like an hallucination, leaving only the sound of late-night traffic, and he is thankful for it.

'What do you mean, there are no more?' The woman stands, hands out in disbelief, staring at Yuri. He shifts from one foot to the other. 'We are sold out, Mrs Sachs,' he says.

The woman fingers her pearl necklace and taps a polished heel. She is most unhappy. 'I've been coming here every week for two months,' she says. 'That salmon is my signature dish. How can I have my friends over tonight without my salmon?'

Her reasoning seems flawless to her own ears, but it makes Alexander smile at the back of the shop.

'Perhaps for next week you'd like to reserve some?' asks Yuri.

'Next week? I need it now, not next week!'

Yuri's face is contorted with uncertainty. He hates to be faced with anyone shouting, which is why his wife gets away with anything she likes so long as she raises her voice.

Alexander comes out from behind his counter. 'I apologise, Mrs Sachs. We had a smaller delivery of salmon today, and I couldn't—'

'It's you?'

'I beg your pardon?'

'Who makes the fish?'

'I make all the food, yes.'

Mrs Sachs has lost her angry demeanour and is filled with interest now that she is faced with the man who can produce meals a hundred times more inviting than her own. She regards him as he stands there in his white apron. She takes in his short dark hair, a damp curl sticking to his wide forehead, his shadowed jaw and his huge brown eyes. He is not overly tall, but his leanness and erect posture give him a length of bone most unlike her husband's meagre stoop. She puts a hand to her wavy red hair and smiles. 'My,' she says. 'And all this time I thought a woman was producing all this food. I can't imagine.'

Alexander smiles briefly, and looks down at the counter, where a brisket of beef lies, ready for trimming and tying.

'What am I going to do about tonight's dinner?' she asks, a petulant sigh in her tone. He meets her look, and she touches her top lip nervously.

'There is a fishmonger on the next block,' he says. 'You can get the salmon there. If you like, I will write down the recipe for you. I can explain how—'

'I don't cook,' she says, with finality.

'Ah,' replies Alexander. He is tired, tempted to frown and hurry the woman out of the shop, but he tries to keep his temper. 'Then I have a new dish, which you may like. It is made with chicken, and has a cream and chive sauce . . .'

'Cream?'

He nods.

'With chicken?'

'Yes.'

'We're Jewish. No mixing meat and dairy.'

'I see.' Alexander smiles politely, and excuses himself.

'What if I ask you to cook the meal – the salmon, I mean – deliver it to my house, and prepare it to be served?'

Alexander stops short, and glances at Yuri, who shrugs.

'Now?'

'Right now.'

'It would cost too much,' says Alexander.

'For who?' Mrs Sachs laughs. 'You name the price, and I'll pay it.'

*

And so he begins. Three and a half hours that pass in a blur, but a happy, adrenaline-packed blur, and culminate in a three-course meal for eight people, prepared, cooled and packed. He makes the drive in Yuri's shuddering red Chevrolet to the lower end of Beacon Hill, a different city from the one he lives in, and he twists and turns up and down the steep streets by the quiet light, soft as butter, of old, ornate street lamps, until he finds Mrs Sachs's house. He gets out and knocks, then enquires to check that he is at the right place. He unloads all of the boxes and dishes, which are covered with crisp aluminium foil and heavy plates, and he carries them straight into the kitchen by the back entrance. Mrs Sachs and her housekeeper are there, one in a black cocktail dress, the other in a grey uniform.

'Wonderful!' Mrs Sachs cries. 'Here,' she says. 'You lay it all out here, on this table, and show Mrs Monks what goes with what.'

She disappears through a swinging door, and as it opens, Alexander can hear laughter dying in a distant room. 'The sauce,' he says, looking at the housekeeper. 'It needs heating.'

The woman evaluates the amount, reaches up to a rack of saucepans above their heads and takes one down.

'A very gentle heat. It shouldn't be hot, just warmed through.'

She nods and turns to the stove while Alexander unwraps the pieces of fish, and the dessert. As he does so he glances about the kitchen, at the rows and rows of pans floating above him – pans for every kind of kitchen work. The serving dishes, white with ornate gilded patterns around the edges, every single piece matching. Rows of utensils, shining silver under the lights, so many gleaming rows that he would not know what to do with most of them.

He bursts into the apartment with more life in him than Yuri has ever seen.

'How was it?'

'Wonderful.'

Yuri smiles and folds up his newspaper. 'She likes you. Mrs Sachs.'

Alexander ignores the comment. 'I like this work, Yuri.'

'You cook every day in the shop.'

'Yes, but tonight I decided a whole menu, and arranged it all on the most beautiful dishes, and she let me stay and make sure that everything was heated and served properly. It was like having those people in my own house.'

'If only you had a house like that! Good. I am happy that you are happy.'

'She asked me to do it again, next Saturday.'

Yuri grins approvingly. 'You know, you can start a good business this way.'

'*We* can.'

'No, Sasha, not me. I have enough to do. You can do the work for this one, and take the profits!'

Which is why Yuri wonders, three months later, why he should be up to his armpits in onions and garlic. True, his bank account is better than it has ever been, but what a price he pays! On days like this he goes to bed reeking of the pungent bulbs – all the milk and lemon juice and soap in the world will not help him – and his wife refuses to touch him. Or to let him near her. Alexander should be doing this job, Yuri thinks. He sleeps alone. No one will care what he smells like.

He leans forward and watches his brother-in-law narrowly, as he works in the kitchen. He sees the fingers and eyes working in perfect harmony, producing dishes that Yuri samples every night, and he knows that he is chopping the onions because he cannot do what Alexander is doing.

The cook looks up. 'Did you get the fresh herbs?'

Yuri wipes away a burning tear. 'Bradshaw is laughing at me. I asked him for fresh rosemary, and he said, "Who uses it fresh?" We have it dried, lots of it . . .'

'He can get it if he wants to. He finds the fruit and vegetables that we need, why not the herbs? Someone somewhere is growing them to dry them.'

'Not here. It's not warm enough.'

'Yuri!'

'Okay, okay. I'll tell him again tomorrow. You are too fussy. It will make your business harder to run.'

'It will make the difference between our business and everyone else's.'

'No one else is doing this!'

Alexander laughs. 'But they will. And we have to be far ahead of them when they do.'

Yuri complains again, but inwardly he is smiling. It's a good thing you made it to the States, Sasha, he muses. This way of thinking would have been wasted at home. With a sidelong glance he watches his brother-in-law at work, and Alexander knows he is being watched, but he feigns a lack of awareness. When Yuri least expects it, Alexander's eyes dart up and catch him, and Yuri smiles and looks away, although he has nothing to be embarrassed about. When he glances back, Alexander is still watching him intently.

'You know, just then . . .'

'What?'

'You looked just like Katya. With your head down, and your eyes . . .'

'I'm her brother.' Yuri shrugs, and he continues with his work, but he is pleased. It is the first time that Alexander has voluntarily mentioned her since he arrived. It must be a good sign, Yuri decides.

A sign that he is getting over it a bit. For no reason, except that he feels suddenly light-hearted and happy, he lobs a clove of garlic at Alexander. Alexander sees it coming, watches the clove's short arc through the air and, with a deft swipe of his sharp knife, halves it before it falls. Yuri laughs, and Alexander bows, sticks the tip of his knife into the wooden chopping board and goes to wash his hands.

Chapter Twenty-three

Boston, March 2001

THERE CAN BE no sleep for Alexander that night, or for many nights to come. The sheer force of emotion has drained him physically, leaving him knotted yet shapeless, as though his muscles and nerves are slack with exhaustion. Lauren takes him up to his bedroom, switches on his reading lamp, brings him water and tea, and he is aware of her moving around him, but his heart and mind are filled with nothing but Katya and Misha. Much later, in the weak light that precedes dawn, he persuades Lauren to go to bed. She is red-eyed from sleeplessness, travel-weary. Reluctantly she leaves him for a few hours, and she sleeps at once, a blank dreamless slumber, and when she wakes, feeling jet-lagged, she forces herself to step under a hot, reviving shower in order to get back to her uncle as quickly as possible.

She finds him in the kitchen, sitting at the table. Or, rather, he is slumped in his chair. She feels a small pain in her heart to see him like this. He does not even look up when she comes in, and when she walks round the table to sit across from him, she realises he has fallen asleep. He looks old now in a way she has never seen before, and the change has happened only hours after she has told him what she learned. Or perhaps it happened in moments. His hair seems lank, despite being short; his eyes and mouth are pursed and his skin is dry and grey.

He opens his eyes and gives her a fair attempt at a smile. 'How are you?' he asks.

'Worried about you.'

She gets up and hugs him, then moves around the kitchen preparing tea and toast. He is watching her; at least, his eyes are following her, but his mind is elsewhere, filling again with the hundreds of questions he has thought of during the night, the questions he has been waiting here to ask her.

'I need to know everything, Lauren,' he says. 'About how he killed her.'

To his dismay, tears are rising to his eyes again. Just saying those words brings back the grief that surrounds him like subtly suffocating fumes.

'I'll tell you whatever I know,' she says.

She is so grateful to Melissa, so pleased that she came with her to Moscow. Not only did she catch hold of Misha before he left the hotel, but after she broke through his silence and got him to talk she ensured that they heard as much detail as he could possibly provide. While Lauren herself sat hardly speaking, overwhelmed with what he had done, Melissa had gone on questioning him with delicacy and intelligence. Lauren had watched her working to fill in the details, to clarify every nuance and suggestion, to sift the reality of what had happened from any wishful thinking on Misha's part, to ensure that every last bitter drop was wrung from his memory. Later she had told Lauren that her subtle interrogation was done partly to satisfy herself that Misha was telling the truth, but mostly to ensure that when they came home, they would be able to give Alexander as much of the story as they could.

'What do you want to know?' Lauren asks gently.

'I want to know how she died. Exactly. How did he betray her? What did they say to each other? How did he do it? *How could he have done it?*'

So she tells him the story of Katya's final hours, as Misha had told it, and she also fills in the details that led up to it. How Misha had been caught by the KGB and he and his family threatened. That he had agreed to give up the names of other American spies in return for his life. That he said he had intended to protect Katya, until she came and asked him for help.

'Do you think that's true?'

'Who knows for sure? Maybe that's how he lives with himself. Pretends he really would have protected her. Blaming her for coming to him for help.'

'Why didn't he just help her? Why tell them?'

'He said they were watching and listening to his every move. Just by contacting him Katya threw suspicion on herself, and they were watching them when they met that day. She had her suitcase with her, it was too obvious. He felt he had no choice.'

Alexander has to grip his cup to stop his hand shaking. He feels incandescent, glowing inside, as if a fire is burning in his stomach, lit by pure rage.

'And then?' he says, and his teeth are clenched.

'And they told him to get rid of her, and followed him when he went back for her. She saw them just before the end, and she tried to persuade him to make a run for it. She tried everything to convince him.' Her voice drops. 'She even told him about the baby.'

He puts a hand over his eyes. She clears dishes for a few minutes, waiting until he is ready for her to continue. There is a loud bang behind her, and she turns to see that his fist has crashed to the table.

327

'He could have run with her,' he says, and his voice is loud. 'He could have tried. They might have caught them, probably they would have but, my God, was it better to stay and live whatever sham of a life he's lived for the last forty years? He could have tried to save her and get out himself. He could have made it out and lived with us . . .'

'That's the other thing.'

He looks up at her, waiting.

'One of the last things he admitted was that he loved Katya.'

At his core, he understands the full implication of this statement at once, but there is something in his mind that prevents him acknowledging it. The betrayal so far, all the revelations, have been so spectacular that he almost wills this one to be a mistake.

'He was her best friend,' he says, with exaggerated calm. 'He should have loved her.'

'No, I mean he was in love with her.'

He looks at Lauren, sadly, helplessly.

'He'd always loved her, for years. And I think watching you and Katya together, so happy, drove him crazy.'

Alexander is thinking back – there are so many years to cross, so many later memories to push through – to any time when he could ever have had the smallest clue that Misha was in love with Katya. He can recall many vague situations, words, gestures, glances, smiles. Misha was always physically demonstrative with both of them, but perhaps Alexander had never wanted to consider that his hugs and friendly teasing of his wife hid a deeper passion. He cannot pick out details – this part of his past is so far away and his memory is simply not good enough – but, somehow, all of this revelation about Misha is not quite as surprising as it should be. Just as Katya's confession of her betrayal had allowed him to feel a certain parallel reality clicking into place, even as it shocked him.

'Why didn't he go after her himself?'

'Because she never wanted him. She wasn't interested, and he wouldn't chase any woman. They chased him, apparently.'

Alexander nods his assent.

'She was never interested in anyone except you, and he hated that. He tried to keep her on track, to push her to marry you just to spy on you, but all the time she was falling more and more in love with you, and turning away from the work he had trained her to do, that she had always wanted to do. After you got married, she refused to do it any more, and he had to blackmail her into it.'

'She told me she had been blackmailed, but I never knew it was *him*.'

'Yes. He had made her steal papers from you when you first met, and he held that over her. She was so scared she'd lose you that it worked, for a while anyway. But he never counted on her loving you enough to confess everything. It drove him crazy that any man could have this effect on her, especially when it wasn't him. By the time you defected he resented you horribly. There was something she said to him, in the last moments, he can't even remember what exactly, something about you, and he felt again how much she adored you, and he says he just felt a blind rage, and it helped him to – to do it.'

Alexander is crying again, silently, except for a slight choking noise. She feels she should stop speaking, but there is one more thing that she hasn't told him, that she knows must be said.

'Her last words were about you, Uncle Alex. She said, "I love you, Sasha." That was the last thing he heard her say.'

Her eyes are so full that her uncle is a blur to her. She grips his hand, and feels him shuddering. His tears are falling in round drops on to the bare wood of the table where they sit, heavy and pooled, as though they will never soak away.

*

After a week, Lauren calls the doctor. During this time, Alexander has been in his bed; he has hardly eaten and hardly spoken. The doctor's tests, as much as Alexander will allow them, show him to be healthy. Lauren sees the doctor out, and goes back upstairs with some soup. Her uncle is sleeping again, has been sleeping most of the days. She hears him sometimes at night, padding about the house. She sits on the edge of the bed and strokes his head. Then she shakes him awake and offers him the soup.

'Thank you,' he says, and he sits up.

'Why don't you go and freshen up, then come downstairs and eat with me?'

'Okay.' He gets out of bed and, pleased with herself, she carries the soup downstairs, and hears him running the shower. But forty minutes later, when he has not joined her, she runs up again to find that he is back in bed, asleep. He has changed his pyjamas and combed his damp hair, but has not bothered to shave. With a sigh she checks her watch. She will wake him again in an hour and try to get him to eat.

'And Estelle? Where is she through all this?' Lauren asks. She is walking with Melissa towards the car, on their way out to dinner.

'In Concord. Not far. She's always loved the little inn there, and that's where she's been staying.'

'Does your father know?'

'Sure. She's been calling him now and then to check in.' Melissa gives a wry smile. 'She can't even leave him properly.'

'Are you sure about that? What if she does leave? What if he ends up losing her?'

'That's the risk he's always taken, I guess. How long can you treat someone offhandedly and get away with it? Maybe for ever.'

'Maybe not,' replies Lauren, sharply.

330

Melissa knows that her father misses her mother, but his routines of living are so defined, and involve Estelle so little, that he can continue practising them with little disruption. Melissa has been buying for him the type of cold food that needs little preparation – she knows that eventually, when he becomes hungry enough, he will remember to come out to the kitchen and eat it. She has felt a chill, standing there in the deserted kitchen of the silent apartment, her father sequestered in his study, unable to reach out for her mother, or even to say anything about what is occurring to his daughter. During the time she was growing up, her father's path always struck her as containing an element of nobility – that devotion to his books, to study, to the delineating of original thought; the passion that was not circumscribed in any way, even by wife and family. But in the last few days, it has appeared to her as a cold, self-absorbed existence, filled with a kind of ultimate loneliness. Perhaps that is simply her own projection, and something of which he is not even aware, but nevertheless the sense of it lies strongly within her, and she finds that she dislikes it intensely.

Lauren gets into the car. 'Can you do me a favour?' she asks. 'Call up Uncle Alex and get him back into working on this deal with you.'

'I hate to push him on that after what he's been through. The deal will wait.'

Lauren is grateful for this, for she knows Melissa was working closely with her uncle just before the trip to Moscow and is impatient to complete the sale – but she is also wondering if a reminder of his other life, his working life, would not be a kind of relief to Alexander at this point. 'He's becoming more and more depressed. I just think it might help. Even a short meeting, here and there.'

'He probably needs more time. But if you want me to, I'll try.'

'Please,' says Lauren. 'He'll be reluctant at first. You'll have to be aggressive about it. Pushy, even.'

'Pushy? *Moi?*' smiles Melissa. Lauren leans over to kiss her.

'I know. Hard to imagine,' she says drily. 'But give it your best shot.'

Alexander has always wondered whether flying out of the Soviet Union with that delegation, leaving Katya behind to try to follow him, was the greatest mistake of his life. He cannot be sure, no one can about such things, because he can never know for certain what the alternative outcome would have been, what would have happened had he stayed. Would they both have been captured and killed, or imprisoned? Would she have been tortured? Would Katya have somehow pulled Misha over to their side and would they have escaped together? The possibilities, likely or unlikely, unfold themselves in his overwrought imagination, forming ever-lengthening, tangled strands. What he does know is that he would have liked to be there with her, would have felt less helpless, more able to try to protect her from harm. To be in America was not simply to be in a separate country from the Soviet Union; rather, it was like being in another universe. There could be no contact, no communication, no news, nothing. Just silence, and then smuggled information filtering through slowly and unreliably. Such isolation he had felt when he learned of her death: not only was she gone but there was no detail, no body for him to grieve over and no one to tell him the terrible story of what had happened. Until now.

Over the years he has imagined countless deaths for her. In his mind he has watched her lose her life over and over and over again, in different ways, all violent, all terrifying. He has been haunted by her last moments, even though he has never known what they were. The most bearable versions of the sickening visions that he has put himself through show her death to be quick. A bullet that she did not know was coming. The idea that she might be aware, caught, tortured – that she would have to wait, knowing what was going to happen to her, is intolerable to him, and yet he has forced himself to tolerate it, day after day, year after year. But now he knows. He knows the details of those last, long minutes, and the idea of Misha, and of Katya's misery and fear, is all he dreams of now, and what he thinks of most often when he is awake.

He spends long hours in the night sitting in the dark under the cool gaze of Katya's portrait. It is a refinement of the agony for him to think about these things while he sees her face right before him, and her eyes upon his. It makes the pain almost unendurable, but not quite; for in the end he is able to sit there, enduring it. He talks to her sometimes, always reverting to the Russian language he has not used for so many years, and after a while he hears her reply to him, and her answers are always kind and well thought-out. It is as if he has trained himself to think and feel as she would, so that he can have some semblance of the dialogue that he has craved for so long. He begs her forgiveness and she accepts his plea, but then he remembers her letter, that last, beautiful letter, and he knows that she does not want his apologies. He knows every word by heart, knows the curve and fall of the letters that her hand wrote; he has traced the lines with his eyes and fingers so many times that he cannot remember ever not knowing the words. There is much in that letter that has made him cry over what she gave up and what she lost – *I am so full of hope for our baby . . . I live to be with you again* – But there is also enough within it to remind him, during these dark, silent days and nights, that she wrote it for a reason. For him to keep and to live by if she were to fail in her attempt to reach him. It is harder for him to recall and consider these parts: *we can tell the truth about our country . . . I rely on you to live the life we dreamed of.*

Has he lived that life well? He tells her, during the nights that pass, of everything he has done with his business. How he has built a career from cooking and food, from the things that he always loved and was good at. How he has set up foundations to help others do the same thing. That he is as a father to Lauren, and how proud of her he is and how happy. It has been a good, full life, but he is conscious now that he has always avoided Katya's death and the reasons for it. He has tried to keep everything that happened to her, and everything associated with their old lives, at a distance. He has not told the truth. He has not lied, but he has never been prepared to face up to the reality of the world he came from and to speak about it openly and widely. Rather, he has kept quietly within him that void where Katya should have been. That this void exists and has always existed is simply the case, as far as he has always known. For forty years he has assumed it to be an unchangeable fact, like the relentless spinning of the earth. But now for the first time, in the light of his wife's words, he understands that he has not continued the work she was so driven to do, and he considers whether she would be happy to see his heart still sealed off and guilty and unspoken, so many years later.

He is far from ready to return to work. In truth, his business and its sale mean comparatively little to him at this time, and he tells Melissa this directly and honestly. He cannot imagine a time in the near future when he will feel able to think of it, so he suggests that she continues to work out a deal with Lauren, and to Lauren he repeats the same thing, assuring her that his finance officers and directors will help her.

'What do you think?' Lauren asks Melissa.

'I think, forget about it.'

'You don't want the company any more?'

'Oh, I want it all right,' Melissa tells her, 'but in any negotiation I will eat you alive. And the directors. You won't get a good deal.'

Lauren cannot help but smile. 'So why not just give me a fair one? It's up to you."

Melissa tries to explain. Her business success until now has been based on making a series of deals weighted in her favour, so that the risk was always lower than usual. Throughout it all she has prided herself on never taking anyone for a ride. She has always been upfront about the deal she requires and if the other side accepts it, at least they know what they're signing.

This preamble confuses Lauren somewhat. 'Why would anyone sign a deal that was bad for them?'

'I'm not saying bad, just not great.'

'Whatever. Why would they?'

'Usually desperation. A company might be on the verge of bankruptcy, for example, so they need to sell fast. Occasionally it can be ignorance. Someone might not recognise that you're offering below the odds.'

Melissa watches Lauren's face. Her reaction is uncertain, but has a definite edge of distaste. For that is what I do, Melissa thinks. Something that is distasteful; at least, it seems that way to her here and now, with Lauren.

'Anyway,' she continues, 'I don't want to work like that any more. I don't think it's wrong, necessarily, but I want to try something new. Maybe it would be nice to look at a company as a business to build and grow, instead of a stack of pieces that can be dismantled and sold for more than the sum of the parts. And in this case, because you are both insisting on things like the charity stuff, there is really no other way to do it.'

Lauren looks relieved. 'Good. Then we can work this thing out, right?'

'No. We can talk about scenarios. Especially how we can keep the philanthropy going, without me losing too much of my margins. Maybe you or Alexander should maintain a stake. I'm not sure. But we'll talk. And then we'll wait. When your uncle is ready to do this, or when he appoints someone as good as he is to advise you, we'll complete.' Melissa smiles. 'I have no intention of giving you a bad deal, Lauren, but this is business, and I don't want you to wonder one day if you really did get the best deal. I don't want what happens here to come between us personally. I'd rather lose the company.'

It is perhaps the least romantic declaration Lauren has ever heard in her life, but she knows it represents a huge step forward for Melissa in every way.

'Thank you,' Lauren tells her.

The courtyard feels surprisingly familiar and comforting. He had assumed that the many weeks that he has been away and the violent emotional storms that he has been through would have made his old offices and the business that he is preparing to sell seem alien and unimportant to him. Alexander looks up at the glass and steel structures that rise up from the paved slabs, at the windows that used to be his, the boardroom from which he did so much of his work. A glance at his watch propels him forwards, to his meeting with Melissa, and he strides into the building and up to the banks of elevators.

'Glad you could make it,' Melissa says, when he knocks on the open door of the boardroom, and she takes the hand he holds out, but also leans to kiss his cheek.

'It's good to be back,' he says, without thinking. It is an automatic, unconsidered reply, but he finds, to his surprise, that it is true. The hum of conversations and computers, the relaxed air of the staff – he has missed all of this, at least a little, and it is good, after all, to be out of the house and thinking of something else.

His afternoon passes quickly, for Melissa has piled up an agenda for him that leaves no room for more than a snatched cup of coffee along the way. But the progress they make is good, and to his relief, he comes to the end of the day with the realisation that for much of the time he has not thought about Katya.

'What's next?' he asks Melissa, as they leave another meeting.

'Nothing. Home time,' she replies.

He smiles. 'And tell me, have you ever gone home at five thirty?'

She shrugs. 'Not that I can remember but, then, I'm hardly your role model.' She walks with him to the exit. 'Go on home,' she says. 'If you feel like it, I'd love to meet you back here tomorrow. But only if you're up for it.'

'What sort of time?' He steps into the glass elevator.

'Since you ask, nine sharp,' she says, with a smile, and the doors close.

He follows the same routine the next day, and the next, and when he leaves for the week on Friday evening, he stops and breathes deeply of the cool courtyard air. People walk purposefully past him and around him, hurrying home for the weekend. He wonders if any of them see that the fading light has a crispness about it, a patina of life that hints at the coming springtime. He stops under the huge tree that dominates the centre of the paved area, and notes the sticky, ripe buds that are already clinging to its upper branches.

'It looked a lot different the last time we were here, didn't it?'

He turns to the bench behind him. Estelle's eyes hold the mischievous smile that he has tried hard to forget. They look at each other for a long moment. He is collecting himself, trying to repress the unseemly crashing of his heart inside his chest. When at last he takes the few steps towards her, she shifts over on the bench and waits for him to sit down. Now that he is so close to her, she finds she cannot quite look at his eyes. Not just yet.

'Are you waiting for Melissa?'

She shakes her head, then gives him a quick glance.

'I'm flattered,' he says.

'Do you wish I hadn't come?'

'Of course not. I just didn't expect it. Didn't dare to expect it.'

The emotion in his voice settles over her residual fears like a soft, warm blanket, easing them away so that she feels able to speak.

'I was wrong to push you away that evening,' she says. 'I didn't want to – I guess I felt I had to.' She waits, unsure how to formulate her next sentences, hoping that he will fill in the gaps with questions that will guide her towards what she wants to say. But he remains silent, his brown eyes fixed on a point just before them.

She wants to touch him, just the sleeve of his coat or the top of his hand or the back of his neck, which even at his age has the slim, shorn look of a little boy's. But she does not dare. Instead, she leans over to her handbag, pulls out a sheaf of paper and offers it to him. He takes it, then holds on to her hand. To her chagrin, she blushes.

'The first few chapters.'

'Is it about Katya?'

'Yes and no.'

'Because I don't know if I can read it just yet,' he says. 'If it is.'

'Well, I started out with her, but then I had a minor problem. I didn't know a thing about the places I was trying to describe. Oh, and half my plot line was missing.'

'So what did you write about?'

'Well, I thought about the characters and story that I knew best. And so, we have the following scenario. Picture it. A mature woman – I hate to say old – who has always lived a safe and easy life. Who has been married for nearly forty years, and who believes that marriage is for life, because there are such things between her and her husband as loyalty and respect, if not the attention and care she would have wanted.'

'I see.'

'But then this woman meets someone. Someone she loves to be with and who maybe sees in her more than there is. And there's another character, you see, though I'm not sure how to bring her in yet. This character is my Katya. Someone whose story proves interesting and then inspirational to my main character.'

'Why inspirational?'

'Because in her young life she has always lived for her passions and ideals and beliefs, no matter what the risks might be for doing that.'

He feels his eyes moisten but, with a breath, he controls the tears.

'How does your story end?' he asks at last.

'That's the thing. I'm not sure. But I think the old lady gets up the courage to live life in the end. I really do.'

He offers her his hand, and together they walk across the courtyard to the main road. They join the line for a cab and his face is handsome and stern and kind as he stands there. She feels lost suddenly, and a trace of panic crosses her face.

'Tell me what you feel, Estelle.'

She laughs nervously. 'It's a lot easier to talk about my characters.'

But he will not let her go so easily. His eyes hold her down until she looks away. Perhaps he is challenging her to show the courage that she just talked about. She swallows and looks up at him. 'While I was away I realised I would never see you again. That my life would just continue the way it had before – except that I've changed. And that's the problem, you see. I don't want my life to be the same as it has been. And I began to understand that – God help me – even with good blood pressure and low cholesterol, I can only have a limited number of years left on this earth. And I don't want to spend them away from you.'

He takes a deep breath, to try to slow his heart – he wonders how many more shocks it can take. 'What about your husband?' he asks.

'I'm not sure,' she says. In her mind she has envisaged packing up, walking out, not returning, but the picture is one of too much brutality and harshness. 'I would have to ask you to bear with me for a while.'

'Yes, I will,' he says.

'Really?'

'Yes.'

There is a weight of compassion in her face as she says, 'Melissa told me you've had a hard few weeks.'

'Yes.'

'I'm sorry.'

'Don't be. It was time for everything to come out. But it brought it all back, with such force. What she gave up for me, what she and I both lost.'

Estelle cannot reply just now. She does not know whether it is tiredness, excitement, relief or uncertainty. Despite her best efforts, a rogue droplet escapes from the edge of her eye and runs over her cheek. His hand reaches up to brush it away.

It is late, perhaps one o'clock in the morning. To be able to sit in her uncle's living room, wrapped in a thick darkness that is scattered away only here and there by the last flickers of the fire seems luxurious to Lauren, like being swathed in the softest velvet. She has waited until Alexander is asleep before methodically turning out all the lights downstairs. Her head feels heavier as she watches the dying flames, but before she falls asleep, she rouses herself and goes over to the easel that stands at the other end of the room. She lifts away the cover, and glances at the beginnings of Estelle's portrait. She can see little of it in the dim light. Lifting it down, she leans it against a second sketch that outlines her uncle's features. Then she wraps the cloth around both.

She watched them both closely tonight at dinner. In Alexander she saw a new softness and peace, a relaxation of the features. And in Estelle she noticed a more determined look in the blue eyes which previously had only masked her inner feelings with irony and laughter. Or perhaps she merely imagined these changes, had wished for them so much that she read them into the faces before her. In any event, she is tired. She does not want to paint for a while, and maybe the time off that she takes will allow those developments to occur that she wants to see in her two latest subjects. She wanders back to the fireplace and looks up at Katya's portrait. The shadows cast on to her face by the glowing embers mean that her eyes and mouth are barely visible. How would her aunt have changed, had she been given the chance? Lauren looks at the painting, trying in her mind to rework the familiar features so that age and experience cause their alterations. But she cannot – the choices that her aunt might have made, the way her character might have developed are too varied to be pinned down so easily. Lauren closes her eyes briefly, but beneath the lids that burn from lack of sleep, the image of Katya still lies, clear and bright. She opens then, pushes down the last embers of the fire with the poker, and turns to leave the room.

'Good night, Katya,' she says. 'Good night.'